# Praise for Jo Nesbo and *The Thirst*

#1 International Bestseller

National Bestseller

Nordic Noir Thriller of the Year

"My favourite thriller writer."　　　　　—Michael Connelly

"His outstanding series featuring Detective Inspector Harry Hole has secured Jo Nesbo the undisputed position of Scandinavia's leading crime writer."

—Carina Nunstedt, head of Sweden's Crimetime Gotland (organization behind the Nordic Noir Thriller Award)

"[*The Thirst*] was satisfying, it was gruesome. I could only read it during the day, it was that scary."

—Shelagh Rogers, CBC Books, *The Next Chapter*

"Nesbo depicts a heartbreakingly conflicted Harry, who both wants to forget the horror he's trying to prevent and knows he has to remember them in all their grim detail."

—*Publishers Weekly* (starred review)

"It's a big-boned, technicolour epic in the current Nesbo style, starting *adagio* and ending *accelerando*, but with the kind of close psychological character readings that distinguished his early work."

—*The Guardian*

"What distinguishes Jo Nesbo . . . is his wry sense of humour. He not only provides a super-complex plot with plenty of twists (two within the first twelve pages), but also skillfully continues the lives of the all-too-fallible characters we have grown to love and hate."

—*Evening Standard*

"Nesbo's greatest strength as a novelist is the way he places two opposing forces in battle: the perverse criminal and the compulsive

detective. In Nesbo's consistently excellent Hole series, *The Thirst* may well be the pinnacle."
—Paste

# Praise for *The Snowman*

### International Bestseller

"Mesmerizing. . . . The brilliance of Nesbo: He takes the simple and cozy, and transforms it into the terrorizing. . . . The characters are marvellous, the plot is tight and the setting perfect—just at the edge of a Norwegian winter—and the concept original."
—The Globe and Mail

"Many authors know how to make the hairs on the back of your neck stand up. Jo Nesbo's one of the few who keeps them there."
—Linwood Barclay

"Another fiendishly complex thriller."
—The New York Times Book Review

"This is crime writing of the highest order."     —*The Times* (UK)

"You may never be able to build a snowman again with quite the same innocent enthusiasm."     —*The Independent*

"[*The Snowman*] could make Nesbo the writer most likely to take the ice-cold crown in the critically acclaimed—and now bestselling—category of Nordic noir."     —*Los Angeles Times*

"*The Snowman* is a standout thriller, capable of disturbing your slumbers long after the first thaw."     —NPR

# THE THIRST

ALSO BY JO NESBO

*Headhunters*

*The Son*

*Blood on Snow*

*Midnight Sun*

The Harry Hole Series

*The Bat*

*Cockroaches*

*The Redbreast*

*Nemesis*

*The Devil's Star*

*The Redeemer*

*The Snowman*

*The Leopard*

*Phantom*

*Police*

# THE THIRST

## JO NESBO

*Translated from the Norwegian by Neil Smith*

VINTAGE CANADA

VINTAGE CANADA EDITION, 2018

Published by Vintage Canada, a division of Penguin Random House Canada
Limited, in 2018. Previously published in hardcover by Random House
Canada, a division of Penguin Random House Canada Limited, in 2017, and
simultaneously in the United States by Alfred A. Knopf, a division of Penguin
Random House LLC, New York. Originally published in Norway as Tørst
by H. Aschehoug & Co. (W.Nygaard), Oslo, 2017. Copyright © 2017 by Jo
Nesbø. This translation originally published in hardcover in Great Britain
by Harvill Secker, an imprint of Vintage Publishing, a division of Penguin
Random House Ltd., London, in 2017. Distributed in Canada by Penguin
Random House Canada Limited, Toronto.

Vintage Canada with colophon is a registered trademark.

www.penguinrandomhouse.ca

Library and Archives Canada Cataloguing in Publication

Nesbø, Jo, 1960–
[Tørst. English]
The thirst / Jo Nesbø ; Neil Smith, translator

(Harry Hole ; 11)
Translation of: Tørst.

ISBN 978-0-7352-7248-4
eBook ISBN 978-0-7352-7249-1

I. Smith, Neil, 1964–, translator  II. Title.  III. Title: Tørst. English.
IV. Series: Nesbø, Jo, 1960–. Harry Hole mystery series ; 11.

PT8951.24.E83T6713 2018          839.82'374          C2017-900475-1

Cover photographs: Arcangel and Alamy Stock Photo

Printed and bound in the United States of America

68975

Penguin
Random
House

# THE THIRST

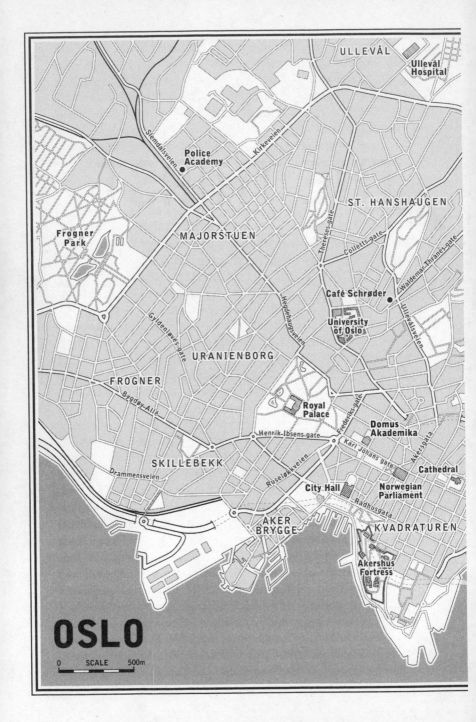

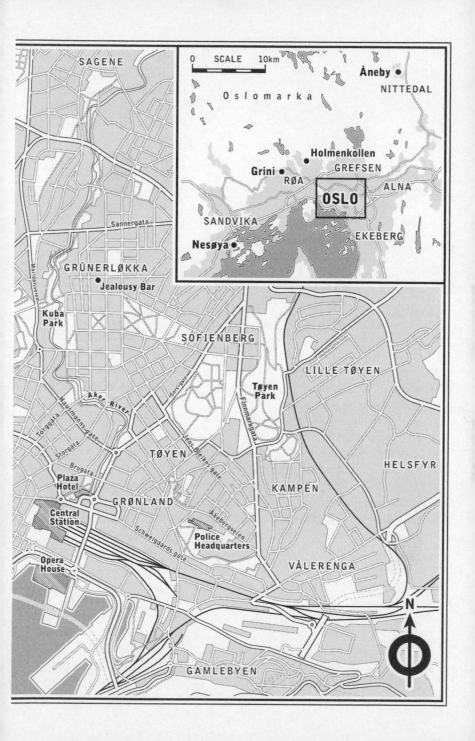

# Prologue

He stared into the white nothingness.

The way he had done for almost three years.

No one saw him, and he saw no one. Apart from each time the door opened and enough steam was sucked out for him to be able to glimpse a naked man for a brief moment before the door closed and everything was shrouded in fog.

The baths would be closing soon. He was alone.

He wrapped the white towelling bathrobe more tightly around him, got up from the wooden bench and walked out, past the empty swimming pool and into the changing room.

No trickling showers, no conversations in Turkish, no bare feet padding across the tiled floor. He looked at himself in the mirror. Ran a finger along the scar that was still visible after the last operation. It had taken him time to get used to his new face. His finger carried on down his throat, across his chest, and came to a halt at the start of the tattoo.

He removed the padlock from his locker, pulled on his trousers and put his coat on over the still damp bathrobe. Tied his shoelaces. He made sure he was definitely alone before going over to a locker with a coded padlock, one with a splash of blue paint on it. He turned the lock until it read 0999. Removed the lock and opened the door. Took a moment to admire the big, beautiful revolver that lay inside before taking hold of the red hilt and putting it in his coat pocket. Then he removed the envelope and opened it. A key. An address, and some more detailed information.

There was one more thing in the locker.

Painted black, made of iron.

He held it up against the light with one hand, looking at the wrought ironwork with fascination.

He would have to clean it, scrub it, but he already felt aroused at the thought of using it.

Three years. Three years in a white nothingness, in a desert of empty days.

Now it was time. Time he drank from the well of life again.

Time he returned.


Harry woke with a start. Stared out at the semi-darkness of the bedroom. It was *him* again, he was back, he was here.

"Nightmare, darling?" The whispered voice by his side was warm and soothing.

He turned towards her. Her brown eyes studied his. And the apparition faded and disappeared.

"I'm here," Rakel said.

"And here I am," he said.

"Who was it this time?"

"No one," he lied, and touched her cheek. "Go back to sleep."

Harry closed his eyes. Waited until he was sure she had closed hers before opening his again. He studied her face. He had seen him in a forest this time. Moorland, wreathed in white fog that swirled around them. He had raised his hand and pointed something towards Harry. He could just make out the demonic, tattooed face on his naked chest. Then the fog had grown thicker, and he was gone. Gone again.

"And here I am," Harry Hole whispered.

# Part I

# I

# Wednesday evening

The Jealousy Bar was almost empty, but even so it was hard to breathe.

Mehmet Kalak looked at the man and woman standing at the bar as he poured wine into their glasses. Four customers. The third was a guy sitting on his own at a table, taking tiny little sips of beer, and the fourth was just a pair of cowboy boots sticking out from one of the booths, where the darkness occasionally gave way to the glow from the screen of a phone. Four customers at half past eleven on a September evening in the best bar district in Grünerløkka. Terrible, and it couldn't go on like this. Sometimes he asked himself why he'd left his job as bar manager at the hippest hotel in the city to go it alone and take over this rundown bar with its pissed-up clientele. Possibly because he thought that by jacking up the prices he could replace the old customers with the ones everyone wanted: the neighbourhood's affluent, trouble-free young adults. Possibly because he needed somewhere to work himself to death after breaking up with his girlfriend. Possibly because the offer from loan shark Danial Banks had looked favourable after the bank rejected his application. Or possibly just because at the Jealousy Bar he was the one who picked the music, not some damn hotel manager who only knew one tune: the ringing of the cash register. Getting rid of the old clientele had been easy— they had long since settled in at a cheap bar three blocks away. But it turned out to be a whole lot harder to attract new customers. Maybe he would have to reconsider the whole concept. Maybe one big television screen on which he showed Turkish football wasn't enough to merit the description "sports bar." And maybe he'd have to change the music and go for reliable classics like U2 and Springsteen for the guys, Coldplay for the girls.

"Well, I haven't been on that many Tinder dates," Geir said, putting his glass of white wine back down on the bar. "But I've worked out that there's a lot of strange people out there."

"Have you?" the woman said, stifling a yawn. She had short fair hair. Slim. Mid-thirties, Mehmet thought. Quick, slightly stressed movements. Tired eyes. Works too hard and goes to the gym in the hope that it will give her the advantage she's never had. Mehmet watched Geir raise his glass with three fingers round the stem, the same way as the woman. On his countless Tinder hook-ups he had always ordered the same thing as his dates, regardless of whether it was whiskey or green tea. Keen to signal that they were a match on that point too.

Geir coughed. Six minutes had passed since she had walked into the bar, and Mehmet knew that this was when he would make his move.

"You're more beautiful than your profile picture, Elise," Geir said.

"So you said, but thanks again."

Mehmet polished a glass and pretended not to listen.

"So tell me, Elise, what do you want from life?"

She gave a rather resigned little smile. "A man who doesn't just judge by appearances."

"I couldn't agree more, Elise, it's what's inside that counts."

"That was a joke. I look better in my profile picture, and, to be honest, so do you, Geir."

"Ha ha," Geir said, and stared down into his wine glass, slightly deflated. "I suppose most people pick a flattering picture. So you're looking for a man. What sort of man?"

"One who'd like to stay at home with three kids." She glanced at the time.

"Ha ha." Sweat hadn't just broken out on Geir's forehead, but all over his large, close-shaven head. And soon rings of sweat would appear under the arms of his black slim-fit shirt, an odd choice given that Geir was neither slim nor fit. He toyed with his glass. "That's exactly my kind of humour, Elise. A dog is family enough for me for the time being. Do you like animals?"

*Tanrim*, Mehmet thought. Why doesn't he just give up?

"If I meet the right person, I can feel it, here . . . and here." He grinned, lowered his voice and pointed towards his crotch. "But obviously you have to find out if that's right. What do you say, Elise?"

Mehmet shuddered. Geir had gone all-in, and his self-esteem was about to take another beating.

The woman pushed her wine glass aside, leaned forward slightly, and Mehmet had to strain to hear. "Can you promise me something, Geir?"

"Of course." His voice and the look in his eyes were as eager as a dog's.

"That when I walk out of here in a moment, you'll never try to contact me again?"

Mehmet had to admire Geir for managing to summon up a smile. "Of course."

The woman leaned back again. "It's not that you seem like a stalker, Geir, but I've had a couple of bad experiences. One guy started following me. He threatened the people I was with as well. I hope you can understand my being a bit cautious."

"I understand." Geir raised his glass and emptied it. "Like I said, there's a lot of strange people out there. But don't worry, you're pretty safe. Statistically speaking, the chances of getting murdered are four times greater for a man than a woman."

"Thanks for the wine, Geir."

"If one of the three of us—"

Mehmet hurried to look away when Geir pointed to him.

"—was going to get murdered tonight, the likelihood of it being you is one in eight. No, hang on, you have to divide that by . . ."

She stood up. "I hope you figure it out. Have a good life."

Geir stared at her wine glass for a while after she left, nodded in time to "Fix You," as if to convince Mehmet and anyone else watching that he had already shaken the experience off, she had been nothing more than a three-minute-long pop song, and just as forgettable. Then he stood up and left. Mehmet looked round. The cowboy boots and the guy who had been dragging out his beer were both gone too. He was alone. And the oxygen was back. He used his mobile phone to change the playlist. To *his* playlist. Bad Company. Given that the group contained members of Free, Mott the Hoople and King Crimson, there was no way it was ever going to be bad. And with Paul Rodgers on vocals, there was no way it could fail. Mehmet turned the volume up until the glasses behind the bar started to rattle against each other.

· · ·

Elise walked down Thorvald Meyers gate, past plain four-storey buildings that had once housed the working classes in a poor part of a poor city, but where one square metre now cost as much as in London or Stockholm. September in Oslo. The darkness was back at last, and the drawn-out, annoyingly light summer nights were long gone, with all the hysterical, cheerful, stupid self-expression of summer. In September Oslo reverted to its true self: melancholic, reserved, efficient. A solid facade, but not without its dark corners and secrets. Much like her, apparently. She quickened her pace; there was rain in the air, mist, the spray when God sneezed, as one of her dates had put it in an attempt to be poetic. She was going to give up Tinder. Tomorrow. Enough was enough. Enough randy men whose way of looking at her made her feel like a whore when she met them in bars. Enough crazy psychopaths and stalkers who stuck like mud, sucking time, energy and security from her. Enough pathetic losers who made her feel like she was one of them.

They said Internet dating was the cool way to meet new people, that it was nothing to be ashamed of anymore, that everyone was doing it. But that wasn't true. People met each other at work, in class-rooms, through friends, at the gym, in cafes, on planes, buses, trains. They met each other the way they were supposed to meet each other, when they were relaxed, no pressure, and afterwards they could cling to the romantic illusion of innocence, purity and quirks of fate. She *wanted* that illusion. She was going to delete her profile. She'd told herself that before, but this time it was definitely going to happen, that very night.

She crossed Sofienberggata and fished out the key to unlock the gate next to the greengrocer's. She pushed the gate open and stepped into the darkness of the archway. And stopped dead.

There were two of them.

It took a moment or two for her eyes to get used to the darkness, and for her to see what they were holding in their hands. Both men had undone their trousers and had their cocks out.

She jerked back. Didn't look round, just prayed that there was no one standing behind her.

"Fucksorry." The combination of oath and apology was uttered by a young voice. Nineteen, twenty, Elise guessed. Not sober.

"Duh," the other one said, "you're pissing all over my shoes!"

"I was startled!"

Elise pulled her coat more tightly around her and walked past the young men, who had turned back to face the wall again. "This isn't a public toilet," she said.

"Sorry, we were desperate. It won't happen again."


Geir hurried over Schleppegrells gate. Thinking hard. It was wrong that two men and one woman gave the woman a one in eight chance of being murdered, the calculation was much more complicated than that. *Everything* was always much more complicated.

He had just passed Romsdalsgata when something made him turn round. There was a man walking fifty metres behind him. He wasn't sure, but wasn't it the same guy who had been standing on the other side of the street looking at a window display when Geir emerged from the Jealousy Bar? Geir sped up, heading east, towards Dælenenga and the chocolate factory; there was no one out on the streets here, just a bus which was evidently running ahead of schedule and was waiting at a bus stop. Geir glanced back. The man was still there, still the same distance. Geir was frightened of dark-skinned people, always had been, but he couldn't see this guy properly. They were on their way out of the white, gentrified neighbourhood, heading towards an area with far more social housing and immigrants. Geir could see the door of his own apartment block one hundred metres away. But when he looked back he saw that the guy had started running, and the thought that he had a Somali, thoroughly traumatised from Mogadishu, on his heels made him break into a run. Geir hadn't run for years, and each time his heels hit the tarmac a jolt ran through his brain and jogged his sight. He reached the door, got the key in the lock at the first attempt, threw himself inside and slammed the heavy wooden door behind him. He leaned against the damp wood and stared out through the glass in the top part of the door. He couldn't see anyone out in the street. Perhaps it wasn't a Somali. Geir couldn't help laughing. It was ridiculous how jumpy you got just because you'd been talking about murder. And what had Elise said about that stalker?

Geir was still out of breath when he unlocked the door to his flat. He got a beer from the fridge, noticed that the kitchen window facing the street was open, and closed it. Then he went into the study and switched the lamp on.

He pressed one of the keys of the PC in front of him, and the twenty-inch screen lit up.

He typed in "Pornhub," then "french' in the search box. He looked through the thumbnails until he found a woman who at least had the same hairstyle and colouring as Elise. The walls of the flat were thin, so he plugged his headphones into the PC before double-clicking the picture, undoing his trousers and pushing them down his thighs. The woman actually resembled Elise so little that Geir shut his eyes instead and concentrated on her groaning while he tried to conjure up the image of Elise's small, tight little mouth, the scornful look in her eyes, her sober but still sexy blouse. There was no way he could ever have had her. Never. Except this way.

Geir stopped. Opened his eyes. Let go of his cock as the hairs on the back of his neck stood up in the cold breeze from behind. From the door he *knew* he had closed properly. He raised his hand to pull off the headphones, but knew it was already too late.


Elise put the security chain on the door, kicked her shoes off in the hallway and, as always, ran her hand over the photograph of herself and her niece Ingvild that was stuck to one side of the mirror. It was a ritual she didn't quite understand, except that it clearly fulfilled some deep-rooted human need, the same way as stories about what happens to us after death. She went into the living room and lay down on the sofa in her small but cosy two-room flat; at least she owned it. She checked her phone. One text from work—tomorrow morning's meeting had been cancelled. She hadn't told the guy she had met this evening that she worked as a lawyer, specialising in rape cases. And that his statistics about men being more likely to be murdered only told half the story. In sexually motivated murders, the victim was four times more likely to be a woman. That was one of the reasons why the first thing she did when she bought the flat was change the locks and have a security chain fitted, a rare concept in Norway, and one she still fumbled with every time she used it. She went onto Tinder. She had matched with three of the men she had right-swiped earlier that evening. Oh, this was what was so nice about it. Not meeting them, but knowing that they were out there, and that they wanted her. Should she allow herself one last flirtation by message, one last virtual threesome with her last two strangers before deleting her account and the app for good?

No. Delete it at once.

She went into the menu, clicked the relevant option and was asked if she was *really* sure she wanted to delete her account?

Elise looked at her index finger. It was trembling. God, had she become addicted? Addicted to being told that someone—someone who had no real idea of who she was or what she was like, but still *someone*—wanted her, just the way she was? Well, the way she was in her profile picture, anyway. Completely addicted, or only a bit? Presumably she'd find out if she just deleted her account and promised to go a month without Tinder. One month, and if she couldn't manage that, then there was something seriously wrong with her. The trembling finger moved closer to the delete button. But, if she *was* addicted, was that such a bad thing? We all need to feel that we've got someone, that someone's got us. She had read that babies could die if they didn't get a minimum of skin-to-skin contact. She doubted that was true, but, on the other hand, what was the point of living if it was just her, doing a job that was eating her up and with friends she socialised with mostly out of a sense of duty, if she was honest, because her fear of loneliness worried her more than their tedious moaning about their children and husbands, or the absence of one or other of these? And perhaps the right man for her was on Tinder right now? So, OK, one last go. The first picture popped up and she swiped left. Onto the scrapheap, to I-don't-want-you. Same thing with the second one. And the third.

Her mind started to wander. She had attended a lecture where a psychologist who had been in close contact with some of the worst criminals in the country had said that men killed for sex, money and power, and women as a result of jealousy and fear.

She stopped swiping left. There was something vaguely familiar about the thin face in the picture, even though it was dark and slightly out of focus. That had happened before, seeing as Tinder matched people who were geographically close to each other. And, according to Tinder, this man was less than a kilometre away, so for all she knew he could be in the same block. The fact that the picture was out of focus meant that he hadn't studied the online advice about Tinder tactics, and that in itself was a plus. The message was a very basic "hi." No attempt to stand out. It may not have been particularly imaginative, but it did at least display a certain confidence. Yes, she would definitely have been pleased if a man came up to her at a party and just said "hi" with a calm, steady gaze that said "Shall we take this any further?". She swiped right. To I'm-curious-about-you.

And heard the happy bleep from her iPhone that told her she had another match.

. . .

Geir was breathing hard through his nose.

He pulled his trousers up and slowly spun his chair round.

The light from the computer screen was the only one in the room, and illuminated just the torso and hands of the person who was standing behind him. He couldn't see a face, just the white hands holding something out towards him. A black leather strap. With a loop at one end.

The figure took a step closer and Geir pulled back automatically.

"Do you know what the only thing I find more disgusting than you is?" the voice whispered in the darkness as the hands pulled at the leather strap.

Geir swallowed.

"The dog," the voice said. "That bloody dog, which you promised *you'd* do everything to look after. Which shits on the kitchen floor because no one can be bothered to take it outside."

Geir coughed. "Kari, please . . ."

"Take it out. And don't touch me when you come to bed."

Geir took the dog leash, and the door slammed behind her.

He was left sitting in the darkness, blinking.

Nine, he thought. Two men and one woman, one murder. The chances of the woman being the murder victim is one in nine, not one in eight.


Mehmet drove the old BMW out of the streets of the city centre, up towards Kjelsås, towards the villas, fjord views and fresher air. He turned into his silent, sleeping street. Discovered that there was a black Audi R8 parked in front of the garage by the house. Mehmet slowed down. Briefly considered accelerating and just driving on. He knew that would only be putting it off. On the other hand, that was exactly what he needed. A delay. But Banks would find him again, and perhaps now was the right time. It was dark and quiet, no witnesses. Mehmet pulled up by the pavement. Opened the glove compartment. Looked at what he had been keeping in there for the past few days, specifically in case this situation arose. Mehmet put it in his jacket pocket and took a deep breath. Then he got out of the car and started to walk towards the house.

The door of the Audi opened and Danial Banks got out. When Mehmet had met him at the Pearl of India restaurant, he knew that the Pakistani first name and English surname were probably just as fake as the signature on the dubious contract they had signed. But the cash in the case he had pushed across the table had been real enough.

The gravel in front of the garage crunched beneath Mehmet's shoes.

"Nice house," Danial Banks said, leaning against the R8 with his arms folded. "Wasn't your bank prepared to take it as collateral?"

"I'm only renting," Mehmet said. "The basement."

"That's bad news for me," Banks said. He was much shorter than Mehmet, but it didn't feel like it as he stood there squeezing the biceps inside his smart jacket. "Because burning it down won't help either of us if you don't get anything from the insurance to repay your debt, will it?"

"No, I don't suppose it would."

"Bad news for you, too, because that means I'm going to have to use the more painful methods instead. Do you want to know what they are?"

"Don't you want to know if I can pay first?"

Banks shook his head and pulled something from his pocket. "The instalment was due three days ago, and I told you punctuality was crucial. And so that *all* my clients, not just you, know that that sort of thing isn't tolerated, I can't make any exceptions." He held the object up in the light of the lamp on the garage. Mehmet gasped for breath.

"I know it isn't very original," Banks said, tilting his head and looking at the pliers. "But it works."

"But—"

"What part of this don't you understand? You can choose which finger. Most people prefer the left little finger."

Mehmet felt it coming. The anger. And he felt his chest expand as he filled his lungs with air. "I've got a better solution, Banks."

"Oh?"

"I know it isn't very original," Mehmet said, sticking his right hand in his jacket pocket. Pulled it out. Held it out towards Banks, clutching it with both hands. "But it works."

Banks stared at him in surprise. Nodded slowly.

"You're right there," Banks said, taking the bundle of notes Mehmet was holding out to him and pulling the elastic band off.

"That covers the repayment and the interest, down to the last krone," Mehmet said. "But feel free to count it."

.   .   .

Ping.

A match on Tinder.

The triumphant sound your phone makes when someone you've already swiped right on swipes *your* picture right as well.

Elise's head was spinning, her heart was racing.

She knew it was the familiar response to the sound of Tinder's matchmaking: increased heart rate as a consequence of excitement. That it released a whole load of happy chemicals that you could become addicted to. But that wasn't why her heart was galloping. It was because the ping hadn't come from *her* phone.

But the ping had rung out at the very moment she'd swiped right on a picture. The picture of a person who, according to Tinder, was less than a kilometre away from her.

She stared at the closed bedroom door. Swallowed.

The sound must have come from one of the neighbouring apartments. There were lots of single people living in the block, lots of potential Tinder users. And everything was quiet now, even on the floor below where the girls had been having a party when she went out earlier that evening. But there was only one way to get rid of imaginary monsters. By checking.

Elise got up from the sofa and walked the four steps over to the bedroom door. Hesitated. A couple of assault cases from work swirled through her head.

Then she pulled herself together and opened the door.

She found herself standing in the doorway gasping for air. Because there wasn't any. None that she could breathe.

The light above the bed was switched on, and the first thing she saw was the soles of a pair of cowboy boots sticking off the end of the bed. Jeans and a pair of long legs, crossed. The man lying there was like the photograph, half in darkness, half out of focus. But he had unbuttoned his shirt to reveal his bare chest. And on his chest was a drawing or a tattoo of a face. That was what caught her eye now. The silently screaming face. As if it were held tight and was trying to pull free. Elise couldn't bring herself to scream either.

As the person on the bed sat up, the light from his mobile phone fell across his face.

"So we meet again, Elise," he whispered.

And the voice made her realise why the profile picture had seemed familiar to her. His hair was a different colour. And his face must have been operated on—she could see the scars left by stitches.

He raised his hand and shoved something into his mouth.

Elise stared at him as she backed away. Then she spun round, got some air into her lungs, and knew she had to use it to run, not scream. The front door was only five steps away, six at most. She heard the bed creak, but he had further to run. If she could just get out into the stairwell she'd be able to scream and get some help. She made it to the hallway and reached the door, tugged the handle down and pushed, but the door wouldn't open properly.

The security chain. She tried to pull the door closed, to grab the chain, but it was all taking too long, like a bad dream, and she knew it was too late. Something was pressed over her mouth and she was dragged backwards. In desperation she stuck her hand through the opening above the security chain, grabbed hold of the door frame outside, tried to scream, but the huge nicotine-stinking hand was clamped tightly over her mouth. Then she was yanked free and the door slammed shut in front of her. The voice whispered in her ear: "Didn't you like me? You don't look as good as your profile picture either, baby. We just need to get to know each other better, we didn't have a chance for that last t-time."

The voice. And that last, solitary stammer. She'd heard it once before. She tried to kick and tear herself free, but he had her in a vice-like grip. He dragged her over to the hall mirror. Rested his head on her shoulder.

"It wasn't your fault I was found guilty, Elise, the evidence was overwhelming. That's not why I'm here. Would you believe me if I said it is a coincidence?" Then he grinned. Elise stared into his mouth. His teeth looked like they were made of iron, black and rusty, with sharp spikes in both upper and lower jaw, like a bear trap.

It creaked gently when he opened his mouth—was it spring-loaded?

She remembered the details of the case now. The photographs from the scene. And knew she would soon be dead.

Then he bit.

Elise Hermansen tried to scream into his hand as she saw the blood spraying from her own throat.

He raised his head again. Looked into the mirror. Her blood was running from his eyebrows, from his hair and down over his chin.

"I'd call that a m-match, baby," he whispered. Then he bit again.

She felt dizzy. He wasn't holding her so tightly now, he didn't need to, because a paralysing chill, an alien darkness was moving slowly over her, into her. She pulled one hand free and reached towards the photograph on the side of the mirror. Tried to touch it, but her fingertips couldn't reach.

# 2

# Thursday morning

The sharp afternoon light reached through the living-room windows and out into the hallway.

Detective Inspector Katrine Bratt was standing in front of the mirror, silent and thoughtful, looking at the photograph that was stuck to the frame. It showed a woman and a young girl sitting on a rock hugging each other, both with wet hair and wrapped in big towels. As if they had just gone swimming in a rather too chilly Norwegian summer and were trying to keep warm by clinging to one another. But now there was something separating them. A dark streak of blood had run down the mirror and across the photograph, right between the two smiling faces. Katrine Bratt didn't have children. She may have wished that she had in the past, but not now. Now she was a newly single career woman, and she was happy with that. Wasn't she?

She heard a low cough and looked up. Met the gaze of a deeply scarred face with a prominent brow and a remarkably high hairline. Truls Berntsen.

"What is it, Constable?" she said. Saw his face cloud over at her deliberate reminder that he was still a constable after fifteen years in the force, and for that and several other reasons would never have been allowed to apply to become a detective with Crime Squad if it hadn't been for the fact that Truls Berntsen had been transferred there by his childhood friend, Police Chief Mikael Bellman.

Berntsen shrugged. "Nothing much, you're in charge of the

investigation." He looked at her with a cold, doggy look that was simultaneously submissive and hostile.

"Talk to the neighbours," Bratt said. "Start with the floor below. We're especially interested in anything they heard or saw yesterday and last night. But seeing as Elise Hermansen lived alone, we also want to know what sort of men she used to hang out with."

"So you think it was a man, and that they already knew each other?" Only now did she see the young man, the lad standing next to Berntsen. An open face. Fair hair. Handsome. "Anders Wyller. This is my first day." His voice was high, and he was smiling with his eyes, which Katrine took to mean that he was confident of charming those around him. His references from his boss at Tromsø Police Station had looked pretty much like a declaration of love. But, to be fair, he had the CV to match. Top grades from Police College two years ago, and good results as a detective constable in Tromsø.

"Go and make a start, Berntsen," Katrine said.

She took his shuffling feet to be a passive protest at being ordered about by a younger, female boss.

"Welcome," she said, holding her hand out to Wyller. "Sorry we weren't there to say hello on your first day."

"The dead take priority over the living," the young man said. Katrine recognised the quote as one of Harry Hole's, saw that Wyller was looking at her hand, and realised that she was still wearing a pair of latex gloves.

"I haven't touched anything disgusting," she said.

He smiled. White teeth. Ten bonus points.

"I'm allergic to latex," he said

Twenty penalty points.

"OK, Wyller," Katrine Bratt said, still holding her hand out. "These gloves are powder-free and low in allergens and endotoxins, and if you're going to work in Crime Squad, you're going to be wearing them pretty often. But obviously we could always get you a transfer to Financial Crime or . . ."

"I'd rather not," he laughed and grasped her hand. She could feel the warmth through the latex.

"My name's Katrine Bratt, and I'm lead detective on this case."

"I know. You worked in the Harry Hole group."

"The Harry Hole group?"

"The boiler room."

Katrine nodded. She had never thought of it as the *Harry Hole group*, the little gang of three detectives who had been thrown together to work on the cop murder cases . . . But the name was fitting enough. Since then Harry had withdrawn to lecture at Police College, Bjørn had moved to work in Forensics out at Bryn, and she had come to Crime Squad where she was now a detective inspector.

Wyller's eyes were shining, and he was still smiling. "Shame Harry Hole isn't—"

"Shame we haven't got time to talk right now, Wyller, but we've got a murder to investigate. Go with Berntsen, and listen and learn."

Anders Wyller gave her a wry smile. "You're saying *Constable* Berntsen has a lot to teach me?"

Bratt raised an eyebrow. Young, self-assured, fearless. All good, but she hoped to God that he wasn't another Harry Hole wannabe.


Truls Berntsen pressed the doorbell with his thumb and heard it ring inside the flat, noted that he ought to stop biting his nails, and let go.

When he had gone to see Mikael and asked to be transferred to Crime Squad, Mikael had asked why. And Truls had given an honest answer: he wanted to sit a bit higher up the food chain, but without having to wear himself out making an effort. Any other police chief would have thrown Truls out on his ear, but this one couldn't. They had too much dirt on each other. When they were young they were connected by something approaching friendship, then a sort of symbiotic relationship, like a suckerfish and a shark. But now they were bound together by their sins and a mutual assurance of silence. That meant Truls Berntsen didn't even have to try to pretend when he presented his request.

But he had started to wonder how sensible that request had been. Crime Squad had two categories of job: detectives and analysts. And when the head of Crime Squad, Gunnar Hagen, had told Truls he could choose for himself what he wanted to be, Truls had realised that he was hardly going to be expected to shoulder much responsibility. Which in and of itself suited him fine. But he had to admit that it had stung when Detective Inspector Katrine Bratt had shown him round the unit, all the time addressing him as "Constable," and taking extra care to explain to him how the coffee machine worked.

The door opened. Three young girls were standing there looking at him with horrified expressions on their faces. They had evidently heard what had happened.

"Police," he said, holding up his ID. "I've got some questions. Did you hear anything between—"

"—questions we wondered if you could help us with," a voice said behind him. The new guy. Wyller. Truls saw some of the horror fall away from the girls' faces, and they almost brightened up.

"Of course," the one who had opened the door said. "Do you know who . . . who did . . . *it*?"

"Obviously we can't say anything about that," Truls said.

"But what we can say," Wyller said, "is that there are no grounds for you to be scared. Am I right in thinking that you're students sharing this flat?"

"Yes," they replied in chorus, as if they all wanted to be first.

"May we come in?" Wyller said, with a smile as white as Mikael Bellman's, Truls noted.

The girls led them into the living room, and two of them began quickly clearing beer bottles and glasses from the table and left the room.

"We had a bit of a party here last night," the door-opener said sheepishly. "It's terrible."

Truls wasn't sure if she meant the fact that their neighbour had been murdered, or that they had been having a party when it happened.

"Did you hear anything last night between ten o'clock and midnight?" Truls asked.

The girl shook her head.

"Did Else—"

"Elise," Wyller corrected as he pulled out a notepad and pen. It occurred to Truls that perhaps he ought to have done the same.

Truls cleared his throat. "Did your neighbour have a boyfriend, someone who used to spend much time here?"

"I don't know," the girl said.

"Thanks, that's all," Truls said, turning towards the door as the other two girls came back.

"Perhaps we should hear what you have to say as well," Wyller said. "Your friend says she didn't hear anything yesterday, and that she isn't aware of anyone Elise Hermansen saw regularly, or even recently. Do either of you have anything to add to that?"

The two girls looked at each other before turning towards him and shaking their blonde heads at the same time. Truls could see the way all their attention was focused on the young detective. It didn't bother him, he'd had a lot of training in being overlooked. He was used to that little pang in his chest, like the time in high school in Manglerud when Ulla finally looked at him, but only to ask if he knew where Mikael was. And—seeing as this was before the days of mobile phones—if he could give Mikael a message. On one occasion Truls replied that that might be difficult seeing as Mikael had gone camping with a girlfriend. Not that the bit about camping was true, but because just for once he wanted to see the same pain, his own pain, reflected in her eyes.

"When did you last see Elise?" Wyller asked.

The three girls looked at each other again. "*We* didn't see her, but . . ."

One of them giggled, then clapped her hand to her mouth when she realised how inappropriate that was. The girl who had opened the door to them cleared her throat. "Enrique rang this morning and said he and Alfa stopped for a pee down in the archway on their way home."

"They're, like, really stupid," the tallest of them said.

"They were just a bit drunk," the third one said. She giggled again.

The girl who had opened the door shot the other two a pull-yourselves-together look. "Whatever. A woman walked in while they were standing there, and they called to say sorry in case their behaviour made us look bad."

"Which was pretty considerate of them," Wyller said. "And they think this woman was . . . ?"

"They *know*. They read online that 'a woman in her thirties' had been murdered, and saw the picture of the front of our building, so they googled and found a photo of her in one of the online papers."

Truls grunted. He hated journalists. Fucking scavengers, the lot of them. He went over to the window and looked down at the street. And there they were, on the other side of the police cordon, with the long lenses of their cameras that made Truls think of vultures' beaks when they held them in front of their faces in the hope of getting a glimpse of the body when it was carried out. Beside the waiting ambulance stood a guy in a Rasta hat with green, yellow and red stripes, talking to his white-clad colleagues. Bjørn Holm, from the Criminal Forensics Unit. He nodded to his people, then disappeared back inside the building again. There was something hunched, huddled about Holm's posture, as if he had stomach ache, and Truls wondered if it had anything to do with the rumours that the fish-eyed, moon-faced bumpkin had recently been dumped by Katrine Bratt. Good. Someone else could experience what it felt like to be ripped to shreds. Wyller's high-pitched voice buzzed in the background: "So their names are Enrique and . . . ?"

"No, no!" The girls laughed. "Henrik. And Alf."

Truls caught Wyller's eye and nodded towards the door.

"Thanks a lot, girls, that's all," Wyller said. "By the way, I'd better get some phone numbers."

The girls looked at him with a mixture of fear and delight.

"For Henrik and Alf," he added with a wry smile.


Katrine was standing in the bedroom behind the forensics medical officer, who was crouched by the bed. Elise Hermansen was lying on her back on top of the duvet. But the blood on her blouse was distributed in a way that showed she had been standing upright when the blood gushed out. She had probably been standing in front of the mirror in the hallway, where the rug was so drenched in blood that it had stuck to the parquet floor underneath. The trail of blood between the hall and the bedroom, and its limited quantity, indicated that her heart had probably stopped beating out in the hallway. Based on body temperature and rigor mortis, the forensics officer had estimated the time of death at between 2300 hours and one o'clock in the morning, and that the cause of death was probably loss of blood after her carotid artery was punctured by one or more of the incisions on the side of her throat, just above the left shoulder.

Her trousers and knickers were pulled down to her ankles.

"I've scraped and cut her nails, but I can't see any traces of skin with the naked eye," the forensics officer said.

"When did you lot start doing Forensics' work for them?" Katrine asked.

"When Bjørn told us to," she replied. "He asked so nicely."

"Really? Any other injuries?"

"She's got a scratch on her lower left arm, and a splinter of wood on the inside of her left middle finger."

"Any signs of sexual assault?"

"No visible sign of violence to the genitals, but there's this . . ." She held a magnifying glass above the body's stomach. Katrine looked through it and saw a thin, shiny line. "Could be saliva, her own or someone else's, but it looks more like precum or semen."

"Let's hope so," Katrine said.

"Let's *hope* she was sexually assaulted?" Bjørn Holm had walked in and was standing behind her.

"If she was, all the evidence suggests that it happened postmortem," Katrine said without turning round. "So she was already gone by then. And I'd really like some semen."

"I was joking," Bjørn said quietly in his amiable Toten dialect.

Katrine closed her eyes. Of course he knew that semen was the ultimate "open sesame" in a case like this. And of course he was only joking, trying to lighten the weird, wounded atmosphere that had existed between them in the three months that had passed since she had moved out. She was trying, too. She just couldn't quite manage it.

The forensics officer looked up at them. "I'm done here," she said, adjusting her hijab.

"The ambulance is here—I'll get my people to take the body down," Bjørn said. "Thanks for your help, Zahra."

The forensics officer nodded and hurried out, as if she had also noticed the strained atmosphere.

"Well?" Katrine said, forcing herself to look at Bjørn. Forcing herself to ignore the sombre look in his eyes that was more sad than pleading.

"There's not much to say," he said, scratching the bushy red beard that stuck out below his Rasta hat.

Katrine waited, hoping that they were still talking about the murder.

"She doesn't seem to have been particularly bothered about housework. We've found hairs from a whole load of people—mainly men—and it's hardly likely that they were all here last night."

"She was a lawyer," Katrine said. "A single woman with a demanding job like that might not prioritise cleaning as highly as you."

He smiled briefly without responding. And Katrine recognised the pang of the guilty conscience he always managed to give her. Obviously they had never argued about cleaning, Bjørn had always been too quick to deal with the washing-up, sweeping the steps, putting the clothes in the machine, cleaning the bath and airing the sheets, without any reproach or discussion. Like everything else. Not one single damn argument during the whole year they had lived together, he always wriggled out of them. And whenever she let him down or just couldn't be bothered, he was there, attentive, sacrificial, inexhaustible, like some fucking irritating robot who made her feel more like a pea-brained princess the higher he built her pedestal.

"How do you know that the hairs come from men?" she sighed.

"A single woman with a demanding job . . ." Bjørn said without looking at her.

Katrine folded her arms. "What are you trying to say, Bjørn?"

"What?" His pale face flushed lightly and his eyes bulged more than usual.

"That I'm easy? OK, if you really want to know, I—"

"No!" Bjørn held his hands up as if to defend himself. "I didn't mean it like that. It was just a bad joke."

Katrine knew she ought to feel pity. And she did, to an extent. Just not the sort of pity that makes you want to give someone a hug. This particular type of pity was more like derision, the sort of derision that made her want to slap him, humiliate him. And that was why she had walked out on him—because she didn't want to see Bjørn Holm, a perfectly good man, humiliated. Katrine Bratt took a deep breath.

"So, men?"

"Most of the hairs are short," Bjørn said. "We'll have to wait and see if the analysis confirms that. We've certainly got enough DNA to keep the National Forensic Lab busy for a while."

"OK," Katrine said, turning back towards the body. "Any ideas about what he could have stabbed her with? Or hacked, seeing as there's a whole load of incisions close together."

"It's not very easy to see, but they form a pattern," he said. "Two patterns, in fact."

"Oh?"

Bjørn went over to the body and pointed towards the woman's neck, beneath her short blonde hair. "Do you see that the incisions form two small, overlapping ovals, one here—and one here?"

Katrine tilted her head. "Now that you mention it . . ."

"Like bite marks."

"Oh, fuck," Katrine blurted out. "An animal?"

"Who knows? But imagine a fold of skin being pulled out and pressed together when upper and lower jaws meet. That would leave a mark like this . . ." Bjørn pulled a piece of semi-transparent paper from his pocket and Katrine instantly recognised it as the wrapper of the packed lunch he took to work each day. "Looks like it matches the bite of someone from Toten, anyway."

"Human teeth can't have done that to her neck."

"Agreed. But the pattern is human."

Katrine moistened her lips. "There are people who file their teeth to make them sharper."

"If it was teeth, we may find saliva around the wounds. Either way, if they were standing on the rug in the hallway when he bit her, the bite marks indicate that he was standing behind her, and that he's taller than her."

"The forensics officer didn't find anything under her nails, so I reckon he was holding her tight," Katrine said. "A strong man of average or above average height, with the teeth of a predator."

They stood in silence, looking at the body. Like a young couple in an art gallery contemplating opinions with which to impress other people, Katrine thought. The only difference was that Bjørn never tried to impress people. She was the one who did that.

Katrine heard steps in the hall. "No more people in here now!" she called.

"Just wanted to let you know there were only people at home in two of the flats, and none of them saw or heard anything." Wyller's high-pitched voice. "But I've just spoken to two lads who saw Elise Hermansen when she came home. They say she was alone."

"And these lads are . . . ?"

"No criminal record, and they had a taxi receipt to prove that they left here just after 11:30. They said she walked in on them while they were urinating in the archway. Shall I bring them in for questioning?"

"It wasn't them, but yes."

"OK."

Wyller's steps receded.

"She returned home alone and there are no signs of a break-in," Bjørn said. "Do you think she let him in voluntarily?"

"Not unless she knew him well."

"No?"

"Elise was a lawyer, she knew the risks, and that security chain on the door looks pretty new. I think she was a careful young woman." Katrine crouched down beside the body. Looked at the splinter of wood sticking out of Elise's middle finger. And the scratch on her lower arm.

"A lawyer," Bjørn said. "Where?"

"Hollumsen & Skiri. They were the ones who called the police when she didn't show up at a hearing and wasn't answering her phone. It's not exactly unusual for lawyers to be the victims of attacks."

"Do you think . . . ?"

"No, like I said, I don't think she let anyone in. But . . ." Katrine frowned. "Do you agree that this splinter looks pinkish white?"

Bjørn leaned over her. "White, certainly."

"Pinkish white," Katrine said, standing up. "Come with me."

They went out into the hall, where Katrine opened the door and pointed at the splintered door frame outside. "Pinkish white."

"If you say so," Bjørn said.

"Don't you see it?" she asked incredulously.

"Research has shown that women usually see more nuances of colour than men."

"You do see *this*, though?" Katrine asked, holding up the security chain that was hanging down the inside of the door.

Bjørn leaned closer. His scent came as a shock to her. Maybe it was just discomfort at the sudden intimacy.

"Scraped skin," he said.

"The scratch on her lower arm. Do you see?"

He nodded slowly. "She scratched herself on the security chain, so it must have been on. So he wasn't trying to push past her, she was fighting to get out."

"We don't usually use security chains in Norway, we rely on locks, that's the general rule. And if she did let him in, if this strong man was someone she knew, for instance . . ."

". . . she wouldn't have fiddled about putting the chain back on after she'd opened the door to let him in. Because she would have felt safe. Ergo . . ."

"Ergo," she took over, "he was already in the flat when she got home."

"Without her knowing," he said.

"That's why she put the security chain on, she thought anything dangerous was *outside*." Katrine shuddered. This was what the expression "horrified delight" was for. The feeling a homicide detective gets when they suddenly *see* and *understand*.

"Harry would have been pleased with you now," Bjørn said. And laughed.

"What?"

"You're blushing."

I'm *so* fucked up, Katrine thought.

# 3

# Thursday afternoon

Katrine had trouble concentrating during the press conference, where they gave a brief account of the victim's identity, age, where and when she was found, but that was about it. The first press conferences immediately after a murder were almost always a matter of saying as little as possible and simply going through the motions, in the name of modern, open democracy.

Alongside her sat the head of Crime Squad, Gunnar Hagen. The camera lights reflected off the shiny bald patch above his ring of dark hair as he read out the short sentences they had composed together. Katrine was happy to let Hagen do the talking. Not that she didn't like the spotlight, but that could come later. At the moment she was so new to the role of lead detective that it felt reassuring to let Hagen deal with the talking until she learned the right way to say things, and watch as an accomplished senior police officer used body language and tone of voice rather than actual content to convince the general public that the police were in control.

She sat there, looking out over the heads of the thirty or so journalists who had gathered in the Parole Hall on the fourth floor, at the large painting that covered the whole of the back wall. It showed naked people swimming, most of them skinny young boys. A beautiful, innocent scene from a time before everything became loaded and interpreted in the worst possible way. And she was no different: she assumed the artist was a pedophile. Hagen was repeating his mantra in response to the journalists' questions: "We aren't in a position to answer that at present," with simple variations to stop the replies sounding arrogant or directly comical. "At this moment in time we can't comment on that." Or a more benevolent: "We'll have to come back to that."

She heard their scratching pens and keyboards write questions that were obviously more elaborate than the answers: "Was the body badly damaged?" "Was there any evidence of sexual assault?" "Do you have a suspect, and, if so, is it someone close to her?" Speculative questions that could lend a certain tremulous subtext to the reply "No comment," if nothing else.

In the doorway at the back of the room she could make out a familiar figure. He had a black patch over one eye, and had put on the Police Chief's uniform that she knew always hung, freshly pressed, in the cupboard in his office. Mikael Bellman. He didn't come all the way inside, just stood there as an observer. She noted that Hagen had also spotted him, and he sat up a little straighter in his chair under the gaze of the rather younger Police Chief.

"We'll leave it there," the head of communications said.

Katrine saw Bellman indicate that he wanted to talk to her.

"When's the next press conference?" asked Mona Daa, *VG*'s crime correspondent.

"We'll get—"

"When we've got something new," Hagen interrupted the head of communications.

*When*, Katrine noted. Not *if*. It was tiny but important choices of words like that which signalled that the servants of the state were working tirelessly, that the wheels of justice were turning, and that it was only a matter of time before the perpetrator was caught.


"Anything new?" Bellman asked as they strode across the floor of the atrium of Police HQ. In the past his almost girlish prettiness, emphasised by his long eyelashes, neat, slightly too long hair and tanned skin with its characteristic white pigmentless marks, could give an impression almost of affectation, of weakness. But the eye-patch, which of course could have made him look theatrical, had the opposite effect. It implied strength, a man who wasn't going to let even losing an eye stop him.

"Forensics have found something in the bite marks," Katrine said as she followed Bellman through the airlock in front of reception.

"Saliva?"

"Rust."

"Rust?"

"Yes."

"As in . . . ?" Bellman pressed the lift button in front of them.

"We don't know," Katrine said, stopping beside him.

"And you still don't know how the perpetrator got into the flat?"

"No. The lock is impossible to pick, and neither the door nor any of the windows has been forced. It's still a possibility that she let him in, but we don't believe that."

"Perhaps he had a key."

"The housing association uses locks where the same key will open both the main entrance to the building and one of the flats. And according to the association's key register, there was only one key to Elise Hermansen's flat. The one that she had. Berntsen and Wyller have spoken to two guys who were by the entrance when she got home, and they're both certain she used her key to get in—she didn't use the entryphone to call someone who was already in the flat to open the front door from there."

"I see. But couldn't he just have got a copy of the key?"

"In that case he would have had to get hold of the original key, and find a key-cutter who had the technical ability to cut that type of key, and was unscrupulous enough to make a copy without the written permission of the housing association. That probably isn't very likely."

"OK. Well, that wasn't actually what I wanted to talk to you about . . ." The lift door in front of them slid open and two officers who were on their way out stopped laughing automatically when they caught sight of the Police Chief.

"It's about Truls," Bellman said, after gallantly letting Katrine get into the empty lift before him. "Berntsen, I mean."

"OK?" Katrine said, detecting a faint scent of aftershave. She'd always assumed men had given up wet shaving and the dowsing with spirits that followed it. Bjørn had used an electric razor and didn't bother with any added flavourings, and the men she had met since . . . well, on a couple of occasions she would have preferred heavy perfume to their natural smell.

"How is he getting on?"

"Berntsen? Fine."

They were standing side by side, facing the lift doors, but from the corner of her eye she caught a glimpse of his crooked smile in the silence that followed.

"Fine?" he eventually repeated.

"Berntsen carries out the orders he's given."

"Which aren't too demanding, I imagine?"

Katrine shrugged. "He has no background as a detective. And he's been posted to the biggest crime squad in the country, outside of Kripos. That means you don't get to sit in the driver's seat, if I can put it like that."

Bellman nodded and rubbed his chin. "I really just wanted to know that he's behaving himself. That he isn't . . . That he's following the rules."

"As far as I'm aware." The lift slowed down. "What rules are we actually talking about here?"

"I just want you to keep an eye on him, Bratt. Truls Berntsen hasn't had it easy."

"You mean the injuries he received from the explosion?"

"I mean his life, Bratt. He's a bit . . . what's the word I'm looking for?"

"Fucked up?"

Bellman let out a brief laugh and nodded towards the open doors. "Your floor, Bratt."

Bellman studied Katrine Bratt's well-shaped rear as she walked off down the corridor towards the Crime Squad Unit, and let his imagination run loose in the seconds it took the lift doors to close again. Then he refocused his thoughts on *the problem*. Which wasn't a problem, of course, but an opportunity. Though it was a dilemma. He had received a speculative and highly unofficial enquiry from the Prime Minister's office. It was rumoured that there was going to be a government reshuffle, and, among others, the position of Justice Minister was up for grabs. The enquiry concerned what Bellman—purely hypothetically—would say if he were to be asked. He had been astonished at first. But on closer consideration he realised that the choice was logical. As Chief of Police he had not only been responsible for the unmasking of the now internationally renowned "cop killer," but had also lost an eye in the heat of battle, thereby becoming in some ways both a national and an international hero. A forty-year-old, articulate Chief of Police with legal training who had already successfully defended the capital against murder, narcotics and criminality: surely it was about time they gave him a greater challenge? And did it do any harm that he was good-looking? That was hardly going to attract *fewer* women to the party. So he had replied that he—hypothetically—would accept.

Bellman got out at the seventh—the top—floor, and walked past the row of photographs of previous chiefs of police.

But until they made their minds up he would have to make sure he didn't get any scratches on his paintwork. Such as Truls doing something stupid and it rebounding on him. Bellman shuddered at the thought of the newspaper headlines: POLICE CHIEF PROTECTED CORRUPT COP AND FRIEND. When Truls had come to his office, he had put his feet up on the desk and said straight out that if he got fired from the police, he would at least have the consolation of dragging an equally tainted chief of police with him. So it had been an easy decision to grant Truls's request to work at Crime Squad. Particularly since—as Bratt had just confirmed—he wasn't going to be given enough responsibility to enable him to fuck things up again any time soon.

"Your lovely wife is sitting in there," Helga said when Mikael Bellman reached the outer office. Helga was well over sixty, and when Bellman was appointed four years ago, the first thing she had said was that she didn't want to be known as his PA, in the way of modern job descriptions. She was and would remain his secretary.

Ulla was sitting on the sofa by the window. Helga was right, his wife was lovely. She was vivacious, sensitive, and giving birth to three children hadn't changed that. But more important, she had backed him up, had realised that his career required nurturing, support, elbow room. And that the occasional misstep in his private life was only human when you had to live with the pressure that went with such a demanding position.

And there was something unspoiled, almost naive about her that meant you could read everything in her face. And right now he could read despair. The first thing Bellman thought was that it was something to do with the children. He was on the point of asking when he detected a hint of bitterness. And he realised that she had found something out. Again. Damn.

"You look very serious, darling," he said calmly, walking towards the cupboard as he unbuttoned the jacket of his uniform. "Has something happened to the children?"

She shook her head. He breathed out in feigned relief. "Not that I'm not pleased to see you, but I always get a bit worried when you turn up unannounced." He hung up his jacket and then sat down in the armchair facing her. "So?"

"You've been seeing her again," Ulla said. He could hear that she had been practising how to say it. Worked out how to say it without crying. But now there were already tears in her blue eyes.

He shook his head.

"Don't deny it," she said in a muffled voice. "I've checked your phone. You've called her three times this week alone, Mikael. You promised . . ."

"Ulla." He leaned forward and took her hand over the table but she pulled away. "I've spoken to her because I need advice. Isabelle Skøyen is currently working as a communications adviser for a company that specialises in politics and lobbying. She's familiar with the workings of power, because she's been there herself. *And* she knows me, too."

"*Knows*?" Ulla's face contorted in a grimace.

"If I—if *we* are going to do this, I need to make the most of anything that can give me an advantage, anything that can help me cross the line ahead of everyone else who wants the job. The *government*, Ulla. There's nothing bigger than that."

"Not even your family?" she sniffed.

"You know very well that I'd never let our family down—"

"Never let us down?" she yelped. "You've already—"

"—and I hope you're not thinking of doing that either, Ulla. Not on the grounds of some unwarranted jealousy towards a woman I've spoken to on the phone for purely professional reasons."

"That woman was only a local politician for a very brief time, Mikael. What could she possibly have to tell you?"

"Among other things, what *not* to do if you want to survive in politics. That was the experience they were buying when they employed her. For instance, you shouldn't betray your ideals. Or those closest to you. Or your responsibilities and obligations. And, if you get it wrong, you apologise and try to get it right next time. It's OK to make mistakes. But betrayal isn't OK. And I don't want to do that, Ulla." He took her hand again, and this time she didn't pull away. "I know I don't have the right to ask for much after what happened, but if I'm going to do this, I'm going to need your trust and support. You have to believe me."

"How can I . . . ?"

"Come." He stood up without letting go of her hand and pulled her over to the window. He positioned her so she was facing the city. Stood behind her and put his hands on her shoulders. Because Police Headquarters was at the top of a hill they could see half of Oslo, which lay bathed in sunshine below them. "Do you want to help make a difference, Ulla? Do you want to help me create a safer future for our children? For our neighbours? For this city? For our country?"

He could feel that his words were having an effect on her. Christ, they were having an effect on him too—he actually felt pretty moved by them. Even if they were more or less lifted straight from notes he had made when he was thinking about what to say to the media. It wouldn't be many more hours before he was officially offered the ministerial post, and said yes, and the newspapers, television, radio all started phoning for a comment.

Truls Berntsen was stopped by a short woman when he and Wyller emerged into the atrium after the press conference.

"Mona Daa, *VG*. I've seen you before." She turned away from Truls. "But you seem to be a new arrival at Crime Squad?"

"Correct," Wyller said. Truls studied Mona Daa from the side. She had a fairly attractive face. Wide—Sami heritage, perhaps. But he had never really made sense of her body. The colourful, loose-fitting outfits she wore made her look more like an old-school opera reviewer than a tough crime reporter. Even though she couldn't be much over thirty, Truls couldn't help thinking that she'd been around for an eternity: strong, persistent and robust, it would take a lot to shake Mona Daa. And she smelled like a man. Rumour had it that she used Old Spice aftershave.

"You didn't exactly give us much to go on in the press conference." Mona Daa smiled. The way journalists smile when they want something. Only this time it looked like she wasn't just after information. Her eyes were glued to Wyller.

"I dare say we didn't have much more," Wyller said, smiling back.

"I'll quote you on that," Mona Daa said, making notes. "Name?"

"Quote me on *what*?"

"That the police really don't know anything beyond what Hagen and Bratt said during the press conference."

Truls saw a brief look of panic in Wyller's eyes. "No, no, that's not what I meant . . . I . . . don't write that, please."

Mona went on writing as she replied: "I introduced myself as a journalist, and it ought to be pretty obvious that I'm here because of my job."

Wyller looked to Truls for help, but Truls said nothing. The young dude certainly wasn't as cocky now as when he was charming those student girls.

Wyller squirmed and tried to make his voice sound lower. "I refuse to let you use that quote."

"I see," Daa said. "Then I'll quote you on that as well, to show that the police are trying to muzzle the press."

"I . . . no, that's . . ." Wyller was blushing furiously now, and Truls had to make a real effort not to laugh.

"Relax, I'm only kidding," Mona Daa said.

Anders Wyller stared at her for a moment before breathing out again.

"Welcome to the game. We play tough but fair. And if we can, we help each other out. Isn't that right, Berntsen?"

Truls grunted something in response and left them to decide how to interpret it.

Daa leafed through her notebook. "I won't bother repeating the question of whether you've identified a suspect, your boss can deal with that one, but let me just ask more generally about the investigation."

"Fire away," Wyller said with a smile, looking like he was already back in the saddle.

"Isn't it the case in a murder investigation like this that the spotlight is always aimed at previous partners or lovers?"

Anders Wyller was about to answer when Truls put a hand on his shoulder and interjected: "I can already see it in front of me, Daa: 'Detectives are unwilling to say if they have a suspect, but a source in the police has told *VG* that the investigation is focusing on previous partners and lovers.'"

"Bloody hell," Mona Daa said, still taking notes. "I didn't know you were that smart, Berntsen."

"And I didn't know you knew my name."

"Oh, all police officers have a reputation, you know. And Crime Squad isn't so big that I can't keep up to date. But I've got nothing on you, the new kid on the block."

Anders Wyller smiled weakly.

"I see you've decided to keep quiet, but you can at least tell me your name."

"Anders Wyller."

"This is how you can get hold of me, Wyller." She handed him a business card and—after an almost imperceptible hesitation—

another to Truls. "Like I said, it's traditional for us to help each other. And we pay well if the tip-off's good."

"You surely don't pay *police officers*?" Wyller said, tucking her card into his jeans pocket.

"Why not?" she said, and her eyes very briefly met Truls's. "A tip-off is a tip-off. So if you come up with anything, just call. Or pop into the Gain Gym, I'm there around nine o'clock most evenings. We could sweat it out together . . ."

"I prefer to do my sweating outdoors," Wyller said.

Mona Daa nodded. "Running with a dog. You look like a dog person. I like that."

"Why?"

"Allergic to cats. OK, guys, in the spirit of collaboration I promise to call if I find out anything I think might help you."

"Thanks," Truls said.

"But I'll need a phone number to call." Mona Daa kept her eyes fixed on Wyller.

"Sure," he said.

"I'll write it down."

Wyller recited several digits until Mona Daa looked up. "That's the number to reception here in Police HQ."

"This is where I work," Anders Wyller said. "And by the way, I've got a cat."

Mona Daa closed her notebook. "We'll be in touch."

Truls watched her as she waddled like a penguin towards the exit and the weirdly heavy metal door with its staring porthole.

"The meeting starts in three minutes," Wyller said.

Truls looked at his watch. The afternoon meeting of the investigative team. Crime Squad would have been great if it weren't for the murders. Murders were shit. Murders meant long hours, writing reports, endless meetings and loads of stressed-out people. But at least they got free food from the cafeteria when they worked overtime. He sighed and turned to walk towards the airlock, but stiffened.

There she was.

Ulla.

She was on her way out, and her eyes swept over him as she passed, without letting on that she had seen him. She did that sometimes. Possibly because it had occasionally been a bit awkward when the two of them met without Mikael being present. In truth, they probably both tried to avoid that, even when they were younger. Him because he would start to sweat and his heart would beat too quickly and because he would always torment himself afterwards with the stupid things he had said and the smart, genuine things he hadn't said. Her because . . . well, probably because he would start to sweat, his heart would beat too quickly, and because he either didn't speak or said stupid things.

Even so, he almost called out her name in the atrium.

But she had already reached the door. In a moment she would be outside and the sunshine would kiss her fine blonde hair.

So he whispered her name silently to himself instead.

Ulla.

# 4

# Thursday, late afternoon

Katrine Bratt looked out across the conference room.

Eight detectives, four analysts, one forensics expert. They were all at her disposal. And they were all watching her like hawks. The new, female lead detective. And Katrine knew that the biggest skeptics in the room were her female colleagues. She had often wondered if she was fundamentally different from other women. They had a testosterone level somewhere between five and ten percent of their male colleagues, whereas hers was closer to twenty-five percent. That hadn't yet turned her into a hairy lump of muscle with a clitoris the size of a penis, but as far back as she could remember it had made her far hornier than any of her female friends had ever admitted to being. Or "angry horny," as Bjørn used to say when things got really bad, and she would break off from work to drive out to Bryn just so he could fuck her in the deserted storeroom behind the laboratory, making the boxes of flasks and test tubes rattle.

Katrine coughed, switched on the recording function of her phone, and began. "1600 hours on Thursday, 22 September, conference room 1 in the Crime Squad Unit, and this is the first meeting of the preliminary investigation into the murder of Elise Hermansen."

Katrine saw Truls Berntsen come lumbering in, and sit down at the back.

She began explaining what most people in the room already knew: that Elise Hermansen had been found murdered that morning, that the probable cause of death was loss of blood as a result of injuries to her neck. That no witnesses had come forward so far. They had no suspect, and no conclusive physical evidence. The organic matter they had found in the flat, which might be human in origin, had been sent for DNA analysis, and they would hopefully be getting the results back within the space of a week. Other potential physical evidence was being examined by Forensics and the forensics officer. In other words: they had nothing.

She saw a couple of them fold their arms and breathe out heavily, on the brink of yawning. And she knew what they were thinking: that this was all obvious, repetitive, there was nothing for them to sink their teeth into, not enough to make them drop everything else they were working on. She explained how she had deduced that the murderer was already in the flat by the time Elise got home, but could hear for herself that it just sounded boastful. A new boss's plea for respect. She started to feel desperate, and thought about what Harry had said when she had called to ask for advice.

"Catch the murderer," he had replied.

"Harry, that's not what I asked. I asked how to *lead* an investigative team that doesn't trust you."

"And I gave you the answer."

"Catching the odd murderer won't solve—"

"It will solve everything."

"Everything? So exactly what has it solved for you, Harry? In purely personal terms?"

"Nothing. But you asked about leadership."

Katrine looked out at the room, came to the end of yet another superfluous sentence, took a deep breath and noticed a hand drumming gently on the arm of a chair.

"Unless Elise Hermansen let this individual into her flat earlier yesterday evening and left him there when she went out, we're looking for someone she knows. So we've been examining her phone and computer. Tord?"

Tord Gren got to his feet. He had been given the nickname Wader, presumably because he resembled a wading bird with his unusually long neck, narrow beak-like nose and a wingspan far greater than his height. His old-fashioned round glasses and curly hair hanging down on both sides of his thin face made him look like something from the 1970s.

"We've got into her iPhone and have checked the lists of texts and calls made and received in the last three days," Tord said, without taking his eyes from his tablet, as if he wasn't big on eye contact in general. "Nothing but work-related calls. Colleagues and clients."

"No friends?" This from Magnus Skarre, a tactical analyst. "Parents?"

"I believe that's what I said," Tord replied. Not unfriendly, just precise. "The same applies to her emails. Work-related."

"The law firm has confirmed that Elise did a lot of overtime," Katrine added.

"Single women tend to," Skarre said.

Katrine looked in resignation at the thickset little detective, even though she knew the comment wasn't directed at her. Skarre was neither malicious nor quick-witted enough for that.

"Her PC wasn't password-protected, but there wasn't much to find on there," Tord went on. "The log shows that she mostly used it to watch the news or to google information. She visited a few porn sites, just the ordinary sort of thing, and there's no sign that she ever contacted anyone via those websites. The only dodgy thing she seems to have done in the past two years is streaming *The Notebook* on Popcorn Time."

Given that Katrine didn't know the IT expert well enough, she wasn't sure if by "dodgy" he meant the use of a pirate server or the choice of film. She would have said the latter if it was up to her. She missed Popcorn Time.

"I tried a couple of obvious passwords for her Facebook account," Tord continued. "No joy, so I've sent a freeze request to Kripos."

"A freeze request?" Anders Wyller asked from the front row.

"An application to the court," Katrine said. "Any request to access a Facebook account has to go through Kripos and the courts, and even with their approval it has to go to a court in the USA, and only *then* to Facebook. At best it will take several weeks, but more likely months."

"That's all," Tord Gren said.

"Just one more question from a rookie," Wyller said. "How did you get into the phone? Fingerprints from the body?"

Tord glanced up at Wyller, then looked away and shook his head.

"How, then? Older iPhones have four-digit codes. That means 10,000 different—"

"Microscope," Tord interrupted, typing something on his tablet

Katrine was familiar with Tord's method, but she waited. Tord

Gren hadn't trained to become a police officer. He hadn't trained to become much at all, really. A few years in information technology in Denmark, but no qualifications. Even so, he had soon been pulled out of Police HQ's IT department and given a job as an analyst, with a particular focus on anything relating to technological evidence. Purely because he was so much better than everyone else.

"Even the toughest glass acquires microscopic indentations where it's touched most often by someone's fingertips," Tord said. "I just have to find out where on the screen the deepest indentations are, and that's the code. Well, the four digits give twenty-four possible combinations."

"The phone locks after three failed attempts, though," Anders said. "So you'd have to be lucky . . ."

"I got the right code on the second attempt," Tord said with a smile, but Katrine couldn't tell if he was smiling because of what he'd just said or something on his tablet.

"Bloody hell," Skarre said. "Talk about luck."

"On the contrary, I was unlucky not to get it on my first attempt. When the number contains the numerals 1 and 9, as in this instance, that usually means a year, and then there are only two possible combinations."

"Enough of that," Katrine said. "We've spoken to Elise's sister, and she says she hadn't had a regular boyfriend for years. And that she probably didn't want one either."

"Tinder," Wyller said.

"Sorry?"

"Did she have the Tinder app on her phone?"

"Yes," Tord said.

"The guys who saw Elise in the archway said she looked a bit dressed up. So she wasn't coming home from the gym, or work, and presumably not from seeing a female friend. And if she didn't want a boyfriend."

"Good," Katrine said. "Tord?"

"We did check the app, and there were plenty of matches, to put it mildly. But Tinder is linked to Facebook, so we can't yet access any further information about people she may have had contact with on there."

"Tinder people meet in bars," a voice said.

Katrine looked up in surprise. It was Truls Berntsen.

"If she had her phone with her, it's just a matter of checking the base stations, then going round the bars in the areas she was in."

"Thanks, Truls," Katrine said. "We've already checked the base stations. Stine?"

One of the analysts sat up in her chair and cleared her throat. "According to the printout from Telenor's operations centre, Elise Hermansen left work at Youngstorget sometime between 6:30 and 7 p.m. She went to an area in the vicinity of Bentsebrua. Then—"

"Her sister told us Elise used the gym at Myrens Verksted," Katrine interrupted. "And they've confirmed that she checked in at 19:32, and left at 21:14, Sorry, Stine."

Stine gave her a brief, slightly stiff smile. "Then Elise moved to the area around her home address, where she—or at least her phone—remained until she was found. That's to say, its signal was picked up by a few overlapping base stations, which confirms that she went out, but no further than a few hundred metres from her home in Grünerløkka."

"Great, so we get to go on a bar crawl," Katrine said.

She was rewarded with a chuckle from Truls, a broad smile from Anders Wyller, but otherwise total silence.

Could be worse, she thought.

Her phone, which was on the table in front of her, began to move. She saw from the screen that it was Bjørn.

It could be something about forensic evidence, in which case it would be good to hear it straight away. But, on the other hand, if that was the case he ought to have called his colleague from Forensics who was attending the meeting, not her. So it could be something personal.

She was about to click 'Reject call' when she realised that Bjørn would be well aware that she was in a meeting. He was good at keeping track of that sort of thing.

She raised the phone to her ear. "We're in the middle of a meeting of the investigative team, Bjørn."

She regretted saying that the moment she felt all eyes on her.

"I'm at the Forensic Medical Institute," Bjørn said. "We've just had the results of the preliminary tests on the shiny substance she had on her stomach. There's no human DNA in it."

"Damn," Katrine blurted out. It had been in the back of her mind the whole time: that if the substance was semen, the case could probably be solved within the magical limit of the first forty-eight hours. All experience indicated that it would be harder after that.

"But it could suggest that he had intercourse with her after all," Bjørn said.

"What makes you think that?"

"It was lubricating gel. Probably from a condom."

Katrine swore again. And she could tell from the way the others were looking at her that she hadn't yet said anything to prove that this wasn't just a private conversation. "So you're saying the perpetrator used a condom?" she said, loudly and clearly.

"Him, or someone else she met yesterday evening."

"OK, thanks." She was keen to end the conversation, but heard Bjørn say her name before she had time to hang up.

"Yes?" she said.

"That wasn't actually why I called."

She swallowed. "Bjørn, we're in the middle—"

"The murder weapon," he said. "I think I might have figured out what it was. Can you keep the group there for another twenty minutes?"


He was lying in bed in the flat, reading on his phone. He'd been through all the newspapers now. It was disappointing, they'd left out all the details, they'd neglected to report everything that was of artistic value. Either because the lead detective, Katrine Bratt, didn't want to reveal them, or because she simply lacked the capacity to see the beauty in it. But *he*, the policeman with murder in his eyes, he would have seen it. Maybe like Bratt he would have kept it to himself, but at least he would have appreciated it.

He looked more closely at the picture of Katrine Bratt in the newspaper.

She was beautiful.

Wasn't there some sort of regulation about them having to wear a uniform for press conferences? If there was, she was breaking it. He liked her. Imagined her wearing her police uniform.

Very beautiful.

Sadly she wasn't on the agenda.

He put the newspaper down. Ran his hand across the tattoo. Sometimes it felt like it was real, that it was bursting, that the skin over his chest was stretched tight and about to split.

To hell with regulations.

He tensed his stomach muscles and used them to get up from the bed. Looked at his reflection in the mirror on the sliding door of the wardrobe. He had got into shape in prison. Not in the gym. Lying on benches and mats soaked in other people's sweat was out of the question. No, in his cell. Not to get muscles, but to acquire *real* strength. Stamina. Tautness. Balance. The capacity to bear pain.

His mother had been solidly built. A big backside. She'd let herself go towards the end. Weak. He must have got his body and metabolism from his father. And his strength.

He pushed the wardrobe door aside.

There was a uniform hanging there. He ran his hand over it. Soon it would come into use.

He thought about Katrine Bratt. In her uniform.

That evening he would go to a bar. A popular, busy bar, not like the Jealousy Bar. It was against the rules to go out among people for anything but food, the baths and the agenda, but he would glide about in tantalising anonymity and isolation. Because he needed to. Needed to, to stop himself going mad. He let out a quiet laugh. Mad. The counsellors said he needed to see a psychiatrist. And of course he knew what they meant by that: that he needed someone who could prescribe medication.

He took a pair of freshly polished cowboy boots from the shoe rack, and looked for a moment at the woman at the back of the wardrobe. She was hung up on the pegs in the wall behind her, and her eyes stared out between the suits. She smelt faintly of the lavender perfume he had rubbed on her chest. He closed the door again.

Mad? They were incompetent idiots, the whole lot of them. He had read the definition of personality disorder in a dictionary, that it was a mental illness that leads to "discomfort and difficulties for the individual concerned and those around them." Fine. In his case that merely applied to those around him. He had just the personality he wanted. Because when you have access to drink, what could be more pleasant, more rational and more normal than feeling thirsty?

He looked at the time. In half an hour it would be dark enough outside.


"This is what we found around the injuries to her neck," Bjørn Holm said, pointing to the image on the screen. "The three fragments on the left are rusted iron, and on the right, black paint."

Katrine had sat down with the others in the conference room. Bjørn had been out of breath when he arrived, and his pale cheeks were still glistening with sweat.

He tapped on his laptop and a close-up of the neck appeared.

"As you can see, the places where the skin has been punctured form a pattern, as if she'd been bitten by someone, but if that was the case, the teeth must have been razor-sharp."

"A satanist," Skarre said.

"Katrine wondered if it was someone who had sharpened his teeth, but we've checked, and where the teeth have almost gone through the other side of the fold of skin, we can see that the teeth don't actually meet, but have slotted in perfectly between the other set of teeth. So this could hardly be an ordinary human bite, where the lower and upper teeth are positioned so that they meet each other, tooth for tooth. The fact that we found rust therefore leads me to think that the perpetrator used some sort of iron dentures."

Bjørn tapped at the computer.

Katrine felt a quiet gasp go through the room.

The screen showed an object which at first put Katrine in mind of an old, rusty animal trap she had once seen at her grandfather's in Bergen, something he called a bear trap. The sharp teeth formed a zigzag pattern, and the upper and lower jaws were fixed together by what looked to be a spring-loaded mechanism.

"This picture is taken from a private collection in Caracas, and is said to date from the days of slavery, when they used to bet on slaves fighting each other. Two slaves would each be given a set of dentures, their hands would be tied behind their backs, and then they would be put in the ring. The one who survived went through to the next round. I assume. But to get back to the point—"

"Please," Katrine said.

"I've tried to find out where you could get hold of a set of iron teeth like these. And it isn't exactly the sort of thing you can get through mail order. So if we were able to find someone who's sold contraptions like this in Oslo or elsewhere in Norway, and who to, I'd say we'd be looking at a very limited number of people."

Katrine realised that Bjørn had gone far beyond the usual duties of a forensics officer, but decided not to comment on the fact.

"One more thing," Bjørn said. "There's not enough blood."

"Not enough?"

"The blood contained in an adult human body makes up, on average, seven percent of bodyweight. It differs slightly from person to person, but even if she was at the low end of the scale, there's almost half a litre missing when we add up what was left in the body, on the carpet in the hallway, on the wooden floor and the small quantity on the bed. So, unless the murderer took the missing blood away with him in a bucket . . ."

". . . he drank it," Katrine concluded, giving voice to what they were all thinking.

For three seconds there was total silence in the conference room. Wyller cleared his throat. "What about the black paint?"

"There's rust on the inside of the flakes of paint, so it came from the same source," Bjørn said, disconnecting his laptop from the projector. "But the paint isn't that old. I'm going to analyse that tonight."

Katrine could see that the others hadn't really absorbed the bit about the paint, they were still thinking about the blood.

"Thanks, Bjørn," Katrine said, standing up and looking at her watch. "OK, about that bar crawl. It's bedtime, so how about we send the people with kids home while us poor barren souls stay behind and split into teams?"

No response, no laughter, not so much as a smile.

"Good, we'll do that, then," Katrine said. She could feel how tired she was. And thrust her weariness aside. Because she had a nagging sense that this was only the beginning. Iron dentures and no DNA. Half a litre of missing blood.

The sound of scraping chairs.

She gathered her papers, glanced up and saw Bjørn disappearing through the door. Recognised the peculiar feeling of relief, guilty conscience and self-loathing. And thought that she felt . . . wrong.

# 5

# Thursday evening and night

Mehmet Kalak looked at the two people in front of him. The woman had an attractive face, an intense look in her eyes, tight hipster clothes and such a finely proportioned body that it didn't seem unlikely that she might have picked up the handsome young man who had to be ten years her junior. They were just the sort of clientele he was after, which was why he had given them an extra generous smile when they walked through the door of the Jealousy Bar.

"What do you think?" the woman said. She spoke with a Bergen accent. He had only managed to see the surname on her ID card. Bratt.

Mehmet lowered his eyes again and looked at the photograph they had put down on the bar in front of him.

"Yes," he said.

"Yes?"

"Yes, she was here. Yesterday evening."

"You're sure?"

"She was sitting right where you're standing now."

"Here? Alone?"

Mehmet could see that she was trying to hide her excitement. Why did people bother? What was so dangerous about showing what you felt? He wasn't particularly keen on selling out the only regular he had, but they had police ID.

"She was with a guy who's here a fair bit. What's happened?"

"Don't you read the papers?" her blond colleague asked in a high voice.

"No, I prefer something with news in it," Mehmet said.

Bratt smiled. "She was found murdered this morning. Tell us about the man. What were they doing here?"

Mehmet felt as if someone had emptied a bucket of ice-cold water over him. Murdered? The woman who had been standing here right in front of him less than twenty-four hours ago was now a corpse? He pulled himself together. And felt ashamed of the next thought that automatically popped into his head: if the bar got mentioned in the papers, would that be good or bad for business? After all, there was a limit to how much worse it could get.

"A Tinder date," he said. "He usually meets his dates here. Calls himself Geir."

"Calls himself?"

"I'd say it's his real name."

"Does he pay by card?"

"Yes."

She nodded towards the till. "Do you think you could find the receipt for his payment last night?"

"That should be possible, yes." Mehmet smiled sadly.

"Did they leave together?"

"Definitely not."

"Meaning?"

"That Geir had set his sights too high, as usual. He'd basically been dumped before I'd even had time to pour their drinks. Speaking of which, can I get you something . . . ?

"No, thanks," Bratt said. "We're on duty. So she left here alone?"

"Yes."

"And you didn't see anyone follow her?"

Mehmet shook his head, got two glasses out, and picked up a bottle of apple juice "This is on the house, freshly pressed, local. Come back another night and have a beer, on the house. The first one's free, you know. Same thing applies if you want to bring any police colleagues. Do you like the music?"

"Yes," the blond policeman said. "U2 are—"

"No," Bratt said. "Did you hear the woman say anything you think might be of interest to us?"

"No. Actually, now you come to mention it, she did say something about someone stalking her." Mehmet looked up from pouring. "The music was on low and she was talking loudly."

"I see. Was anyone else here showing any interest in her?"

Mehmet shook his head. "It was a quiet night."

"Like tonight, then?"

Mehmet shrugged. "The other two customers who were here had gone by the time Geir left."

"So it might not be too difficult to get their card details as well?"

"One of them paid cash, I remember. The other one didn't buy anything."

"OK. And where were you between 10 p.m. and one o'clock this morning?"

"Me? I was here. Then at home."

"Anyone who can confirm that? Just so we can get it out of the way at the start."

"Yes. Or no."

"Yes or no?"

Mehmet thought hard. Getting a loan shark with previous convictions mixed up in this could mean more trouble. He should hold on to that card in case he needed it later.

"No. I live alone."

"Thanks." Bratt raised her glass, and Mehmet thought at first she was drinking a toast, until he realised she was gesturing towards the till with it. "We'll sample these local apples while you look, OK?"


Truls had quickly worked his way through his bars and restaurants. Had shown the photograph to bartenders and waiters, and moved on as soon as he got the answer he expected, "No" or "Don't know." If you don't know, you don't know, and the day had already been more than long enough. Besides, he had one final item on his agenda.

Truls typed the last sentence on the keyboard and looked at the brief but, in his opinion, concise report. "See attached list of licensed premises visited by the undersigned at the times specified. None of the staff reported having seen Elise Hermansen on the evening of the murder." He pressed Send and stood up.

He heard a low buzz and saw a light flash on the desk telephone. He could tell from the number on the screen that it was the duty officer. They dealt with any tip-offs and only forwarded the ones that seemed relevant. Damn, he didn't have time for any more chat right now. He could pretend he hadn't seen it. But, on the other hand, if it was a tip-off, he might end up with more to pass on than he had thought.

He picked up.

"Berntsen."

"At last! No one's answering, where is everyone?"

"Out at bars."

"Haven't you got a murder to—?"

"What is it?"

"We've got a guy who says he was with Elise Hermansen last night."

"Put him through."

There was a click and Truls heard a man who was breathing so hard it could only mean he was frightened.

"DC Berntsen, Crime Squad. What's this about?"

"My name is Geir Sølle. I saw the picture of Elise Hermansen on *VG*'s website. I'm phoning because I had a very short encounter yesterday with a lady who looked a lot like her. And she said her name was Elise."

It took Geir Sølle five minutes to give an account of his date at the Jealousy Bar, and how he had gone straight home afterwards, and was home before midnight. Truls vaguely remembered that the pissing boys had seen Elise alive after 11:30.

"Can anyone confirm when you got home?"

"The log on my computer. And Kari."

"Kari?"

"My wife."

"You've got family?"

"Wife and dog." Truls heard him swallow audibly.

"Why didn't you call earlier?"

"I've only just seen the picture."

Truls made a note, swearing silently to himself. This wasn't the murderer, just someone they needed to rule out, but it still meant writing a full report, and now it was going to be ten o'clock before he managed to get away.


Katrine was walking down Markveien. She had sent Anders Wyller home from his first day at work. She smiled at the thought that he was bound to remember it for the rest of his life. First the office, then straight to the scene of a murder—and a serious one at that. Not the sort of boring drug-related murder that people forgot the next day, but what Harry called a could-have-been-me murder. Which was the murder of a so-called ordinary person in ordinary circumstances, the sort that led to packed press conferences and guaranteed front pages. Because familiarity made it easier for the public to empathise. That was why a terrorist attack in Paris got more media coverage than one in Beirut. And the media was the media. That was why Police Chief Bellman was taking the effort to keep himself informed. He was going to have to deal with questions. Not right away, but if the murder of a young, well-educated, hard-working female citizen wasn't cleared up within the next few days, he would have to make a statement.

It would take her half an hour to walk from here to her flat in Frogner, but that was fine, she needed to clear her head. And her body. She pulled her phone out of her jacket pocket and opened the Tinder app. She walked on with one eye on the pavement and the other on the phone as she swiped to right and left.

They had guessed right. Elise Hermansen had got home from a Tinder date. The man the bartender had described to them sounded harmless enough, but she knew from experience that some men had the strange idea that a quick shag gave them the right to more. An old-fashioned attitude that the act itself constituted a form of female submission which could be taken as purely sexual, perhaps. But for all she knew, there might be just as many women out there with equally old-fashioned ideas that men were automatically under some sort of moral obligation the moment they kindly consented to penetrate them. But enough of that—she'd just got a match.

*I'm 10 minutes from Nox on Solli plass*, she tapped.

*OK, I'll be waiting*, came the reply from Ulrich, who from his profile picture and description seemed to be a very straightforward man.


Truls Berntsen stopped and looked at Mona Daa looking at herself.

She no longer reminded him of a penguin. Well, she actually reminded him of a penguin that was being tightly squeezed around the middle.

Truls had detected a certain reluctance when he had asked the girl in gym gear behind the counter at Gain Gym to let him in so he could take a look at the facilities. Possibly because she didn't buy the idea that he was considering joining, and possibly because they didn't want people like him as members. Because a long life as someone who aroused other people's disapproval—often on good grounds, he had to admit—had taught Truls Berntsen to perceive disapproval in most faces he encountered. Either way, after passing machines that were supposed to tighten stomachs and buttocks, rooms for Pilates, rooms for spinning and rooms containing hysterical aerobics instructors (Truls had a vague idea it wasn't called aerobics anymore), he found her in the boys' area. The weights room. She was doing deadlifts. Her squat, splayed legs were still a bit penguiny. But the combination of broad backside and the wide leather belt that was squeezing her waist and making her bulge out both above and below made her look more like a number 8.

She let out a hoarse, almost frightening roar as she straightened her back and took the strain, staring at her own red face in the mirror. The weights clanked against each other as they left the floor. The bar didn't bend as much as he'd seen them do on television, but he could see that it was heavy from the two grunting Paki types who were doing curls to get biceps that were big enough for their pathetic gang tattoos. Christ, how he hated them. Christ, how they hated him.

Mona Daa lowered the weights. Roared and raised them again. Down. Up. Four times.

She stood there trembling afterwards. Smiled the way that crazy woman out in Lier did when she'd had an orgasm. If she hadn't been quite so fat and lived quite so far away, maybe something could have come of that. She said she'd dumped him because she was starting to like him. That once a week wasn't enough. At the time he had been relieved, but Truls still found himself thinking about her from time to time. Not the way he thought about Ulla, of course, but she had been nice, no question.

Mona Daa caught sight of him in the mirror. Pulled out her earphones. "Berntsen? I thought you had a gym in Police HQ?"

"We have," he said, going closer. Gave the Paki types an I'm-a-cop-so-get-lost look, but they didn't seem to understand. Perhaps he'd been wrong about them. Some of those kids were even in Police College these days.

"So what brings you here?" She loosened the belt and Truls couldn't help staring to see if she was going to balloon back out and become an ordinary penguin again.

"I thought we might be able to help each other."

"With what?" She squatted down in front of the weights and undid the nuts holding them on each side.

He crouched down beside her and lowered his voice. "You said you paid well for tip-offs."

"We do," she said, without lowering hers. "What have you got?"

"It'll cost fifty thousand."

Mona Daa laughed out loud. "We pay well, Berntsen, but not that well. Ten thousand is the maximum. And then we're talking a *really* tasty morsel."

Truls nodded slowly as he moistened his lips. "This isn't a tasty morsel."

"What did you say?"

Truls raised his voice a bit more. "I said: this isn't a tasty morsel."

"What is it, then?"

"It's a three-course meal."


"Not going to happen," Katrine cried over the cacophony of voices and took a sip of her White Russian. "I've got a partner and he's at home. Where do you live?"

"Gyldenløves gate. But there's nothing to drink, it's a real mess, and—"

"Clean sheets?"

Ulrich shrugged.

"You change the sheets while I take a shower," she said. "I've come straight from work."

"What do you—?"

"Let's just say that all you need to know about my job is that I have to be up early tomorrow, so shall we . . . ?" She nodded towards the door.

"OK, but maybe we could finish our drinks first?"

She looked at the cocktail. The only reason she'd started drinking White Russians was because that's what Jeff Bridges drinks in *The Big Lebowski*.

"That depends," she said.

"On what?"

"On what effect alcohol has . . . on you."

Ulrich smiled. "Are you trying to give me performance anxiety, Katrine?"

She shivered at the sound of her own name in this stranger's mouth. "Do you get performance anxiety, then, *Ul-rich*?"

"No," he grinned. "But do you know what these drinks cost?"

Now she smiled. Ulrich was OK. Thin enough. That was the first and really the only thing she looked for in a profile. Weight. And height. She could calculate their BMI as quickly as a poker player figured out the odds. A 26.5 was OK. Before she met Bjørn she'd never have believed she'd accept anyone over 25.

"I need to go to the toilet," she said. "Here's my cloakroom ticket, black leather jacket, wait by the door."

Katrine stood up and walked across the floor, assuming—seeing as this was his first chance to look at her from behind—that he was checking out what people where she came from usually called her arse. And knew that he'd be happy.

The back of the bar was more crowded and she had to push her way through, seeing as "Excuse me!" didn't have the open-sesame effect it had in what she considered to be the more civilised parts of the world. Bergen, for instance. And she must have been getting squeezed harder than she thought between the sweaty bodies, because suddenly she couldn't breathe. She broke free, and the giddy feeling of a lack of oxygen disappeared after a few steps.

In the corridor beyond there was the usual queue for the women's toilet and no one waiting for the men's. She looked at her watch again. Lead detective. She wanted to get to work first tomorrow. What the hell. She yanked open the door to the men's toilet, marched in and walked past the row of urinals, unnoticed by two men standing there, and locked herself in one of the cubicles. Her few female friends had always said they'd never set foot in a men's toilet, that they were much dirtier than the ladies'. That wasn't Katrine's experience.

She had pulled her trousers down and was sitting on the toilet when she heard a cautious knock on the door. That struck her as odd—it ought to be obvious from the outside that the cubicle was occupied, and, if you thought it was empty, why knock? She looked down. In the gap between the bottom of the door and the floor she saw the toes of a pair of pointed snakeskin boots. Her next thought was that someone must have seen her go into the men's toilet and had followed her to see if she was the more adventurous sort.

"Get los—" she began, but the 't' at the end vanished in a shortness of breath. Was she coming down with something? Had one single day heading up what she already knew was going to be a big murder investigation turned her into a nervous wreck who could hardly breathe? Christ . . .

She heard the door to the men's open and two squawking man-boys came in.

"It's, like, so fucking sick, man!"

"*Totally* sick!"

The pointed boots disappeared from below the door. Katrine listened, but couldn't hear any footsteps. She finished off, opened the door and went over to the washbasins. The conversation between the man-boys at the urinals tailed off as she turned the tap.

"What are you doing here?" one of them asked.

"Having a piss and washing my hands," she said. "Try to do it in that order."

She shook her hands and walked out.

Ulrich was waiting by the door. He reminded her of a dog wagging its tail with a stick in its mouth as he stood there holding her jacket. She pushed the image aside.


Truls was driving home. He turned the radio up when he heard them playing the Motörhead song he had always thought was called "Ace of Space" until Mikael yelled out at a high-school party: "Beavis here thinks Lemmy's singing Ace of . . . *Space!*" He could still hear the roars of laughter drowning out the music, and see the twinkle in Ulla's beautiful, laughing eyes.

That was fine, Truls still thought "Ace of Space" was a better title than "Ace of Spades." One day when Truls had taken the risk of sitting down at the same table as the others in the cafeteria, Bjørn Holm had been in the middle of explaining—in that ridiculous Toten dialect of his—that he thought it would have been more poetic if Lemmy had lived till he was seventy-two. When Truls asked why, Bjørn replied: "Seven and two, two and seven, right? Morrison, Hendrix, Joplin, Cobain, Winehouse, the whole lot."

Truls had merely nodded when he saw the others nodding. He still didn't know what it meant. Only that he had felt excluded.

Still, excluded or not, this evening Truls had become thirty thousand kroner richer than Bjørn fucking Holm and all his nodding cafeteria buddies.

Mona had brightened up considerably when Truls told her about the teeth, or iron dentures, as Holm had put it. She had called her editor and got him to agree that it was precisely what Truls had said: a three-course meal. The starter was the fact that Elise Hermansen had been on a Tinder date. The main course that the killer was probably already inside her flat when she got home. And the dessert that he had murdered her by biting her throat with teeth made of iron. Ten thousand for each course. Thirty. Three and zero, zero and three, right?

"Ace of space, the ace of space!" Truls and Lemmy roared.


"Not going to happen," Katrine said, pulling her trousers back up. "If you haven't got a condom, you can forget it."

"But I got checked out two weeks ago," Ulrich said, sitting up in bed. "Cross my heart, hope to die."

"Try that on someone else . . ." Katrine had to take a deep breath before buttoning her trousers. "Anyway, that's hardly going to stop me getting pregnant."

"Don't you use anything, then, girl?"

*Girl*? Oh, she did like Ulrich. It wasn't that. It was . . . God knows what it was.

She went out into the hall and put her shoes on. She'd made a note of where he'd hung her leather jacket, and had checked that there was just an ordinary lock on the inside of the door. Yep, she was good at planning her escape. She walked out and went down the stairs. When she emerged onto Gyldenløves gate the fresh autumn air tasted of freedom and a sense of having had a narrow escape. She laughed. Walked down the path that ran between the trees in the middle of the wide, empty street. God, how stupid. But if she was really so good at escaping, if she had already made sure she had a way out when she and Bjørn moved in together, why hadn't she had a coil fitted, or at least gone on the pill? She remembered a conversation in which she explained to Bjørn that her already brittle psyche didn't need the mood swings that were the inevitable consequence of that sort of hormone manipulation. And it was true, she had stopped taking the pill when she got together with Bjørn. Her thoughts were interrupted when her phone rang, the opening riff of "O My Soul" by Big Star, installed by Bjørn, of course, who had gone to great lengths to explain the significance of the largely forgotten Southern States band from the seventies to her, and complained that the Netflix documentary had deprived him of his mission in life. "Fuck them! Half the pleasure of secret bands is the fact that they *are* secret!" There wasn't much chance of him growing up any time soon.

She answered. "Yes, Gunnar."

"*Murdered with iron teeth*?" Her otherwise placid boss sounded upset.

"Sorry?"

"That's the lead story on *VG*'s website. It says the murderer was already inside Elise Hermansen's flat, and that he bit through her carotid artery. From a reliable source in the police, it says."

"What?"

"Bellman has already called. He's . . . what's the word I'm looking for? Livid."

Katrine stopped walking. Tried to think. "To start with, we don't *know* that he was already there, and we don't *know* that he bit her, or that it was a he."

"*Un*reliable source in the police, then! I don't give a damn about that! We need to get to the bottom of this. Who's the leak?"

"I don't know, but I know that *VG* will protect the identity of its source as a matter of principle."

"Principles be damned—they want to protect their source because they want more inside information. We need to plug this leak, Bratt."

Katrine was more focused now. "So Bellman's worried the leak might harm the investigation?"

"He's worried it'll make the whole force look bad."

"I thought as much."

"You thought what?"

"You know what, and you're thinking the same."

"We'll deal with this first thing tomorrow," Hagen said.

Katrine Bratt put her phone in her jacket pocket and looked ahead along the path. One of the shadows had moved. Probably just a gust of wind in the trees.

For a moment she considered crossing the road to the well-lit pavement, before deciding against it and walking on, quicker than before.


Mikael Bellman was standing by the living-room window. From their house in Høyenhall he could see the whole of the centre of Oslo, stretching out westward towards the low hills below Holmenkollen. And tonight the city was sparkling like a diamond in the moonlight. His diamond.

His children were sleeping soundly. His city was sleeping relatively soundly.

"What is it?" Ulla wondered, looking up from her book.

"This latest murder, it needs solving."

"So do all murders, surely?"

"This one's a big case now."

"It's one single woman."

"It's not that."

"Is it because *VG* is running so hard with it?"

He could hear the trace of derision in her voice, but it didn't bother him. She had calmed down, she was back in her place. Because, deep down, Ulla knew her place. And she wasn't the sort of person who looked for conflict. What his wife liked more than anything was looking after the family, fussing over the children and reading her books. So the tacit criticism in her voice didn't really demand an answer. And she would hardly have understood it anyway—that if you want to be remembered as a good king, you have two choices. Either you are a king in good times, with the good fortune to sit on the throne during years of plenty. Or you're the king who leads the country out of a time of crisis. And if it isn't a time of crisis, you can pretend, start a war and show how deep a crisis the country would be in if it *didn't* go to war, and make out that things are really terrible. It didn't matter if it was only a small war, the important thing was winning it. Mikael Bellman had opted for the latter when he had appeared in the media and in front of the City Council, exaggerating the amount of crime committed by migrants from the Baltic States and Romania, and making dire predictions about the future. And he had been granted extra resources to win what was actually a very small war, albeit a big one in the media. And with the latest figures he had provided twelve months later, he had been able indirectly to declare himself the triumphant victor.

But this new murder case was a war he wasn't in charge of, and—judging from *VG*'s coverage that evening—he knew it was no longer a small war. Because they all danced to the media's tune. He remembered a landslide on Svalbard which had left two people dead and many more homeless. A few months before there had been a fire in Nedre Eiker, in which three people had died and far more been left homeless. The latter story had received the usual modest coverage granted to house fires and road accidents. But a landslide on a distant island was a far more media-friendly story, just like these iron jaws, meaning that the media had leapt into action as if it was a national disaster. And the Prime Minister—who jumps whenever the media says jump—had addressed the country in a live broadcast. And the viewers and residents of Nedre Eiker might well have wondered where she was when their homes were burning. Mikael Bellman knew where she had been. She and her advisers had, as usual, had their ears to the ground, listening out for tremors in the media. And there hadn't been any.

But Mikael Bellman could feel the ground shaking now.

And now—just as he, as victorious Chief of Police, had a chance to enter the corridors of power—this was already starting to turn into a war he couldn't afford to lose. He needed to prioritise this single murder as if it were an entire crime wave, simply because Elise Hermansen was a wealthy, well-educated, ethnically Norwegian woman in her thirties, and because the murder weapon wasn't a steel bar, a knife or a pistol, but a set of teeth made out of iron.

And that was why he felt obliged to take a decision he really didn't want to have to take. For so many reasons. But there was no way round it.

He had to bring him in.

# 6

# Friday morning

Harry woke up. the echo of a dream, a scream, died away. He lit a cigarette and reflected. Upon what sort of awakening this was. There were basically five different types. The first was waking up to work. For a long time that had been the best sort. When he could slip straight into the case he was investigating. Sometimes sleep and dreams had done something to his way of seeing things and he could lie there going through what they had revealed, piece by piece, from this new perspective. If he was lucky he might be able to catch a glimpse of something new, see part of the dark side of the moon. Not because the moon had moved, but because he had.

The second sort was waking up alone. That was characterised by an awareness that he was alone in bed, alone in life, alone in the world, and it could sometimes fill him with a sweet sensation of freedom, and at other times with a melancholy that could perhaps be called loneliness, but which was perhaps just a glimpse of what anyone's life *really* is: a journey from the attachment of the umbilical cord to a death where we are finally separated from everything and everyone. A brief glimpse at the moment of awakening before all our defence mechanisms and comforting illusions slot into place again and we can face life in all its unreal glory.

Then there was waking up full of angst. That usually happened if he'd been drunk for more than three days in a row. There were different gradations of angst, but it was always there instantly. It was hard to identify a specific external danger or threat, it was more a sense of panic at being awake at all, being alive, being *here*. But every so often he could sense an internal threat. A fear of never feeling afraid again. Of finally and irrevocably going mad.

The fourth was similar to waking up full of angst: the there-are-other-people-here awakening. That set his mind working in two directions. One backwards: how the hell did this happen? One forwards: how do I get out of here? Sometimes this fight-or-flight impulse would settle down, but that always came later and therefore fell outside the frame of waking up.

And then there was the fifth. Which was a new type of waking up for Harry Hole. Waking up content. At first he had been surprised that it was possible to wake up happy, and had automatically thought through all the parameters, what this ridiculous "happiness" actually consisted of, and if it was just an echo of some wonderful, stupid dream. But that night he hadn't had any nice dreams, and the echo of the scream had come from the demon, the face on his retina which belonged to the murderer who got away. Even so, Harry had woken up happy. Hadn't he? Yes. And when this variety of awakening had been repeated, morning after morning, he had begun to get used to the idea that he might actually be a relatively content man who had found happiness somewhere towards the end of his forties, and actually seemed capable of clinging on to this newly conquered territory.

The main reason for this lay less than an arm's length away from him, and was breathing calmly and evenly. Her hair lay spread out on the pillow, like the rays of a raven-black sun.

What is happiness? Harry had read an article about research into happiness which had shown that if you take the happiness of blood, its serotonin level, as your starting point, then there are relatively few external factors that can either reduce or increase that level. You can lose a foot, you can find out you're infertile, your house can burn down. Your serotonin level sinks at first, but six months later you're pretty much as happy or unhappy as you were to start with. Same thing if you buy a bigger house or a more expensive car.

But the researchers had discovered that there were a few things that were important in feeling happiness. One of the most important was a good marriage.

And that was just what he had. It sounded so banal that he couldn't help smiling sometimes when he told himself or—very occasionally—the tiny number of people he called friends yet still hardly ever saw: "My wife and I are very happy together."

Yes, he was in control of his own happiness. If he could have, he would have been more than happy to copy and paste the three years that had passed since the wedding and relive those days over and over again. But obviously that wasn't an option, and perhaps that was the cause of the tiny trace of anxiety he still felt? That time couldn't be stopped, that things happened, that life was like the smoke from a cigarette, moving even in the most airtight of rooms, changing in the most unpredictable ways. And seeing as everything was perfect now, any change could only be for the worse. Yes, that was it. Happiness was like moving on thin ice, it was better to crack the ice and swim in cold water and freeze and struggle to get out than simply to wait until you plunged into it. That was why he had started to program himself to wake up earlier than he had to. Like today, when his lecture on murder investigation didn't start until eleven o'clock. Waking up just to have more time to lie and experience this peculiar happiness, for as long as it lasted. He suppressed the image of the man who had got away. That wasn't Harry's responsibility. Wasn't Harry's hunting ground. And the man with the demon's face was appearing in his dreams less and less frequently.

Harry crept out of bed as quietly as he could, even though her breathing was no longer as regular and he suspected she might be pretending to still be asleep because she didn't want to spoil things. He pulled on a pair of trousers and went downstairs, put her favourite capsule in the espresso machine, added water, and opened the little glass jar of instant coffee for himself. He bought small jars because fresh, newly opened instant coffee tasted so much better. He switched the kettle on, stuck his bare feet in a pair of shoes and went outside onto the steps.

He breathed in the biting autumn air. The nights had already started to get colder here on Holmenkollveien, up in the hills of Besserud. He looked down towards the city and the fjord, where there were still a few sailing boats, standing out as tiny white triangles against the blue water. In two months, maybe just a matter of weeks, the first snow would be falling up here. But that was fine, the big house with its brown timber walls was built for winter rather than summer.

He lit his second cigarette of the day and walked down the steep gravel drive. He picked his feet up carefully to avoid treading on the untied laces. He could have put on a jacket, or at least a T-shirt, but that was part of the pleasure of having a warm house to come back to: freezing, just a little bit. He stopped by the mailbox. Took out the copy of *Aftenposten*.

"Good morning, neighbour."

Harry hadn't heard the Tesla pull out onto his neighbour's tar-macked drive. The driver's window slid open and he saw the always immaculately blonde fru Syvertsen. She was what Harry—who came from the east of the city and had only been here in the west a rela-tively short time—thought of as a typical Holmenkollen wife. A housewife with two children and two home helps, and no plans to get a job even though the Norwegian state had invested five years of university education in her. To put it another way, what other people saw as a leisure activity, she saw as her job: keeping herself in shape (Harry could only see her tracksuit top, but knew she was wearing tight-fitting gym gear underneath, and yes, she looked bloody good considering that she was well past forty), logistics (when which of the home helps should take care of the children, and when the family should go on holiday, and where: the house outside Nice, the ski-ing cabin in Hemsedal, the summer cottage in Sørlandet?), and net-working (lunch with friends, dinners with potentially advantageous contacts). And her most important task was already done. Securing herself a husband with enough money to finance this so-called job of hers.

That was where Rakel had failed so miserably. Even though she had grown up in the big wooden house in Besserud, where children were taught how to maneuver through society at a young age, and even though she was smart and attractive enough to get anyone she wanted, she had ended up with an alcoholic murder detective on a low salary, who was currently a sober lecturer at Police College on an even lower salary.

"You should stop smoking," fru Syvertsen said, studying him. "That's all I've got to say. Which gym do you go to?"

"The cellar," Harry said.

"Have you installed a gym? Who's your trainer?"

"I am," Harry said, taking a deep drag and looking at his reflection in the window in the back door of the car. Thin, but not as skinny as a few years ago. Three kilos more muscle. Two kilos of stress-free days. And a healthier lifestyle. But the face looking back at him bore witness to the fact that this hadn't always been the case. The deltas of thin red veins in the whites of his eyes and just under the skin of his face betrayed a past characterised by alcohol, chaos, lack of sleep and other bad habits. The scar running from one ear to the corner of his mouth spoke of desperate situations and a lack of control. And the fact that he was holding his cigarette between his index and ring fingers, and that he no longer had a middle finger, was yet further evidence of murder and mayhem written in flesh and blood.

He looked down at the newspaper. Saw the word "murder" across the fold. And for a moment the echo of the scream was back again.

"I've been thinking of installing a gym of my own," fru Syvertsen said. "Why don't you pop round one morning next week and give me some advice?"

"A mat, some weights, and a beam to hang from," Harry said. "That's my advice."

Fru Syvertsen gave him a wide smile. Nodded as if she understood. "Have a good day, Harry."

The Tesla whistled off on its way, and he walked back towards the place he called home.

When he reached the shade of the big fir trees he stopped and looked at the house. It was solid. Not impregnable, nothing was impregnable, but it would take some effort. There were three locks in the heavy oak door, and there were iron bars over the windows. Herr Syvertsen had complained, said the fortified house looked like something out of Johannesburg, and that it made their safe area look dangerous and would depress property values. Rakel had had the bars installed at a time when they had been necessary. When Harry's work as a murder detective had put her and her son Oleg in danger. Oleg had grown up since then. He had moved out and was now living with his girlfriend, and had enrolled at Police College. It was up to Rakel to decide when the bars were removed. Because they were no longer needed. Harry was just an underpaid teacher now.

"Oh, break-fuss," Rakel mumbled with a smile, did an exaggerated yawn and sat up in bed.

Harry put the tray down in front of her.

Break-fuss was their word for the hour they spent in bed every Friday morning when he started late and she had the whole day off from her job as a lawyer in the Foreign Ministry. He crept in under the covers and, as usual, gave her the section of *Aftenposten* containing the domestic news and sport, while he kept the international news section and culture. He put on the glasses he had belatedly accepted that he needed, and immersed himself in a review of Sufjan Stevens's latest album while he thought about Oleg's invitation to go with him to a Sleater-Kinney concert next week. Enervating, slightly neurotic rock, just the way Harry liked it. Oleg really preferred harder stuff, which only made Harry appreciate the gesture all the more.

"Anything new?" Harry asked as he turned the page.

He knew she was reading about the murder he had seen on the front page, but also that she wasn't going to mention it to him. One of their silent agreements.

"Over thirty percent of American Tinder users are married," she said. "But Tinder are denying it. How about you?"

"Sounds like the new Father John Misty album's a bit crap. Either that or the reviewer's just got old and grumpy. I'd guess the latter. It's had good reviews in *Mojo* and *Uncut*."

"Harry?"

"I prefer young and grumpy. Then slowly but surely getting more amenable over the years. Like me. Don't you think?"

"Would you be jealous if I was on Tinder?"

"No."

"No?" He noticed her sitting up in bed. "Why not?"

"I suppose I'm just unimaginative. I'm stupid, and believe I'm more than enough for you. Being stupid isn't all that stupid, you know."

She sighed. "Don't you ever get jealous?"

Harry turned another page. "I do get jealous, but Ståle Aune has recently given me a number of reasons to try to minimise it, darling. He's actually giving a guest lecture about morbid jealousy to my students today."

"Harry?" He could tell from the tone of her voice that she wasn't going to give up.

"Don't start with my name, please, you know it makes me nervous."

"You've got good reason to be, because I'm thinking about asking if you ever fancy anyone apart from me."

"You're thinking about it? Or you're asking now?"

"I'm asking now."

"OK." His eyes settled on a picture of Police Chief Mikael Bellman and his wife at a film premiere. Bellman suited the black eyepatch he had started to wear, and Harry knew that Bellman knew it. The young Police Chief had declared that the media and crime films such as the one in question created a false picture of Oslo, and that during his time as Chief of Police the city was safer than ever. The statistical risk of someone killing themselves was far greater than them being killed by someone else.

"Well?" Rakel said, and he felt her move closer. "Do you fancy other women?"

"Yes," Harry said, stifling a yawn.

"All the time?" she asked.

He looked up from the paper. Stared in front of him with a frown. He considered the question. "No, not *all* the time." He resumed reading. The new Munch Museum and Public Library were starting to take shape next to the Opera House. In a country of fishermen and farmers, which had spent the past two hundred years sending any dodgy deviants with artistic ambitions to Copenhagen and Europe, the capital city would soon resemble a city of culture. Who would have believed it? Or, more pertinently: who *did* believe it?

"If you could choose," Rakel teased playfully, "if it didn't have any consequences at all, would you rather spend tonight with me or your dream woman?"

"Haven't you got a doctor's appointment?"

"Just one night. No consequences."

"Are you trying to get me to say that you're my dream woman?"

"Come on."

"You'll have to help me with suggestions."

"Audrey Hepburn."

"Necrophilia?"

"Don't try to wriggle out of it, Harry."

"OK. I suspect you of suggesting a dead woman because you assume I'll think you'd find it less of a threat if it's a woman I can't spend the night with, in purely practical terms. But fine, thanks to your manipulative help and *Breakfast at Tiffany's*, my answer is a loud and clear yes."

Rakel let out a half-stifled yelp. "In that case, why don't you just do it? Why not have a fling?"

"To start with, I don't even know if my dream woman would say yes, and I'm no good at dealing with rejection. And secondly, because the bit about 'no consequences' doesn't apply."

"Really?"

Harry focused on the newspaper again. "You might leave me. Even if you don't, you won't look at me the same way anymore."

"You could keep it secret."

"I wouldn't have the energy." The former Councillor for Social Affairs, Isabelle Skøyen, had criticised the current City Council for not having a contingency plan in advance of the so-called tropical storm that was forecast to hit the west coast early next week, with a force the country had never before experienced. Even more unusual was the fact that the storm was predicted to hit Oslo at only a marginally diminished strength a few hours later. Skøyen claimed that the Council Leader's response ("We don't live in the tropics, so we don't set money aside for tropical storms") betrayed an arrogance and irresponsibility bordering on lunacy. "Evidently he believes that climate change is something that only affects other countries," Skøyen had said, beside a photograph of her in a characteristic pose which told Harry she was planning to make a political comeback.

"When you say you wouldn't have the energy to keep an affair secret, do you mean 'couldn't keep up the pretence'?" Rakel asked.

"I mean 'couldn't be bothered.' Keeping secrets is exhausting. And I'd feel guilty." He turned the page. No more pages. "Having a guilty conscience is exhausting."

"Exhausting for *you*, sure. What about me, haven't you thought about how hard it would be for me?"

Harry glanced at the crossword before putting the newspaper down on the duvet and turning towards her. "If you don't know about the affair, then surely you won't feel anything at all, darling?"

Rakel took hold of his chin and held it while her other hand fiddled with his eyebrows. "But what if I found out? Or you found out that I'd slept with another man. Wouldn't that upset you?"

He felt a sudden flash of pain as she plucked a straggly grey hair from one eyebrow.

"Of course," he said. "Hence the guilty conscience if it was the other way round."

She let go of his chin. "Darn it, Harry, you talk as if you were trying to figure out a murder case. Don't you *feel* anything?"

"*Darn it?*" Harry gave a crooked smile and peered at her over his glasses. "Do people still say 'darn it'?"

"Just answer, dar— oh, tarnation!"

Harry laughed. "I feel that I'm trying to answer your questions as honestly as I can. But in order to do that, I need to think about them, and be realistic. If I were to follow my initial emotional instinct, I'd have said what I thought you wanted to hear. So here's a warning. I'm not honest, I'm a slippery sod. My honesty now is merely a long-term investment in my own plausibility. Because there may come a day when I *really* need to lie, and then it might be handy if you think I'm honest."

"Wipe that grin off your face, Harry. So what you're actually saying is that you'd be an adulterous bastard if it wasn't so much bother?"

"Looks like it."

Rakel gave him a shove, swung her legs out of bed and shuffled out through the doorway in her slippers with a derisive snort.

Harry heard her snort again on the stairs.

"Can you put the kettle on?" he called.

"Cary Grant," she called back. "And Kurt Cobain. At the same time."

He heard her moving about downstairs. The rumbling sound of the kettle. Harry moved the newspaper to the bedside table and put his hands behind his head. Smiled. Happy. As he got up he caught sight of her part of the paper, still on her pillow. He saw a picture, a crime scene behind a police cordon, closed his eyes and went over to the window. He opened them again and looked out at the fir trees. He felt he could manage it now. Could manage to forget the name of the one who got away.

He woke up. He had been dreaming about his mother again. And a man who claimed to be his father. He wondered what sort of awakening this was. He was rested. He was calm. He was content. The main reason lay less than an arm's length away from him. He turned towards her. He had gone into hunting mode yesterday. That hadn't been the intention, but when he saw her—the policewoman—in the bar, it was as if fate had grabbed the wheel for a moment. Oslo was a small city, people were always bumping into each other, but all the same. He hadn't run amok, though, he had learned the art of self-control. He studied the lines on her face, her hair, the arm lying at a slightly unnatural angle. She was cold, and she wasn't breathing; the smell of lavender was almost gone, but that was OK, she had done her job.

He threw the covers back and went over to the wardrobe, and took the uniform out. He brushed it down. He could already feel the blood pumping faster through his body. It was going to be another good day.

# 7

# Friday morning

Harry Hole was walking down the corridor in Police College with Ståle Aune. At 192cm tall, Harry was some twenty centimetres taller than his friend, who was twenty years older than him and a good deal fatter.

"I'm surprised that you can't solve such an obvious case," Aune said, checking that his spotted bow tie was in the right place. "There's no mystery, you became a teacher because your parents were. Or, to be more accurate, because your father was. Even post-mortem, you're still trying to get his approval, which you never got as a police officer, and never actually wanted as a police officer, seeing as your rebellion against your father was about not being the same as him, whom you saw as a feeble individual because he hadn't been able to save your mother's life. You projected your own inadequacies onto him. And joined the police to make up for the fact that you weren't able to save your mother either. You wanted to save us all from death, or, more precisely, from being murdered."

"Hm. How much do people pay per appointment to listen to stuff like that?"

Aune laughed. "Speaking of appointments, how did Rakel get on about her headaches?"

"The appointment's today," Harry said. "Her dad suffered from migraines, and they only started later in life."

"Heredity. It's like going to a fortune-teller and regretting it. As human beings, we tend not to like things we can't avoid. Death, for instance."

"Heredity isn't unavoidable. My grandfather said he became an alcoholic the first time he ever had a drink, just like his father. Whereas my father enjoyed—as in actually *enjoyed*—alcohol all his life without becoming a alcoholic."

"So alcoholism skipped a generation. That sort of thing happens."

"Unless me blaming my genes is just an easy excuse for my own weak character."

"OK, but then you ought to be allowed to blame your weak character on your genes as well."

Harry smiled and a female student walking in the other direction misread it and smiled back.

"Katrine's sent me some photographs of the crime scene in Grünerløkka," Aune said. "What do you think about it?"

"I don't read about crime."

The door to lecture theatre 2 stood open ahead of them. The lecture formed part of the syllabus for the final-year students, but Oleg had said that he and a couple of others in the first year were going to try to sneak in. Sure enough, the auditorium was packed. There were students and even a few of the other lecturers sitting on the steps and standing by the walls.

Harry walked up to the podium and switched the microphone on. Looked out at the audience. Found himself searching automatically for Oleg's face. Conversation died away and silence settled on the room. The most peculiar thing wasn't that he'd become a teacher, but that he *liked* it. That he, like most people usually regarded as taciturn and introverted, felt less inhibited in front of a gathering of demanding students than when the guy at the only open checkout in the 7-Eleven put a packet of Camel Lights down on the counter and Harry thought about repeating his request for "Camels," before noticing the restlessness of the queue behind him. Sometimes, on bad days when his nerves were twitchy, he would actually walk out with the Camel Lights, smoke one and throw the rest of the pack away. But here he was in his comfort zone. Work. Murder. Harry cleared his throat. He hadn't found Oleg's face, always so serious, but he had spotted another one he knew well. One with a black patch over one eye. "I see that some of you must be here by mistake—this is a level-three course in detective work for final-year students."

Laughter. No one showed any inclination to leave the room.

"OK," Harry said. "I'm afraid anyone who's here for yet another of my bone-dry lectures on how to investigate murders is going to be disappointed. Our guest lecturer today has been an adviser to the Crime Squad Unit in Police Headquarters for many years, and is Scandinavia's foremost psychologist in the field of violence and murder. But before I give the floor to Ståle Aune, and because I know he won't give it back voluntarily, can I remind you that there's going to be a fresh cross-examination next Wednesday? The 'devil's star' investigation. As usual, the case description, crime-scene reports and interview transcripts are all on the intranet. Ståle?"

Applause broke out and Harry walked towards the steps, as Aune swaggered up to the podium with his stomach out and a contented smile on his lips.

"Othello syndrome!" Aune declared, then lowered his voice when he reached the microphone. "Othello syndrome is another term for what we call morbid jealousy, and it's the motive for most murders in this country. Just as jealousy is in William Shakespeare's play *Othello*. Roderigo is in love with General Othello's new bride, Desdemona, while the sly Iago hates Othello because he feels he was overlooked when the general didn't appoint him as his new lieutenant. Iago sees a chance to advance his own career by destroying Othello, so with Roderigo he sows discord between Othello and his wife. And Iago does this by planting a virus in Othello's brain and in his heart, a lethal and tenacious virus that comes in many guises. Jealousy. Othello gets sicker and sicker, his jealousy causes epileptic attacks, leaving him shaking on the stage. Othello ends up killing his wife, and finally he kills himself too." Aune tugged at the sleeves of his tweed jacket. "The reason why I am telling you the plot is not because Shakespeare is part of the curriculum here at Police College, but because you need a bit of general education." Laughter. "So what, my unjealous ladies and gentlemen, is Othello syndrome?"

"To what do we owe this visit?" Harry whispered. He had gone to stand at the back of the lecture theatre next to Mikael Bellman. "Interested in jealousy?"

"No," Bellman said. "I want you to investigate this latest murder case."

"Then I'm afraid you've had a wasted journey."

"I want you to do what you've done in the past: lead a small team that works in parallel to and independently of the larger investigative team."

"Thanks for the offer, Chief, but the answer's no."

"We need you, Harry."

"Yes. Here."

Bellman let out a laugh. "I don't doubt that you're a good teacher, but you're not the only one. Whereas you happen to be unique as a detective."

"I'm through with murders."

Mikael Bellman shook his head with a smile. "Come off it, Harry. How long do you think you can hide yourself away here, pretending to be something you're not? You're not a herbivore like him down there. You're a predator. Just like me."

"The answer's still no."

"And it's a well-known fact that predators have sharp teeth. That's what puts them at the top of the food chain. I see Oleg's sitting down near the front. Who'd have thought he'd end up at Police College?"

Harry felt the hairs on the back of his neck stand up in warning. "I've got the life I want, Bellman. I can't go back. My answer's final."

"Especially as a clean record is an essential prerequisite to being admitted."

Harry didn't respond. Aune harvested more laughter, and Bellman chuckled too. He put a hand on Harry's shoulder, leaned in and lowered his voice a bit more. "It may be a few years ago now, but I've got connections who would swear on oath that they saw Oleg buying heroin that time. The penalty for that is a maximum of two years. He wouldn't get a custodial sentence, but he could never become a police officer."

Harry shook his head. "Not even you would do that, Bellman."

"No? It might look like shooting sparrows with a cannon, but it really is very important to me that this case is solved."

"If I say no, you have nothing to gain by ruining things for my family."

"Maybe not, but let's not forget that I . . . what's the word? *Hate* you."

Harry looked at the backs of the people in front of him. "You're not the sort of man who lets himself be governed by his feelings, Bellman, you don't have enough of them for that. What would you say when it came out that you'd been sitting on this information about Police College student Oleg Fauke for so long without doing anything about it? There's no point bluffing when your opponent knows what bad cards you're holding, Bellman."

"If you want to stake the boy's future on the fact that I'm bluffing, go ahead, Harry. It's just this one case. Solve it for me, and all the rest will disappear. You can have until this afternoon to give me your answer."

"Out of curiosity, Bellman—why is this particular case so important to you?"

Bellman shrugged. "Politics. Predators need meat. And remember that I'm a tiger, Harry. And you're only a lion. The tiger weighs more and has even more brain per kilo. That's why the Romans in the Coliseum knew a lion would always be killed if they sent it out to fight a tiger."

Harry saw a head turn round down towards the front. It was Oleg, smiling and giving him the thumbs up. The lad would soon turn twenty-two. He had his mother's eyes and mouth, but his straight black hair came from the Russian father no one remembered any longer. Harry returned the thumbs up and tried to smile. When he turned back to Bellman, he was gone.

"It's mostly men who are afflicted with Othello syndrome," Ståle Aune's voice rang out. "While male murderers with Othello syndrome have a tendency to use their hands, female Othellos use knives or blunt instruments."

Harry listened. To the thin, thin ice on top of the black water beneath him.

"You look serious," Aune said when he came back to Harry's office from the toilet. He drank the last of his coffee and put his coat on. "Didn't you like my lecture?"

"Oh, I did. Bellman was there."

"So I saw. What did he want?"

"He tried to blackmail me into investigating this latest murder."

"And what did you say?"

"No."

Aune nodded. "Good. It eats away at your soul, having as much close contact with evil as you and I have had. It may not look like it to other people, but it's already destroyed parts of us. And it's high time our nearest and dearest got the same attention that the sociopaths have had. Our shift is over, Harry."

"Are you saying you're throwing in the towel?"

"Yes."

"Hm. I see what you're saying in general terms, but are you sure there isn't something more specific?"

Aune shrugged. "Only that I've worked too much and spent too little time at home. And when I work on a murder case, I'm not at home even when I am there. Well, you know all about that, Harry. And Aurora, she's . . ." Aune filled his cheeks with air and blew it out. "Her teachers say it's a bit better now. Children sometimes shut themselves off at that age. And they try things out. The fact that they have a scar on their wrist doesn't necessarily mean that they're engaged in systematic self-harm, it could just be natural curiosity. But it's always upsetting when a father realises he can no longer get through to his child. Maybe all the more upsetting when he's supposed to be a hotshot psychologist."

"She's fifteen now, isn't she?"

"And this could all be over and forgotten by the time she turns sixteen. Phases, phases, that's what that age is all about. But you can't put off caring for your loved ones until after the next case, or your next day at work, you have to do it *now*. Wouldn't you say, Harry?"

Harry rubbed his unshaven top lip with his thumb and forefinger as he nodded slowly. "Mm. Of course."

"Well, I'll be off," Aune said, reaching for his briefcase and picking up a pile of photographs. "These are the pictures from the crime scene that Katrine sent. Like I said, they're no use to me."

"Why would I want them?" Harry wondered, looking down at a woman's body on a bloodstained bed.

"For one of your classes, maybe. I heard you mention the devil's star case, so you obviously use real murder cases, and real documents."

"In that instance it works as a template," Harry said, trying to tear his eyes away from the woman's picture. There was something familiar about it. Like an echo. Had he seen her before? "What's the victim's name?"

"Elise Hermansen."

The name didn't ring any bells. Harry looked at the next picture. "These wounds on her neck, what are they?"

"You really haven't read a thing about the case? It's on all the front pages, it's hardly surprising that Bellman's trying to pressgang you. Iron teeth, Harry."

"*Iron teeth*? A satanist?"

"If you read *VG*, you'll see that they refer to my colleague Hallstein Smith's tweet about it being the work of a vampirist."

"A vampirist? A vampire, then?"

"If only," Aune said, taking a page torn out of *VG* from his case. "A vampire does at least have some basis in zoology and fiction.

According to Smith and a few other psychologists around the world, a vampirist is someone who takes pleasure from drinking blood. Read this . . ."

Harry read the tweet Aune held up in front of him. He stopped at the last sentence. *The vampirist will strike again.*

"Mm. Just because there are only a few of them doesn't mean that they're not right."

"Are you mad? I'm all for going against the flow, and I like ambitious people like Smith. He made a big mistake when he was a student and landed himself with his nickname, 'the Monkey', and I'm afraid that means he still doesn't have much credibility among other psychologists. But he was actually a very promising psychologist until he got into this business with vampirism. His articles weren't bad either, but obviously he couldn't get them published in any peer-reviewed journals. Now he's got something printed at last. In *VG*."

"So why don't you believe in vampirism?" Harry said. "You yourself have said that if you can think of any form of deviancy, there'll be someone out there who's got it."

"Oh yes, it's all out there. Or will be. Our sexuality is all about what we're capable of thinking and feeling. And that's pretty much unlimited. Dendrophilia means being sexually excited by trees. Kakorrhaphiophilia means finding failure sexually arousing. But before you can define something as a -philia or an -ism, it has to have reached a degree of prevalence, and have a certain number of common denominators. Smith and his group of mythomaniac psychologists have invented their own -ism. They're wrong, there isn't a group of so-called vampirists who follow any predictable pattern of behaviour for them or anyone else to analyse." Aune buttoned up his coat and walked towards the door. "Whereas the fact that you suffer from a fear of intimacy, and are incapable of giving your best friend a hug before he leaves, is decent material for a psychological theory. Give Rakel my love, and tell her I'll magic those headaches away. Harry?"

"What? Yes, of course. I'll tell her. Hope things work out OK with Aurora."

Harry was left staring into space after Aune had gone. The previous evening he had walked into the living room while Rakel was watching a film. He had glanced at the screen and asked if it was a James Gray film. It was a perfectly neutral picture of a street with no actors in it, without any specific cars or camera angles, two seconds of a film Harry had never seen. OK, a picture can never be completely neutral, but Harry still had no idea what made him think of that particular director. Apart from the fact that he had watched a James Gray film a few months ago. That could be all it was, an automatic and trivial connection. A film he had seen, then a two-second clip that contained one or two details that swirled through his brain so quickly that he couldn't identify what the points of recognition were.

Harry took out his mobile phone.

Hesitated. Then he pulled up Katrine Bratt's number. It had been over six months since the last time they were in touch, when she had sent him a text on his birthday. He had replied with "thanks," no capital letter or full stop. He knew she knew that didn't mean he didn't care, just that he didn't care about long text messages.

His call went unanswered.

When he rang her internal number at Crime Squad, Magnus Skarre picked up. "So, Harry Hole himself." The sarcasm was so heavy that Harry was left in no doubt. Harry hadn't had many fans at Crime Squad, and Skarre certainly hadn't been one of them. "No, I haven't seen Bratt today. Which is pretty odd for a new lead detective, because we've got a hell of a lot to do here."

"Hm. Can you tell her I—?"

"Better to call back, Hole, we've got enough to think about."

Harry hung up. Drummed his fingers on the desk and looked at the pile of essays at one end of it. And at the sheaf of photographs at the other. He thought about Bellman's analogy about predators. A lion? OK, why not? He'd read that lions that hunt alone have a success rate of only fifteen percent or so. And that when lions kill large prey, they don't have the strength to rip their throats open, so they have to suffocate them. They clamp their jaws around the animal's neck and squeeze the windpipe. And that can take time. If it's a big animal, a water buffalo for instance, the lion sometimes has to hang there, tormenting itself and the water buffalo for hours, yet still has to let go in the end. And that's one way of looking at a murder investigation. Hard work and no reward. He had promised Rakel that he wouldn't go back. Had promised himself.

Harry looked at the bundle of photographs again. Looked at the picture of Elise Hermansen. Her name had stuck in his mind automatically. As had the details of the photograph of her lying on the bed. But it wasn't the details. It was the whole. The film Rakel had been watching the night before had been called *The Drop*. And the director wasn't James Gray. Harry had been wrong. Fifteen percent. All the same . . .

There was something about the way she was lying. Or had been lain out. The arrangement. It was like an echo from a forgotten dream. A cry in the forest. The voice of a man he was trying not to remember. The one who got away.

Harry remembered something he had once thought. That when he fell, when he pulled the cork from the bottle and took the first swig, it wasn't the way he imagined, because that wasn't the decisive moment. The decision had already been taken long before. And from that moment on, the only question was what the trigger would be. It was bound to come. At some point the bottle would be standing there in front of him. And it would have been waiting for him. And he for it. The rest was just opposite charges, magnetism, the inevitability of the laws of physics.

Shit. Shit.

Harry stood up quickly, grabbed his leather jacket and hurried out.


He looked in the mirror, checked that the jacket was sitting the way it should. He had read the description of her one last time. He disliked her already. A "w" in a name that should be spelled with a "v," like his, was a good enough reason for punishment on its own. He would have preferred a different victim, one more to his own taste. Like Katrine Bratt. But the decision had already been taken for him. The woman with a "w" in her name was waiting for him.

He fastened the last button on the jacket. Then he left.

# 8

# Friday afternoon

"How did Bellman manage to persuade you?" Gunnar Hagen was standing by the window.

"Well," the unmistakable voice said behind him, "he made me an offer I couldn't refuse." There was a bit more gravel to it now than when he had last heard it, but it had the same depth and calmness. Hagen had heard one of his female colleagues say that the only beautiful thing about Harry Hole was his voice.

"And what was the offer?"

"Fifty percent extra for overtime and double pension contributions."

The head of Crime Squad smiled briefly. "And you don't have any conditions?"

"Just that I'm allowed to pick the members of my group myself. I only want three."

Gunnar Hagen turned round. Harry was slouched in the chair in front of Hagen's desk with his long legs stretched out in front of him. His thin face had gained some more lines, and his thick, short blond hair had started to turn grey at the temples. But he was no longer as thin as the last time Hagen had seen him. The whites around his intense blue irises may not have been clear, but they weren't marbled with red the way they had been when things had been at their worst.

"Are you still dry, Harry?"

"As a Norwegian oil well, boss."

"Hm. You do know that Norwegian oil wells aren't dry, don't you? They've just been shut down until the price of oil rises again."

"That was the image I was trying to convey, yes."

Hagen shook his head. "And there was me thinking that you'd get more mature with age."

"Disappointing, isn't it? We don't get wiser, just older. Still nothing from Katrine?"

Hagen looked at his phone. "Not a thing."

"Shall we try calling her again?"


"Hallstein!" The call came from the living room. "The kids want you to be the hawk again!"

Hallstein Smith let out a resigned but happy sigh and put his book, Francesca Twinn's *Miscellany of Sex*, down on the kitchen table. It was interesting enough to read that biting off a woman's eyelashes is regarded as an act of passion in the Trobriand Islands of Papua New Guinea, but he hadn't found anything he could use in his PhD, and making his kids happier was certainly more fun. It didn't matter that he was still tired from the last game, because birthdays only came round once a year. Well, four times a year when you had four children. Six, if they insisted on their parents having birthday parties too. Twelve, if you celebrate half birthdays as well. He was on his way to the living room, where he could already hear the children cooing like doves, when the doorbell rang.

The woman standing outside on the step stared openly at Hallstein Smith's head when he opened the door.

"I managed to eat something with nuts the day before yesterday," he said, scratching the irritating outbreak of livid red hives on his forehead.

He looked at her and realised that she wasn't staring at the hives.

"Oh, that," he said, taking off his hat. "It's supposed to be a hawk's head."

"Looks more like a chicken," the woman said.

"It is actually an Easter chicken, so we call it a chickenhawk."

"My name is Katrine Bratt, I'm from Crime Squad, Oslo Police."

Smith tilted his head. "Of course, I saw you on the news last night. Is this about what I said on Twitter? The phone hasn't stopped ringing. It wasn't my intention to cause such a fuss."

"Can I come in?"

"Of course, but I hope you don't mind slightly, er . . . boisterous children."

Smith explained to the children that they were going to have to come up with their own hawk for a while, then led the policewoman into the kitchen.

"You look like you could do with some coffee," Smith said, pouring a cup without waiting for an answer.

"It ended up being a late night," the woman said. "I overslept, so I've come straight from bed. And I managed to leave my mobile at home, so I was wondering if I could borrow yours to call the office?"

Smith passed her his mobile and watched as she gazed helplessly at the ancient Ericsson. "The kids call it a stupid-phone. Do you want me to show you?"

"I think I remember," Katrine said. "Tell me, what do you make of this picture?"

As she tapped at the phone, Smith studied the photograph she had handed him.

"Iron dentures," he said. "From Turkey?"

"No, Caracas."

"Right. There are similar sets of iron teeth in the Museum of Archaeology in Istanbul. They're supposed to have been used by soldiers in Alexander the Great's army, but historians doubt that, and think instead that the upper classes used them in some sort of sado-masochistic games." Smith scratched his hives. "So he used something like this?"

"We're not sure. We're just working from the bite marks on the victim, some rust and a few flakes of black paint."

"Aha!" Smith exclaimed. "Then we need to go to Japan!"

"We do?" Bratt put the phone to her ear.

"You might have seen Japanese women with their teeth dyed black? No? Well, it's a tradition known as *ohaguro*. It means 'the darkness after the sun has gone down,' and first appeared during the Heian period, around the year AD 800. And . . . er, shall I go on?"

Bratt gestured impatiently.

"It's said that in the Middle Ages there was a shogun in the north who made his soldiers use iron teeth that were painted black. They were mostly to scare people, but could also be used in close combat. If the fighting got so crowded that the soldiers couldn't use weapons or punch and kick their adversaries, they could use the teeth to bite through their enemies' throats."

The detective indicated that her call had been answered. "Hi,

Gunnar, this is Katrine. I just wanted to let you know that I've come straight from home to talk to Professor Smith . . . yes, the one who sent the tweet. And that I left my phone at home, so if anyone's been trying to get hold of me . . ." She listened. "Harry? You're kidding." She listened for a few more seconds. "He just walked in and said he'd do it? Let's talk about it later." She handed the phone back to Smith. "So, tell me, what's vampirism?"

"For that," Smith said, "I think we should go for a walk."

Katrine walked alongside Hallstein Smith down the gravel track that led from the house to the barn. He was explaining that his wife had inherited the farm and almost a hectare of land, and that only two generations ago there were cows and horses grazing here in Grini, just a few kilometres from the centre of Oslo. Even so, a smaller plot containing a boathouse on Nesøya that had also formed part of the inheritance was worth more. At least if you were to believe the offers they had received from their filthy rich neighbours.

"Nesøya's really too far away to be practical, but we don't want to sell for the time being. We've only got a cheap aluminium boat with a twenty-five horsepower engine, but I love it. Don't tell my wife, but I prefer the sea to this bit of farmland."

"I come from the coast too," Katrine said.

"Bergen, right? I love the dialect. I spent a year working in a psychiatric ward in Sandviken. Beautiful, but so much rain."

Katrine nodded slowly. "Yes, I've got drenched in Sandviken before."

They reached the barn. Smith pulled out a key and undid the padlock.

"Big lock for a barn," Katrine said.

"The last one was too small," Smith said, and Katrine could hear the bitterness in his voice. She stepped through the doorway and let out a small yelp when she put her foot on something that moved. She looked down and saw a rectangular metal plate, one metre by one and a half, set into the cement floor. It felt like it was on springs as it swayed and knocked against the cement edge before settling again.

"Fifty-eight kilos," Smith said.

"What?"

He nodded to his left, towards a large arrow that was quivering between 50 and 60 on a half-moon-shaped dial, and she realised she was standing on old-fashioned cattle scales. She squinted.

"Fifty-seven point six-eight."

Smith laughed. "A long way below slaughter weight, anyway. I have to admit that I try to jump across the scales every morning, I don't like the idea that every day could be my last."

They carried on past a row of stalls and stopped in front of the door to an office. Smith unlocked it. The room contained a desk with a PC, a window looking out across the field, a drawing of a vampire with big, thin bat's wings, a long neck and square face. The bookcase behind the desk was half full with files and a dozen or so books.

"What you see before you is everything that has ever been published on vampirism," Smith said, running his hand over the books. "So it's pretty easy to get an overview. But to answer your question, let's start with Vandenbergh and Kelly, from 1964."

Smith pulled out one of the books, opened it and read: "'*Vampirism is defined as the act of drawing blood from an object (usually a love object), and receiving resultant sexual excitement and pleasure.*' That's the dry definition. But you're after more than that, aren't you?"

"I think so," Katrine said, and looked at the picture of the vampire. It was a fine piece of art. Simple. Lonely. And it seemed to radiate a chill that instinctively made her pull her jacket tighter.

"Let's go a bit deeper," Smith said. "To start with, vampirism isn't some newfangled invention. The word obviously refers to the myth about bloodthirsty creatures in human guise, going way back through history, especially in Eastern Europe and Greece. But the modern concept of vampires comes mainly from Bram Stoker's *Dracula* in 1897 and the first vampire films of the 1930s. Some researchers mistakenly believe that vampirists—ordinary but sick individuals—are largely inspired by these myths. They forget that vampirism had already been mentioned in this . . . ." Smith pulled out an old book with a half-disintegrated brown cover. "Richard von Krafft-Ebing's *Psychopathia Sexualis* from 1887—in other words, *before* the myth became widely known." Smith put it back carefully and pulled out another book.

"My own research is based on the idea that vampirism is related to such conditions as necrophagia, necrophilia and sadism, just as the author of this book, Bourguignon, also thought." Smith opened it. "This is from 1983: '*Vampirism is a rare compulsive disorder with an irresistible urge for blood ingestion, a ritual necessary to bring mental relief; like other compulsions, its meaning is not understood by the participant.*'"

"So a vampirist just does what vampirists do? They simply can't act differently?"

"That's an oversimplification, but yes."

"Can any of these books help us to put together a profile of a murderer who extracts blood from his victims?"

"No," Smith said, replacing Bourguignon's book. "One's been written, but it's not on the shelf."

"Why not?"

"Because it's never been published."

Katrine looked at Smith. "Yours?"

"Mine," Smith said with a sad smile.

"What happened?"

Smith shrugged. "The time wasn't right for that sort of radical psychology. After all, I was flying in the face of this." He pointed at one of the spines on the shelf. "Herschel Prins and his article in the *British Journal of Psychiatry*, 1985. And you don't get away with that unpunished. I was dismissed because my results were based on case studies rather than empirical evidence. But of course that was impossible when there are so few cases of real vampirism, and the few that are recorded have been diagnosed as schizophrenia because there hasn't been enough research. I tried, but even newspapers that are more than happy to publish articles about B-list American celebrities thought vampirism was frivolous, sensationalist. And when I had finally collected enough research evidence, that's when the break-in happened." Smith gestured towards the empty shelves. "Taking my computer was one thing, but they took all my patient notes too, my entire archive of clients, the whole lot. And now certain malicious colleagues are claiming that I was saved by the bell, and that if my material had been published I would only have exposed myself to more ridicule, because it would have become obvious that vampirists don't exist."

Katrine ran her finger across the frame of the picture of the vampire. "Who would break in here to steal medical records?"

"God knows. I assumed it was a colleague. I waited for someone to step forward with my theories and results, but it never happened."

"Maybe they were after your patients?"

Smith laughed. "I wish them luck with that. They're so crazy no one else wants them, believe me. They're only useful as research subjects, not as a way of making a living. If my wife hadn't been doing so well with her yoga school we wouldn't have been able to keep hold of the farm and boathouse. Speaking of which, there's a birthday party going on up at the house that needs a hawk."

They walked back outside and as Smith locked the door to the office Katrine noticed a small surveillance camera fixed to the wall above the stalls.

"You know the police don't investigate ordinary break-ins any more?" she said. "Even if you've got security camera footage."

"I know." Smith sighed. "That's for my own peace of mind. If they come back for any of my new material, I want to know which of my colleagues I'm dealing with. I've got a camera outside by the gate as well."

Katrine couldn't help laughing. "I thought academics were bookish, cosy types, not common thieves."

"Oh, I'm afraid we do just as many stupid things as less intelligent people," Smith said, shaking his head sadly. "Myself included, I have to admit."

"Really?"

"Nothing interesting. Just a mistake my colleagues rewarded with a nickname. And it was a long time ago." Maybe it was a long time ago, but Katrine still saw the flash of pain dart across his face.

On the steps in front of the farmhouse Katrine handed him a card. "If the media call, I'd be very grateful if you don't mention the fact that we've had this conversation. People will only get frightened if they think the police believe there's a vampire on the loose."

"Oh, the media won't call," Smith said, looking at her card.

"Really? But *VG* printed what you wrote on Twitter."

"They didn't bother to interview me. Presumably someone remembered that I've cried wolf before."

"Cried wolf?"

"There was a murder back in the nineties where I'm pretty certain a vampirist was involved. And another case three years ago, I don't know if you remember it?"

"I don't think so."

"No, that one didn't get many headlines either. Which was lucky, I suppose."

"So this would be the third time you've cried wolf?"

Smith nodded slowly and looked at her. "Yes. This is the third time. So the list of my failings is pretty long."

"Hallstein?" called a woman's voice from inside the house. "Are you coming?"

"Just a moment, darling! Sound the hawk alarm! Caw, caw, caw!"

As Katrine walked towards the gate she heard the sound of voices getting louder behind her. Hysteria in advance of a massacre of doves.

# 9

# Friday afternoon

At 3 p.m. Katrine had a meeting with Krimteknisk, at 4 p.m with the forensics officer, both equally depressing, then at 5 p.m with Bellman in the Police Chief's office.

"I'm pleased you've responded positively to us bringing in Harry Hole, Bratt."

"Why wouldn't I? Harry's our most experienced murder detective."

"Some detectives might regard it as—what's the word I'm looking for?—*challenging*, to have such a big name from the past looking over their shoulder."

"Not a problem—I always play with my cards on the table, sir." Katrine gave a brief smile.

"Good. Anyway, Harry's going to be leading his own small, independent team, so you needn't worry about him taking over. Just a bit of healthy competition." Bellman put his fingertips together. She noticed that one of the white patches formed a band around his wedding ring. "And naturally, I'll be cheering on the female participant. I hope we can count on a quick result, Bratt."

"I see," Katrine Bratt said, and glanced at her watch.

"I see, what?"

She heard the irritation in his voice. "I see: you're hoping for a quick result."

She knew she was provoking the Chief of Police. Not because she wanted to. Because she couldn't help it.

"And you should be hoping for the same thing, Detective Inspector Bratt. Positive discrimination or not, jobs like yours don't grow on trees."

"I'll have to do my best to prove that I deserve it, then."

She kept her eyes fixed on his. It was as if the eyepatch emphasised his uninjured eye, its intensity and beauty. And the hard, ruthless glint in it.

She held her breath.

Then he suddenly laughed. "I like you, Katrine. But let me give you a piece of advice."

She waited, ready for anything.

"At the next press conference, you should do the talking, not Hagen. I want you to underline the fact that this is an extremely difficult case, that we have no leads, and that we need to be prepared for a lengthy investigation. That will make the media less impatient and they'll give us more room for maneuver."

Katrine folded her arms. "It might also embolden the killer and make him more likely to strike again."

"I don't think the killer is governed by what the papers say, Bratt."

"If you say so. Well, I have to prepare the next meeting of the investigative team."

Katrine saw the note of warning in the way he looked at her.

"Go ahead. And do as I say. Tell the media that this case is the most difficult you've had."

"I . . ."

"In your own words, obviously. When's the next press conference?"

"We've cancelled today's seeing as we haven't got anything new."

"OK. Remember, if the case is presented as difficult, the glory will be all the greater when we solve it. And we won't be lying, because we haven't actually got anything, have we? Besides, the media love a big, horrifying mystery. See it as a win-win situation, Bratt."

Win-fucking-win, Katrine thought as she walked down the stairs to Crime Squad on the sixth floor.

At 6 p.m., Katrine opened the meeting of the investigative team by stressing the importance of reports being written and registered in the system promptly, because this hadn't been done after the first interview with Geir Sølle, Elise Hermansen's Tinder date the night she was murdered, with the result that a second detective had contacted Geir Sølle.

"For one thing, it makes extra work, as well as giving the public the impression that the police are disorganised, and that our right hand doesn't know what the left hand is doing."

"There must be something wrong with the computers, or the system," Truls Berntsen said, even though Katrine hadn't mentioned him by name. "I know I sent it."

"Tord?"

"There haven't been any system failures reported in the last twenty-four hours," Tord Gren said, adjusting his glasses and noting the look in Katrine's eye, which he interpreted correctly. "But of course there may be something wrong with your computer, Berntsen—I'll take a look at it."

"Seeing as you've started, Tord, could you take us through your latest strokes of genius?"

The IT expert blushed, nodded, and went on in a stiff, unnatural tone of voice, as if he were reading from a script. "Location services. Most people who have a mobile phone permit one or more of the apps on their device to collect data on where they are at all times, many of them without knowing that they've allowed this."

Pause. Tord swallowed. And Katrine realised that he was doing precisely that: reading from a script he had written and learned off by heart after Katrine had said she would be asking him to give a presentation to the group.

"Many of the apps demand, as part of their terms and conditions, the right to be able to send details of the phone's location to third parties, but not to the police. One such commercial third party is Geopard. They gather location data, and have no clause in their own contract prohibiting them from selling the information to the public sector or, in other words, to the police. When people who have served prison sentences for sexual offences are released, we gather contact details—address, mobile number, email address—because we routinely want to be able to get hold of these individuals in the event of further offences similar to those for which they were convicted. Because it used to be generally assumed that sex offenders are the most likely to reoffend. New research has shown this to be completely wrong: rape actually has one of the lowest reoffending rates. BBC Radio 4 recently reported that the chance of offenders being rearrested is sixty percent in the U.S.A. and fifty percent in the UK. And often for the same offence. But *not* for rape. Statistics from the U.S. Justice Department show that 78.8 percent of those convicted of stealing a motor vehicle are rearrested for the same offence within three years, for those convicted of trading in stolen goods the figure is 77.4 percent, and so on. But the same thing only applies to 2.5 percent of convicted rapists." Tord paused again. Katrine presumed he had noticed that the group had limited patience for this sort of discursive presentation. He cleared his throat. "Anyway, when we send our batch of contact data to Geopard, they can map the movements of these people's phones, assuming they use location-tracking apps, at any given time and at any given place. On Wednesday evening, for instance."

"How precisely?" Magnus Skarre called.

"Down to a few square metres," Katrine said. "But the GPS is only two-dimensional, so we can't see elevation. In other words, we don't know what floor the phone is on."

"Is this actually legal?" wondered Gina, one of the analysts. "I mean, privacy legislation—"

"—is struggling to keep up with technology," Katrine interrupted. "I've spoken to our legal department, and they say it's a grey area, but that it isn't covered by existing legislation. And, as we know, if something isn't illegal, then . . ." She held her hands out, but no one in the room was willing to finish the sentence for her. "Go on, Tord."

"Once we received authorisation from our lawyers and financial authorisation from Gunnar Hagen, we bought a set of location data. The maps from the night of the murder give us GPS positions for ninety-one percent of people who have previously been convicted of sex offences." Tord stopped, and seemed to think.

Katrine realised that he had reached the end of his script. She didn't understand why a gasp of delight hadn't gone round the room.

"Don't you understand how much work this has saved us? If we used the old method to write off this many potential suspects from a case—"

She heard a low cough. Wolff, the oldest of the detectives. Should have been pensioned off by now. "Seeing as you said 'write off,' presumably that means the map didn't show a match for Elise Hermansen's address?"

"Correct," Katrine said. She put her hands on her hips. "And it means that we only have to check the alibis of nine percent."

"But the location of your phone doesn't exactly give you an alibi," Skarre said, and looked round for support.

"You know what I mean," Katrine said with a sigh. What was it with this lot? They were here to solve a murder, not suck all the energy out of each other.

"Krimteknisk," she said, and sat down at the front so she wouldn't have to look at them for a while.

"Not much," Bjørn Holm said, getting to his feet. "The lab's examined the paint left in the wound. It's pretty specific stuff. We think it's made of iron filings in a vinegar solution, with added vegetable-based tannic acid from tea. We've looked into it, and it could stem from an old Japanese tradition of dying teeth black."

"*Ohaguro*," Katrine said. "The darkness after the sun's gone down."

"Correct," Bjørn said, giving her the same appreciative look that he used to when they were having breakfast at a cafe and she would get the better of him for once in the quiz in *Aftenposten*.

"Thanks," Katrine said, and Bjørn sat down. "Then there's the elephant in the room. What *VG* is calling 'a source' and we call a leak."

The already quiet room grew even more so.

"One thing is the damage that's already been done: now the murderer knows what we know, and can plan accordingly. But what's worse is that we in this room no longer know if we can trust each other. Which is why I want to ask a very blunt question: who talked to *VG*?"

To her surprise she saw a hand in the air.

"Yes, Truls?"

"Müller and I spoke to Mona Daa right after the press conference yesterday."

"You mean Wyller?"

"I mean the new guy. Neither of us said anything. But she gave you her card, didn't she, Müller?"

All eyes turned to look at Wyller, whose face was glowing bright red beneath his blond fringe.

"Yes . . . but . . ."

"We all know that Mona Daa is *VG*'s crime reporter," Katrine said. "You don't need a business card to call the paper and get hold of her."

"Was it you, Wyller?" Magnus Skarre asked. "Look, all rookies are allowed a certain number of fuck-ups."

"I *haven't* talked to *VG*," Wyller said, with desperation in his voice.

"Berntsen just said that you did," Skarre replied. "Are you saying that Berntsen's lying?"

"No, but—"

"Out with it!"

"Look . . . she said she was allergic to cats, and I said I've got a cat."

"See, you *did* talk! What else?"

"You could be the leak, Skarre." The calm, deep voice came from the very back of the room, and everyone turned round. No one had heard him come in. The tall man was more lying than sitting in a chair against the back wall.

"Speaking of cats," Skarre said. "Look what it's just dragged in. I haven't talked to *VG*, Hole."

"You or anyone else in here could have unconsciously given away a bit too much information to a witness you were talking to. And they could have called the paper and said that they got it directly from the cops. Hence 'a source in the police.' Happens all the time."

"Sorry, but no one believes that, Hole," Skarre snorted.

"You should," Harry said. "Because no one here is going to admit to talking to *VG*, and if you end up thinking you've got a mole, your investigation isn't going to go anywhere."

"What's he doing here?" Skarre wondered, turning to Katrine.

"Harry is here to set up a group that's going to work in parallel to us," Katrine said.

"So far it's a one-man group," Harry said. "And I'm here to order some materials. Those nine percent whose location you don't know for the time of the murder, can I have a list of them, in order of the length of their most recent sentence?"

"I can do that." Tord said, then paused and looked questioningly at Katrine.

She nodded. "What else?"

"A list of which sex offenders Elise Hermansen helped put away. That's all."

"Noted," Katrine said. "But seeing as we've got you here, any initial thoughts?"

"Well." Harry looked round. "I know the forensics officer has found lubricant which probably comes from the murderer, but we can't rule out the possibility of revenge as the main motive, and anything sexual as a bonus. The fact that the murderer was probably already inside the flat when she got home doesn't mean that she let him in or that they knew each other. I don't think I'd have restricted the investigation at such an early stage. But I'm assuming that you've already thought of that yourselves."

Katrine gave a crooked smile. "Good to have you back, Harry."

Possibly the best, possibly the worst, but certainly the most mythologised murder detective in the Oslo Police managed to perform a perfectly acceptable bow from his almost prone position. "Thanks, boss."


"You meant that," Katrine said. She and Harry were standing in the lift.

"What?"

"You called me boss."

"Of course."

They got out in the garage and Katrine pressed the key fob. There was a bleep and some lights flashed somewhere in the darkness. Harry had persuaded her that she ought to make use of the car that was automatically at her disposal during a murder case like this one. And then that she ought to drive him home, stopping for coffee at Schrøder's Restaurant on the way.

"What's happened to your taxi driver?" Katrine asked.

"Øystein? He got fired."

"By you?"

"Course not. By the taxi firm. There was an incident."

Katrine nodded. And thought about Øystein Eikeland, the long-haired beanpole with teeth like a junkie's, a voice like a whiskey drinker, who looked about seventy but was actually one of Harry's childhood friends. One of only two, according to Harry. The other one was called Tresko, and he was, if possible, an even more bizarre character: an overweight, unpleasant office worker who turned into a Mr. Hyde of a poker player at night.

"What sort of incident?" Katrine wondered.

"Do you really want to know?"

"Not really, but go on."

"Øystein doesn't like panpipes."

"No, who does?"

"So he got a long job driving to Trondheim with this guy who has to go by taxi because he's terrified of both trains and planes. And the guy has trouble with aggression too, so he's got this CD with him, panpipe versions of old pop songs that he has to listen to while he's doing breathing exercises to stop him losing control. What happens is that in the middle of the night, up on the Dovre Plateau, when the panpipe version of 'Careless Whisper' comes round for the sixth time, Øystein pulls the CD out, opens the window and chucks it out. That's when the fisticuffs started."

"Fisticuffs is a nice word. And that song's bad enough in the original."

"In the end Øystein managed to kick the guy out of the car."

"While it was moving?"

"No. But in the middle of the plateau, in the middle of the night, twenty kilometres from the nearest house. In his defence, Øystein did point out that it was July, mild weather, and that the guy couldn't possibly be terrified of walking as well."

Katrine laughed. "And now he's out of a job? You ought to employ him as your private chauffeur."

"I'm trying to get him a job, but Øystein is—to quote his own words—pretty much made for unemployment."

Schrøder's Restaurant was, in spite of its name, basically just a bar. The usual early-evening clientele was in place and nodded good-naturedly to Harry without actually saying anything.

The waitress, on the other hand, lit up as if the prodigal son had just returned home. And served them a coffee that definitely wasn't the reason why foreign visitors had recently started to count Oslo among the best cities in the world for coffee.

"Sorry it didn't work out with you and Bjørn," Harry said.

"Yeah." Katrine didn't know if he wanted her to elaborate. Or if she wanted to elaborate. So she just shrugged.

"Yeah," Harry said, and raised his cup to his lips. "So what's it like being single again?"

"Curious about the single life?"

He laughed. And she realised she'd missed that laugh. She'd missed *making* him laugh, it felt like a reward every time she managed it.

"Single life is fine," she said. "I'm seeing guys." She looked for a reaction. Was she *hoping* for a reaction?

"Well, I hope Bjørn's seeing people too, for his sake."

She nodded. But she hadn't really given it much thought. And, like an ironic comment, the cheery ping indicating a Tinder match rang out, and Katrine saw a woman dressed in desperation red hurry towards the door.

"Why are you back, Harry? The last thing you said to me was that you were never going to work on another murder."

Harry turned his coffee cup. "Bellman threatened to get Oleg thrown out of Police College."

Katrine shook her head. "Bellman really is the biggest heap of shit on two legs since the Emperor Nero. He wants me to tell the press that this is an almost impossible case. To make him look better when we solve it."

Harry looked at his watch. "Well, maybe Bellman's right. A murderer who bites people with iron teeth and drinks half a litre of blood from the victim . . . This is probably more about the act of killing than who the victim is. And that instantly makes the case harder."

Katrine nodded. The sun was shining on the street outside, but she still thought she could hear the rumble of thunder in the distance.

"The pictures of Elise Hermansen from the crime scene," Harry said. "Did they remind you of anything?"

"The bite marks on her neck? No."

"I don't mean the details, I mean . . ." Harry stared out of the window. "As a whole. Like when you hear music you've never heard before, by a group you don't know, but you still know who wrote the track. Because there's something there. Something you can't put your finger on."

Katrine looked at his profile. His brush of short hair was sticking up, as messily as before, but not quite as thick. His face had acquired some new lines, the wrinkles and furrows had deepened, and even if he had laughter lines around his eyes, the more brutal aspects of his appearance were more prominent. She had never understood why she thought he was so handsome.

"No," she said, shaking her head.

"OK."

"Harry?"

"Mm?"

"*Is* Oleg the reason you came back?"

He turned and looked at her with one eyebrow raised. "Why do you ask that?"

And she felt it now as she had back then, the way that look could hit her like an electric shock, the way he—a man who could be so reserved, so distant—could bulldoze everything else aside just by looking at you for a second, and demand—and get—all of your attention. In that one second there was only one man in the whole world.

"Never mind," she said, and laughed. "Why am I asking that? Let's get going."

"Ewa with a 'w.' Mum and Dad wanted me to be unique. Then it turned out to be really common in those old Iron bloc countries."

She laughed and drank a sip of her beer. Then opened her mouth and used her forefinger and thumb to wipe the lipstick from the corners of her mouth.

"Iron *Curtain* and *Eastern* bloc," the man said.

"Huh?" She looked at him. He was quite cute. Wasn't he? Nicer than the ones she was usually matched with. There was probably something wrong with him, something that would show up later. There usually was. "You're drinking slowly," she said.

"You like red." The man nodded towards the coat she'd draped over her chair.

"So does that vampire guy," Ewa said, pointing at the news bulletin on one of the enormous televisions in the bar. The football match had ended and the bar, which had been full five minutes ago, had started to empty. She could feel she was a bit tipsy, but not too much. "Did you read *VG*? He *drank* her blood."

"Yes," the man said. "Do you know, she had her last drink a hundred metres down the road from here, at the Jealousy Bar?"

"Is that true?" She looked round. Most of the other customers seemed to be in groups or pairs. She had noticed one man who had been sitting on his own watching her, but he was gone now. And it wasn't the Creep.

"Yes, quite true. Another drink?"

"Yes, I think I'd better," she said with a shiver. "Ugh!"

She gestured to the bartender, but he shook his head. The minute hand had just passed the magic boundary.

"Looks like it'll have to be another day," the man said.

"Just when you've managed to terrify me," Ewa said. "You'll have to walk me home now."

"Of course," the man said. "Tøyen, you said?"

"Come on," she said, and buttoned her red coat over her red blouse.

She tottered slightly on the pavement outside, and felt him discreetly holding her up.

"I had one of those stalkers," she said. "I call him the Creep. I met him one time, and we . . . well, we had quite a nice time. But when I didn't want to take it any further, he got jealous. He started to show up in different places when I was out meeting other people."

"That must have been unpleasant."

"Yes. But it's quite funny as well, being able to bewitch someone so that all they can think about is you."

The man let her put her hand through his arm, and listened politely as she talked about other men she had bewitched.

"I looked stunning, you see. So at first I wasn't really surprised when he showed up, I just assumed he'd been following me. But then I realised that he couldn't possibly have known where I'd be. And you know what?" She stopped abruptly and swayed.

"Er, no."

"Sometimes I had a feeling that he'd been *inside* my flat. You know, your brain registers how people smell and recognises them even when you're not consciously aware of it."

"Sure."

"What if he's this vampire?"

"That would be quite a coincidence. Is this where you live?"

She looked up in surprise at the building in front of her. "It is. Goodness, that was quick."

"As they say, time flies when you're in good company, Ewa. Well, this is where I say—"

"Can't you come up for a bit? I think I've got a bottle tucked away in the cupboard."

"I think we've both had enough . . ."

"Just to make sure he isn't there. Please."

"That's really not very likely."

"Look, the light's on in the kitchen," she said, pointing at one of the first-floor windows. "I'm sure I switched it off before I left!"

"Are you?" the man said, stifling a yawn.

"Don't you believe me?"

"Look, I'm sorry, but I really do need to get home and go to bed." She stared at him coldly. "What's happened to all the real gentlemen?"

He smiled tentatively. "Er . . . maybe they all went home to bed?"

"Ha! You're married, you succumbed to temptation, and now you regret it, is that it?"

The man looked at her thoughtfully. As if he felt sorry for her.

"Yes," he said. "That's it. Sleep well."

She unlocked the front door. Went up the stairs to the first floor. Listened. She couldn't hear anything. She didn't know if she'd turned the kitchen light off, it was just something she'd said to get him to come with her. But now that she'd said it, it was as if she'd talked it up. Maybe the Creep really was in there.

She heard shuffling footsteps behind the door to the basement, heard the lock turn and a man in a security guard's uniform came out. He locked the door with a white key, turned round, caught sight of her looking down and seemed to start back in surprise.

He let out a laugh. "I didn't hear you. Sorry."

"Is there a problem?"

"There've been a few break-ins in basement storerooms recently, so the housing association have ordered extra patrols."

"So you work for us?" Ewa tilted her head a little. He wasn't bad-looking. And he wasn't as young as most other security guards either. "In that case, could I maybe ask you to check my flat? I've had a break-in too, you know. And now I can see that there's a light on, even though I know I turned everything off before I went out."

The guard shrugged. "We're not supposed to go into people's flats, but OK."

"Finally, a man who's useful for something," she said, and looked him up and down once more. A grown-up security guard. Probably not all that smart, but solid, safe. And easy to handle. The common denominator for the men in her life had been that they had everything: came from good families, were looking at a decent inheritance, education, a bright future. And they had worshipped her. But sadly they had also drunk so much that their mutually bright future vanished into the depths with them. Maybe it was time to try something new. Ewa half turned away and bobbed her hip rather provocatively as she went through her keys. God, so many keys. And maybe she was a tiny bit drunker than she had thought.

She found the right one, unlocked the door, didn't bother to kick her shoes off in the hall, and went into the kitchen. She heard the security guard follow her.

"No one here," he said.

"Except you and me," Ewa smiled, leaning back against the worktop.

"Nice kitchen." The guard was standing in the doorway, running his hand over his uniform.

"Thanks. If I'd known I'd be having a visitor I'd have tidied up."

"And maybe done the washing-up." Now he smiled.

"Yeah, yeah, there are only twenty-four hours in a day." She brushed a lock of hair away from her face, and stumbled slightly on her high heels. "Would you mind checking the rest of the flat while I mix us a cocktail. What do you say?" She put her hand on the smoothie blender.

The guard looked at his watch. "I need to be at the next address in twenty-five minutes, but we've probably got time to check if anyone's hiding."

"A lot can happen in that time," she said.

The guard met her gaze, chuckled quietly, rubbed his chin and walked out of the room.

He headed towards what he assumed was the bedroom door, and was struck by how thin the walls were. He could make out individual words being spoken by a man in the next flat. He opened the door. Dark. He found a light switch. A weak ceiling lamp came on.

Empty. Unmade bed. Empty bottle on the bedside table.

He carried on, opened the door to the bathroom. Dirty tiles. A mouldy shower curtain pulled in front of the bath. "Looks like it's safe!" he called back towards the kitchen.

"Sit yourself down in the living room," she called back.

"OK, but I have to leave in twenty minutes." He went into the living room and sat down on the sagging sofa. Heard the chink of glasses in the kitchen, then her shrill voice.

"Would you like a drink?

"Yes." He thought how unpleasant her voice was, the sort of voice that could make a man wish he had a remote control. But she was voluptuous, almost a bit motherly. He fiddled with something in the pocket of his guard's uniform, it had got caught on the lining.

"I've got gin, white wine," the voice whined from the kitchen. Like a drill. "A bit of whiskey. What would you like?"

"Something else," he said in low voice to himself.

"What did you say? I'll bring everything!"

"D-do, Mother," he whispered, freeing the metal contraption from the lining of his pocket. He put it down gently on the coffee table in front of him, where he was sure she would see it. He could feel his erection already. Then he took a deep breath. It felt like he was emptying the room of oxygen. He leaned back in the sofa and put his cowboy boots up on the table, next to the iron teeth.

Katrine Bratt let her eyes wander over the pictures in the light of the desk lamp. It was impossible to tell that they were sex offenders just by looking at them. That they had raped women, men, children, old people, in some instances torturing them, and in a few cases murdering them. OK, if you were told what they had done in the most gruesome detail, you could probably see something in the downcast and often frightened eyes in these custody photographs. But if you passed them in the street, you would walk on without having the faintest idea that you had been observed, evaluated and hopefully rejected as a victim. She recognised some of the men from her time in Sexual Offences, but not others. There were a lot of new ones. A new perpetrator was born every day. An innocent little bundle of humanity, the child's cries drowned out by its mother's screams, linked to life by an umbilical cord, a gift to make its parents weep with joy, a child who in later life would slice open the crotch of a bound woman while he masturbated, his hoarse groans drowned out by the woman's screams.

Half the investigative team had started to contact these offenders, those with the most brutal records first. They were gathering and checking alibis, but hadn't yet managed to place a single one in the vicinity of the crime scene. The other half were busy interviewing former boyfriends, friends, colleagues and relatives. The murder statistics for Norway were very clear: in eighty percent of cases the murderer knew the victim, and in over ninety percent if the victim was a woman killed in her own home. Even so, Katrine didn't expect to find him in that statistic. Because Harry was right. This wasn't that sort of murder. The identity of the victim was less important than the act itself.

They had also been through the list of offenders that Elise's clients had testified against, but Katrine didn't think the perpetrator—as Harry had suggested—was killing two birds with one stone: sweet revenge and sexual gratification. Gratification, though? She tried to imagine the murderer lying with one arm round the victim after the hideous act, with a cigarette in his mouth, smiling as he whispered, "That was wonderful." In marked contrast, Harry used to talk about the serial killer's frustration at never *quite* being able to attain what he was after, making it necessary to keep going, in the hope that next time he would manage it, everything would be perfect, he would be delivered and born again to the sound of a screaming woman before he severed the umbilical cord to the rest of humanity.

She looked at the picture of Elise Hermansen on her bed again. Tried to see what Harry could have seen. Or heard. Music—wasn't that what he said? She gave up and buried her face in her hands. What was it that had made her think she had the right mentality for a job like this? "Bipolarity is never a good starting point for anyone but artists," her psychiatrist had said the last time they'd met, before he wrote a fresh prescription for the little pink pills that kept her afloat.

It was almost the weekend, normal people were doing normal things, they weren't sitting in an office looking at terrible crime-scene photographs and terrible people because they thought one of the faces might reveal something, only to move on to looking for a Tinder date to fuck and forget. But right now she desperately longed for something to connect her to normality. A Sunday lunch. When they were together, Bjørn had invited her to Sunday lunch with his parents out at Skreia several times, it was only half an hour's drive away, but she had always found an excuse to say no. Right now, though, there was nothing she would have liked more than to be sitting round a table with her in-laws, passing the potatoes, complaining about the weather, boasting about the new sofa, chewing dried-up elk steak as the conversation ground on tediously but comfortingly, and the looks and the nods would be warm, the jokes old, the moments of irritation bearable.

"Hi."

Katrine jumped. There was a man standing in the doorway.

"I've ticked the last of mine off the list," Anders Wyller said. "So if there's nothing else, I'll head home and get some sleep."

"Of course. Are you the only one left?"

"Looks like it."

"Berntsen?"

"He finished early. He must just be more efficient."

"Right," Katrine said, and felt like laughing, but couldn't be bothered. "I'm sorry to ask you this, Wyller, but would you mind double-checking his list? I've a feeling—"

"I've just done it. It seemed OK."

"It was *all* OK?" Katrine had asked Wyller and Berntsen to contact the various telephone companies to get hold of lists of numbers and names of people the victim had spoken to in the past six months, then divide them up and check their alibis.

"Yes. There was one guy in Åneby up in Nittedal, first name ending in 'y.' He called Elise a few too many times early in the summer, so I double-checked his alibi."

"Ending in 'y'?"

"Lenny Hell. Yes, really."

"Wow. So do you suspect people based on the letters in their names?"

"Among other things. It's a fact that '-y' names are over-represented in crime statistics."

"And?"

"So when I saw that Berntsen had made a note that Lenny's alibi was that he had been with a friend at Åneby Pizza & Grill at the time Elise Hermansen was murdered, and that this could only be confirmed by the owner of the pizzeria, I called the local sheriff to hear for myself."

"Because the guy's name is Lenny?"

"Because the owner of the pizzeria's name is Tommy."

"And what did the sheriff say?"

"That Lenny and Tommy were extremely law-abiding and trustworthy citizens."

"So you were wrong."

"That remains to be seen. The sheriff's name is Jimmy."

Katrine laughed out loud. Realised that she needed that. Anders Wyller smiled back. Maybe she needed that smile too. Everyone tries to make a good first impression, but she had a feeling that if she hadn't asked, Wyller wouldn't have told her he was doing Berntsen's work as well. And that showed that Wyller—like her—didn't trust Truls Berntsen. There was one thought that Katrine had been trying to ignore since it first appeared, but now she changed her mind.

"Come in and close the door behind you."

Wyller did as she asked.

"There's something else I'm sorry to have to ask you to do, Wyller. The leak to *VG*. You're the one who's going to be working most closely with Berntsen. Can you . . . ?"

"Keep my eyes and ears open?"

Katrine sighed. "Something like that. This stays between us, and if you do discover something, you *only* talk to me about it. Understood?"

"Understood."

Wyller left, and Katrine waited a few moments before picking up her phone from the desk. Looked up Bjørn. She had added a photograph of him that popped up in conjunction with his number. He was smiling. Bjørn Holm was no oil painting. His face was pale, slightly puffy, his red hair eclipsed by a shining white moon. But it was Bjørn. The antidote to all these other pictures. What had she really been so scared of? If Harry Hole could manage to live with someone else, why couldn't she? Her forefinger was getting close to the call button beside the number when the warning popped into her head again. The warning from Harry Hole and Hallstein Smith. The next one.

She put the phone down and concentrated on the pictures again. The next one.

What if the murderer was already thinking about the next one?

"You need to t-try harder, Ewa," he whispered.

He hated it when they didn't make an effort.

When they didn't clean their flats. When they didn't look after their bodies. When they didn't manage to keep hold of the man whose child they had given birth to. When they didn't give the child any supper and locked it in the wardrobe and said it needed to be really quiet, and then it would it get chocolate afterwards, while they received visits from men who were given supper, and all the chocolate, and all the things they played with, shrieking with joy, the way the mother never played with the child.

Oh no.

So the child would have to play with the mother instead. And others like the mother.

And he had played. Played hard. Up until the day when they had taken him away and locked him in another wardrobe, at Jøssingveien 33: Ila Prison and Detention Centre. The statutes said it was a facility for male prisoners from all around the country who had "specific intervention requirements."

One of the faggot psychiatrists there had told him that both the rapes and his stammer were the consequence of psychological trauma while he was growing up. Idiot. He had inherited the stammer from a father he had never met. The stammer and a filthy suit. And he had dreamt of raping women for as long as he could remember. And then he had done what these women never managed. He had tried harder. He had almost stopped stammering. He had raped the female prison dentist. And he had escaped from Ila. And he had gone on playing. Harder than ever. The fact that the police were after him only gave an edge to the game. Right up to the day when he had stood face-to-face with that policeman and had seen the determination and hatred in his eyes, and had realised that this man was capable of catching him. Was capable of sending him back to the darkness of his childhood in the closed wardrobe where he tried to hold his breath so as not to have to breathe in the stench of sweat and tobacco from his father's thick, greasy woollen suit that was hanging up in front of him, and which his mother said she was keeping in case his father showed up again one day. He knew he couldn't handle being locked up again. So he had hidden. Had hidden from the policeman with murder in his eyes. Had sat still for three years. Three years without playing. Until that too had started to become a wardrobe. Then he had been presented with this opportunity. A chance to play safely. It shouldn't be *too* safe, obviously. He needed to be able to detect the smell of fear in order to get properly turned on. Both his own *and* theirs. It didn't matter how old they were, what they looked like, if they were big or small. As long as they were women. Or potential mothers, as one of the idiot psychiatrists had said. He tilted his head and looked at her. The walls of the flat may have been thin, but that no longer bothered him. Only now, when she was so close and in this light, did he notice that Ewa with a "w" had little pimples around her open mouth. She was evidently trying to scream, but there was no way she was going to manage that, no matter how hard she tried. Because beneath her open mouth she had a new one. A bleeding, gaping hole in her throat where her larynx had been. He was holding her tightly against the living-room wall, and there was a gurgling sound as pink bubbles of blood burst where her severed airway protruded. Her neck muscles tensed and relaxed as she tried desperately to get air. And because her lungs were still working, she would live a few more seconds. But that wasn't what fascinated him most right now. It was the fact that he had managed to put a conclusive stop to her insufferable chatter by biting through her vocal cords with his iron teeth.

And as the light in her eyes dimmed, he tried to find something in them that betrayed a fear of dying, a desire to live another second. But he found nothing. She ought to have tried harder. Maybe she didn't have enough imagination. Didn't love life enough. He hated it when they gave up on life so easily.

# 10

# Saturday morning

Harry was running. Harry didn't like running. Some people ran because they liked it. Haruki Murakami liked it. Harry liked Murakami's books, apart from the one about running—he had given up on that one. Harry ran because he liked stopping. He liked *having* to run. He liked weight training: a more concrete pain that was limited by the performance of his muscles, rather than a desire to have more pain. That probably said something about the weakness of his character, his inclination to flee, to look for an end to the pain even *before* it had started.

A skinny dog, the sort the wealthy people of Holmenkollen kept even if they didn't go hunting more than one weekend every other year, leapt away from the path. Its owner came jogging along a hundred metres behind it. That year's Under Armour collection. Harry had time to notice his running technique as they approached each other like passing trains. It was a shame they weren't running in the same direction. Harry would have tucked in behind him, breathing down his neck, then pretended to lose ground only to crush him on the climb up towards Tryvann. Would have let him see the soles of his twenty-year-old Adidas trainers. Oleg said Harry was incredibly childish when they ran, that even though they had promised to jog calmly all the way, it would end with Harry suggesting they race up the last hill. In Harry's defence, it should be pointed out that he was asking for a thrashing, because Oleg had inherited his mother's unfairly high oxygen absorption rate.

Two overweight women who were more walking than running were talking and panting so loudly that they didn't hear Harry approaching, so he turned off onto a narrower path. And suddenly he was in unknown territory. The trees grew more densely there, shutting out the morning light, and Harry had a fleeting taste of something from his childhood. The fear of getting lost and never being able to find his way back home again. Then he was out in open country again, and he knew exactly where he was now, where home was.

Some people liked the fresh air up here, the gently rolling forest paths, the silence and smell of pine needles. Harry liked the view of the city. Liked the sound and smell of it. The feeling of being able to touch it. The certainty that you could drown in it, sink to the bottom of it. Oleg had recently asked Harry how he'd like to die. Harry had replied that he wanted to go peacefully in his sleep. Oleg had chosen suddenly and relatively painlessly. Harry had been lying. He wanted to drink himself to death in a bar in the city below them. And he knew that Oleg had also been lying—he would have chosen his former heaven and hell and taken a heroin overdose. Alcohol and heroin. Infatuations they could leave but never forget, no matter how much time passed.

Harry put in a final spurt on the driveway, heard the gravel kick up behind his trainers, caught a glimpse of fru Syvertsen behind the curtain of the house next door.

Harry showered. He liked showering. Someone ought to write a book about showering.

When he was finished he went into the bedroom, where Rakel was standing by the window in her gardening clothes: Wellington boots, thick gloves, a pair of tatty jeans and a faded sun hat. She half turned towards him and brushed aside a few strands of hair sticking out from under the hat. Harry wondered if she knew how good she looked in that outfit. Probably.

"Eek!" she said quietly, with a smile. "A naked man!"

Harry went and stood behind her, put his hands on her shoulders and massaged her gently. "What are you doing?"

"Looking at the windows. Should we do something about them before Emilia arrives, do you think?"

"Emilia?"

Rakel laughed.

"What?"

"You stopped that massage very abruptly, darling. Relax, we're not having visitors. Just a storm."

"Oh, *that* Emilia. I reckon this fortress could cope with a natural disaster or two."

"That's what we think, living up here on the hill, isn't it?"

"What do we think?"

"That our lives are like fortresses. Impregnable." She sighed. "I need to go shopping."

"Dinner at home? We haven't tried that Peruvian place on Bad-stugata yet. It's not that expensive."

That was one of Harry's bachelor habits that he'd tried to get her to adopt: not cooking dinner for themselves. She had more or less bought his argument that restaurants are one of civilisation's better ideas. That even back in the Stone Age they had figured out that cooking and eating together was smarter than the entire popula-tion spending three hours every day planning, buying, cooking and washing-up. When she objected that it felt a bit decadent, he had replied that ordinary families installing kitchens that cost a million kroner, *that* was decadent. That the most healthy, un-decadent use of resources was to pay trained cooks what they deserved to prepare food in large kitchens, so that they could pay for Rakel's help as a lawyer, or Harry's work training police officers.

"It's my day today, so I'll pay," he said, catching hold of her right arm. "Stay with me."

"I need to go shopping," she said, and grimaced as he pulled her towards his still damp body. "Oleg and Helga are coming."

He held her even tighter. "Are they? I thought you said we weren't having visitors."

"Surely you can cope with a couple of hours with Oleg and—"

"I'm joking. It'll be nice. But shouldn't we—?"

"No, we're *not* taking them to a restaurant. Helga hasn't been here before, and I want to get a proper look at her."

"Poor Helga," Harry whispered, and was about to nip Rakel's ear-lobe with his teeth when he saw something between her breast and her neck.

"What's that?" He put the tip of his finger very gently on a red mark.

"What?" she asked, feeling for herself. "Oh, that. The doctor took a blood sample."

"From your neck?"

"Don't ask me why." She smiled. "You look so sweet when you're worried."

"I'm not worried," Harry said. "I'm jealous. This is *my* neck, and of course we know you've got a weakness for doctors."

She laughed, and he held her closer.

"No," she said.

"No?" he said, and heard her breathing suddenly get deeper. Felt her body somehow give in.

"Bastard," she groaned. Rakel was troubled by what she herself called a "very short sex fuse," and swearing was the most obvious sign.

"Maybe we should stop now," he whispered, letting go of her. "The garden calls."

"Too late," she hissed.

He unbuttoned her jeans and pushed them and her pants down to her knees, just above her boots. She leaned forward and grabbed hold of the windowsill with one hand, and was about to take the sun hat off with the other.

"No," he whispered, leaning forward so that his head was next to hers. "Leave it on."

Her low, burbling laugh tickled his ear. God, how he loved that laugh. Another sound merged into the laughter. The buzz of a vibrating phone that was lying next to her hand on the windowsill.

"Throw it on the bed," he whispered, averting his eyes from the screen.

"It's Katrine Bratt," she said.


Rakel pulled her trousers up as she watched him.

There was a look of intense concentration on his face.

"How long?" he asked. "I see."

She saw him disappear from her at the sound of the other woman's voice on the phone. She wanted to reach out to him, but it was too late, he was already gone. The thin, naked body with muscles that twined like roots beneath his pale skin, it was still there, right in front of her. The blue eyes, their colour almost washed out after years of alcohol abuse, were still fixed on her. But he was no longer seeing her, his gaze was focused somewhere inside himself. He had told her why he had had to take the case the previous evening. She hadn't protested. Because if Oleg was thrown out of Police College he might lose his footing again. And if it came to a choice between losing Harry or Oleg, she would rather lose Harry. She'd had several years' training at losing Harry, she knew she could survive without him. She didn't know if she could survive without her son. But while he had been explaining that it was for Oleg's sake, an echo of something he had said recently drifted through her head: *There may come a day when I really need to lie, and then it might be handy if you think I'm honest.*

"I'll come now," Harry said. "What's the address?"

Harry ended the call and started to get dressed. Quickly, efficiently, each movement carefully measured. Like a machine that's finally doing what it was built for. Rakel studied him, memorising everything, the way you memorise a lover you're not going to be seeing for a while.

He walked quickly past Rakel without looking at her, without a word of farewell. She was already sidelined, pushed from his consciousness by one of his two lovers. Alcohol and murder. And this was the one she feared the most.

Harry was standing outside the orange-and-white police cordon when a window on the first floor of the building in front of him opened. Katrine Bratt stuck her head out.

"Let him through," she called to the young uniformed officer who was blocking his way.

"He hasn't got any ID," the officer protested.

"That's Harry Hole!" Katrine shouted.

"Is it?" The policeman quickly looked him up and down before raising the cordon tape. "I thought he was a myth," he said.

Harry went up the steps to the open door of the flat. Inside, he followed the path between the crime-scene investigators' little white flags, marking where they had found something. Two forensics officers were on their knees picking at a gap in the wooden floor.

"Where . . . ?"

"In there," one of them said.

Harry stopped outside the door indicated by the officer. Took a deep breath and emptied his mind of thoughts. Then he went in.

"Good morning, Harry," Bjørn Holm said.

"Can you move?" Harry said in a low voice.

Bjørn took one step away from the sofa he had been leaning over, revealing the body. Instead of moving closer, Harry took a step back. The scene. The composition. The whole. Then he went closer and started to note the details. The woman was sitting on the sofa, with her legs spread in such a way that her skirt had slid up to show her black underwear. Her head was resting against the back of the sofa, so that her long, bleached blonde hair hung down behind it. Some of her throat was missing.

"She was killed over there," Bjørn said, pointing at the wall beside the window. Harry's eyes slid across the wallpaper and bare wooden floor.

"Less blood," Harry said. "He didn't bite through the carotid artery this time."

"Maybe he missed it," Katrine said, coming in from the kitchen.

"If he bit her, he's got strong jaws," Bjørn said. "The average force of a human bite is seventy kilos, but he seems to have removed her larynx and part of her windpipe in one bite. Even with sharpened metal teeth, that would take a *lot* of strength."

"Or a lot of rage," Harry said. "Can you see any rust or paint in the wound?"

"No, but perhaps anything that was loose came off when he bit Elise Hermansen."

"Hm. Possibly, unless he didn't use the iron teeth this time, but something else. The body wasn't moved to the bed either."

"I see what you're getting at, Harry, but it *is* the same perpetrator," Katrine said. "Come and see."

Harry followed her back to the kitchen. One of the forensics officers was taking samples from the inside of the glass jug from a blender that was standing in the sink.

"He made a smoothie," Katrine said.

Harry swallowed and looked at the jug. The inside of it was red.

"Using blood. And some lemons he found in the fridge, from the looks of it." She pointed at the yellow strips of peel on the worktop.

Harry felt nausea rising. And thought that it was like your first drink, the one that made you sick. Two more drinks and it was impossible to stop. He nodded and walked out again. He took a quick look at the bathroom and bedroom before going back into the living room. He closed his eyes and listened. The woman, the position of the body, the way she had been displayed. The way Elise Hermansen had been displayed. And there it was, the echo. It was him. It had to be him.

When he opened his eyes again, he found himself looking directly into the face of a fair-haired young man he thought he recognised.

"Anders Wyller," the young man said. "Detective."

"Of course," Harry said. "You graduated from Police College a year ago? Two years?"

"Two years ago."

"Congratulations on getting top marks."

"Thanks. That's impressive, remembering what marks I got."

"I don't remember a thing, it was a deduction. You're working at Crime Squad as a detective after just two years of service."

Anders Wyller smiled. "Just say if I'm in the way, and I'll go. The thing is, I've only been here two and a half days, and if this is a double murder, no one's going to have time to teach me anything for a while. So I was wondering about asking if I could shadow you for a bit. But only if it's OK?"

Harry looked at the young man. Remembered him coming to his office, full of questions. So many questions, sometimes so irrelevant that you might have thought he was a Holehead. Holehead was college slang for students who had fallen for the myth of Harry Hole, which in a few extreme cases was the main reason why they had enrolled. Harry avoided them like the plague. But, Holehead or not, Harry realised that with those grades, as well as his ambition, smile and unforced social skills, Anders Wyller was going to go far. And before Anders Wyller went far, a talented young man like him might have time to do a bit of good, such as helping to solve a few murders.

"OK," Harry said. "The first lesson is that you're going to be disappointed in your colleagues."

"Disappointed?"

"You're standing there all drilled and proud because you think you've made it to the top of the police food chain. So the first lesson is that murder detectives are pretty much the same as everyone else. We aren't especially intelligent, some of us are even a bit stupid. We make mistakes, a lot of mistakes, and we don't learn a great deal from them. When we get tired, sometimes we choose to sleep instead of carrying on with the hunt, even though we know that the solution could be just around the next corner. So if you think we're going to open your eyes, inspire you and show you a whole new world of ingenious investigative skills, you're going to be disappointed."

"I know all that already."

"Really?"

"I've spent two days working with Truls Berntsen. I just want to know how you work."

"You took my course in murder investigation."

"And I know you don't work like that. What were you thinking?"

"Thinking?"

"Yes, when you stood there with your eyes closed. I don't think that was part of the course."

Harry saw that Bjørn had straightened up. That Katrine was standing in the doorway with her arms folded, nodding in encouragement.

"OK," Harry said. "Everyone has their own method. Mine is to try to get in touch with the thoughts that go through your brain the first time you enter a crime scene. All the apparently insignificant connections the brain makes automatically when we absorb impressions the first time we visit a place. Thoughts that we forget so quickly because we don't have time to attach meaning to them before our attention is grabbed by something else, like a dream that vanishes when you wake up and start to take in all the other things around you. Nine times out of ten those thoughts are useless. But you always hope that the tenth one might mean something."

"What about now?" Wyller said. "Do any of the thoughts mean anything?"

Harry paused. Saw the absorbed look on Katrine's face. "I don't know. But I can't help thinking that the murderer has a thing about cleanliness."

"Cleanliness?"

"He moved his last victim from the place where he killed her to the bed. Serial killers usually do things in roughly the same way, so why did he leave this woman in the living room? The only difference between this bedroom and Elise Hermansen's is that here the bedclothes are dirty. I inspected Hermansen's flat yesterday when Forensics picked up the sheets. It smelt of lavender."

"So he committed necrophilia with this woman in the living room because he can't deal with dirty sheets?"

"We're coming to that," Harry said. "Have you seen the blender in the kitchen? OK, so you saw that he put it in the sink after he used it?"

"What?"

"The sink," Katrine said. "Youngsters don't know about washing up by hand, Harry."

"The sink," Harry said. "He didn't have to put it there, he wasn't going to do any washing-up. So maybe it was a compulsive act, maybe he has an obsession with cleanliness? A phobia of bacteria? People who commit serial killings often suffer from a whole host of phobias. But he didn't finish the job, he didn't do the washing-up, he didn't even run the tap and fill the jug with water so that the remnants of his blood-and-lemon smoothie would be easier to wash off later. Why not?"

Anders Wyller shook his head.

"OK, we'll come back to that, too," Harry said, then nodded towards the body. "As you can see, this woman—"

"A neighbour has identified her as Ewa Dolmen," Katrine said. "Ewa with a 'w.'"

"Thanks. Ewa is, as you can see, still wearing her knickers, unlike Elise, whom he undressed. There are empty tampon wrappers at the top of the bin in the bathroom, so I assume that Ewa was on her period. Katrine, can you take a look?"

"The forensics officer is on her way."

"Just to see if I'm right, and the tampon is still there."

Katrine frowned. Then did as Harry asked while the three men looked away.

"Yes, I can see the string from a tampon."

Harry pulled a pack of Camels from his pocket. "Which means that the murderer—assuming he didn't insert the tampon himself—didn't rape her vaginally. Because he's . . ." Harry pointed at Anders Wyller with a cigarette.

"Obsessed with cleanliness," Wyller said.

"That's *one* possibility, anyway," Harry went on. "The other is that he doesn't like blood."

"Doesn't like blood?" Katrine said. "He *drinks* it, for God's sake."

"With lemon," Harry said, putting the unlit cigarette to his lips.

"What?"

"I'm asking myself the same question," Harry said. "What? What does that mean? That the blood was too sweet?"

"Are you trying to be funny?" Katrine asked.

"No, I just think it's odd that a man we think seeks sexual gratification by drinking blood doesn't take his favourite drink neat. People add lemon to gin, and to fish, because they claim it makes the taste more pronounced. But that's wrong, lemon paralyses the taste buds and drowns everything else. We add lemon to hide the taste of something we don't actually like. Cod liver oil started to sell much better when they began to add lemon. So maybe our vampirist doesn't like the taste of blood, maybe his consumption of blood is also a compulsion."

"Maybe he's superstitious and drinks to absorb his victims' strength," Wyller said.

"He certainly seems to be driven by sexual depravity, yet appears able to refrain from touching this woman's genitals. And that *could* be because she's bleeding."

"A vampirist who can't bear menstrual blood," Katrine said. "The tangled pathways of the human mind . . ."

"Which brings us back to the glass jug," Harry said. "Have we got any other physical evidence left by the perpetrator, apart from that?"

"The front door," Bjørn said.

"The door?" Harry said. "I took a look at the lock when I arrived, and it looked untouched."

"Not a break-in. You haven't seen the outside of it."

The other three were standing out in the stairwell, looking on as Bjørn untied the rope that had been holding the door open, back against the wall. It swung slowly shut, revealing its front.

Harry looked. Felt his heart beating hard in his chest as his mouth went dry.

"I tied the door back so that none of you touched it when you arrived," Bjørn said.

On the door the letter "V" was written in blood, about a metre high. It was uneven at the bottom where the blood had run.

The four of them stared at the door.

Bjørn was the first to break the silence. "V for victory?"

"V for vampirist," Katrine said.

"Unless he was just ticking off another victim," Wyller suggested.

They looked at Harry.

"Well?" Katrine said impatiently.

"I don't know," Harry said.

The sharp look returned to her eyes. "Come on, I can see that you're thinking something."

"Mm. V for vampirist might not be a bad suggestion. It could fit with the fact that he's putting a lot of effort into telling us precisely this."

"Precisely what?"

"That he's something special. The iron teeth, the blender, this letter. He regards himself as unique, and is giving us the pieces of the puzzle so that we too will appreciate that. He wants us to get closer."

Katrine nodded.

Wyller hesitated, as if he realised that his time to speak had passed, but still ventured: "You mean that deep down the murderer wants to reveal who he is?"

Harry didn't answer.

"Not who he is, but what," Katrine said. "He's raising a flag."

"Can I ask what that means?"

"Of course," Katrine said. "Ask our expert on serial killers."

Harry was looking at the letter. It was no longer an echo of a scream, it was the scream itself. The scream of a demon.

"It means . . ." Harry flicked his lighter and held it to his cigarette, then inhaled deeply. He let the smoke out again. "He wants to play."

"You think the V stands for something else," Katrine said when she and Harry left the flat an hour later.

"Do I?" Harry said, looking along the street. Tøyen. The immigrant district. Narrow streets, Pakistani carpet shops, cobblestones, Norwegian-language teachers on bikes, Turkish cafes, swaying mothers in hijabs, youngsters getting by on student loans, a tiny record shop pushing vinyl and hard rock. Harry loved Tøyen. So much so that he couldn't help wondering what he was doing up in the hills with the bourgeoisie.

"You just didn't want to say it out loud," Katrine said.

"Do you know what my grandfather used to say when he caught me swearing? 'If you call for the devil, he'll come.' So . . ."

"So, what?"

"Do you want the devil to come?"

"We've got a double murder, Harry, maybe a serial killer. Can it really get any worse?"

"Yes," Harry said. "It can."

# 11

# Saturday evening

"We're assuming that we're dealing with a serial killer," Detective Inspector Katrine Bratt said, and looked out at the conference room and her entire investigative team. Plus Harry. They had agreed that he would participate in meetings until he'd set up his own group.

There was a different, more focused atmosphere than during their previous meetings. This was obviously to do with the development of the case, but Katrine was pretty sure that Harry's presence also made a difference. He may well have been Crime Squad's drunk, arrogant *enfant terrible*, someone who had directly or indirectly caused the deaths of other officers, and whose working methods were highly questionable. But he still made them sit up and pay attention. Because he still had the same dour, almost frightening charisma, and his achievements were beyond question. Off the top of her head, she could only think of one person he had failed to catch. Maybe Harry was right when he said that longevity bestowed respect, even upon a whorehouse madam if she kept going for long enough.

"This sort of perpetrator is very difficult to find for a number of reasons, but primarily because—as in this case—he plans carefully, chooses his victims at random, and doesn't leave any evidence at the scene except what he wants us to find. That's why the folders in front of you containing the analysis from Forensics, the forensics medical officer and our own tactical analysts is so thin. We still haven't managed to link any known sex offender to Elise Hermansen or Ewa

Dolmen, or either of the crime scenes. But we have managed to identify the methodology behind the murders. Tord?"

The IT expert let out a short, inappropriate laugh, as if he had found what Katrine had said funny, before saying: "Ewa Dolmen sent a message from her mobile phone which tells us that she had a Tinder date at a sports bar called Dicky's."

"Dicky's?" Magnus Skarre exclaimed. "That's more or less opposite the Jealousy Bar."

A collective groan ran round the room.

"So we could be on to something, if the murderer's MO is to use Tinder and arrange to meet in Grünerløkka," Katrine said.

"What, though?" one of the detectives asked.

"An idea of how it might happen next time."

"What if there isn't a next time?"

Katrine took a deep breath. "Harry?"

Harry rocked back on his chair. "Well, serial killers who are still learning the ropes usually leave a long gap between their first murders. It can be months, years, even. The classic pattern is that after a killing there's a cooling-down period, before his sexual frustration starts to build up again. These cycles typically get shorter and shorter between each murder. With a cycle that's already as short as two days, it's tempting to assume that this isn't the first time he's committed this type of offence."

A silence followed, during which everyone waited for him to go on. He didn't.

Katrine cleared her throat. "The problem is that we can't find any serious crimes in Norway during the past five years that show any similarities to these two murders. We've checked with Interpol to see if it's possible that any likely perpetrator may have switched hunting grounds and moved to Norway. There are a dozen candidates, but none of them appears to have moved recently. So we have no idea who he is. But we do know that experience indicates that it's likely to happen again. And in this case, soon."

"How soon?" a voice asked.

"Hard to say," Katrine said, glancing at Harry, who discreetly held up one finger. "But the gap could be as short as one day."

"And there's nothing we can do to stop him?"

Katrine shifted her weight to the other foot. "We've contacted the Chief of Police to ask for permission to issue a public warning in conjunction with the press conference at 1800 hours. With a bit of luck the perpetrator will cancel or at least postpone any plans for another murder if he thinks people are going to be more wary."

"Would he really do that?" Wolff wondered.

"I think—" Katrine began, but was interrupted.

"With all due respect, Bratt, I was asking Hole."

Katrine swallowed and tried not to get annoyed. "What do you say, Harry? Would a public warning stop him?"

"I don't know," Harry said. "Forget what you've seen on television, serial killers aren't robots with the same software who follow the same pattern of behaviour, they're as diverse and unpredictable as everyone else."

"Smart answer, Hole." Everyone in the room turned towards the door, where the new arrival, Police Chief Bellman, was leaning against the door frame with his arms folded. "No one knows what effect a public warning might have. Maybe it would only encourage this sick murderer, give him a feeling that he's in control of the situation, that he's invulnerable and can just carry on. But what we *do* know, on the other hand, is that a public warning would give the impression that we here at Police Headquarters have *lost* control of the situation. And the only people who would be scared by that are the city's inhabitants. More scared, we should probably say, because—as those of you who have read what the papers have been saying online in the past few hours will have noticed—there is already a lot of speculation about these two murders being linked. So I have a better suggestion." Mikael Bellman pulled at his shirtsleeves so that the white cuffs stuck out from the sleeves of his jacket. "And that is that we catch this guy before he does any more damage." He smiled at them all. "What do you say, good people?"

Katrine saw a few of them nod their heads.

"Good," Bellman said. "Carry on, Detective Inspector Bratt."


The bells of the City Hall signalled that it was eight o'clock as an unmarked police car, a VW Passat, drove slowly past.

"That was the worst fucking press conference I've ever held," Katrine said as she steered the Passat towards Dronning Mauds gate.

"Twenty-nine times," Harry said.

"What?"

"You said 'We can't comment on that' twenty-nine times," Harry said. "I counted."

"I was *so* close to saying 'Sorry, the Chief of Police has muzzled us.' What's Bellman playing at? No warning, no saying we've got a serial killer on the loose and that people should watch out?"

"He's right when he says it would spread irrational fear."

"Irrational?" Katrine snapped. "Look around you! It's Saturday night, and half the women you can see wandering about are on their way to meet a man they don't know, a prince they hope will change their lives. And if your idea of a gap of a single day is correct, one of them is going to be *really* fucking right about that."

"Did you know there was a serious bus crash in the centre of London the same day as the terror attacks in Paris? Almost as many people were killed as in Paris. Norwegians who had friends in Paris started calling, worried they might be among the dead. But no one was particularly worried about their friends in London. After the terror attacks people were frightened of going to Paris, even though the police there were on high alert. No one was worried about travelling by bus in London even though traffic safety hadn't improved."

"What's your point?"

"That people are more scared than the likelihood of meeting a vampirist ought to make them. Because it's all over the front pages of the newspapers, and because they've read that he drinks blood. But at the same time they light cigarettes that are pretty much certain to kill them."

"So tell me, do you actually *agree* with Bellman?"

"No," Harry said, gazing out at the street. "I'm just musing. Because I'm trying to put myself in Bellman's shoes to work out what he wants. Bellman always has something in mind."

"And what is it this time?"

"I don't know. But he wants this kept as low-key as possible, and solved as fast as possible. Like a boxer defending his title."

"What are you talking about now, Harry?"

"Once you've got hold of a belt, you really want to try to avoid fights. Because the best thing you can achieve is holding on to what you've already got."

"Interesting theory. What about that other theory of yours?"

"I said I wasn't sure."

"He painted the letter V on Ewa Dolmen's door. That's his initial, Harry. And you said you recognised the crime scene from when he was active."

"Yes, but like I said, I can't put my finger on what it is that I recognised." Harry paused as a split-second shot of a neutral street scene flashed through his mind.

"Katrine, listen: biting throats, iron teeth, drinking blood—that isn't his MO. Serial attackers and murderers might be unpredictable when it comes to details, but they don't change their whole MO."

"He's got a lot of different MOs, Harry."

"He likes pain, and he likes their fear. Not blood."

"You said the killer put lemon in the blood because he didn't like it."

"Katrine, it wouldn't even help us to know that it *is* him. How long have you and Interpol been looking for him now?"

"Getting on for four years."

"That's why I think it would be counterproductive to tell the others about my suspicions and risk the investigation narrowing down to focus on just one person."

"Or else you want to catch him yourself."

"What?"

"He's the reason you're back, isn't he, Harry? You got his scent right from the start. Oleg was just an excuse."

"We're dropping this conversation now, Katrine."

"Because Bellman would never have gone public about Oleg's past—the fact that he hadn't done anything before now would bounce back and hit him."

Harry turned the radio up. "Heard this one? Aurora Aksnes, it's pretty . . ."

"You hate synth-pop, Harry."

"I like it more than this conversation."

Katrine sighed. They pulled up at a red light. She leaned forward towards the windscreen.

"Look. It's a full moon."


"It's a full moon," Mona Daa said, looking out of the kitchen window at the rolling fields. The moonlight made it look like they were shimmering, as if they were covered with fresh snow. "Does that increase the likelihood of him striking for a third time as early as tonight, do you think?"

Hallstein Smith smiled. "Hardly. From what you've told me about the two murders, this vampirist's paraphilias are necrophilia and sadism rather than mythomania or any delusion that he's a supernatural being. But he will strike again, that much is certain."

"Interesting." Mona Daa was writing in her notebook, which was lying on the kitchen table next to the cup of freshly brewed green chilli tea. "And where and when will that happen, do you think?"

"You said the second woman had also been on a Tinder date?"

Mona Daa nodded as she continued to take notes. Most of her colleagues used recording devices, but—even though she was the youngest of the crime reporters—she preferred to do it the old-fashioned way. Her official explanation was that in the race to be first with the news, she saved time in comparison to the others because she edited her stories while taking notes. That was a particular advantage when she was covering press conferences. Although this afternoon at Police HQ you could have managed without a Dictaphone or notebook. Katrine Bratt's refrain of "We can't comment" had eventually managed to provoke even the most experienced crime reporters.

"We haven't printed anything about it being a Tinder date in the paper yet, but we've received a tip-off from a source in the police saying that Ewa Dolmen had sent a text message to a friend telling her that she was on a Tinder date at Dicky's in Grünerløkka."

"Right." Smith adjusted his glasses. "I'm pretty sure he'll stick to the method that's proved successful for him so far."

"So what would you say to people who are thinking of meeting new men via Tinder over the next few days?"

"That they ought to wait until the vampirist is caught."

"But do you think he'll go on using Tinder himself after he's read this and realised that everyone knows that's his method?"

"This is a psychosis, he won't let himself be stopped by rational considerations when it comes to risk. This isn't a classic serial killer, calmly planning what he does, a cold-blooded psychopath who doesn't leave any evidence, who hides in corners spinning his web and taking his time between murders."

"Our source says the detectives leading the investigation believe he *is* a classic serial killer."

"This is a different sort of madness. The murder is less important to him than the biting, the blood—*that's* what's driving him. And all he wants is to carry on, he's on a roll now, his psychosis is fully developed. The hope is that he—unlike the classic serial killer—actually wants to be identified and caught because he's so out of control, so indifferent to being found. The classic serial killer and the vampirist are both natural disasters in the sense that they are perfectly ordinary people who happen to be mentally ill. But while the serial killer is a storm that can rage and rage and you don't know when it's over, the vampirist is like a landslide. It's over after a very short time. But in that time he could have wiped out an entire community, OK?"

"OK," Mona said, scribbling away. *Wipe out an entire community.* "Well, thanks very much, I've got all I need."

"Don't mention it. I'm actually surprised that you came out here for so little."

Mona Daa opened her iPad. "We had to come anyway, to get a picture, so I came along as well. Will?"

"I was thinking of taking a picture out on the field," the photographer said, having sat quietly and listened to the interview. "You, the open landscape and the light of the moon."

Mona knew exactly what the photographer was thinking, of course. Man alone outside in the dark, full moon, vampire. She nodded almost imperceptibly to him. Sometimes it was best not to tell the subject of a photograph what your ideas were, because then you only ran the risk of them objecting.

"Any chance my wife can be in the picture too?" Smith wondered, looking rather taken aback. "*VG* . . . this is a pretty big deal for us."

Mona Daa couldn't help smiling. Sweet. For a moment an idea flashed through her head, of them taking a picture of the psychologist biting his wife's neck to illustrate the case, but that would obviously be taking it too far, too much slapstick for a serious murder story.

"My editor would probably prefer to have you on your own," she said.

"I understand, I just had to ask."

"I'll stay here and write, then maybe we can get it up on the website before we leave. Have you got Wi-Fi?"

She got the password, *freudundgammen*, and was already halfway through by the time she saw the camera flash out on the field.

The unofficial explanation of why she avoided recordings was that they were incontrovertible evidence of what had *really* been said. Not that Mona Daa ever consciously wrote anything that contradicted what she believed her interviewee had meant. But it gave her the freedom to emphasise certain points. Translating quotes into a tabloid form that the readers would understand. And would click to read.

PSYCHOLOGIST: VAMPIRIST CAN WIPE OUT WHOLE CITIES!

She glanced at the time. Truls Berntsen had said he'd call at ten o'clock if anything new had cropped up.

. . .

"I don't like science-fiction films," said the man sitting opposite Penelope Rasch. "The most irritating thing is the sound as the spaceship passes the camera." He pursed his lips and made a quick whooshing sound. "There's no air in space, there's no sound, just complete silence. We're being lied to."

"Amen," Penelope said, and raised her glass of mineral water.

"I like Alejandro González Iñárritu," the man said, raising his own glass of water. "I prefer *Biutiful* and *Babel* to *Birdman* and *The Revenant*. I'm afraid he's getting a bit mainstream now."

Penelope felt a little shiver of pleasure. Not so much because he had just mentioned both her favourite films, but because he had included Iñárritu's rarely used middle name. And he had already mentioned her favourite author (Cormac McCarthy) and city (Florence).

The door opened. They had been the only customers in the neglected little restaurant he had suggested, but now another couple walked in. He turned round. Not towards the door to look, but away from it. And she got a couple of seconds in which to study him unobserved. She had already noted that he was slim, about the same height as her, well mannered, nicely dressed. But was he attractive? It was hard to say. He certainly wasn't ugly, but there was something slippery about him. And something made her doubt he was as young as the forty years he claimed to be. His skin looked tight around his eyes and neck, as if he'd had a facelift.

"I didn't know this restaurant was here," she said. "Very quiet."

"T-too quiet?" he smiled.

"It's nice."

"Next time we can go to this place I know that serves Kirin beer and black rice," he said. "If you like that."

She very nearly squealed. This was fantastic. How could he know that she *loved* black rice? Most of her friends didn't know it even existed. Roar had hated it, he said it tasted of health-food shops and snobbery. And, to be fair, those were both fair accusations: black rice contained more antioxidants than blueberries and was served alongside the forbidden sushi that was reserved for the emperor and his family.

"I love it," she said. "What else do you like?"

"My job," he said.

"Which is?"

"I'm a visual artist."

"How exciting! What . . . ?"

"Installations."

"Roar—my ex—he was a visual artist too, perhaps you know him?"

"I doubt it, I operate outside conventional artistic circles. And I'm self-taught, so to speak."

"But if you can make a living as an artist, it's odd that I haven't heard of you. Oslo's so small."

"I do other things to survive."

"Such as?"

"Caretaker."

"But you exhibit?"

"It's mostly private installations for a professional clientele, where the press aren't invited."

"Wow. It sounds great that you're able to be exclusive. I told Roar that he ought to try that. What do you use in your installations?"

He wiped his glass with a napkin. "Models."

"Models as in . . . living people?"

He smiled. "Both. Tell me about yourself, Penelope. What do you like?"

She put a finger under her chin. Yes, what did she like? Right now she had a sense that he had covered everything.

"I like people," she said. "And honesty. And my family. Children."

"And being held, tight," he said, glancing over at the couple who were sitting two tables away from them.

"Sorry?"

"You like being held tight, and playing rough games." He leaned across the table. "I can see it in you, Penelope. And that's fine, I like that too. This place is starting to get a bit crowded, so shall we go back to yours?"

It took Penelope a moment to realise that it wasn't a joke. She looked down and saw that he had put his hand so close to hers that their fingertips were almost touching. She swallowed. What was it about her that meant she always ended up with nutters? It was her friends who had suggested that the best way to get over Roar was to meet other men. And she had tried, but they were either bumbling, socially inadequate IT nerds where she had to do all the talking, or men like this one, who were only after a quick shag.

"I think I'll go home alone," she said, and looked around for the waiter. "I'm happy to settle up." They had barely been there twenty minutes, but according to her friends, that was the third, and most important, rule of Tinder: *Don't play games, leave if you don't click.*

"I can manage two bottles of mineral water," the man smiled, and tugged gently at his pale blue shirt collar. "Run, Cinderella."

"In that case, thank you."

Penelope picked up her bag and hurried out. The sharp autumn air felt good against her warm cheeks. She crossed Bogstadveien. Because it was Saturday night the streets were full of happy people and there was a queue at the taxi rank. Which was just as well—the price of taxis in Oslo was so high that she avoided them unless it was pouring with rain. She passed Sorgenfrigata, where she had once dreamt that she and Roar would some day live in one of the lovely buildings. They had agreed that the flat didn't need to be more that seventy or eighty square metres in size, as long as it had been recently renovated, the bathroom at least. They knew that it would be incredibly expensive, but both her and Roar's parents had promised to help out financially. And by "help out" they obviously meant paying for the whole flat. She was, after all, a recently qualified designer on the hunt for a job, and the art market hadn't yet discovered Roar's immense talent. Except that bitch of a gallery owner who had set her trap for him. After Roar moved out, Penelope had been convinced that he would see through the woman, realise she was a wrinkled puma who just wanted a young trophy boyfriend to play with for a while. But that hadn't happened. On the contrary, they had just announced their engagement in the form of a hideous art installation made of candyfloss.

At the metro station in Majorstua Penelope took the first train heading west. She got off at Hovseter, known as the eastern edge of the west side of the city. A cluster of apartment blocks and relatively cheap flats where she and Roar had rented the cheapest they could find. The bathroom was disgusting.

Roar had tried to console her by giving her a copy of Patti Smith's *Just Kids*, an autobiographical account of two ambitious artists living on hope, air and love in New York in the early 1970s, and who obviously end up making a success of things. OK, they lost each other along the way, but . . .

She walked from the station towards the building rising up in front of her, which looked like it had a halo. Penelope realised that there was a full moon tonight, that must be what was glowing behind the building. Four. She had slept with four men since Roar left her, eleven months and thirteen days ago. Two of them had been better than Roar, two worse. But she didn't love Roar for the sex. But because . . . well, because he was Roar, the bastard.

She found herself quickening her pace as she passed the little clump of trees on the left-hand side of the road. The streets of Hovseter grew empty early each evening, but Penelope was a tall, fit young woman, and until now it hadn't even occurred to her that it might be dangerous to walk here after dark. Perhaps it was because of that murderer who was in all the papers. No, it wasn't that. It was because someone had been inside her flat. It was three months ago now, and at first she had dared to hope that Roar had come back. She realised someone had been there when she found mud in the hallway that didn't match her shoes. And when she found some more in the bedroom, in front of the chest of drawers, she had counted her knickers in the idiotic hope that Roar had taken a pair. But no, that didn't seem to be the case. Then she realised what was missing. The engagement ring in its box, the one Roar had bought her in London. Could it just have been a run-of-the-mill burglary, after all? No, it was Roar. He had snuck in and taken it, and had given it to that bitch of a gallery owner! Naturally, Penelope had been furious, and had called Roar and confronted him with it. But he swore he hadn't been back, and claimed to have lost the keys to the flat during the move, because otherwise he would have posted them to her. A lie, of course, like everything else, but she had still gone to the effort of getting the locks changed, both the front door and the door to her flat on the fourth floor.

Penelope took her keys out of her handbag—they were next to the pepper spray she had bought—unlocked the front door, heard the low hiss of the hydraulics as it swung behind her, saw that the lift was on the sixth floor, and started to walk up the stairs. She passed the Amundsens' door. Stopped. Felt that she was out of breath. Funny, she was in good shape, these stairs had never tired her out before. Something was wrong. What?

She stared up at the door to her flat.

It was an old building, built for the working classes of western Oslo, now long gone, and they had been sparing with the lighting. There was just one large, metal-framed light on each floor, jutting out from high up on the wall above the stairs. She held her breath and listened. She hadn't heard a sound since she came into the building.

Not since the hiss of the hydraulics.

Not a sound.

That was what was wrong.

She hadn't heard the door close.

Penelope didn't have time to turn round, didn't have time to put her hand in her bag, didn't have time to do anything before an arm swung round her, locking her arms and pressing her chest so hard that she couldn't breathe. Her bag fell onto the stairs and was the only thing she managed to hit as she kicked out wildly around her. She screamed soundlessly into the hand that was clamped over her mouth. It smelt of soap.

"There, there, Penelope," a voice whispered in her ear. "In space, no one c-can hear you scream, you know." He made the whooshing sound.

She heard a noise from down near the front door, and for a moment hoped someone was coming, before realising that it was her bag, her keys—and the pepper spray—sailing through the railings and hitting the floor downstairs.

"What is it?" Rakel asked, without turning round or stopping chopping the onion for the salad. She had seen from the reflection in the window above the kitchen worktop that Harry had stopped laying the table and had gone over to the living-room window.

"I thought I heard something," he said.

"Probably Oleg and Helga."

"No, it was something else. It was . . . something else."

Rakel sighed. "Harry, you've only just got home, and already you're climbing the walls. Look at what it's doing to you."

"Just this one case, then it's over." Harry walked over to the worktop and kissed the back of her neck. "How are you feeling?"

"Fine," she lied. Her body ached, her head ached. Her heart ached.

"You're lying," he said.

"Am I good liar?"

He smiled and massaged her neck.

"If I ever disappeared," she said, "would you look for someone new?"

"Look for? That sounds tiring. It was bad enough trying to persuade you."

"Someone younger. Someone you could have kids with. I wouldn't be jealous, you know."

"You're not *that* good a liar, darling."

She smiled and let go of the knife, leaned her head forward and felt his warm, dry fingers massage the aches away, giving her a break from the pain.

"I love you," she said.

"Mm?"

"I love you. Especially if you make me a cup of tea."

"Aye aye, boss."

Harry let go and Rakel stood there waiting. Hoping. But no, the pain came back again, punching her like a fist.

Harry stood with both hands on the kitchen worktop, staring at the kettle. Waiting for the low rumble. Which would get louder and louder until the whole thing shook. Like a scream. He could hear screams. Silent screams that filled his head, filled the room, filled his body. He shifted his weight. Screams that wanted to get out, that *had* to get out. Was he going mad? He looked up at the glass of the window. All he could see in the darkness was his own reflection. There he was. He was out there. He was waiting for them. He was singing. Come out and play!

Harry closed his eyes.

No, he wasn't waiting for *them*. He was waiting for him, for Harry. Come out and play!

He could feel that she was different from the others. Penelope Rasch wanted to live. She was big and strong. And the keys to her flat lay three floors below them. He could feel her relinquishing the air from her lungs and tightened his grasp round her chest. Like a boa constrictor. A muscle tightening a little more each time the prey lets air out of its lungs. He wanted her alive. Alive and warm. With this wonderful desire to survive. Which he would break, little by little. But how? Even if he managed to drag her all the way downstairs to get the key, there was a risk that one of the neighbours would hear them. He felt his rage growing. He should have skipped Penelope Rasch. Should have taken that decision three days ago when he discovered that she'd changed the locks. But then he had been lucky, had made contact with her on Tinder, she had agreed to meet at that discreet place, and he had thought that it was going to work out after all. But a small, quiet place also means that the few people who are there pay more attention to you. One customer had stared at him a little too hard. And he had panicked, had decided to get out of there, and had rushed things. Penelope had turned him down and walked out.

He had been prepared for that eventuality and had the car nearby. He had driven fast. Not so fast that he risked being stopped by the police, but fast enough to reach the cluster of trees before she emerged from the metro. She hadn't turned round when he was following her, nor when she got her keys out of her bag and went in. He had managed to stick his foot in the gap before the door clicked shut.

He felt a shudder run through her body and knew that she would soon lose consciousness. His erection rubbed against her buttocks. A broad, fleshy woman's arse. His mother had had a similar backside.

He could feel the boy coming, eager to take over, and he was screaming inside, wanting to be fed. Now. Here.

"I love you," he whispered in her ear. "I really do, Penelope, and that's why I'm going to make an honest woman of you before we go any further."

She went limp in his arms and he hurried, holding her up with one arm as he fumbled in his jacket pocket with the other.

Penelope Rasch came to, and realised that she must have passed out. It had got darker. She was floating, and there was something tugging and pulling at her arms, something cutting into her wrists. She looked up. Handcuffs. And something on one of her ring fingers, shimmering dully.

Then she felt the pain between her legs and looked down just as he pulled his hand out of her.

His face was partially shaded, but she saw him put his fingers to his nose and sniff. She tried to scream, but couldn't.

"Good, my darling," he said. "You're clean, so we can begin."

He unbuttoned his jacket and shirt, pushed his shirt aside, revealing his chest. A tattoo became visible, a face screaming as soundlessly as her. He was thrusting his chest out, as if the tattoo had something to say to her. Unless it was the other way round. Perhaps *she* was the one on display. On display to this snarling image of the devil.

He felt for something in his jacket pocket, pulled it out and showed her. Black. Iron. Teeth.

Penelope managed to get some air. And screamed.

"That's right, darling," he laughed. "Just like that. Music to work to."

Then he opened his mouth wide and inserted the teeth.

And they echoed and sang between the walls: his laughter and her screaming.

There was a buzz of voices and international news broadcasts on the big television screens that hung on the walls of *VG*'s offices, where the head of news and the duty manager were working on updates to the online edition.

Mona Daa and the photographer were standing behind the head of news's chair, studying the image on his console.

"I tried everything, but I just couldn't make him look creepy," the photographer sighed.

And Mona realised that he was right, Hallstein Smith simply looked far too jovial, standing there with the full moon above him.

"It's still working," the head of news said. "Look at the traffic. Nine hundred per minute now."

Mona saw the counter to the right of the screen.

"We've got a winner," her boss said. "We'll move it to the top of the website. Maybe we should ask the night editor if she wants to change the front page."

The photographer raised his clenched fist towards Mona and she dutifully touched her knuckles to his. Her father claimed it was Tiger Woods and his caddie who had popularised the gesture. They had switched from the obligatory high five after the caddie had injured the golfer's hand by high-fiving him a bit too enthusiastically when Woods pitched the sixteenth hole in the final round of the Masters. It was one of her father's greatest regrets that Mona's congenital hip defect meant she could never be the great golfer he had hoped. She, on the other hand, had hated golf from the first time he took her to a driving range, but because the standard was so comically low she had won everything there was to win with a swing that was so short and ugly that the coach of the national junior team refused to select her on the grounds that it was better to get beaten with a team that at least looked like it was playing golf. So she had dumped her golf clubs in the basement at her dad's and headed for the weight room instead, where no one had any objections to the *way* she lifted 120 kilos off the floor. The number of kilos, the number of blows, the number of clicks. Success was measured in numbers, anyone who claimed otherwise was just scared of the truth and seriously believed that delusion was an essential fact of life for the average person. But right now she was more interested in the comments section. Because something had struck her when Smith said the vampirist didn't care about the risks. That it was possible he might read *VG*. That he *might* post some sort of comment online.

Her eyes scanned the comments as they appeared.

But it was the usual stuff.

The sympathetic, expressing pity for the victims.

The self-appointed guardians of truth, explaining how a particu-lar political party bore responsibility for a society that had produced a particular type of undesirable person, in this instance a vampirist.

The executioners, shrieking for the death penalty and castration the moment they got a chance.

And then there were the wannabe stand-up comedians whose role models had popularised the idea that anything could be joked about. "New band, Wampire." "Sell Tinder shares now!"

And if she did see a comment that looked suspicious, what was she going to do? Report it to Katrine Bratt & co.? Maybe. She owed Truls Berntsen that much. Or she could call the blond one, Wyller. Make him indebted to her. Even if you're not on Tinder, you still swipe left and right.

She yawned. Walked over to her desk and picked up her bag.

"I'm going to the gym," she said.

"Now? It's practically the middle of the night!"

"Call me if anything happens."

"Your shift ended an hour ago, Daa, other people can—"

"This is my story, so you call me, OK?"

She heard someone laugh as the door closed behind her. Maybe they were laughing at her walk, maybe at her provocative clever-girl-can-do-it-all-herself attitude. She didn't care. She *did* have a funny walk. And she *could* do it all herself.

Lift, airlock, swing doors, then she was outside the building, its glass facade lit up by the moonlight. Mona breathed in. Something big was going on, she just knew it. And she knew that she was going to be part of it.


Truls Berntsen had parked the car beside the steep, winding road. The brick buildings below him lay silent in the darkness: Oslo's abandoned industrial district, railway tracks with grass growing between the sleepers. And, further away, the architects' new toy building blocks, Barcode, the playground of the new business world, in marked contrast to the sombre seriousness of the working life of the past, where minimalism was a matter of cost-saving practicality, not an aesthetic ideal.

Truls looked up at the house bathed in moonlight, up on the crest of the hill.

There were lights in the windows and he knew that Ulla was in there. Maybe she was sitting in her usual place, on the sofa with her legs tucked beneath her, reading a book. If he took his binoculars in among the trees further up the hill he'd find out. And if she was doing that, he'd see her brush her blonde hair behind one ear, as if she were listening out for something. In case the children woke up. In case Mikael wanted something. Or perhaps just listening out for predators, like a gazelle at a watering hole.

There was a buzz and a crackle and voices relaying short messages before disappearing again. The sounds of the city conveyed through a police radio soothed him more than music.

Truls looked at the glove compartment he'd just opened. The binoculars were tucked behind his service pistol. He had promised himself that he was going to stop. That it was time, that he didn't need this anymore, not now he'd found out there were other fish in the sea. OK. Monkfish, sculpins and weevers. Truls heard himself grunt. It was his laugh that had earned him the nickname Beavis. That, and his heavy lower jaw. And there she was, up there, imprisoned in that oversized, overpriced house with a terrace that Truls had helped construct, and where he had buried the corpse of a drug dealer in wet cement, a corpse that only Truls knew about, and which had never given him so much as one sleepless night.

A scraping sound on the radio. The voice from Emergency Control.

"Have we got any cars near Hovseter?"

"Car 31, in Skøyen."

"Hovseterveien 44, doorway B. We got a pretty hysterical resident saying there's a madman in the stairwell assaulting a woman there, but that they daren't intervene because he's smashed the light on the stairs and it's pitch-black."

"Assaulting with a weapon?"

"They don't know. They say they saw him bite her before it went dark. The caller's name was Amundsen."

Truls reacted instantly and pressed the "speak" button on the radio. "Detective Constable Truls Berntsen here, I'm closer, I'll take it."

He had already started the engine, and revved it hard as he pulled out onto the road, hearing a car coming round the bend behind him blow its horn angrily.

"Copy," Emergency Control said. "And where are you, Berntsen?"

"Just round the corner, I said. 31, I want you as backup, so wait if you get there first. Suspect that the assailant is armed. Repeat, armed."

Saturday night, almost no traffic. If he drove through the Opera

Tunnel at full speed, cutting straight through the centre beneath the fjord, he wouldn't be more than seven or eight minutes behind car 31. Those minutes *could*, of course, be critical, both for the victim and for the perpetrator to get away, but Detective Constable Truls Berntsen *could* also be the officer who arrested the vampirist. And who knew what *VG* would be willing to pay for a report from the first man on the scene. He blew the car's horn repeatedly and a Volvo swerved out of his way. Dual carriageway now. Three lanes. Foot on the floor. His heart was pounding against his ribs. A speed camera in the tunnel flashed. Police officer on duty, a licence to tell everyone in this whole damn city to fuck off. On duty. His blood was pulsing through his veins, brilliant, as if he was about to get a hard-on.

"Ace of space!" Truls roared. "Ace of space!"


"Yes, we're car 31. We've been waiting!" The man and woman were standing behind the patrol car parked in front of doorway B.

"Slow lorry that wouldn't let me pass," Truls said, checking that his pistol was loaded and the cartridge full. "Heard anything?"

"It's all quiet in there. No one's entered or left."

"Let's go." Truls pointed to the male officer. "You come with me, and bring a torch." He nodded to the woman. "You stay here."

The two men walked up to the entrance. Truls peered through the window at the darkened stairwell. He pressed the button beside the name Amundsen.

"Yes?" a voice whispered.

"Police. Have you heard anything since you called?"

"No, but he could still be out there."

"OK. Open the door."

The lock clicked and Truls pulled the door open. "You go first with the torch."

Truls heard the officer swallow. "I thought you said backup, not up front."

"Just be grateful you're not here on your own," Truls whispered. "Come on."


Rakel looked at Harry.

Two murders. A new serial killer. His type of hunt.

He was sitting there eating, making out that he was following the conversation around the table, was polite towards Helga, listened with apparent interest to Oleg. Perhaps she was wrong, perhaps he really was interested. Perhaps he wasn't completely enchained by it after all, perhaps he had changed.

"Gun licences are pointless when people will soon be able to buy a 3D printer and make their own pistols," Oleg said.

"I thought 3D printers could only make things out of plastic?" Harry said.

"Home printers, yes. But plastic is durable enough if you just want a weapon and you're only going to use it once to murder someone." Oleg leaned across the dining table. "You don't even need an original pistol as the template, you just borrow one for five minutes, dismantle it, take wax copies of the pieces, then use those to make a 3D model that you feed into the computer that controls the printer. Once the murder has been committed, you just melt the whole plastic pistol down. And if anyone *did* work out that that was the murder weapon, it wouldn't be registered to anyone."

"Hm. But the pistol could still be traced back to the printer that produced it. Forensics can already do that with inkjet printers."

Rakel looked at Helga, who was looking rather lost.

"Boys . . ." Rakel said.

"Whatever," Oleg said. "It's really crazy—they can make practically anything. So far there are just over two thousand 3D printers in Norway, but imagine when everyone's got one, when terrorists can 3D-print a hydrogen bomb."

"Boys, can't we talk about something more pleasant?" Rakel said, feeling strangely breathless. "Something a bit more cultured, just for once, seeing as we've got a guest?"

Oleg and Harry turned towards Helga, who smiled and shrugged, as if to say that she was fine with anything.

"OK," Oleg said. "What about Shakespeare?"

"That sounds better," Rakel said, looking at her son suspiciously as she passed the potatoes to Helga.

"OK, Ståle Aune and Othello syndrome," Oleg said. "I haven't told you that Jesus and I recorded the entire lecture. I was wearing a hidden microphone and transmitter under my shirt, and Jesus was in the next room recording it. Do you think Ståle would be OK if we uploaded it to the Net? What do you think, Harry?"

Harry didn't answer. Rakel studied him. Was he drifting away again?

"Harry?" she said.

"Well, obviously I can't answer that," he said, looking down at his plate. "But why didn't you just record it on your phone? It isn't forbidden to record lectures for private use."

"They're practising," Helga said.

The others turned towards her.

"Jesus and Oleg dream of working as undercover agents."

"Wine, Helga?" Rakel picked up the bottle.

"Thanks. But aren't you having any?"

"I've taken a headache pill," Rakel said. "And Harry doesn't drink."

"I'm a so-called alcoholic," Harry said. "Which is a shame, because that's supposed to be a really good wine."

Rakel saw Helga's cheeks burn, and hurried to ask: "So Ståle's teaching you about Shakespeare?"

"Yes and no," Oleg said. "Othello syndrome implies that jealousy is the main reason for the murders in the play, but that isn't true. Helga and I read *Othello* yesterday—"

"You read it together?" Rakel put her hand in Harry's arm. "Isn't that sweet?"

Oleg looked up at the ceiling. "Either way, my interpretation is that the real, underlying cause of all the murders isn't jealousy but a humiliated man's envy and ambition. In other words, Iago. Othello is just a puppet. The play ought to be called *Iago*, not *Othello*."

"And do you agree with that, Helga?" Rakel liked the slim, slightly anaemic, well-mannered girl, and she seemed to have found her feet pretty quickly.

"I like *Othello* as the title. And maybe there isn't a deep-seated reason. Maybe it's like Othello himself says. That the full moon is the real cause, because it drives men mad."

"*No reason*," Harry declaimed solemnly in English. "*I just like doing things like that.*"

"Impressive, Harry," Rakel said. "You can quote Shakespeare."

"Walter Hill," Harry said. "*The Warriors*, 1979."

"Yeah," Oleg laughed. "Best gang film *ever*."

Rakel and Helga laughed. Harry raised his glass of water and looked across the table at Rakel. Smiled. Laughter round the family dinner table. And she thought that he was here now, he was with them. She tried to hold on to his gaze, hold on to him. But imperceptibly, as the sea turns from green to blue, it happened. His eyes turned inward again. And she knew that even before the laughter had died out, he was on his way again, into the darkness, away from them.

. . .

Truls walked up the stairs in the dark, crouching with his pistol behind the big, uniformed police officer with the torch. The silence was only broken by a ticking sound, like a clock somewhere further up inside the building. The cone of light from the torch seemed to push the darkness ahead of them, making it denser, more compact, like the snow Truls and Mikael used to shovel for pensioners in Manglerud. Afterwards they would snatch the hundred-krone note from gnarled, trembling hands, and say they would come back with the change. If they ever did wait for them, they were waiting still.

Something crunched beneath their feet.

Truls grabbed the back of the policeman's jacket, and he stopped and pointed the torch at the floor. Splinters of glass sparkled, and between them Truls could see indistinct footprints in what he was fairly sure was blood. The heel and front of the sole were clearly divided, but he thought the print was too big to be a woman's. The prints were pointing down the stairs, and he was sure he would have seen them if there had been any further down. The ticking sound had got louder.

Truls gestured to the policeman to go on. He looked at the stairs, saw that the bloody prints were getting clearer. Looked up the stairs. Stopped and raised his pistol. Let the policeman carry on. Truls had seen something. Something that had fallen through the light. Something that sparkled. Something red. It wasn't ticking they had heard, it was the sound of blood dripping and hitting the stairs.

"Shine the torch upward," he said.

The police officer stopped, turned round, and for a moment looked surprised that the colleague whom he had thought was right behind him had stopped a few steps below and was looking up at the ceiling. But he did as Truls said.

"Oh my God . . ." he whispered.

"Amen," Truls said.

There was a woman hanging from the wall above them.

Her checked skirt had been pulled up, revealing the edge of her white knickers. On one thigh, level with the policeman's head, blood was dripping from a large wound. It ran down her leg, into her shoe. The shoe was evidently full, because the blood was running down the outside and gathering in drops at the point of the shoe, then falling to join a red puddle on the stairs. Her arms were pulled up above her lolling head. Her wrists were tied with a peculiar set of cuffs which had been hooked over the lamp bracket. Whoever had put her there had to be strong. Her hair was covering her face and neck, so Truls couldn't see if there was a bite mark, but the amount of blood in the puddle and the terrible dripping told him that she was empty, dry.

Truls looked hard at her. Memorised every detail. She looked like a painting. He would use that expression when he spoke to Mona Daa. *Like a painting hung on the wall.*

A door opened slightly on the landing above them. A pale face peered out. "Has he gone?"

"Looks like it. Amundsen?"

"Yes."

Light streamed out when the door on the other side of the hallway opened. They heard a gasp of horror.

An elderly man stumbled out while a woman who was presumably his wife stayed behind and looked out anxiously from the doorway. "That was the devil himself," the man said. "Look what he's done."

"Please, don't come any closer," Truls said. "This is a murder scene. Does anyone know where the perpetrator went?"

"If we'd known he was gone, we'd have come out to see if there was anything we could do," the old man said. "But we did see a man from the living-room window. He left the building and headed off towards the metro. We don't know if it was him though. Because he was walking so calmly."

"How long ago was this?"

"Quarter of an hour, at most."

"What did he look like?"

"Now you're asking . . ." He turned to his wife for help.

"Ordinary," she said.

"Yes," the man agreed. "Neither tall nor short. Neither fair nor dark hair. A suit."

"Grey," his wife added.

Truls nodded to the policeman, who understood the signal and began talking into the radio that was clipped to the top pocket of his jacket. "Request assistance to Hovseterveien 44. Suspect observed heading on foot towards the metro, fifteen minutes ago. Approximately 1 metre 75, possibly ethnic Norwegian, grey suit."

Fru Amundsen had come out from behind the door. She seemed even less steady on her feet than her husband, and her slippers dragged on the floor as she pointed a trembling finger at the woman on the wall. She reminded Truls of one of those pensioners they used to clear snow for. He raised his voice: "I said, don't come any closer!"

"But—" the woman began.

"Inside! Murder scenes mustn't be contaminated before Forensics gets here, we'll ring on the door if we have any questions."

"But . . . but she's not dead."

Truls turned round. In the light from the open door, he saw the woman's right foot quiver, as if it was cramping. And the thought popped into his head before he could stop it. That she was infected. She had become a vampire. And now she was waking up.

# 12

# Saturday night

There was a loud noise of metal on metal as the bar carrying the weights hit the cradle above the narrow bench. Some people would think it a terrible sound, but for Mona Daa it was like bells chiming. And she wasn't bothering anyone else either, she was on her own at Gain Gym. They'd switched to twenty-four-hour opening six months ago, presumably inspired by gyms in New York and Los Angeles, but Mona still hadn't seen anyone else exercising there after midnight. Norwegians simply didn't work enough hours for it to be a problem finding time for the gym during the day. She was the exception. She *wanted* to be the exception. A mutant. Because it was like evolution, it was the exceptions who drove the world forward. Who perfected things.

Her phone rang, and she got up from the bench.

It was Nora. Mona put her earphone in and took the call.

"You're at the *gym*, bitch," her friend groaned.

"I haven't been here long."

"You're lying, I can see that you've been there for two hours."

Mona, Nora and a few of their other friends from college could find each other using the GPS on their mobiles. They'd activated a service that allowed them to voluntarily track the others' phones. It was both sociable and reassuring. But Mona couldn't help thinking that it felt a bit claustrophobic at times. Professional sisterhood was all well and good, but they didn't have to follow each other about like fourteen-year-olds going to the toilet together. It was high time they realised that the world was full of career opportunities for intelligent young women, and that the only thing holding them back was their own lack of courage and ambition, ambition to make a difference, not just get the others' validation of their own smartness.

"I hate you just a tiny bit when I think of all the calories that are falling off you right now," Nora said. "While I'm sitting here on my fat arse consoling myself with another piña colada. Listen . . ."

Mona felt like pulling the earphone out as the sound of drawn-out slurping through a straw battered her eardrum. Nora believed that a piña colada was the only antidote to premature autumn depression.

"Did you actually want to talk about anything, Nora? I'm in the middle of—"

"Yep," Nora said. "Work."

Nora and Mona had been at the College of Journalism together. A few years ago the college had had stricter entrance requirements than any other higher education establishment in Norway, and it had seemed as if every other clever little boy or girl's dream was to get their own newspaper column or a job on television. That had certainly been the case for Nora and Mona. Cancer research and running the country were for people who weren't quite as bright. But Mona had noticed that the College of Journalism now had competition from all the local high schools that were using their state funding to offer Norwegian youngsters popular courses in journalism, film, music and beauty therapy, with no consideration of the kind of qualifications the country lacked and actively needed. Which meant that the richest country in the world had to import those skills while the nation's carefree, unemployed, film-studying sons and daughters were left sitting at home with their drinking straws stuck deep in the state's milkshake while they watched—and, if they could be bothered, criticised—films made abroad. Another reason for the falling entrance requirements was of course that the boys and girls had discovered the blog market and no longer needed to work hard for the grades with which to achieve the same level of attention offered by the more traditional route of television and the newspapers. Mona had written about this, about the fact that the media no longer demanded professional qualifications from its journalists, with the result that aspiring reporters no longer made the effort to acquire them. The new media environment, with its increasingly banal focus on celebrity, had reduced the role of journalists to that of the town gossip. Mona had used her own newspaper, the biggest in Norway, as an example. The article never got published. "Too long," the features editor had said, referring her to the magazine editor. "Well, if there's one thing the so-called critical press doesn't like, it's being criticised," as one more positively inclined colleague explained. But Mona had a feeling that the magazine editor hit the nail on the head when she said: "But, Mona, you haven't got any quotes from celebrities here."

Mona went over to the window and looked out over Frognerparken. It had clouded over, and apart from the illuminated paths an almost tangible darkness had settled on the park. It was always like that in autumn, before the trees lost their leaves and everything became more transparent, and the city once again became hard and cold. But from late September to late October, Oslo was like a soft, warm teddy bear that she just wanted to hug and cuddle.

"I'm all ears, Nora."

"It's about the vampirist."

"You've been told to get him on as a guest. Do you think he does chat shows?"

"For the last time, *The Sunday Magazine* is a serious discussion program. I've called Harry Hole but he said no, and told me that Katrine Bratt is leading the investigation."

"But isn't that good? You're always complaining about how hard it is to find good female guests."

"Yes, but Hole is, like, the most famous detective we've got. You must remember that time when he was drunk live on air? A scandal, obviously, but people loved it!"

"Did you tell him that?"

"No, but I said that television needs celebrities, and that a famous face could attract more attention to the work the police do in this city."

"Ingenious. But he didn't go for it?"

"He said if I wanted to get him on *Let's Dance* to represent the police, he'd start practising his slow fox-trot tomorrow. But that this was about a murder investigation, and that Katrine Bratt was the one with all the facts and the mandate to speak."

Mona laughed.

"What?"

"Nothing. All I can see now is Harry Hole on *Let's Dance*."

"What? Do you think he meant it?"

Mona laughed even louder.

"I was just calling to hear what you think of this Katrine Bratt, seeing as you move in those circles."

Mona picked up a pair of light dumbbells from the rack in front of her and did some quick bicep curls to keep her circulation going and to shift waste products out of her muscles. "Bratt's intelligent. And articulate. A bit severe, maybe."

"But do you think she'd reach beyond the screen? In footage from press conferences she seems a bit . . ."

"Grey? Yes, but she can look great when she wants to. Some of the guys in the newsroom think she's the hottest thing they've got over in Police HQ. But she's one of those women who suppress it and would rather look professional."

"I can feel myself starting to hate her already. What about Hallstein Smith?"

"Now *he's* got the potential to be one of your regulars. He's eccentric enough, indiscreet enough, but smart with it. Run with that one."

"OK, thanks. Sisters are doing it for themselves, right?"

"Aren't we a bit past saying stuff like that?"

"Yeah, but these days it's ironic."

"Right. Ha ha."

"Ha ha yourself. How about you?"

"What?"

"He's still out there."

"I know."

"I mean, literally. It's not that far from Hovseter to Frognerparken."

"What are you talking about?"

"Shit, haven't you heard? He's struck again."

"Fuck!" Mona yelled, and from the corner of her eye saw the guy in reception look up. "My bastard head of news said he'd call me. He's given it to someone else. Bye, Nora."

Mona went to the locker room, stuffed her clothes in her bag, then ran down the steps and onto the street. She carried on towards the *VG* building as she looked for a free taxi on the road. She was lucky and got hold of one at a red light. She threw herself into the back seat and pulled out her phone. Brought up Truls Berntsen's number. After just two rings she heard his weird, grunting laugh.

"What?" she said.

"I was wondering how long it would take you," Truls Berntsen said.

# 13

# Saturday night

"She'd lost over a litre and a half of blood by the time they got her down," the doctor said as he walked along the corridor in Ullevål Hospital with Harry and Katrine. "If the bite had hit the artery higher up in her thigh, where it's thicker, we wouldn't have been able to save her life. We wouldn't usually let a patient in her condition be questioned by the police, but seeing as other people's lives are at risk . . ."

"Thanks," Katrine said. "We won't ask more than we absolutely have to."

The doctor opened the door and he and Harry waited outside while Katrine went over to the bed and the nurse who was sitting beside it.

"It's pretty impressive," the doctor said. "Don't you think, Harry?"

Harry turned towards him and raised an eyebrow.

"You don't mind me using your first name, do you?" the doctor said. "Oslo's a small city, and seeing as I'm your wife's doctor."

"Really? I didn't know her appointment was here."

"I only realised when she filled in one of our forms and I saw she'd put your name as next of kin. And of course I remember the name from the papers."

"You've got a good memory . . ." Harry said, and looked at the name badge on the white coat. ". . . Senior Consultant John D. Steffens. Because it's been a long while since they printed my name. What is it you think is impressive?"

"That a human being can bite through a woman's thigh like that. A lot of people think modern man has weak jaws, but in comparison with most mammals we've got a fairly sharp bite. Did you know that?"

"No."

"How hard do you think we bite, Harry?"

Harry realised after a few seconds that Steffens really was expecting an answer. "Well, our criminal forensics experts say seventy kilos."

"Well, then—you already know the answer."

Harry shrugged. "The number doesn't mean anything to me. If I'd been told 150, I wouldn't have been any more or less impressed. Speaking of numbers, how do you know that Penelope Rasch lost a litre and a half? I didn't think pulse and blood pressure were such accurate indicators?"

"I was sent pictures from the crime scene," Steffens said. "I buy and sell blood, so I've got a pretty accurate eye."

Harry was about to ask him to elaborate, but at that moment Katrine waved him over.

Harry went in and stood beside Katrine. Penelope Rasch's face was as white as the pillowcase that framed it. Her eyes were open but her gaze was clouded.

"We won't trouble you for long, Penelope," Katrine said. "We've spoken to the policeman who talked to you at the scene, so we know that you met the assailant in the city just before, that he attacked you in the stairwell and that he used metal teeth to bite you. But can you tell us anything about who he is? Did he give you any other name apart from Vidar? Did he say where he lives, where he works?"

"Vidar Hansen. I didn't ask where he lives," she said. Her voice made Harry think of fragile porcelain. "He said he's an artist, but works as a caretaker."

"Did you believe him?"

"I don't know. He could well have been a guard. Someone who has access to keys, anyway, because he'd been inside my flat."

"Oh?"

With what looked like a great effort, she pulled her left hand out from under the covers and held it up. "The engagement ring I got from Roar. He took it from the drawer in my bedroom."

Katrine stared skeptically at the matt gold ring. "You mean . . . he put it on you in the stairwell?"

Penelope nodded and closed her eyes tightly again. "And the last thing he said . . ."

"Yes?"

"Was that he wasn't like other men, that he'd come back and marry me." She let out a sob.

Harry could see that Katrine was shaken, but still focused.

"What does he look like, Penelope?"

Penelope opened her mouth, then closed it again. Stared at them in despair. "I don't remember. I . . . I must have forgotten. How can . . . ?" She bit her bottom lip and tears welled up in her eyes.

"It's OK," Katrine said. "It's not unusual in your situation, you'll be able to remember more later. Do you remember what he was wearing?"

"A suit. And a shirt. He unbuttoned it. He had . . ." She stopped.

"Yes?"

"A tattoo on his chest."

Harry saw Katrine gasp. "What sort of tattoo, Penelope?" He said.

"A face."

"Like a demon that's trying to get out?"

Penelope nodded. A single tear ran down her cheek. As if she didn't have enough liquid inside her for two, Harry thought.

"And it was as if he . . ." Penelope sobbed again. "As if he wanted to show it to me."

Harry closed his eyes.

"She needs to rest," the nurse said.

Katrine nodded and put her hand on Penelope's milk-white arm. "Thank you, Penelope, you've been a great help."

Harry and Katrine were on their way out when the nurse called them back. They returned to the bed.

"I do remember one more thing," Penelope whispered. "He looked like he'd had his face operated on. And I can't help wondering . . ."

"What?" Katrine said, leaning in to hear the barely audible voice.

"Why didn't he kill me?"

Katrine looked at Harry for help. He took a deep breath, nodded to her and leaned closer to Penelope.

"Because he couldn't," he said. "Because you didn't let him."

"Well, now we know for sure that it's him," Katrine said as they walked along the corridor towards the exit.

"Mm. And he's changed his MO. And his preferences."

"How does that make you feel?"

"That it's him?" Harry shrugged. "No feelings. He's a murderer, and he needs to be caught. Full stop."

"Don't lie, Harry. Not to me. He's the reason you're here."

"Because he might take more lives. Catching him is important, but it isn't personal. OK?"

"I hear you."

"Good," Harry said.

"When he says he'll come back and marry her, do you think that's . . . ?"

"Meant as a metaphor? Yes. He's going to haunt her dreams."

"But that means he . . ."

"Deliberately didn't kill her."

"You lied to her."

"I lied." Harry pushed the door open and they got in the car that was waiting for them right outside. Katrine in the front, Harry in the back.

"Police HQ?" Anders Wyller asked from the driver's seat.

"Yes," Katrine said, picking up the mobile that she'd left charging. "Bjørn's texted to say that those bloody footprints on the stairs were probably left by cowboy boots."

"Cowboy boots," Harry repeated from the backseat.

"Those ones with a narrow high heel and—"

"I know what cowboy boots look like. They were mentioned in one of the witness statements."

"Which one?" Katrine said, skimming through the other texts she'd received while she was inside the hospital.

"The bartender at the Jealousy Bar. Mehmet Something."

"I must say, your memory is still intact. It says here that they want me as a guest on *The Sunday Magazine*, to talk about the vampirist." She tapped at her phone.

"And?"

"No, obviously. Bellman has said loud and clear that he wants the least possible publicity for this case."

"Even if it's been solved?"

Katrine turned to Harry. "What do you mean?"

"Firstly: the Chief of Police can boast on national television about having solved the case in three days. And secondly: we might need the publicity to catch him."

"Have we solved the case?" Wyller's eyes met Harry's in the rearview mirror.

"Solved," Harry said. "Not finished."

Wyller turned to Katrine. "What does he mean?"

"That we know who the perpetrator is, but that the investigation isn't over until the long arm of the law has caught him. And in his case, that arm has turned out to be too short. This individual has been wanted across the whole world for almost four years."

"Who is he?"

Katrine gave a deep sigh. "I can't even say his name. Harry, you tell him."

Harry looked out through the window. Katrine was right, of course. He could deny it, but he was here for one single selfish reason. Not for the victims, not for the good of the city, not for the reputation of the force. Not even for his own reputation. Not for anything but this one single thing: that he had got away. Oh, Harry certainly felt guilty at not having been able to stop him before, for all the murder victims, for every day that this man had gone free. Even so, this was the only thing he could think about: that he had to catch him. That he, Harry, had to catch him. He didn't know why. Did he really need the worst serial killer and offender in order to validate his own life? God alone knew. And God alone knew if it was the other way round as well. That this man had emerged from his hiding place because of Harry. He had drawn the V on Ewa Dolmen's door, and shown Penelope Rasch the demon tattoo. Penelope had asked why he hadn't killed her. And Harry had lied. The reason the man hadn't killed her was because he wanted her to talk. Talk about what she'd seen. Tell Harry what he already knew. That he needed to come out and play.

"OK," Harry said. "Do you want the long version or the short one?"

# 14

# Sunday morning

"Valentin Gjertsen," Harry Hole said, pointing at the face staring out at the investigative team from the huge screen.

Katrine looked intently at the thin face. Brown hair, deep-set eyes. Unless it just appeared that way because he was jutting his forehead forward, meaning that the light fell in a particular way. Katrine couldn't help thinking it was odd that the police photographer had let Valentin get away with it. And then there was his expression. Custody pictures usually showed fear, confusion or resignation. But he looked contented. As if Valentin Gjertsen knew something they didn't know. Didn't know *yet*.

Harry let the face sink in for a few seconds before he went on. "At the age of sixteen he was charged with molesting a nine-year-old girl he'd lured onto a rowing boat. At seventeen a neighbour reported him for trying to rape her in the basement laundry room. When Valentin Gjertsen was twenty-six and serving time for assaulting a minor, he had an appointment to see the dentist at Ila Prison. He used one of the dentist's own drills to force her to take off her nylon stockings and put them over her head. First he raped her in the dentist's chair, then he set fire to the stockings."

Harry tapped at the computer and the image changed. A muffled groan ran through the group, and Katrine saw that even some of the most experienced detectives looked down at their laps.

"I'm not showing this for fun, but so that you know what sort of individual we're dealing with. He let the dentist live. Just like Penelope Rasch. And I don't think that's workplace negligence. I think Valentin Gjertsen is playing a game with us."

Harry clicked again, and the same picture of Valentin appeared, this time taken from Interpol's website. "Valentin escaped from Ila almost four years ago, in a quite spectacular fashion. He beat another prisoner, Judas Johansen, until he was unrecognisable, then had a copy of the demon's face he has tattooed on his own chest tattooed onto the chest of the corpse, and hid the body in the library where he worked, so that Judas was reported missing when he didn't report for inspection. On the night that Valentin himself escaped, he dressed the corpse in his own clothes and laid it on the floor of his cell. The prison guards who discovered the unrecognisable body, and naturally assumed that it was Valentin, weren't particularly surprised. Like any inmate convicted of paedophilia, Valentin Gjertsen was hated by the other prisoners. No one thought to check fingerprints or conduct a DNA test on the body. And so for a long time we assumed that Valentin Gjertsen was history. Until he showed up again in connection with another murder. Obviously we don't know exactly how many people he killed or assaulted, but it's definitely more than he's been suspected or found guilty of. We do know that his last victim before he disappeared for good was his former landlady, Irja Jacobsen." Another click. "This picture is from the commune where she had gone into hiding from Valentin. Unless I'm mistaken, it was you, Berntsen, who was first on the scene where we found her strangled beneath a pile of children's surfboards, with, as you can see, pictures of sharks on them."

A grunt of laughter from the back of the conference room. "Correct. The surfboards were stolen goods that the poor junkies hadn't managed to sell."

"Irja Jacobsen was probably murdered because she could have passed information about Valentin to the police. That may explain why it's been so hard to get anyone to say a word about where he might be. Anyone who knows him simply doesn't dare talk." Harry cleared his throat. "Another reason why Valentin has been impossible to find is that he's undergone several rounds of extensive plastic surgery since his escape. The person you see in this picture doesn't look like the person we observed later in a grainy surveillance picture from a football match at Ullevål Stadium. And he intentionally let us see that surveillance picture. So, because we haven't managed to find him, we suspect that he may have had further operations after that, probably abroad seeing as we've checked anything that moves in Scandinavia as far as plastic surgery is concerned. Our suspicion that his face has changed again is reinforced by the fact that Penelope Rasch doesn't recognise Valentin from the pictures we've shown her. Unfortunately she isn't able to give a good alternative description of him, and the Tinder profile picture of this so-called Vidar on her phone is unlikely to be him."

"Tord has also checked out this Vidar's Facebook profile," Katrine said. "Not surprisingly, it's fake, set up recently on a device that we haven't managed to trace. Tord believes this suggests that he must have a reasonable level of IT skills."

"Or else he had help," Harry said. "But we do at least have one person who saw and spoke to Valentin Gjertsen, just before he disappeared off the radar three years ago. Ståle has retired from his job as a consultant to Crime Squad, but he's agreed to come here today."

Ståle Aune stood up, fastening a button on his tweed jacket.

"For a short time I had the questionable pleasure of seeing a patient who called himself Paul Stavnes. He was unusual as a schizophrenic psychopath insofar as he was aware of his own illness, at least to a certain extent. He also succeeded in manipulating me so that I didn't realise who he was or what he was doing. Until the day when he let his cover slip quite by chance, then tried to kill me before disappearing for good."

"Ståle's description formed the basis for this photofit picture." Harry tapped the computer. "So this is also fairly old now, but at least it's better than the surveillance picture from the football match."

Katrine tilted her head. The drawing showed that his hair, nose and the shape of his eyes were different, and the shape of his face was more angular than in the photograph. But the look of contentment was still there. Presumed contentment. Like the way you *think* a crocodile is grinning.

"How did he become a vampirist?" a voice by the window asked.

"To start with, I'm not convinced that there's any such thing as vampirists," Aune said. "But of course there could be plenty of reasons why Valentin Gjertsen drinks blood, without me being able to give an answer here and now."

A long silence followed.

Harry cleared his throat. "We haven't seen any sign of biting or drinking blood in any previous case that can be linked to Gjertsen. And yes, perpetrators do usually stick to a specific pattern, revisiting the same fantasies again and again."

"How certain are we that this really is Valentin Gjertsen?" Skarre asked. "And not just someone trying to make us think that it's him?"

"Eighty-nine percent." This from Bjørn Holm.

Skarre laughed. "Exactly eighty-nine?"

"Yes. We found strands of body hair on the handcuffs he used on Penelope Rasch, possibly from the back of his hand. With DNA analysis it doesn't take too long to confirm a match with eighty-nine percent probability. It's the last ten percent that takes time. We'll get the final answer in two days. The handcuffs are a type that are available online, by the way, a replica of handcuffs from the Middle Ages. Hence the iron, rather than steel. Apparently popular with people who like to do up their love nests to make them look like medieval dungeons."

A single grunt of laughter.

"What about the iron teeth?" one of the female detectives asked. "Where could he have got those from?"

"That's more difficult," Bjørn Holm said. "We haven't found anyone who manufactures teeth like this, at least not out of iron. He must have commissioned them specially from a blacksmith. Or made them himself. It's certainly something new—we haven't seen anyone use a weapon like this before."

"New behaviour," Aune said, undoing his jacket to free his stomach. "Fundamental changes of behaviour hardly ever happen. Human beings are notorious, they insist on making the same mistakes over and over again, even after they've received new information. That's my opinion, anyway, and it's become so contentious among psychologists that it's even been given its own name, Aune's Thesis. When we see individuals change their behaviour, it usually relates to a change in their surroundings, something the individual is adapting to. While the individual's underlying motivation for that behaviour remains the same. It's by no means unique for a sex offender to discover new fantasies and pleasures, but that's because his taste gradually develops, not because the individual undergoes a fundamental change. When I was a teenager my father said that when I was older I would start to appreciate Beethoven. At the time I hated Beethoven and was convinced he was wrong. Even at a young age, Valentin Gjertsen had a wide-ranging appetite when it came to sexuality. He raped both young and old women, possibly boys, no adult men that we know of, but that could be for practical reasons, seeing as they're more likely to be able to defend themselves. Paedophilia, necrophilia, sadism, all this was on Valentin Gjertsen's menu. The Oslo Police have been able to link him to more sexually motivated crimes than anyone apart from Svein Finne, "the Fiancé." The fact that he's now acquiring a taste for blood merely means that he scores highly on what we call "openness," and is willing to try new experiences. I say "acquiring" because certain observations, such as the fact that he added lemon, suggest that Valentin Gjertsen is experimenting with blood rather than being obsessed with it."

"Not obsessed?" Skarre called. "He's up to a victim a day now! While we're sitting here he's probably out on the hunt again. Wouldn't you say, Professor?" He pronounced the title without trying to conceal his sarcasm.

Aune threw his short arms out. "Once again, I don't know. We don't know. No one knows."


"Valentin Gjertsen," Mikael Bellman said. "Are we completely sure about that, Bratt? If so, give me ten minutes to think it over. Yes, I can see that it's urgent."

Bellman ended the call and put his mobile down on the glass table. Isabelle had just told him it was made of mouth-blown glass from ClassiCon, more than fifty thousand kroner. That she would rather have a few quality pieces than fill her new apartment with rubbish. From where he was sitting he could see an artificial beach and the ferries gliding back and forth across the Oslo Fjord. Strong winds lashed the almost violet water further out.

"Well?" Isabelle asked from the bed behind him.

"The lead detective wants to know if she should agree to take part in *The Sunday Magazine* this evening. The subject is the vampirist murders, obviously. We know who the perpetrator is, but not where he is."

"Simple," Isabelle Skøyen said. "If you already had the guy, you should do it yourself. But seeing as it's only a partial success, you should send a representative. Remind her to say 'we' rather than 'I.' And it wouldn't do any harm if she were to suggest that the perpetrator may have managed to get across the border."

"The border? Why?"

Isabelle Skøyen sighed. "Don't pretend to be more stupid than you are, darling, that's just irritating."

Bellman went over to the door to the veranda. He stood there, looking down at the Sunday tourists streaming towards Tjuvholmen.

Some to visit the Astrup Fearnley Museum of Contemporary Art, some to look at the hyper-modern architecture and drink overpriced cappuccino. And some to dream about one of the laughably expensive apartments that hadn't yet been sold. He had heard that the museum had exhibited a Mercedes with a big, brown human turd in place of the Mercedes star on the bonnet. OK, so for some people solid excrement was a status symbol. Others needed the most expensive apartment, the latest car or the biggest yacht to feel good. And then you had people—like Isabelle and he himself—who wanted absolutely everything: power, but without any suffocating obligations. Admiration and respect, but enough anonymity to be able to move freely. Family, to provide a stable framework and help their genes survive, but also free access to sex outside the four walls of the home. The apartment and the car. *And* solid shit.

"So," Mikael Bellman said. "You're thinking that if Valentin Gjertsen goes missing for a while, the public will automatically think that he's left the country, instead of the Oslo Police being unable to catch him. But if we *do* catch him, we've been smart. And if he commits another murder, anything we've said will be forgotten anyway."

He turned towards her. He had no idea why she had chosen to put her big double bed in the living room when she had a perfectly adequate bedroom. Particularly as it was possible for the neighbours to see in. Although he had a suspicion that that was why. Isabelle Skøyen was a big woman. Her long, powerful limbs were spread out under the gold-coloured silk sheet that lay draped over her sensuous body. The sight alone made him feel ready to go again.

"Just one word, and you've sown the idea of him leaving the country," she said. "In psychology it's called anchoring. It's simple, and it always works. Because people *are* simple." Her eyes roamed down his body and she smiled. "Especially men."

She shoved the silk sheet onto the floor.

He looked at her. Sometimes he thought he preferred just looking at her body to touching it, while the opposite was true of his wife. Which was odd, because Ulla's body, purely objectively, was more beautiful than Isabelle's. But Isabelle's violent, raging desires turned him on far more than Ulla's tenderness and quiet, sob-racked orgasms.

"Wank," she commanded, spreading her legs so that her knees resembled the half-furled wings of a bird of prey, and touched two of her long fingers to her genitals.

He did as she said. Closed his eyes. And heard the glass table buzz.

Damn, he'd forgotten Katrine Bratt. He grabbed the vibrating phone and pressed answer.

"Yes?"

The female voice at the other end said something, but Mikael couldn't hear anything because one of the ferries blew its horn at the same time.

"The answer's yes," he shouted impatiently. "You're to go on *The Sunday Magazine*. I'm busy at the moment, but I'll call you with instructions later."

"It's me."

Mikael Bellman stiffened. "Darling, is that you? I thought it was Katrine Bratt."

"Where are you?"

"Where? At work, of course."

And in the far too long pause that followed, he realised that she had obviously also heard the sound of the ferry, and that that was why she had asked. He breathed hard through his mouth as he looked down at his drooping erection.

"Dinner won't be ready before half past five," she said.

"OK," he said. "What—?"

"Steak," she said, and hung up.


Harry and Anders Wyller got out of the car in front of Jøssing-veien 33. Harry lit a cigarette and looked up at the red-brick building surrounded by a tall fence. They had driven from Police HQ in sunshine and shimmering autumn colours, but on the way up here the clouds had gathered and were now skimming the hills like a cement-coloured ceiling, draining the colour from the landscape.

"So this is Ila Prison," Wyller said.

Harry nodded and sucked hard on the cigarette.

"Why is he called the Fiancé?"

"Because he got his rape victims pregnant and made them promise to give birth to the baby."

"Or else . . . ?"

"Or else he'd come back and perform a Caesarean section himself." Harry took one last drag, rubbed the cigarette out against the packet and tucked the butt inside. "Let's get this done."

. . .

"The regulations don't allow us to keep him tied up, but we'll be watching you on the surveillance camera," said the guard who had buzzed them in and led them to the end of the long corridor, lined with grey-painted steel doors on both sides. "One of our rules is never to get within one metre of him."

"Christ," Wyller said. "Does he attack you?"

"No," the guard said, inserting a key into the lock of the last door. "Svein Finne hasn't had a single black mark against his name in the twenty years he's been here."

"But?"

The prison guard shrugged and turned the key. "I think you'll see what I mean."

He opened the door, stepped aside and Wyller and Harry walked into the cell.

The man on the bed was sitting in shadow.

"Finne," Harry said.

"Hole." The voice from the shadow sounded like crushed rock.

Harry gestured towards the only chair in the room. "OK if I sit down?"

"If you think you've got time for that. I heard you've got your hands full."

Harry sat down. Wyller stood behind him, just inside the door.

"Hm. Is it him?"

"Is it who?"

"You know who I mean."

"I'll answer that if you give me an honest answer—have you missed it?"

"Missed what, Svein?"

"Having a playmate who's up to your level? Like you had with me?"

The man in the shadows leaned forward, into the light from the window near the top of the wall, and Harry heard Wyller's breathing speed up behind him. The bars laid strips of shadow across a pockmarked face with leathery, red-brown skin. It was covered with wrinkles, so deep and close together that they looked as if they'd been carved by a knife, right down to the bone. He had a red handkerchief tied round his forehead, like a Native American, and his thick, wet lips were framed by a moustache. His tiny pupils sat within brown irises, and the whites of his eyes looked yellow, but he had the muscular, sinewy body of a twenty-year-old. Harry did the math. Svein Finne, "the Fiancé," had to be seventy-five now.

"You never forget your first. Isn't that right, Hole? My name will always be at the top of your list of achievements. I took your virginity, didn't I?" His laugh sounded like he was gargling with gravel.

"Well . . ." Harry said, folding his arms. "If my honesty is the price for yours, then the answer is that I don't miss it. And that I'll never forget you, Svein Finne. Or any of the people you maimed and killed. You all visit me fairly regularly at night."

"Me, too. They're very faithful, my fiancées." Finne's thick lips slipped apart as he smiled, and he put his right hand over his right eye. Harry heard Wyller step back and hit the door. Finne's eye stared at Wyller through the hole in his hand that was big enough to hit a golf ball through. "Don't be scared, son," Finne said. "It's your boss you should be frightened of. He was just as young as you are now, and I was already lying on the ground, unable to defend myself. Even so, he held his pistol to my hand and fired. Your boss has a black heart, lad. Remember that. And now he's thirsty again. Just like him out there. And your thirst is like a fire, that's why you have to *quench* it. And until it's quenched, it'll keep growing, devouring everything it comes into contact with. Isn't that right, Hole?"

Harry cleared his throat. "Your turn, Finne. Where's Valentin hiding?"

"You lot have been here to ask about that before, and I can only repeat myself. I barely spoke to Valentin when he was here. And it's been almost four years since he escaped."

"His methods resemble yours. Some people claim that you taught him."

"Nonsense. Valentin was born ready-taught. Believe me."

"Where would you have hidden, if you were him?"

"Close enough to be in your sights, Hole. I'd have been prepared for you this time."

"Does he live in the city? Move about the city? New identity? Is he alone or is he working with anyone else?"

"He's doing it differently now, isn't he? Biting and drinking blood. Maybe it isn't Valentin?"

"It's Valentin. So how do I catch him?"

"You don't catch him."

"No?"

"He'd rather die than end up here again. His imagination was never enough for him, he had to *do* it."

"Sounds like you do know him after all."

"I know what he's made of."

"The same as you? Hormones from hell."

The old man shrugged. "Everyone knows that moral choice is an illusion, it's only the chemistry of the brain that directs your and my behaviour, Hole. Some people's behaviour gets diagnosed as ADHD or anxiety and is treated with drugs and sympathy. Others are diagnosed as criminal and evil and are locked up. But it's the same thing. An unholy mixture of substances in the brain. And I agree that we should be locked up. We rape your daughters, for God's sake." Finne let out a rasping laugh. "So clear us off the streets, threaten us with punishment so we don't head off in the direction the chemicals in our brain would otherwise tell us to go in. But what makes that pathetic is that you're so weak that you need a moral excuse to lock us up. You create a history of lies about free will and some sort of divine punishment that fits into a system of divine justice based on some unchanging, universal morality. But morality can hardly be unchanging or universal, it's entirely dependent upon the spirit of the age, Hole. Men fucking men was completely OK a few thousand years ago, then they were put in prison, and now politicians go on parades with them. Everything gets decided according to what society needs or doesn't need at any given time. Morality is flexible and utilitarian. My problem is that I was born in an age and in a country where men who scatter their seed so wantonly are undesirable. But after a pandemic, when the species needs to get back on its feet again, Svein "the Fiancé" Finne would have been a pillar of the community and a saviour of humanity. Don't you think, Hole?"

"You raped women and made them give birth to your children," Harry said. "Valentin kills them. So why don't you want to help me catch him?"

"Am I not being helpful?"

"You're giving me general answers and half-baked moral philosophy. If you help us, I'll put in a good word to the parole board."

Harry heard Wyller shuffle his feet.

"Really?" Finne stroked his moustache. "Even though you know I'd start raping again as soon as I got out? I appreciate that it must be very important for you to catch Valentin, seeing as you're prepared to sacrifice so many innocent women's honour. But I don't suppose you have a choice." He tapped his temple with one finger. "Chemistry . . ."

Harry didn't respond.

"Well, then," Finne said. "To start with, I'll have served my sentence on the first Saturday of March next year, so it's too late to get a reduction that makes much difference. And I was taken outside a couple of weeks ago, and you know what? I wanted to get back here. So, thanks but no thanks. Tell me how you're doing instead, Hole. I heard that you got married. And have a bastard son, yes? Do you live in a safe place?"

"Was that all you had to say, Finne?"

"Yes. But I shall follow your collective progress with interest."

"Me and Valentin?"

"You and your family. Hope to see you in the welcoming committee when I'm released." Finne's laugh turned into a wet cough.

Harry stood and gestured to Wyller to bang on the door. "Thanks for sparing some of your precious time, Finne."

Finne raised his right hand in front of his face and waved. "See you again, Hole. Nice to be able to talk about f-future plans."

Harry saw his grin flit back and forth behind the hole in his hand.

# 15

# Sunday evening

Rakel was sitting at the kitchen table. The pain, drowned out by the noise and distraction of urgent jobs, became harder to ignore whenever she stopped. She scratched her arm. The rash had barely been noticeable yesterday evening. When the doctor asked if she was urinating regularly she had answered yes automatically, but now that she was more aware of it, she realised that she had hardly peed at all in the past couple of days. And then there was her breathing. As if she was out of shape, and she definitely wasn't.

There was a clatter of keys at the front door and Rakel stood up.

The door opened and Harry came in. He looked pale and tired.

"Just popped in to change clothes," he said, stroked her cheek and carried on towards the stairs.

"How's it going?" she asked as she watched him disappear upstairs to their bedroom.

"Good!" he called. "We know who it is."

"Time to come home, then?" she said halfheartedly.

"What?" She heard footsteps on the floor and knew he'd taken his trousers off, like a little boy or a drunk man.

"If you and your great big brain have solved the case . . ."

"That's just it." He appeared in the doorway at the top of the stairs. He was wearing a thin woollen sweater and leaning against the door frame as he pulled on a pair of thin woollen socks. She had teased him about that, saying that only old men insisted on wearing wool all year round. He had replied that the best survival strategy was always to copy old men, because they, after all, were the winners, the survivors. "I didn't solve anything. He chose to reveal himself." Harry straightened up. Patted his pockets. "Keys," he said, and vanished into the bedroom again. "I met Dr. Steffens at Ullevål," he called. "He said he's *treating* you."

"Really? Darling, I think you should try to get a few hours' sleep— your keys are still in the door down here."

"All you said was that they'd examined you?"

"What's the difference?"

Harry came out, ran down the stairs, and hugged her. "*Examined* is past tense," he whispered in her ear. "*Treating* is present tense. And, as far as I know, treatment is what happens after an examination comes up with something."

Rakel laughed. "I came up with the headaches myself, and that's what needs treating, Harry. And the treatment's called paracetamol."

He held her out in front of him and looked at her intently. "You wouldn't hide anything from me, would you?"

"So you've got time for this sort of nonsense, have you?" Rakel leaned into him, forced the pain away, bit him on the ear and pushed him towards the door. "Go and get the job finished, then come straight home to Mummy. If not, I'll 3D-print myself a home-loving man made out of white plastic."

Harry smiled and walked over to the door. Pulled his keys out of the lock. Stopped and looked at them.

"What is it?" Rakel said.


"He had the key to Elise Hermansen's flat," Harry said, slamming the passenger door behind him. "And presumably also to Ewa Dolmen's."

"Really?" Wyller said, taking the handbrake off and rolling down the drive. "We definitely checked every key-cutter in the city, and none of them has made any new keys to any of the buildings."

"That's because he made them himself. Out of white plastic."

"White plastic?"

"Using an ordinary 3D printer costing fifteen thousand kroner which you can keep on your desk. All he needed was access to the original key for a few seconds. He could have taken a photograph of it, or made a wax impression of it, and used that to produce a 3D data file. So when Elise Hermansen came home, he had already locked himself inside her flat. That's why she put the security chain on, she thought she was alone."

"And how do you think he got hold of the keys? None of the buildings the victims lived in used a security company, they each had their own caretaker. And they've all got alibis, and they all swear they haven't lent any keys to anyone."

"I know. I don't know *how* it happened, just that it *did* happen."

Harry didn't have to look at his young colleague to see how skeptical he was. There were hundreds of other explanations as to why Elise Hermansen's safety chain had been on. Harry's deduction didn't rule out a single one of them. Tresko, Harry's poker-playing friend, claimed that probability theory and how to play your cards according to the rulebook was the easiest thing in the world. But that what separated smart players from the not-so-smart was the ability to understand how their opponent was thinking, and that meant dealing with so much information that it felt like listening for a whispered answer in a howling storm. Maybe it was. Because through the storm of everything Harry knew about Valentin Gjertsen, all the reports, all his experience of other serial murders, all the ghosts of previous murder victims he hadn't managed to save over the years, a voice was whispering. Valentin Gjertsen's voice. That he had taken them from inside. That he had been inside their field of vision.

Harry pulled out his phone. Katrine answered on the second ring.

"I'm sitting in makeup," she said.

"I think Valentin has a 3D printer. And that could lead us to him."

"How?"

"Shops selling electronic equipment register their customers' names and addresses if the price is above a certain amount. There've only been a couple of thousand 3D printers sold in Norway. If everyone in the team drops what they're doing, we might be able to get a good overview within a day, and have checked ninety-five percent of the buyers within two. Which would mean we were left with a list of twenty buyers. Fake names or aliases, we'd find out if we couldn't see them in the population register at the stated address, or called people to find that they denied buying a 3D printer. Most shops selling electronic equipment have security cameras, so we can check anyone suspicious using the time of the purchase. There's no reason why he wouldn't have gone to the shop closest to where he lives, so that would give us an area to search. And by releasing the security camera images, we can get the public to point us in the right direction."

"How did you come up with the idea of the 3D printer, Harry?"

"I was talking to Oleg about printers and guns and—"

"Drop everything else, Harry? To focus on something that occurred to you when you were talking to Oleg?"

"Yep."

"This is precisely the sort of alternative angle you're supposed to be exploring with your guerrilla team, Harry."

"Which still only consists of me, and I need your resources."

Harry heard Katrine burst into laughter. "If you weren't Harry Hole, I'd already have hung up."

"Good job I am, then. Listen, we've been trying to find Valentin Gjertsen for four years without succeeding. This is the only new lead we've got."

"Let me think about it after the program. It's going out live and my head's full of things I need to remember to say and not say. And my stomach's full of butterflies, if I'm honest."

"Mm."

"Any tips for a television debutante?"

"Lean back and be relaxed, genial and witty."

He heard her chuckle. "The way you used to be?"

"I was none of those. Oh yeah—be sober."

Harry put his phone in his jacket pocket. They were getting close to the place. Where Slemdalsveien crossed Rasmus Winderens vei in Vinderen. And the lights turned red. They stopped. And Harry couldn't help looking. He could never help it. He glanced at the platform on the other side of the metro track. The place where, half a lifetime ago, he'd lost control of his police car during a chase, sailed across the track and hit the concrete. The officer who had been sitting in the passenger seat died. How drunk had he been? Harry was never made to take a breath test, and the official report said he'd been in the passenger seat rather than driving. Anything, for the good of the force.

"Did you do it to save lives?"

"What?" Harry asked.

"Working at Crime Squad," Wyller said. "Or did you do it to catch murderers?"

"Hm. Are you thinking about what the Fiancé said?"

"I remember your lectures. I thought you were a murder detective simply because you loved the job."

"Really?"

Harry shrugged as the lights turned green. They carried on

towards Majorstua and the evening darkness that seemed to be rolling towards them from the cauldron of Oslo.

"Let me out at the bar," Harry said. "The one the first victim went to."


Katrine was in the wings looking at the little desert island in the middle of the circle of light. The island was a black platform holding three chairs and a table. In one of these chairs sat the presenter of *The Sunday Magazine*, who was about to bring her on as the first guest. Katrine tried not to think about the sea of eyes. Not think about how hard her heart was beating. Nor think about the fact that Valentin was out there right now, and that there was nothing they could do about that, even though they knew full well that it was him. Instead she kept repeating to herself what Bellman had told her: to be credible and reassuring when she said the case had been solved, but that the perpetrator was still at large, and that there was a possibility he had fled the country.

Katrine looked at the director, who was standing between the cameras and the island wearing headphones and clutching a clipboard, shouting that there was ten seconds to go before they began the broadcast, then she started counting down. And suddenly a silly thing that had happened earlier in the day popped into her head. Possibly because she was exhausted and nervous, possibly because the brain takes refuge in silly things when it ought to be concentrating on things that are overwhelming and terrifying. She had called in to see Bjørn at Krimteknisk to ask him to fast-track analysis of the evidence they had found in the stairwell, so that she could use it on television to make herself more convincing. Naturally there hadn't been many other people there on a Sunday: those who were there were all working on the vampirist murders. Perhaps this emptiness was the reason the situation had made such a strong impression on Katrine. When she walked straight into Bjørn's office, as usual, a woman had been standing by his chair, almost leaning over him. And one of them must have said something funny, because both she and Bjørn were laughing. When they turned towards Katrine, she had realised that the woman was the recently appointed head of Krimteknisk something-or-other Lien. Katrine remembered Bjørn mentioning her appointment, and remembered thinking she was far too young and inexperienced, and that he should have got the job. Or rather: Bjørn should have *taken* the job, because he had actually been offered it. But his response had been classic Bjørn Holm: why lose a pretty decent criminal forensics expert to gain a pretty bad boss? Looked at that way, fru or frøken Lien had been a good choice, because Katrine had never heard of anyone called Lien who had excelled in any case. When Katrine had presented her request for quicker results, Bjørn had calmly replied that that was up to his boss, she was the one who decided what was a priority. And something-or-other Lien had given her an ambiguous smile and said she'd check with the other forensics officers and see when they might have the work finished. So Katrine had raised her voice and said that "checking" wasn't good enough, that the vampirist murders were the priority just now, that anyone with any experience could understand that. And that it would look bad on television if she was forced to say that she couldn't answer because the new head of Krimteknisk didn't think it was important enough.

And Berna Lien—yes, that was her name, and she did look a bit like Bernadette in *The Big Bang Theory*, short with glasses and breasts that were too big for her—had replied: "And if I prioritise this, do you *promise* not to tell anyone that I don't think the child abuse case in Aker or the honour killings in Stovner are important enough?" Katrine hadn't realised that the pleading note in her voice was fake, until Lien went on in her normal, serious voice: "Naturally, I agree with you that it's extremely urgent if it can prevent more murders, Bratt. And it's that—and not the fact that you're appearing on television—that weighs most heavily. I'll get back to you within twenty minutes, OK?"

Katrine had merely nodded and walked away. She went straight to Police HQ, locked herself in the toilet and wiped off the makeup she had put on before heading off to Krimteknisk.

The theme music began to play, and the presenter—who was already sitting up—sat up even straighter as he warmed up his facial muscles with a couple of exaggeratedly wide smiles that he wasn't likely to need given the subject matter of that evening's program.

Katrine felt her phone vibrate in her trouser pocket. As lead investigator, she needed to be accessible at all times, and had ignored the demand to switch her phone off altogether during the broadcast. It was a text from Bjørn.

*Found a match for fingerprints on the front door of Penelope's building. Valentin Gjertsen. Watching TV. Break a leg.*

Katrine nodded to the girl beside her who was telling her again that she should walk towards the presenter as soon as she heard her name, and which chair she should sit in. *Break a leg.* As if she were about to go onstage. But Katrine realised that she was smiling inside anyway.


Harry stopped inside the door of the Jealousy Bar. And realised that the sound of a noisy crowd wasn't real. Because, unless there were people hiding in the booths along one wall, he was the only customer. Then he caught sight of the football match on the television behind the bar. Harry sat down on one of the bar stools and watched.

"Beşiktaş–Galatasaray," the bartender smiled.

"Turkish teams," Harry said.

"Yes," the bartender said. "Interested?"

"Not really."

"That's fine. It's all crazy anyway. In Turkey, if you support the visitors and they win, you have to rush home at once so you don't get shot."

"Hm. Religious differences or class?"

The bartender stopped polishing glasses and looked at Harry. "It's about winning."

Harry shrugged. "Of course. My name's Harry Hole, I'm . . . I *used* to be a detective with Crime Squad. I've been brought back in to—"

"Elise Hermansen."

"Precisely. I read in your witness statement that you had a customer who was wearing cowboy boots at the same time Elise and her date were here."

"That's right."

"Can you tell me anything else about him?"

"Not really. Because as I remember it, he came in just after Elise Hermansen and sat in that booth over there."

"Did you get a look at him?"

"Yes, but not long enough or carefully enough to give much of a description. Look, you can't see into the booths from here, and he didn't order anything before he was suddenly gone again. That happens fairly often—presumably they think the place is a bit too quiet. That's the way with bars—you need a crowd to attract a crowd. But I didn't see when he left, so I haven't really thought about it. Anyway, she was murdered inside her flat, wasn't she?"

"She was."

"You think he might have followed her home?"

"It's a possibility, at least." Harry looked at the bartender. "Mehmet, isn't it?"

"That's right."

There was something about the guy that Harry liked instinctively, which made him decide to come straight out and say what he was thinking. "If I don't like the look of a bar, I turn at the door, and if I go in, I order something. I don't just sit in a booth. He might have followed her here, then—once he'd read the situation and realised she was likely to be going home without the guy soon—he may have gone to her flat and waited for her there."

"Seriously? Sick man. And poor girl. Speaking of poor sods, here comes her date from that night." Mehmet inclined his head towards the door and Harry turned round. The Galatasaray fans had drowned out the entrance of a bald, rather overweight man in a padded vest and black shirt. He sat down at the bar and nodded to the bartender with a stiff expression on his face. "A large one."

"Geir Sølle?" Harry asked.

"Preferably not," the man said with a hollow laugh, without changing his expression. "Journalist?"

"Police. I'd like to know if either of you recognise this man." Harry put a copy of the photofit picture of Valentin Gjertsen down on the bar. "He's probably had extensive plastic surgery since this was produced, so use your imagination."

Mehmet and Sølle studied the picture. They both shook their heads.

"You know what, forget the beer," Sølle said. "I just remembered I need to get home."

"As you can see, I've already poured it," Mehmet said.

"The dog needs walking—give it to our police officer here, he looks thirsty."

"One last question, Sølle. In your witness statement, you said she told you about a stalker who had been following her and threatening men she was with. Did you get the impression that was true?"

"True?"

"It wasn't just something she was saying to keep you away?"

"Ha, right. You tell me. Presumably she had her own methods of getting rid of frogs." Geir Sølle's attempt at a smile turned into a grimace. "Like me."

"And do you think she'd had to kiss a lot of frogs?"

"Tinder can be disappointing, but you never give up hope, do you?"

"This stalker, did you get the impression he was just a passing nutter, or someone she'd had a relationship with?"

"No." Geir pulled the zip of his vest all the way up to his chin, even though it was mild outside. "I'm going now."

"A man she'd had a relationship with?" the bartender said, giving him his change. "I thought these murders were just about drinking blood. And sex."

"Maybe," Harry said. "But it's usually about jealousy."

"And if it isn't?"

"Then it might be about what you said."

"Blood and sex?"

"About winning." Harry looked down into the glass. Beer had always made him feel bloated and tired. He used to like the first few sips, but after that it just tasted dull. "Talking of winning. Looks like Galatasaray are going to lose, so would you mind turning over to *The Sunday Magazine* on NRK1 instead?"

"What if I'm a Beşiktaş fan?"

Harry nodded to the corner of the top shelf in front of the mirror. "Then you probably wouldn't have a Galatasaray banner up there next to that bottle of Jim Beam, Mehmet."

The bartender looked at Harry. Then he grinned, shook his head and pressed the remote.


"We can't say with one hundred percent certainty that the man who attacked the woman in Hovseter yesterday is the same person who killed Elise Hermansen and Ewa Dolmen," Katrine said, and it struck her how *quiet* the studio was, as if everything around them was listening. "But what I can say is that we have physical evidence and witness statements linking a specific individual to the attack. And because this person is already a wanted man, an escaped prisoner who was convicted of sex offences, we've decided to go public with his name."

"And this is the first time you've done that, here on *The Sunday Magazine*?"

"That's right. His real name is Valentin Gjertsen, but he's probably using a different name."

She saw that the presenter looked a bit disappointed because she'd said the name so quickly, without any buildup. He would clearly have liked to have had time to do a verbal drumroll beforehand.

"And this is an artist's impression that shows what he looked like three years ago," she said. "He's probably had extensive plastic surgery since then, but it does at least give an idea." Katrine held up the picture towards the rows of seats containing the audience of some fifty or so people who, according to the director, were there to give the program more "edge." Katrine waited, saw the red light of the camera in front of her come on, and let the picture sink in with the people watching at home in their living rooms. The presenter was gazing at her with a look of satisfaction.

"We would ask anyone with any information to call our hotline," she said. "This picture, his name and known aliases, as well as our phone number, can all be found on the Oslo Police District website."

"And of course it's urgent," the presenter said, addressing the camera. "Because there's a risk that he might strike again as early as this evening." He turned to Katrine. "At this very moment, even. That's a possibility, isn't it?"

Katrine saw that he wanted her help to implant the image of a vampire drinking fresh blood right now.

"We don't want to rule anything out," she said. That was the phrase Bellman had drummed into her, word for word. He had explained that, unlike "we *can't* rule anything out," "we don't *want* to" gave the impression that the Oslo Police had a good enough over-view of the situation to be able to rule things out, but nonetheless chose not to. "But I have received reports suggesting that in the time between the most recent attack and the results of the analysis which has now identified him, Valentin Gjertsen may have left the country. It's highly plausible that he has a hiding place outside Norway, a place he has been using since his escape from prison four years ago."

Bellman hadn't needed to explain this choice of words to her, she was a fast learner. "I have received reports" prompted thoughts of sur-veillance, secret informants and thorough police work, and the fact that she was talking about a time frame when there would have been plenty of options for flights, trains and ferries didn't necessarily mean that she was lying. The claim that it was plausible that he had been out of the country was defensible, as long as it wasn't directly improb-able. It also had the advantage of discreetly nudging responsibility for the fact that Valentin Gjertsen hadn't been caught in the past four years onto "outside Norway."

"So how do you go about catching a vampirist?" the presenter said, turning towards the second chair. "We've brought in Hallstein Smith, a professor of psychology and author of a series of articles about vampirism. Can you answer that for us, Professor Smith?"

Katrine looked at Smith, who had sat down on the third chair off-camera. He was wearing large glasses and a fancy, colourful jacket that looked as if it was homemade. It was in stark contrast to the sombreness of Katrine's black leather trousers, fitted black jacket and glossy, slicked-back hair. She knew she looked good, and that there would be comments and invitations on their website when she checked later that evening. But she didn't care, Bellman hadn't said anything about how to dress. She just hoped that Lien bitch was watching.

"Er," Smith said, smiling dumbly.

Katrine could see that the presenter was worried that the psychologist had frozen and was about to jump in.

"To start with, I'm not a professor, I'm still working on my PhD. But if I pass, I'll let you know."

Laughter.

"And the articles I've written haven't been published in professional journals, just in dubious magazines dedicated to the more obscure corners of psychology. One of them was called *Psycho*, after the film. That probably marks the low point of my academic career."

More laughter.

"But I am a psychologist," he said, turning to the audience. "A graduate of Mykolas Romeris University in Vilnius, with grades well above average. And I have got the sort of couch where you can lie and look up at the ceiling for fifteen hundred kroner an hour while I pretend to take notes."

For a moment it looked like the amused audience and presenter had forgotten the seriousness of the subject. Until Smith brought them back.

"But I don't know how to catch vampirists."

Silence.

"At least not in general terms. Vampirists are rare, and they come up to the surface even more rarely than that. Let me just point out, to start with, that we need to differentiate between two types of vampirist. One is relatively harmless—people who feel attracted by the myth of the immortal, bloodsucking demigod upon which modern vampire stories such as *Dracula* are based. This type of vampirism has clear erotic undertones and even drew comment from dear old Sigmund Freud himself. They rarely kill anyone. Then there are people who suffer from what we call clinical vampirism, or Renfield's syndrome, which means that they're obsessed with drinking blood. Most of the articles on this subject have been published in journals of forensic psychiatry, because they generally deal with extremely violent crimes. But vampirism as a phenomenon has never been acknowledged within established psychology, it gets rejected as sensationalist, an arena for charlatans. In fact it isn't even mentioned in psychiatric reference books. Those of us researching vampirism have been accused of inventing a type of human being that doesn't exist. And for the past three days I have wished that they were right. Unfortunately, they are wrong. Vampires don't exist, but vampirists do."

"How does someone become a vampirist, herr Smith?"

"Obviously there's no simple answer to that, but the classic case would start with an incident in childhood in which the subject sees themselves or someone else bleed heavily. Or with them drinking blood. And finding this exciting. That was the case with vampirist and serial killer John George Haigh, for instance, when he was beaten with a hairbrush as punishment by his fanatically religious mother, and licked up the blood afterwards. Later, in puberty, blood becomes a source of sexual excitement. Then the nascent vampirist starts experimenting with blood, often by so-called auto-vampirism, cutting themselves and drinking their own blood. Then at some point they take the decisive step and drink someone else's blood. It's also common that after they have drunk a person's blood, they kill them. By this point they are full-blown vampirists."

"And rape, where does that come into it? Elise Hermansen was sexually assaulted, after all."

"Well, the experience of power and control speaks very strongly to the adult vampirist. John George Haigh was, for instance, very interested in sex, and said he felt forced to drink his victims' blood. He used to use a glass, by the way. But I'm fairly certain that for our vampirist here in Oslo, the blood is more important than the sexual assault."

"Detective Inspector Bratt?"

"Er, yes?"

"Do you agree? Does it seem as if blood is more important than sex for this vampirist?"

"I have no comment to make about that."

Katrine saw the presenter take a quick decision and turn back to Smith. Presumably he thought there were richer pickings there.

"Herr Smith, do vampirists believe that they're vampires? In other words, that they're immortal as long as they avoid sunlight, that they can convert others by biting them, and so on?"

"Not the clinical vampirist with Renfield's syndrome. It's actually rather unfortunate that the syndrome is named after Renfield, who of course was Count Dracula's servant in Bram Stoker's novel. It should be called Noll's syndrome, after the psychiatrist who first identified it. On the other hand, Noll didn't take vampirism seriously either: the article in which he wrote about the syndrome was intended as a parody."

"Is it out of the question that this individual might not actually be sick, but taking a drug that makes them thirst for human blood, in the same way that MDPV, so-called 'bath salts,' made its users attack other people and eat them in Miami and New York in 2012?"

"No. When people who take MDPV become cannibalistic they are extremely psychotic, unable to think rationally or plan, the police can catch them red-handed—pardon the pun—because they make no attempt to hide. Now, the typical vampirist is so driven by a thirst for blood that escape isn't the first thing they think of, but in this case the planning is so thorough that he or she hasn't left any evidence behind, if we're to believe *VG*."

"She?"

"I, er, was just trying to be politically correct. Vampirists are almost always men, especially when the attacks are violent, as in this instance. Female vampirists usually make do with auto-vampirism, seek out like-minded souls to swap blood with, get blood from slaughterhouses, or hang around near blood banks. I did have a female patient in Lithuania who actually ate her mother's canaries while they were still alive . . ."

Katrine noticed the first yawn of the evening in the audience, and a solitary laugh that quickly fell silent.

"At first my colleagues and I thought we were dealing with what is known as species dysphoria, which is when a patient believes they were born the wrong species and is actually something else: in this instance, a cat. That was until we realised we were looking at a case of vampirism. Unfortunately *Psychology Today* didn't agree, so if you want to read the article about the case you'll have to go to hallstein.psychologist.com."

"Detective Inspector Bratt, can we say that this is a serial killer?"

Katrine thought for a couple of seconds. "No."

"But *VG* is saying that Harry Hole, who of course isn't exactly unknown as a specialist in serial murders, has been brought onto the case. Doesn't that suggest that—?"

"We sometimes consult firemen even when there isn't a fire."

Smith was the only person who laughed. "Good answer! Psychiatrists and psychologists would starve to death if we only saw patients when there was actually something wrong with them."

That got a lot of laughs, and the presenter smiled gratefully at

Smith. Katrine had a feeling that Smith was the more likely out of the pair of them to be asked back.

"Serial killer or not, do you both consider that the vampirist is going to strike again? Or will he wait until the next full moon?"

"I don't want to speculate about that," Katrine said, and caught a glimpse of irritation in the presenter's eyes. What the hell, did he really expect her to join in with his tabloid parlour games?

"I'm not going to speculate either," Hallstein Smith said. "I don't need to, because I know. A paraphile—what we rather imprecisely call a sexually perverted person—who doesn't get treatment very rarely stops of his own accord. And a vampirist never does. But I think the fact that the most recent attempted murder took place at a full moon is a complete coincidence, and was enjoyed more by you in the media than the vampirist."

It didn't look like the presenter felt put out by Smith's barb. He asked with a serious frown: "Herr Smith, would you say we should be critical of the police for not warning the public earlier that a vampirist was on the loose, like you yourself did in *VG*?"

"Mm." Smith grimaced and looked up at one of the spotlights. "That becomes a question about what one ought to have known, doesn't it? Like I said, vampirism is tucked away in one of the less familiar corners of psychology, rarely troubled by the light. So, no. I'd say it was unfortunate, but they shouldn't be criticised for it."

"But now the police do know. So what should they do?"

"Find out more about the subject."

"And finally: how many vampirists have you met?"

Smith puffed his cheeks out and exhaled. "Genuine ones?"

"Yes."

"Two."

"How do you personally react to blood?"

"It makes me feel queasy."

"Yet you still research and write about it."

Smith smiled wryly. "Perhaps that's why. We're all a bit crazy."

"Does that apply to you as well, Detective Inspector Bratt?"

Katrine started. For a moment she'd forgotten she wasn't just watching but was actually on television.

"Er, sorry?"

"A bit crazy?"

Katrine searched for an answer. Something quick-witted and genial, like Harry had advised. She knew she'd think of something when she got into bed later that night. Which couldn't come soon enough, seeing as she could feel her tiredness seeping through now that the adrenalin rush of being on television was starting to fade. "I . . ." she began, then gave up and plumped for a "Well, who knows?"

"Crazy enough that you could envisage meeting a vampirist? Not a murderer, as in this tragic case, but one who might just bite you a little bit?"

Katrine suspected that was a joke, possibly one alluding to her vaguely S&M-inspired outfit.

"A little bit?" she repeated, and raised one black, made-up eyebrow. "Yes, why not?"

And without actually trying, she too was rewarded with laughter this time.

"Good luck with catching him, Detective Inspector Bratt. The last word to you, herr Smith. You didn't answer the question about how to find vampirists. Any advice for Detective Inspector Bratt here?"

"Vampirism is such an extreme paraphilia that it often occurs in conjunction with other psychiatric diagnoses. So I would encourage all psychologists and psychiatrists to help the police by going through their lists to see if they have patients who demonstrate behaviour that might fit the criteria for clinical vampirism. I think we can agree that a case like this has to take precedence over our oath of confidentiality."

"And with that, this edition of *The Sunday Magazine* . . ."

The television screen behind the counter went dark.

"Nasty stuff," Mehmet said. "But your colleague looked good."

"Hm. Is it always this empty here?"

"Oh, no." Mehmet looked around the bar. Cleared his throat. "Well, yes."

"I like it."

"Do you? You haven't touched your beer. Look at it, going flat there."

"Good," the policeman said.

"I could give you something with a bit more life in it." Mehmet nodded towards the Galatasaray banner.

Katrine was hurrying along one of the empty, labyrinthine corridors in Television Centre when she heard heavy footsteps and breathing behind her. She glanced back without stopping. It was Hallstein Smith. Katrine noted a running style that was as unorthodox as his research, unless he was just unusually knock-kneed.

"Bratt," Smith called.

Katrine stopped and waited.

"I'd like to start by apologising," Smith said as he caught up with her, gasping for breath.

"What for?"

"For talking far too much. I get a bit high from the attention, my wife's always telling me. But much more importantly, that picture . . ."

"Yes?"

"I couldn't say anything in there, but I think I might have had him as a patient."

"Valentin Gjertsen?"

"I'm not sure, it must be at least two years ago, and it was only a couple of hours of therapy at the office I used to rent in the city. There's not really that much of a similarity, but I thought of this particular patient when you mentioned plastic surgery. Because, if I remember rightly, he had a scar left by stitches under his chin."

"Was he a vampirist?"

"What do I know? He didn't mention it, and if he had I'd have included him in my research."

"Maybe he came to see you because he was curious, if he knew that you were conducting research into his . . . what was that word?"

"Paraphilia. That's not impossible. Like I said, I'm pretty sure we're dealing with an intelligent vampirist who's aware of his own illness. Either way, this makes the fact that my patient records were stolen even more annoying."

"You don't remember what this patient said his name was, where he worked, where he lived?"

Smith sighed deeply. "I'm afraid my memory isn't what it used to be."

Katrine nodded. "We can always hope that he's seen other psychologists and that they remember something. And that they're not too Catholic when it comes to the oath of confidentiality."

"A bit of Catholicism isn't to be sniffed at."

Katrine raised an eyebrow. "What do you mean by that?"

Smith screwed his eyes shut in frustration and looked like he was trying not to swear. "Nothing."

"Come on, Smith."

The psychologist threw his hands out. "I'm putting two and

two together here, Bratt. Your reaction when the presenter asked if you were crazy, combined with what you said to me about getting drenched in Sandviken. We often communicate non-verbally, and what you were communicating was the fact that you had been treated in the psychiatric unit in Sandviken. And for you as a lead detective at Crime Squad, it's probably a good idea for us to keep an oath of confidentiality that's in part designed to protect people seeking help for problems from having it come back to haunt them later in their careers."

Katrine Bratt felt her mouth hang open as she tried in vain to think of something to say.

"You don't actually have to respond to my idiotic guesses," Smith said. "I'm actually under an oath of confidentiality when it comes to them too. Goodnight, Bratt."

Katrine watched Hallstein trudge off along the corridor, as knock-kneed as the Eiffel Tower. Her phone rang.

It was Bellman.


He was naked, locked into an impenetrable, burning fog that stung the parts of his skin where he had scrubbed through it, making the blood run onto the wooden bench beneath him. He closed his eyes, felt a sob rising, and visualised how it would happen. The fucking rules. They limited the enjoyment, limited the pain, stopped him from expressing himself the way he would like to. But things would change. The police had received his message, and were after him now. Right now. Trying to sniff him out, but they couldn't. Because he was clean.

He started when he heard someone clear their throat in the fog and realised that he was no longer alone.

"*Kapatiyoruz.*"

"Yes," Valentin Gjertsen replied in a thick voice, but remained seated, trying to stifle the sob.

Closing time.

He touched his genitals carefully. He knew exactly where she was. How she should be played with. He was ready. Valentin breathed moist air into his lungs. And there was Harry Hole, thinking he was the hunter.

Valentin Gjertsen stood up suddenly and walked towards the door.

# 16

# Sunday night

Aurora got out of bed and crept into the hall. Went past her mum and dad's bedroom and the stairs that led down to the living room. She couldn't help listening to the rumbling, silent darkness down there as she crept into the bathroom and turned the light on. She locked the door, pulled her pyjamas down and sat on the toilet. Waited, but nothing happened. She had been so desperate to pee that she couldn't sleep, so why couldn't she go now? Was it because she didn't really need to, and had just persuaded herself that she did because she couldn't sleep? And because it was so quiet and safe in here? She had locked the door. When she was a child, her parents had told her she wasn't allowed to do that unless they had guests. Said they needed to be able to get in if anything happened to her.

Aurora closed her eyes. Listened. What if they had guests? Because it had been a sound that had woken her, she remembered that now. The sound of creaking shoes. No, boots. Long, pointed boots that creaked and bent as he crept forward. Stopped and waited outside the bathroom door. Waiting for her. Aurora felt that she couldn't breathe and looked automatically at the bottom of the door. But it was hidden by the threshold, so she couldn't see if anything outside was casting a shadow. Anyway, it was pitch-black out there. The first time she saw him she had been sitting on the swing in the garden. He'd asked for a glass of water, and had almost followed Aurora into the house, then vanished when they'd heard her mum's car coming. The second time had been in the ladies' toilet during the handball tournament.

Aurora listened. She knew he was there. In the darkness outside the door. He had told her he would come back. If she said anything. So she had stopped talking. That was the safest option. And she knew why she couldn't pee now. Because then he'd know she was sitting here. She closed her eyes and listened as hard as she could. No. Nothing. And she could breathe again. He had gone.

Aurora pulled her pyjamas up, unlocked the door and hurried out. She ran past the top of the stairs to the door of her mum and dad's room. She cautiously pushed it open and peered in. A strip of moonlight coming through a gap in the curtains lay across her dad's face. She couldn't see if he was breathing, but his face was so white, just like her grandmother's when Aurora had seen her in the coffin. She crept closer to the bed. Her mum's breathing reminded Aurora of the rubber pump they used to blow up the inflatable mattresses at the cottage. She went over to her dad and put her ear as close to his mouth as she dared. And felt her heart skip with joy when she felt his warm breath on her skin.

When she was lying in bed again it was as if it had never happened. As if it was all just a nightmare she could escape by closing her eyes and falling asleep.

Rakel opened her eyes.

She had been having a nightmare. But that wasn't what had woken her. Someone had opened the front door downstairs. She looked at the space beside her. Harry wasn't there. Presumably he had just got home. She heard his footsteps on the stairs, and listened automatically for their familiar sound. But no, these sounded different. And they didn't sound like Oleg's either, if he had decided to drop in for some reason.

She stared at the closed bedroom door.

The footsteps came closer.

The door opened.

A huge, dark silhouette filled the opening.

And Rakel remembered what she had been dreaming about. It was a full moon, and he had chained himself to the bed and the sheet had been torn to shreds. He had been twisting in agony, tugging at the chain, howling at the night sky as if he'd been hurt, before finally tearing off his own skin. And from beneath it his other self emerged. A werewolf with claws and teeth, with hunting and death in his crazed, ice-blue eyes.

"Harry?" she whispered.

"Did I wake you?" His deep, calm voice was the same as always.

"I was dreaming about you."

He slipped into the room without turning the light on as he undid his belt and pulled his T-shirt over his head. "About me? That's a waste of a dream, I'm already yours."

"Where have you been?"

"At a bar."

The unfamiliar rhythm of his steps. "Have you been drinking?"

He slid into bed beside her. "Yes, I've been drinking. And you've gone to bed early."

She held her breath. "What have you been drinking, Harry? And how much?"

"Turkish coffee. Two cups."

"Harry!" She hit him with the pillow.

"Sorry," he laughed. "Did you know that Turkish coffee isn't supposed to boil? And that Istanbul has three big football clubs that have hated each other like the plague for a hundred years but everyone's forgotten why? Apart from the fact that it's probably very human to hate someone because they hate you."

She curled up next to him and put her arm round his chest. "All this is news to me, Harry."

"I know you like getting regular updates about how the world actually works."

"I don't know how I'd survive without."

"You didn't say why you've gone to bed so early?"

"You didn't ask."

"I'm asking now."

"I was so tired. And I've got an early appointment at Ullevål before work tomorrow."

"You haven't mentioned that."

"No, I only heard today. Dr. Steffens called in person."

"Sure it's an appointment and not just an excuse?"

Rakel laughed quietly, turned away from him and pushed back into his embrace. "Sure you're not just pretending to be jealous to make me happy?"

He bit her gently on the back of her neck. Rakel closed her eyes and hoped that her headache would soon be drowned out by lust, wonderful, pain-relieving lust. But it didn't come. And perhaps Harry could feel it, because he lay there quietly, just holding her. His breathing was deep and even, but she knew he wasn't asleep. He was somewhere else. With his other love.

Mona Daa was running on the treadmill. Because of her damaged hip, her running style looked like a crab's, so she never used the treadmill until she was completely sure she was alone. But she liked jogging a few kilometres after a hard session in the gym, feeling the lactic acid drain from her muscles while she looked out across the darkness of Frognerparken. The Rubinoos, a power-pop group from the seventies who had written a song for one of her favourite films, *The Revenge of the Nerds*, were singing bittersweet pop songs through the earphones that were connected to her phone. Until they were interrupted by a call.

She realised that she had been half expecting it.

It wasn't that she *wanted* him to strike again. She didn't want anything. She merely reported what happened. That was what she told herself, anyway.

The screen said "Unknown number." So it wasn't the newsroom. She hesitated. A lot of weird types popped up during big murder cases like this one, but curiosity got the better of her and she clicked "answer."

"Good evening, Mona." A man's voice. "I think we're alone now."

Mona looked round instinctively. The girl on reception was immersed in her own phone. "What do you mean?"

"You've got the whole of the gym to yourself, I've got the whole of Frognerparken. Actually, it feels like we've got the whole of Oslo to ourselves, Mona. You with your unusually well-informed articles, me as the main character in those articles."

Mona looked at the pulse monitor on her wrist. Her pulse rate had gone up, but not by much. All her friends knew she spent her evenings at the gym, and that she had a view of the park. This wasn't the first time someone had tried to fool her, and it probably wasn't the last either.

"I don't know who you are or what you want. You've got ten seconds to convince me not to hang up."

"I'm not entirely happy with the coverage, a lot of the detail of my work seems to be passing you by completely. I'm offering you a meeting where I shall tell you what I'm trying to show you. And what's going to happen in the near future."

Her pulse rate rose a bit further.

"Tempting, I must say. Apart from the fact that you probably don't want to be arrested, and I don't want to be bitten."

"There's an old abandoned cage from the zoo at Kristiansand down at the container port at Ormøya. There's no lock on it, so take a padlock with you, lock yourself in, and I'll come and talk to you from outside. That means I've got control of you at the same time as you're safe. You can take a weapon to defend yourself with if you like."

"Like a harpoon, you mean?"

"A harpoon?"

"Yes, seeing as we're going to be playing great-white-shark-and-diver-in-a-cage."

"You're not taking me seriously."

"Would *you* take you seriously if you were me?"

"If I were you, I would—before I made up my mind—ask for information about the killings that only the person who committed them could know."

"Go ahead, then."

"I used Ewa Dolmen's blender to mix myself a cocktail, a Bloody Ewa, if you will. You can check that with your police source, because I didn't wash up after me."

Mona was thinking hard. This was mad. And it could be the scoop of the century, the story that would define her journalistic career for all time.

"OK, I'm going to contact my source now, can I call you back in five minutes?"

Low laughter. "You don't build trust by trying cheap tricks like that, Mona. I'll call *you* back in five minutes."

"Fine."

It took a while for Truls Berntsen to answer. He sounded sleepy.

"I thought you were all working?" Mona said.

"Someone has to have some time off."

"I've just got one question."

"There's a discount for bulk if you've got more."

When Mona hung up she knew she'd struck gold. Or, to be more accurate, that gold had struck her.

When the unknown number called again, she had two questions. Where, and when.

"Havnegate 3. Tomorrow evening, eight o'clock. And, Mona?"

"Yes?"

"Don't tell a soul until it's over."

"Any reason why we can't just do this over the phone?"

"Because I want to see you the whole time. And you want to see me. Sleep well. If you're done on that treadmill."


Harry lay on his back, staring at the ceiling. Obviously he could blame those two cups of Mehmet's bitumen-strength coffee, but knew that wasn't the cause. He knew he was there again, unable to switch his brain off until it was over. It just went on working and working until the perpetrator was caught, and sometimes far beyond that. Four years. Four years without so much as a sign of life. Or a sign of death. But now Valentin Gjertsen had shown himself. And not just a glimpse of his devil's tail—he had voluntarily stepped out into the spotlight, like a self-obsessed actor, scriptwriter and director rolled into one. Because this *was* being directed, it wasn't simply the actions of a raving psychotic. This wasn't someone they were going to catch by chance. They just had to wait until he made his next move, and pray to God that he made a mistake. In the meantime, they had to keep looking in the hope of unearthing the tiny mistakes he had already made. Because everyone makes mistakes. Almost everyone.

Harry listened to Rakel's regular breathing, then slipped out from under the covers, crept to the door and downstairs to the living room.

His call was answered on the second ring.

"I thought you'd be asleep," Harry said.

"And you still called?" Ståle Aune said in a sleepy voice.

"You have to help me find Valentin Gjertsen."

"Help *me*? Or help *us*?"

"Me. Us. The city. Humanity, for fuck's sake. He has to be stopped."

"I've told you, my watch is over, Harry."

"He's awake, and he's out there right now, Ståle. While we're lying asleep."

"And with a guilty conscience. But we're sleeping. Because we're tired. *I'm* tired, Harry. *Too* tired."

"I need someone who understands him, who can predict his next move, Ståle. See where he's going to make mistakes. Identify his weakness."

"I can't—"

"Hallstein Smith," Harry said. "What do you make of him?"

There was a pause.

"You didn't actually call to persuade me," Ståle said, and Harry could hear that he felt a bit hurt.

"This is plan B," Harry said. "Hallstein Smith was the first person to say that this was the work of a vampirist, and that he'd strike again. He was right about Valentin Gjertsen sticking to the method that had worked, Tinder dating. Right about him taking the risk of leaving evidence. Right about Valentin's ambivalence towards being identified. And he said early on that the police should be looking for a sex offender. Smith has hit the target pretty well so far. The fact that he goes against the flow is good, because I'm thinking of recruiting him to my little against-the-flow team. But, most importantly of all, you told me he was a smart psychologist."

"He's that all right. Yes, Hallstein Smith could be a good choice."

"There's just one thing I'm wondering about. That nickname of his . . ."

"The Monkey?"

"You said it was connected to the fact that he's still struggling for credibility among his colleagues."

"Bloody hell, Harry, it's more than half a lifetime ago."

"Tell me."

It sounded like Ståle was thinking. Then he mumbled quietly into the phone: "That nickname was partly my fault, I'm afraid. And his too, of course. While he was a student here in Oslo we discovered that there was money missing from the little safe in the psychology department bar. Hallstein was our prime suspect because he was suddenly able to afford to come on a study trip to Vienna that he hadn't initially signed up to because he didn't have the cash. The problem was that it was impossible to prove that Hallstein had got hold of the code to the safe, which was the only way he could have got the money. So I set a monkey trap."

"A what?"

"Daddy!" Harry heard a high-pitched girl's voice at the other end of the phone. "Is everything OK?"

Harry heard Ståle's hand scrape against the microphone. "I didn't mean to wake you, Aurora. I'm talking to Harry."

Then her mother, Ingrid's voice: "Oh, sweetie, you look terrified. A nightmare? Come with me and I'll tuck you in. Or perhaps we could make some tea?" Footsteps moved off across the floor.

"Where were we?" Ståle Aune said.

"The monkey trap."

"Ah, yes. Have you read Robert Pirsig's *Zen and the Art of Motorcycle Maintenance*?"

"All I know is that it's not really about motorcycle maintenance."

"True. First and foremost it's a book about philosophy, but also philosophy and the struggle between feelings and the intellect. Like the monkey trap. You make a hole in a coconut, big enough for the monkey to stick its hand in. You fill the coconut with food and fix it to a pole. Then you hide and wait. The monkey picks up the smell of food, comes and sticks its hand in the hole, grabs the food, and that's when you jump out. The monkey wants to get away, but realises that it can't get its hand out without letting go of the food. The interesting thing is that even though the monkey ought to be intelligent enough to realise that if it gets caught it's unlikely to be able to enjoy the food, it still refuses to let go. Instinct, starvation, desire are stronger than the intellect. And that's the monkey's downfall. Every time. So I and the manager of the bar arranged a psychology quiz and invited everyone in the department. It was a large gathering, with a lot at stake, a lot of tension. Once the bar manager and I had been through the results, I announced that it was a dead heat between the two second-best minds in the department, Smith and a guy called Olavsen, and that the winner would be decided by testing the students' skill at detecting lies. So I introduced a young woman as being one of the bar staff, sat her down on a chair, and asked the two finalists to find out as much as they could about the code to the safe. Smith and Olavsen had to sit opposite her while she was asked about the first number in the four-digit code, from one to nine in a random order. Then the second one, and so on. The young woman had been told to reply 'No, that's not the right number' each time, while Smith and Olavsen studied her body language, the dilation of her pupils, signs of increased heart rate, changes in the modulation of her voice, perspiration, involuntary eye movement, everything an ambitious psychologist takes pride in being able to interpret correctly. The winner would be the one who guessed the most digits correctly. The two of them sat there making notes, concentrating hard while I asked the forty questions. Because remember what was at stake: the title of second-smartest psychologist in the department."

"Obviously, because everyone knew that the smartest—"

"—couldn't take part because he had organised the quiz. Quite. When I'd finished, they each handed me a note with their suggestion. It turned out that Smith had got all four digits right. Great rejoicing all around the room! Because of course this was very impressive. Suspiciously impressive, one might say. Now, Hallstein Smith is more intelligent than the average monkey, and I'm not ignoring the possibility that he may actually have realised what was going on. Even so, he couldn't help trying to win. He just couldn't! Possibly because at the time Hallstein Smith was an impoverished, spotty, largely overlooked young man who didn't have much luck with the ladies, or anything else come to that, and was therefore more desperate for this sort of victory than most people. Or perhaps because he knew it might arouse the suspicion that it was he who had taken the money from the safe, but that it wouldn't *prove* it, because of course it could be the case that he really was brilliant at reading people and interpreting the human body's many signals. But . . ."

"Hm."

"What?"

"Nothing."

"No, what is it?"

"The young woman in the chair. She didn't know the code."

Ståle murmured in agreement. "She didn't even work in the bar."

"How did you know Smith would walk into the monkey trap?"

"Because I'm brilliant at reading people and so on. The question is, what do you think now that you know that your candidate has a background as a thief?"

"How much are we talking about?"

"If I remember rightly, two thousand kroner."

"Not much. And you said there was money missing from the safe, which means he didn't empty it completely, doesn't it?"

"At the time we thought that was because he hoped it wouldn't be noticed."

"But since then you've been thinking that he only took what he needed to be able to join the rest of you on that study trip?"

"He was asked, very politely, to surrender his place on the course in return for the matter not being referred to the police. He got onto a psychology course in Lithuania."

"He went into exile, now with the nickname 'the Monkey' as a result of your stunt."

"He came back and did a postgraduate degree in Norway. Qualified as a psychologist. He did OK."

"You're aware that you sound like you've got a guilty conscience?"

"And you sound like you're thinking about employing a thief."

"I've never had anything against thieves with acceptable motives."

"Hah!" Ståle exclaimed. "You like him even more now. Because you understand the idea of the monkey trap: you can never give up either, Harry. You're losing the bigger prize because you can't let go of the smaller one. You're *determined* to catch Valentin Gjertsen, even though you're actually aware that it might well cost you everything you hold dear, yourself and those around you—you simply can't let go."

"A neat parallel, but you're wrong."

"Am I?"

"Yes."

"If that's the case, then I'm pleased. Now I ought to go and see how my womenfolk are getting on."

"If Smith does join us, could you give him a brief introduction into what's expected of him as a psychologist?"

"Of course, it's the least I can do."

"For Crime Squad? Or because you're why he got nicknamed 'the Monkey'?"

"Goodnight, Harry."

Harry went back upstairs and lay down in bed. Without actually touching Rakel, he lay close enough to feel the heat radiating from her sleeping body. He closed his eyes.

And after a while he glided away. Out of bed, out through the window, through the night, down towards the glittering city where the lights never went out, down onto the streets, into the alleys, over the rubbish bins, where the light of the city never reached. And there, there he was. His shirt was open and from his bare chest a face screamed at him as it tried to rip the skin apart and get out.

It was a face he knew.

Hunter and hunted, scared and hungry, hated and full of hate.

Harry quickly opened his eyes.

He had seen his own face.

# 17

# Monday morning

Katrine looked out at the investigative team's collection of pale faces. Some of them had worked through the night, and those who hadn't probably hadn't got much sleep either. They had already been through the list of Valentin Gjertsen's known contacts, most of them criminal, some of them in prison, some of them dead, it turned out. Then Tord Gren had briefed them about the call lists provided by Telenor, which showed the names of everyone the three victims had been in contact with by phone in the hours and days before they were attacked. So far there hadn't been anything to link them in the numbers, or any suspicious-looking calls or texts. In fact the only thing that was suspicious at all was an unanswered call from an unregistered number, made to Ewa Dolmen's phone two days before her murder. It had come from a pay-as-you-go mobile which couldn't be traced, which could mean that it was switched off, had been destroyed, had had its SIM card removed, or that the balance on the card had simply run out.

Anders Wyller had presented the current state of the investigation into the sale of 3D printers, saying that there were just too many of them, and the percentage that weren't registered to names and addresses in the stores that sold them was too great for there to be any point carrying on with that line of inquiry.

Katrine had looked at Harry, who had shaken his head at the result, before nodding to her that he agreed with the conclusion.

Bjørn Holm had explained that now that the forensic evidence from the last crime scene pointed towards a suspect, Krimteknisk would concentrate on securing further evidence that could tie Valentin Gjertsen to the three crime scenes and victims.

Katrine was ready to allocate the day's work when Magnus Skarre stuck his hand up and said, before she had given him permission to speak: "Why did you decide to go public with the news that Valentin Gjertsen is the suspect?"

"Why? To get tip-offs about where he might be, of course."

"And now we're going to get hundreds, thousands of them, based on a pencil sketch of a face that could easily have belonged to two of my uncles. And we'll have to check every single one of them, because imagine if it later emerged that the police had received a tip-off about Gjertsen's new identity and where he was living before he bit and killed victims number four and five." Skarre looked round as if to gather support. Or, Katrine realised, because he was already speaking on behalf of several of them.

"That's always the dilemma, Skarre, but that's what we decided."

Skarre nodded towards one of the female analysts, who picked up the baton and ran with it. "Skarre's right, Katrine. What we could really do with right now is some time to get on with our work in peace. We've asked the public for information about Valentin Gjertsen before and it didn't get us anywhere, it just took the focus away from things which *might* have been able to get us somewhere."

"And now he knows that we know, we may have frightened him off. He's got a hideaway where he's managed to stay out of sight for three years, and now we risk him sneaking back into his hole. Just saying." Skarre folded his arms with a triumphant look on his face.

"*Risk*?" The voice came from the back of the room, followed by a snort of laughter. "Surely the ones at risk are the women you want to use as bait while we keep quiet about the fact that we know who it is, Skarre. And if we don't catch the bastard, we might as well chase him back to his hole, in my opinion."

Skarre shook his head with a smile. "You'll learn, Berntsen, when you've been in the unit for a *bit* longer, that men like Valentin Gjertsen don't stop. He'll just do what he's doing somewhere else. You heard what our boss—" he pronounced *our boss* with exaggerated slowness—"said on television last night. That Valentin might have already left the country. But if you're hoping that he's sitting at home with his popcorn and knitting, a little more experience will make you realise you're wrong."

Truls Berntsen looked down at his palms and muttered something Katrine couldn't hear.

"We can't hear you, Berntsen," Skarre called, without turning to look at him.

"I said that those pictures that were shown the other day, of the Jacobsen woman under that pile of surfboards, didn't reveal everything," Truls Berntsen responded in a loud, clear voice. "When I got there she was still breathing. But she couldn't talk because he'd used pliers to rip her tongue out of her mouth and stuff it you know where. Do you know how much more comes out if you rip someone's tongue out instead of cutting it off, Skarre? Either way, it sounded like she was begging me to shoot her. And if I'd had a pistol, I'm pretty fucking sure I'd have considered it. But she died soon after that, so that was OK. Just thought I'd mention it while we're talking about experience."

In the silence that followed, as Truls took a deep breath, Katrine found herself thinking that one day she might end up liking Constable Berntsen. That thought was immediately punctured by Truls Berntsen's concluding remarks.

"And as far as I know, our responsibility is Norway, Skarre. If Valentin fucks wogs and coons in other countries, they can deal with it. Better that than him helping himself to our girls."

"And that's where we stop," Katrine said firmly. The looks of surprise revealed that they were at least awake again now. "We'll gather for the afternoon meeting at 1600 hours, then there's a press conference at 1800 hours. I want people to be able to reach me over the phone, so keep your reports as short and concise as possible. And, just so we're all still aware, *everything* is urgent. The fact that he didn't strike again yesterday doesn't mean that he won't today. After all, even God took a breather on Sunday."

The conference room emptied quickly. Katrine gathered her papers, shut her laptop and got ready to leave.

"I want Wyller and Bjørn." Harry said. He was still seated, hands behind his head, legs stretched out in front of him.

"No problem with Wyller, but you'll have to ask the new head of Krimteknisk about Bjørn. Something Lien."

"I've asked Bjørn, and he says he's going to talk to her."

"Yes, I'm sure he is," Katrine found herself saying. "Have you spoken to Wyller?"

"Yes. He got quite excited."

"And the last person?"

"Hallstein Smith."

"Really?"

"Why not?"

"An eccentric with a nut allergy and no experience of police work?"

Harry leaned back in his chair, dug in his trouser pocket and pulled out a crumpled pack of Camels. "If there's a new creature in the jungle called a vampirist, I want the person who knows most about that creature by my side the whole time. But you seem to be saying that the fact that he's allergic to nuts should count against him?"

Katrine sighed. "I just mean that I'm getting fed up of all these allergies. Anders Wyller's allergic to rubber, he can't use latex gloves. Or condoms, I assume. Imagine that."

"I'd rather not," Harry said, looking down into the packet and sticking a sad, broken little cigarette between his lips.

"Why don't you just keep your cigarettes in your jacket pocket like other people, Harry?"

Harry shrugged. "Broken cigarettes taste better. By the way, I'm assuming that because the boiler room hasn't officially been designated an office, the smoking ban doesn't apply there?"

"Sorry," Hallstein Smith said over the phone. "Thanks for asking, though."

He hung up, put his phone in his pocket and looked at his wife May, who was sitting on the other side of the kitchen table.

"Is something wrong?" she asked with a worried expression.

"That was the police. They asked if I wanted to join a small group working to catch this vampirist."

"And?"

"And I've got a deadline for my PhD. I haven't got time. And I'm not interested in that sort of manhunt. We have quite enough hawks and doves at home."

"And you told them that?"

"Yes. Apart from the bit about hawks and doves."

"And what did they say?"

"He. It was a man. Harry." Hallstein Smith laughed. "He said he understood, and that police investigations are boring and full of painstaking work, and not at all like they're depicted on television."

"Well, then," May said, and raised her cup to her lips.

"Well, then," Hallstein said, and did the same.

. . .

Harry's and Anders Wyller's footsteps echoed, drowning out the gentle sound of water dripping from the brick roof of the tunnel.

"Where are we?" Wyller asked. He was carrying the screen and keyboard of a desktop computer of older vintage.

"Under the park, somewhere between Police HQ and Bots Prison," Harry said. "We call it the Culvert."

"And there's a secret office here?"

"Not secret. Just vacant."

"Who'd want an office here, underground?"

"No one. That's why it's vacant." Harry stopped in front of a metal door. Inserted a key in the lock and turned it. Pulled the handle.

"Still locked?" Wyller asked.

"Swollen." Harry braced one foot on the wall next to the door and yanked it open. They were hit by a warm, damp smell of brick cellar. Harry breathed it in happily. Back in the boiler room.

He switched the lights on inside. After a few moments' hesitation, fluorescent lights on the ceiling began to flicker. Once the lights had settled down they looked around the square room with its grey-blue linoleum floor. No windows, just bare concrete walls. Harry glanced over at Wyller. Wondered if the sight of their workplace might dampen the spontaneous joy the young detective had shown when Harry invited him to join his team of guerrillas. It didn't look like it.

"Rock 'n' roll," Anders Wyller said, and grinned.

"We're first, so you get to choose." Harry nodded towards the desks. On one of them stood a scorched brown coffee machine, a water container and four white mugs with names written on them by hand.

Wyller had just installed the computer and Harry had started up the coffee machine when the door was tugged open.

"Wow, it's warmer than I remember," Bjørn Holm laughed. "Here's Hallstein."

A man with big glasses, messy hair and a checked jacket appeared behind Bjørn Holm.

"Smith," Harry said, holding his hand out. "I'm pleased you changed your mind."

Hallstein Smith took Harry's hand. "I've got a weakness for counter-intuitive psychology," he said. "If that's what it was. If not, you're the worst telephone salesman I've ever encountered. But it's the first time I've called the salesman *back* to accept an offer."

"No point pushing anyone, we only want people who are motivated to be here," Harry said. "Do you like your coffee strong?"

"No, preferably a bit . . . I mean, I'll take it however you all do."

"Good. Looks like this is yours." Harry handed Smith one of the white mugs.

Smith adjusted his glasses and read the handwritten name on the side. "Lev Vygotsky."

"And this is for our forensics expert," Harry said, passing Bjørn Holm one of the other mugs.

"Still Hank Williams," Bjørn read cheerfully. "Does that mean it hasn't been washed for three years?"

"Indelible marker," Harry said. "Here's yours, Wyller."

"Popeye Doyle? Who's that?"

"Best cop ever. Look him up."

Bjørn turned the fourth mug round. "So why doesn't it say Valentin Gjertsen on your mug, Harry?"

"Forgetfulness, probably." Harry took the jug from the coffee maker and filled all four mugs.

Bjørn noticed the bemused expressions on the others' faces. "It's a tradition that we have our heroes on our mugs, and Harry the name of the main suspect. Yin and yang."

"It doesn't really matter," Smith said. "But just for the record, Lev Vygotsky isn't my favourite psychologist. He was, admittedly, a pioneer, but—"

"You've got Ståle Aune's mug," Harry said, putting the last chair in place so that all four formed a circle in the middle of the floor. "OK, we're free, we're our own bosses and we don't report to anyone. But we keep Katrine Bratt informed, and vice versa. Sit down. Let's start with each of us saying honestly what we think of this case. Base it on facts and experience, or gut feeling, one single stupid detail or nothing at all. None of what you say will ever be used against you later, and it's OK to go way off beam. Who wants to start?" The four of them sat down.

"Obviously I'm not making the decisions," Smith said. "But I think . . . well, you start, Harry." Smith wrapped his hands around him as if he was freezing, even though they were sitting next door to the boiler that heated the whole prison. "Maybe tell us why you think it isn't Valentin Gjertsen."

Harry looked at Smith. Took a sip from his mug. Swallowed. "OK, I'll start. I *don't* think it *isn't* Valentin Gjertsen. Even if the thought has occurred to me. A killer carries out two murders without leaving any evidence. That takes planning and a cool head. But then he suddenly carries out an assault where he liberally scatters evidence and proof, all of which points towards Valentin Gjertsen. There's something insistent about that, as if the person responsible wants to announce who he is. And that obviously arouses suspicions. Is someone trying to manipulate us into thinking it's someone else? If so, Valentin Gjertsen is the perfect scapegoat." Harry looked at the others, noted Anders Wyller's concentrated, wide-eyed expression, Bjørn Holm looking almost sleepy, and Hallstein Smith looking friendly, inviting, as if in a setting like this he had automatically slipped into his role as psychologist. "Valentin Gjertsen is a plausible culprit, given his past," Harry went on. "And he is also one the murderer knows we're unlikely to find, seeing as we've already tried for so long without any result. Or because the killer knows that Valentin Gjertsen is dead and buried. Because he himself killed and buried him. Because a Valentin who's been buried in secret can't deny our suspicions with an alibi or anything like that, but even from the grave he can carry on drawing attention away from alternative perpetrators."

"Fingerprints," Bjørn Holm said. "The tattoo of the demon face. The DNA on the handcuffs."

"Right." Harry took another sip. "The perpetrator could have planted the fingerprints by cutting off one of Valentin's fingers and taking it with him to Hovseter. The tattoo could be a copy that can be washed off. The hairs on the handcuffs could come from Valentin Gjertsen's corpse, and the handcuffs left there on purpose."

The silence in the boiler room was only broken by a last rattle from the coffee machine.

"Bloody hell," Anders Wyller laughed.

"That could have gone straight into my top ten of paranoid patients' conspiracy theories," Smith said. "That's, er . . . meant as a compliment."

"And that's why we're here," Harry said, leaning forward on his chair. "We're supposed to think differently, look at possibilities that Katrine's investigative team don't touch. Because they've created a scenario of what happened, and the bigger the group is, the harder it is to break free from prevailing ideas and assumptions. They work a bit like a religion, because you automatically think that so many other people around you can't be wrong. Well." Harry raised his unnamed mug. "They can. And they are. All the time."

"Amen," Smith said.

"So let's move on to the next bad theory," Harry said. "Wyller?"

Anders Wyller looked down into his mug. Took a deep breath and began. "Smith, you described on television how a vampirist develops, from one phase to the next. Here in Scandinavia young people are monitored so closely that if they showed such extreme tendencies, it would be picked up by the health service before they reached the final phase. The vampirist isn't Norwegian, he's from some other country. That's my theory." He looked up.

"Thanks," Harry said. "I can add that in the recorded criminal history of serial killers, there isn't a single blood-drinking Scandinavian."

"The Atlas Murder in Stockholm, 1932," Smith said.

"Hm. I don't know about that one."

"That's probably because the vampirist was never found, and it was never ascertained that he was a serial killer."

"Interesting. And the victim was a woman, as in this case?"

"Lilly Lindeström, a thirty-two-year-old prostitute. And I'd eat the straw hat I've got at home if she was the only one. More recently it's become known at the Vampire Murder."

"Details?"

Smith blinked a couple of times, his eyes almost closed and he began to speak as if he were reciting from memory, word for word: "4 May, Walpurgis Eve, Sankt Eriksplan 11, one-room flat. Lilly had received a man there. She had been down to see her friend on the first floor and asked to borrow a condom. When the police broke into Lilly's flat they found her dead, lying on an ottoman. No fingerprints or other clues. It was obvious that the murderer had cleaned up after him, even Lilly's clothes were neatly folded. In the kitchen sink they found a sauce ladle covered in blood."

Bjørn exchanged a glance with Harry before Smith went on.

"None of the names in her address book, which admittedly only contained a load of first names, led the police to any suspects. They never came close to finding the vampirist."

"But if it was a vampirist, surely he would have struck again?" Wyller said.

"Yes," Smith said. "And who's to say he didn't? And cleaned up after himself even better."

"Smith's right," Harry said. "The number of people who go missing each year is greater than the number of recorded murders. But might Wyller have a point in that a vampirist in the making would be identified at an early stage?"

"What I described on television was the *typical* development," Smith said. "There are people who discover their inner vampirist later in life, just like it can take time for ordinary people to discover their true sexual orientation. One of the most famous vampirists in history, Peter Kürten, the so-called 'Vampire of Düsseldorf,' was forty-five years old the first time he drank the blood of an animal, a swan he killed outside the city in December 1929. Less than two years later he had killed nine people and tried to kill another seven."

"So you don't think it strange that Valentin Gjertsen's otherwise pretty horrifying track record has never included blood-drinking or cannibalism?"

"No."

"OK. What are your thoughts, Bjørn?"

Bjørn Holm straightened up on his chair and rubbed his eyes. "The same as you, Harry."

"Which is?"

"That Ewa Dolmen's murder is a copy of the killing in Stockholm. The sofa, the fact that the place had been tidied up, that the blender he used to drink the blood from was left in the sink."

"Does that sound plausible, Smith?" Harry asked.

"A copycat? If so, it would be something new. Er, paradox not intended. There have, certainly, been vampirists who have regarded themselves as the reincarnation of Count Dracula, but the notion that a vampirist would take it upon himself to re-create the Atlas Murder seems a little unlikely. A more plausible explanation would be that there are certain personality traits that are typical of vampirists."

"Harry thinks our vampirist seems to be obsessed with cleanliness," Wyller said.

"I understand that," Smith said. "The vampirist John George Haigh was obsessed with clean hands, and wore gloves all year round. He hated dirt and only drank his victims' blood from freshly washed glasses."

"How about you, Smith?" Harry said. "Who do you think our vampirist is?"

Smith put two fingers between his lips and moved them up and down, making a flapping sound as he breathed in and out.

"I think that like a lot of vampirists he's an intelligent person who has tortured animals and possibly people since he was young, that he comes from a well-adapted family where he was the only one who didn't fit in. He'll soon want blood again, and I think he gets sexual satisfaction not only from drinking blood, but from seeing blood. That he is seeking the perfect orgasm he thinks a combination of rape and blood can give him. Peter Kürten—the swan killer from

Düsseldorf—said that the number of times he stabbed his victims with a knife depended on how much blood came out, which in turn determined how quickly he reached orgasm."

A gloomy silence settled on the room.

"And where and how do we find a person like that?" Harry asked.

"Maybe Katrine was right last night on television," Bjørn said. "Perhaps Valentin has fled the country. Taken a trip to Red Square, maybe."

"Moscow?" Smith said in surprise.

"Copenhagen," Harry said. "Multicultural Nørrebro. There's a park there that's frequented by people engaged in human trafficking. Mostly import, a bit of export. You sit down on one of the benches or swings and hold up a ticket—a bus ticket, plane ticket, anything. A guy comes over and asks where you're going. Then he asks more, nothing that would give him away, while a colleague sitting elsewhere in the park takes your picture without you noticing, and checks online that you're who you say you are and not a detective. This travel agency is discreet and expensive, but even so, no one gets to travel business class. The cheapest seats are in a shipping container."

Smith shook his head. "But vampirists don't calculate risk as rationally as we do, so I don't think he's gone."

"Nor do I," Harry said. "So where is he? Is he hiding in a crowd, or does he live alone in some secluded place? Has he got friends? Can we imagine him having a partner?"

"I don't know."

"Everyone here understands that no one can know, Smith, whether or not they're a psychologist. All I'm asking for is your hunch."

"We researchers aren't good at hunches. But he's alone. I'm pretty certain of that. Very alone, even. A loner."

There was a knock.

"Pull hard and come in!" Harry called.

The door opened.

"Good day, bold vampire hunters," Ståle Aune said, stepping inside, paunch first, hand in hand with a round-shouldered girl with so much dark hair hanging in front of her face that Harry couldn't see it. "I've agreed to give you a crash course in the role of the psychologist in police work, Smith."

Smith lit up. "I'd really appreciate that, dear colleague."

Ståle Aune rocked on his heels. "You should. But I have no intention of working in these catacombs again, so I've arranged to borrow

Katrine's office." He put one hand on the girl's shoulder. "Aurora came with me because she needs a new passport. Could you help her jump the queue while Smith and I talk, Harry?"

The girl pulled her hair aside. At first Harry couldn't believe the pale face with greasy skin and red spots belonged to the pretty little girl he remembered from just a couple of years before. Looking at her dark clothes and heavy makeup, he guessed she was now a goth, or what Oleg called an emo. But there was no defiance or rebellion in her eyes. Nor the weariness of youth, or any sign of joy at seeing Harry again. Her favourite not-uncle, as she used to call him. There was nothing there. Actually, there was something there. Something he couldn't put his finger on.

"Queue-jumping it shall be. That's how corrupt we are here," Harry said, and got a little smile from Aurora. "Let's go up to the passport department."

The four of them left the boiler room. Harry and Aurora walked silently along the culvert while Ståle Aune and Hallstein Smith chatted away two steps behind them.

"So, I had this patient who talked so indirectly about his own problems that I didn't put two and two together," Aune said. "When, quite by chance, I realised that he was the missing Valentin Gjertsen, he attacked me. If Harry hadn't come to my rescue he would have killed me."

Harry noticed Aurora tense at this.

"He got away, but while he was threatening me I got a clearer picture of him. He held a knife to my throat as he tried to force me to make a diagnosis. He called himself 'damaged goods.' And said that if I didn't answer, he'd drain me of blood while his own cock swelled."

"Interesting. Could you see if he did actually get an erection?"

"No, but I could feel it. As well as the jagged edge of the hunting knife. I remember hoping that my double chin might save me." Ståle chuckled.

Harry heard a stifled gasp from Aurora and half turned to give Aune a pointed look.

"Oh, sorry, sweetheart!" her father exclaimed.

"What did you talk about?" Smith wondered.

"A lot," he said, lowering his voice. "He was interested in the voices in the background of Pink Floyd's *Dark Side of the Moon*."

"Now I remember! I don't think he said his name was Paul. But all my patient records have been stolen, sadly."

"Harry, Smith says—"

"I heard."

They went up the steps to the ground floor, where Aune and Smith stopped in front of the lift and Harry and Aurora carried on into the atrium. A notice on the glass in front of the counter announced that their camera was out of action, and that anyone applying for a passport should use the photograph booth towards the rear of the building.

Harry led Aurora to the booth, which looked like an outside toilet, pulled the curtain aside and gave Aurora some coins before she sat down.

"Oh yes," he said. "You're not supposed to show your teeth." Then he closed the curtain.

Aurora looked at her reflection in the black glass that concealed the camera.

Felt tears welling up.

It had seemed like a good idea, telling her dad that she wanted to go with him when he went to Police HQ to see Harry. That she needed a new passport before a class trip to London. He never had a clue about that sort of thing, her mum did all that. The plan had been to get Harry on his own for a few minutes and tell him everything. But now that they were alone she found she couldn't do it. It was what her dad had said in the tunnel, about the knife, it had frightened her so much that the trembling had started again, and her legs almost gave way beneath her. It was the same jagged knife the man had held to her throat. And he was back. Aurora closed her eyes to avoid seeing her own terrified reflection. He was back, and he was going to kill them all if she talked. And what good would talking do? She didn't know anything that could help them find him. That wouldn't save her dad, or anyone else out there. Aurora opened her eyes again. Looked around the cramped booth, just like the toilet at the sports hall that time. She found herself looking down automatically, at the bottom of the curtain. The pointed boots on the floor, right outside. They were waiting for her, wanted to get in, wanted . . .

Aurora yanked the curtain aside, pushed her way past Harry and headed for the exit. Heard him call her name behind her. Then she was out in daylight and open ground. She ran across the grass, through the park, off towards Grønlandsleiret. She heard her hiccoughed sobs mixed with gasping breath, as if there wasn't enough air, even out here. But she didn't stop. She ran. Knew she was going to keep running until she dropped.

"Paul, or Valentin, didn't mention any particular attraction to blood as such," Aune said. He had settled down behind Katrine's desk. "But considering his history, we can probably conclude that he's not a man with any inhibitions about acting out his sexual preferences. And someone like that is unlikely to discover new sexual sides to himself as an adult."

"Maybe the preference was always there," Smith said. "He just hadn't found a way to act out the fantasy. If his real desire was to bite people until they bled, and then drink straight from the well, so to speak, maybe it was the discovery of these iron teeth that made it possible for him to put that into action?"

"Drinking other people's blood is an ancient tradition with connotations of assuming the powers and abilities of other people, usually enemies, isn't it?"

"Agreed."

"If you're going to put together a profile of this serial killer, Smith, I'd suggest taking as your starting point a person who is driven by a need for control, like we see in more conventional rapists and sexually motivated murderers. Or, to be more accurate, regaining control, reclaiming a power that was taken from him at some point. Restitution."

"Thanks," Smith said. "Restitution. I agree, I'll definitely include that aspect."

"What does 'restitution' mean?" Katrine asked, who was sitting on the windowsill after being granted leave to stay by the two psychologists.

"We all want to repair injuries inflicted on us," Aune said. "Or take revenge, which is much the same thing. I, for instance, decided to become the genius psychologist I am because I was so bad at playing football that no one ever wanted me on their team. Harry was just a boy when his mother died, and he decided to be become a murder detective to punish people who take lives."

There was a knock on the door frame.

"Speak of the devil . . ." Aune said.

"Sorry to interrupt," Harry said. "But Aurora's run off. I don't know what happened, but it was definitely something."

A cloud swept across Ståle Aune's face and he heaved himself up from the chair with a groan. "God knows with teenagers. I'll go and find her. This was a bit brief, Smith—give me a call and we'll carry on."

"Anything new?" Harry asked when Aune had gone.

"Yes and no," Katrine said. "The Forensic Medical Institute has confirmed that there's a hundred percent match between the DNA found on the handcuffs and Gjertsen. Only one psychologist and two sexologists have contacted us after Smith's plea to check their patient records, but the names they gave us have already been dismissed from the investigation. And, as expected, we've received several hundred calls from people reporting anything from scary neighbours and dogs with bite marks on them, to vampires, werewolves, gnomes and trolls. But also a few that are worth checking out. By the way, Rakel has been calling, trying to get hold of you."

"Yes, I just saw the missed calls. There's not much of a signal down in our bunker. Would it be possible to do anything about that?"

"I'll ask Tord if we could set up a relay or something. So can I have my office back now?"

Harry and Smith were alone in the lift.

"You're avoiding eye contact," Smith said.

"That's the rule in lifts, isn't it?" Harry said.

"I meant generally."

"If not making eye contact is the same as avoiding it, you're probably right."

"And you don't like lifts."

"Mm. Is it that obvious?"

"Body language doesn't lie. And you think I talk too much."

"This is your first day, you're bound to be a bit nervous."

"No, I'm like this most of the time."

"OK. By the way, I haven't thanked you for changing your mind."

"Don't mention it. I should be apologising for the fact that my initial response was so selfish when people's lives are at stake."

"I can understand that your doctorate means a lot to you."

Smith smiled. "Yes, you understand because you're one of us."

"One of who?"

"The half-crazy elite. Maybe you've heard of the Goldman Dilemma from the 1980s? Elite athletes were asked if they'd be prepared to take a drug that would guarantee a gold medal, but they'd die five years later. More than half answered yes. When the rest of the population were asked the same question, only two out of 250 said yes. I know it sounds sick to most people, but not to people like you and me, Harry. Because you'd sacrifice your life to catch this murderer, wouldn't you?"

Harry looked at the psychologist for a long while. Heard the echo of Ståle's words. *Because you understand the idea of the monkey trap: you can never give up either.*

"Anything else you're wondering about, Smith?"

"Yes. Has she put on weight?"

"Who?"

"Ståle's daughter."

"Aurora?" Harry raised an eyebrow. "Well, she probably used to be thinner."

Smith nodded. "You're not going to like my next question, Harry."

"We'll see."

"Do you think Ståle Aune might have an incestuous relationship with his daughter?"

Harry stared at Smith. He had picked him because he wanted people who were prepared to think original thoughts, and as long as Smith came up with the goods Harry was prepared to tolerate almost anything. *Almost* anything.

"OK," Harry said in a low voice. "You've got twenty seconds to explain yourself. Use them wisely."

"I'm just saying that—"

"Eighteen."

"OK, OK. Self-harming behaviour. She was wearing a long-sleeved T-shirt that hid the scars on her lower arms which she kept scratching the whole time. Hygiene. When you stood close to her you could tell that her personal hygiene wasn't great. Eating. Extreme eating or dieting is typical in abuse victims. Mental state. She seemed depressed generally, may be suffering from angst. I realise that the clothes and makeup can be misleading, but body language and facial expressions don't lie. Intimacy. I could see in your body language that you were open to the idea of a hug in the boiler room. But she pretended not to notice, that was why she'd pulled her hair in front of her face before she came in—you know each other well, you've hugged each other before, so she predicted what would happen. Abuse victims avoid intimacy and bodily contact. Is my time up?"

The lift stopped with a jolt.

Harry took a step forward, so that he towered over Smith, and pressed the button to keep the lift doors closed. "Let's assume for a moment that you're right, Smith." Harry lowered his voice to a whisper. "What the hell has that got to do with Ståle? Apart from the fact that back in the day he got you kicked off your psychology degree in Oslo and landed you with the nickname 'the Monkey.'"

Harry saw tears of pain in Smith's eyes, as if he'd been slapped. Smith blinked and swallowed. "Oh. You're probably right, Harry. I'm just seeing something I subconsciously want to see because I'm still angry. It was a hunch, and like I said, I'm not good at them."

Harry nodded slowly. "And you know that, so this wasn't your first hunch. What did you see?"

Hallstein Smith straightened up. "I saw a father holding his daughter's hand when she's what, sixteen, seventeen years old? And my first thought is that it's sweet that they're still doing that, that I hope my daughters and I will still be holding hands well into their teenage years."

"But?"

"But you can look at it from the other side, that the father is exerting power and control by holding on to her, keeping her in her place."

"And what makes you think that?"

"Because she runs off the moment she gets the chance. I've worked on cases where there are suspicions of incest, Harry, and running away from home is precisely one of the things we look at. The symptoms I mentioned can mean a thousand other things, but if there's one chance in a thousand that she's being abused at home, it would be a dereliction of my professional duty not to share my thoughts, don't you think? I understand that you're a friend of the family, but that's also the reason I'm sharing these thoughts with you. You're the only person who can talk to her."

Harry let go of the button, the doors slid open and Hallstein Smith slipped out.

Harry waited until the doors started to close again, stuck one foot between them and was going after Smith, down the stairs towards the culvert, when his phone buzzed in his pocket.

He answered.

"Hello, Harry." Isabelle Skøyen's masculine voice, simultaneously chirping and teasing, was unmistakable. "You're back in the saddle, I hear."

"I don't know about that."

"We did ride together for a while, Harry. It was fun. Could have been more fun."

"I thought it was as much fun as it could have been."

"Well, water under the bridge, Harry. I'm calling to ask for a favour. Our communications bureau is doing some work for Mikael, and you might have seen that *Dagbladet* has just published an article online which is pretty hard on Mikael?"

"No."

"They write, quote: 'The city is now paying the price for the fact that the Oslo Police under Mikael Bellman has failed to do what we have the police for, to catch people like Valentin Gjertsen. It is a scandal, a sign of professional bankruptcy, that Gjertsen has played cat and mouse with the police for four years. And now he's tired of being the mouse, so he's playing at being the cat instead.' What do you think?"

"Could have been better written."

"What we want is for someone to come forward and explain how unreasonable this criticism of Mikael is. Someone who can remind people of the clear-up rate for serious crime under Bellman, someone who has been personally responsible for many murder investigations, someone who is held in high esteem. And because you're now a lecturer at Police College you can't be accused of sycophancy either. You're perfect, Harry. What do you say?"

"Obviously I want to help you and Bellman."

"You do? That's great!"

"The best way I can. Which is by catching Valentin Gjertsen. Something I'm pretty busy with right now, so if you'll excuse me, Skøyen."

"I know you're all working hard, Harry, but that could take time."

"And why is it so urgent to polish Bellman's reputation right now? Let me save us both some time. I will *never* stand in front of a microphone and say anything dictated by a PR agent. If we hang up now we can say that we had a civilised conversation which didn't end with me being forced to tell you to go to hell."

Isabelle Skøyen laughed loudly. "You haven't changed, Harry. Still engaged to that sweet lawyer with the black hair?"

"No."

"No? Maybe we should have a drink one evening?"

"Rakel and I are no longer engaged because we're married."

"Ah. Well, I never. But is that necessarily a problem?"

"It is for me. For you it's probably more of a challenge."

"Married men are best, they never give you any trouble."

"Like Bellman?"

"Mikael's lovely, and he's got the most kissable lips in the city. Well, this conversation's getting boring now, Harry, so I'm hanging up. You've got my number."

"No, I haven't. Bye."

Rakel. He'd forgotten that she'd called. He brought up her number as he checked his reaction, just for the hell of it. Had Isabelle Skøyen's invitation had any effect on him, had it managed to turn him on at all? No. Well. A bit. Did that mean anything? No. It meant so little that he couldn't be bothered to work out what sort of bastard he was. Not that it meant that he *wasn't* a bastard, but that tiny little tingle, that involuntary, half-dreamt fragment of a scene—with her long legs and broad hips—which was there one moment, then gone, wasn't enough for a guilty verdict. Bloody hell. He'd rejected her. Even though he knew that rejection made Isabelle Skøyen more likely to call him again.

"Rakel Fauke's phone, you're talking to Dr. Steffens."

Harry felt the back of his neck begin to prickle. "This is Harry Hole, is Rakel there?"

"No, Hole, she isn't."

Harry felt his throat tighten. Panic was creeping up on him. The ice was creaking. He concentrated on breathing. "Where is she?"

In the long pause that followed, which he suspected was there for a reason, Harry had time to think a lot of things. And of all the conclusions his brain automatically came to, there was one he knew he would remember. That it ended here, that he would no longer be able to have the one thing he wanted: for today and tomorrow to be a copy of the day he had yesterday.

"She's in a coma."

In confusion, or in sheer, utter desperation, his brain tried to tell him that a coma was a city or a country.

"But she tried to call me. Less than an hour ago."

"Yes," Steffens said. "And you didn't answer."

# 18

# Monday afternoon

Senseless. Harry was sitting in a hard chair and trying to concentrate on what the man on the other side of the desk was saying. But the words made as much sense as the birdsong outside the open window behind the man in glasses and a white coat. As senseless as the blue sky and the fact that the sun had decided to shine brighter today than it had done for weeks. As senseless as the posters on the walls depicting people with grey organs and bright red blood vessels on show, or, beside them, a cross with a bleeding Christ on it.

Rakel.

The only thing in his life that made any sense.

Not science, not religion, not justice, not a better world, not pleasure, not intoxication, not the absence of pain, not even happiness. Only those five letters. R-a-k-e-l. It wasn't the case that if it hadn't been her, it would have been someone else. If it hadn't been her, it would have been no one.

And having no one would have been better than this.

They can't take no one away from you.

So in the end Harry cut through the torrent of words.

"What does it mean?"

"It means," Senior Consultant John D. Steffens said, "that we don't know. We know that her kidneys aren't working the way they should. And that could be caused by a number of things, but, like I said, we've ruled out the most obvious."

"So what do you think?"

"A syndrome," Steffens said. "The problem is that there are thousands, each one rarer and more obscure than the last."

"Which means?"

"That we need to keep looking. For the time being we've put her in a coma, because she was starting to have difficulty breathing."

"How long . . . ?"

"For the time being. We don't just need to find out what's wrong with your wife, we need to be able to treat it as well. Only when we're sure she'll be able to breathe independently will we bring her out of the coma."

"Could she . . . could she . . ."

"Yes?"

"Could she die while she's in the coma?"

"We don't know."

"Yes, you do."

Steffens put his fingertips together. Waited, as if to force the conversation into a lower gear.

"She could die," he said eventually. "We could all die. The heart can stop at any moment, but obviously it's a question of probability."

Harry knew that the rage he felt bubbling up wasn't really anything to do with the doctor and the platitudes he was coming out with. He had spoken to enough next of kin in murder cases to know that frustration sought a target, and the fact that it couldn't find one only made him more furious. He took a deep breath. "And what sort of probability are we talking about here?"

Steffens threw his hands out. "Like I said, we don't know the cause of her kidney failure."

"You don't know, and that's why it's called probability," Harry said. Stopped. Swallowed. Lowered his voice. "So just tell me what you think the probability is, based on the little you do know."

"Kidney failure isn't the fault, in and of itself, it's a symptom. It could be a blood disease, or poisoning. It's the season for mushroom poisoning, but your wife said you haven't eaten any recently. And you've eaten the same things. Are you feeling unwell, Hole?"

"Yes."

"You . . . Okay, I understand. What we're left with, some sort of syndrome, is invariably a serious problem."

"Over or under fifty percent, Steffens?"

"I can't—"

"Steffens, I know we're in no-man's-land here, but I'm begging you. Please."

The doctor stared at Harry for a long time before seeming to make a decision.

"As things stand, based on her test results, I think the risk of losing her is a little over fifty percent. Not much more than fifty, but slightly more. The reason I don't like telling relatives these percentages is that they usually read too much into them. If a patient dies during an operation where we estimated the risk of death at twenty-five percent, they often accuse us of having misled them."

"Forty-five percent? A forty-five percent chance of her surviving?"

"At the moment. Her condition is deteriorating, so a bit lower if we can't identify the cause within a day or two."

"Thanks." Harry stood up. Dizzy. And the thought came automatically: a hope that everything would go completely dark. A fast and pain-free exit, stupid and banal, yet no less senseless than everything else.

"It would be useful to know how to get hold of you if . . ."

"I'll make sure you can reach me at any time," Harry said. "I'll go back to her now, if there isn't anything else I should know."

"Let me come with you, Harry."

They headed back to room 301. The corridor stretched away and vanished into shimmering light. Presumably a window, with the low autumn sun shining directly through it. They passed nurses in ghostly white, and patients in dressing gowns, slowly moving towards the light with their living-dead shuffle. Yesterday he and Rakel had been embracing in the big bed with its slightly too soft mattress, and now she was here, in the land of coma, among ghosts and spirits. He needed to call Oleg. He needed to work out how to tell him. He needed a drink. Harry didn't know where the thought came from, but there it was, as if someone had shouted it, spelling it out, straight into his ear. The thought needed to be drowned out, quickly.

"Why were you Penelope Rasch's doctor?" he said in a loud voice. "She wasn't a patient here."

"Because she needed a blood transfusion," Steffens said. "And I'm a haematologist and bank manager. But I also do shifts in A&E."

"Bank manager?"

Steffens looked at Harry. And perhaps he realised that Harry's mind needed distracting, a brief pause from everything he found himself in the middle of.

"The local branch of the blood bank. I should probably be called bath manager, because we took over the old rheumatic baths that used to be in the basement beneath this building. We call it the bloodbath. Don't try to tell me that haematologists haven't got a sense of humour."

"Hm. So that's what you meant about buying and selling blood."

"Sorry?"

"You said that was why you were able to use pictures from the crime scene in Penelope Rasch's stairwell to calculate how much blood she'd lost. By eye."

"You've got a good memory."

"How is she doing?"

"Oh, Penelope Rasch is recovering physically. But she's going to need psychological help. Coming face-to-face with a vampire—"

"Vampirist."

"—it's an omen, you know."

"An omen?"

"Oh yes. He was predicted and described in the Old Testament."

"The vampirist?"

Steffens smiled thinly. "Proverbs 30:14. *A sort whose teeth are swords, and whose jaws are set with knives, who devour the poor from the earth and the needy out of house and home.'* Here we are."

Steffens held the door open and Harry walked in. Into the night. On the other side of the closed curtain the sun was shining, but in here the only light was a shimmering green line jumping across a black screen, over and over again. Harry gazed down at her face. She looked so peaceful. And so far away, floating in a dark space where he couldn't reach her. He sat down on the chair beside the bed, waited until he heard the door close behind him. Then he took hold of her hand and pressed his face to the covers.

"No further away now, darling," he whispered. "No further."


Truls Berntsen had moved the screens in the open-plan office so that the corner he shared with Anders Wyller was completely hidden from view. Which is why he was annoyed that the only person who could see him, Wyller, was so damn curious about everything, and especially who he was talking to on the phone. But right now the snooper was out at some tattoo and piercing parlour, because they'd had a tip-off saying they were importing vampire accessories, among them denture-like metal objects with pointed canine teeth, and Truls was planning to make the most of the break. He'd downloaded the final episode of the second season of *The Shield*, and had turned the volume so low that only he could hear it. For that reason he definitely wasn't at all pleased when his phone started to flash and buzz like a vibrator on the desk in front of him as it played the start of Britney Spears's "I'm Not a Girl," which Truls, for reasons that weren't entirely clear, was very fond of. The words, about her not being a woman yet, prompted vague thoughts of a girl who was under the age of consent, and Truls hoped that wasn't why he had it as his ringtone. Or was it? Britney Spears in that school uniform, was it perverse to wank off to that? OK, in that case he was a perv. But what worried Truls more was that the number on the screen was vaguely familiar. The City Treasurer's department? Internal Investigations? Some questionable old contact he'd done a burner job for? Someone he owed money or a favour? It wasn't Mona Daa's number anyway. Most likely it was a work call, and probably one that meant he was going to have to do something. Either way, he concluded that this was unlikely to be a call he had anything to win by answering. He put the phone in a drawer and concentrated on Vic Mackey and his colleagues on the STRIKE team. He loved Vic, *The Shield* really was the only cop series that showed how people in the force actually thought. Then all of a sudden he realised why the number had seemed familiar. He yanked the drawer open and grabbed the phone. "Detective Constable Berntsen."

Two seconds passed before he heard anything at the other end, and he thought she had hung up. But then the voice was there, right by his ear, soft and tantalising.

"Hello, Truls, this is Ulla."

"Ulla . . . ?"

"Ulla Bellman."

"Oh, hi, Ulla, is that you?" Truls hoped he sounded convincing. "How can I help you?"

She let out a little laugh. "I don't know about 'help.' I saw you in the atrium of Police HQ the other day, and realised how long it had been since we last had a proper chat. You know, like we used to."

We never had a *proper* chat, Truls thought.

"Could we meet up sometime?"

"Yeah, sure." Truls tried to stifle his grunting laughter.

"Great. How about tomorrow? Mum's got the kids then. We could go for a drink or a bite to eat?"

Truls could hardly believe his ears. Ulla wanted to meet him. To interrogate him about Mikael again? No, she must know they didn't see much of each other these days. Besides: a drink or a bite to eat? "That would be great. Is there something on your mind?"

"I just thought it would be nice to meet up, I don't really have much contact with too many people from the old days."

"No, of course," Truls said. "So, where?"

Ulla laughed. "I haven't been out for years. I don't know what there is in Manglerud these days. You do still live there, don't you?"

"Yes. Er . . . Olsen's is still there, down in Bryn."

"Is it? Right, then. Let's say there. Eight o'clock?"

Truls nodded dumbly, then remembered to say "Yes."

"And, Truls?"

"Yes?"

"Don't mention it to Mikael, please."

Truls coughed. "No?"

"No. See you tomorrow at eight o'clock, then."

He stared at the phone after she'd hung up. Had that really happened or was it just an echo of the daydreams he had cooked up when he was sixteen, seventeen? Truls felt a happiness so intense that his chest felt like it was going to burst. And then panic hit. It was going to be a disaster. One way or another, it was obviously going to be a disaster.


It was all a disaster.

Obviously, it couldn't have lasted, it was only a matter of time before he was chucked out of paradise.

"Beer," he said, looking up at the young freckled girl who was standing at his table.

She wasn't wearing any makeup, her hair was pulled up in a simple ponytail, and she'd rolled up the sleeves of her white blouse like she was ready for a fight. She wrote on her pad, as if she were expecting a longer order, which made Harry think she was new, seeing as they were at Schrøder's, where nine out of ten orders stopped there. She'd hate the job for the first few weeks. The coarse jokes from the male customers, the ill-concealed jealousy from the most alcoholic of the women. Poor tips, no music to sway her hips to as she moved round the bar, no nice guys to be seen by, just argumentative old drunks to chuck out at closing time. She'd wonder if it was worth the boost it gave her student loan, which meant she could afford to live in a shared student house in such a relatively central location. But Harry knew that if she got through the first month without giving up and handing in her notice, things would gradually change. She'd start to laugh at the senseless humour in the comments, learn to give as good as she got in the same tacky way. When the women realised she wasn't threatening their territory they'd start to confide in her. And she'd get tips. Not much, but they'd be genuine tips, as well as gentle encouragement and the occasional declaration of love. And they'd give her a name. Something that might be uncomfortably close to the bone, but it would still be meant affectionately, something that ennobled you among this ignoble company. Short-Kari, Lenin, Backscreen, She-Bear. In her case it would probably be something to do with her freckles and red hair. And as people moved in and out of the collective, and presumptive boyfriends came and went, little by little it would become her family. A kind, generous, irritating, lost family.

The girl looked up from her pad. "Is that all?"

"Yes," Harry smiled.

She hurried to the bar as if someone was timing her. And who knows, maybe Rita was standing behind the bar doing just that.

Anders Wyller had texted to say that he was waiting for Harry at Tattoos & Piercings on Storgata. Harry started to write a reply, saying that Anders would have to deal with it on his own, when he suddenly heard someone sit down in front of him.

"Hello, Rita," he said without looking up.

"Hello, Harry. Bad day?"

"Yes." He tapped in the old-fashioned smiley: colon, right-hand bracket.

"And now you're here to make it even worse?"

Harry didn't answer.

"Know what I think, Harry?"

"What do you think, Rita?" His finger tried to find the Send button.

"I don't think this is a crack in the ice."

"I've just ordered a beer from Freckly-Fia."

"Who we're still calling Marte. And I've cancelled that beer. The devil on your right shoulder might want a drink, Harry, but the angel on your left steered you to a place where they don't serve spirits, but where there is a Rita who you know will serve you coffee instead of beer, have a chat with you, then send you home to Rakel."

"She's not at home, Rita."

"Aha, so that's why. Harry Hole has managed to fuck up again. You men always seem to find a way."

"Rakel's sick. And I need a beer before I call Oleg." Harry looked down at his phone. Looked again for the Send button as he felt Rita's stubby warm hand settle on his.

"Things usually turn out OK in the end, Harry."

He stared at her. "Of course they don't. Unless you actually know someone who made it out alive?"

She laughed. "*In the end* is somewhere between what's dragging you down today, and the day when nothing can drag us down any more, Harry."

Harry looked at his phone again. Then he tapped in Oleg's name instead and pressed the Call button.

Rita stood up and left him alone.

Oleg answered after the first ring. "It's good that you called! We're in a seminar, discussing paragraph 20 of the Police Act. You have to interpret it to mean that if the situation demands it, every police officer is subordinate to one of a higher rank and must obey orders from that higher rank even if they don't work in the same department, or even at the police station, don't you? Paragraph 20 says that the ranking officer decides if the situation is precarious and requires that. Come on, tell me I'm right! I've just bet these two idiots here a drink . . ." Harry could hear laughter in the background.

Harry closed his eyes. Of course there was something to hope for, something to look forward to: the time that comes after what's dragging you down today. The day when nothing can drag you down any more.

"Bad news, Oleg. Your mum's in Ullevål."


"I'll have the fish," Mona said to the waiter. "Skip the potatoes, sauce and vegetables."

"Then there's only the fish left," the waiter said.

"Precisely," Mona said, handing him the menu. She looked around the lunchtime customers at the new but already popular restaurant where they had got hold of the last table for two.

"Just fish?" Nora said, after ordering the Caesar salad with no dressing, but Mona already knew her friend would capitulate and order dessert to go with coffee.

"Deffing," Mona said.

"Deffing?"

"Getting rid of subcutaneous fat so that the muscles stand out better. It's the Norwegian Championships in three weeks."

"Bodybuilding? You're really going to take part?"

Mona laughed. "With these hips, you mean? I'm hoping my legs and upper body will get me enough points. And my winning personality, obviously."

"You seem nervous."

"Of course."

"That's three weeks away, and you *never* get nervous. What is it? Something to do with the vampirist murders? Thanks for the advice, by the way—Smith was great. And Bratt came up with the goods too, in her own way. Have you seen Isabelle Skøyen, that former Councillor for Social Affairs? She called us to ask if *The Sunday Magazine* would be interested in having Mikael Bellman on as a guest."

"So he could answer criticism of the fact that Valentin Gjertsen was never caught? Yes, she's called us about that too. Quite an intense woman, to put it mildly!"

"Are you running it? Christ, anything even vaguely related to the vampirist gets published."

"*I* wouldn't have taken it. But my colleagues aren't quite so fussy." Mona tapped on her iPad and passed it to Nora, who read out loud from *VG*'s online edition:

"'Former Councillor for Social Affairs, Isabelle Skøyen, rejects criticism of the Oslo Police and says that the Chief of Police is firmly in charge: *Mikael Bellman and his police officers have already identified the vampirist murderer, and are now deploying all their resources to find him. Among other things, the Chief of Police has brought in renowned murder detective Harry Hole, who was more than willing to help his former senior officer, and is looking forward to slapping a pair of handcuffs on this wretched pervert.*'" Nora passed the iPad back. "That's pretty tawdry. So what do you think of Hole? Would you kick him out of bed?"

"Definitely. Wouldn't you?"

"Don't know." Nora stared into space. "Not kick. Maybe just a little push. Sort of please-leave-and-don't-touch-me-there-and-not-there-and-definitely-not-there." She giggled.

"Bloody hell," Mona said, shaking her head. "It's people like you who are driving up the figures for misunderstanding-rapes."

"Misunderstanding-rapes? Is that a thing? And what does it actually mean?"

"You tell me. No one's ever misunderstood me."

"Which reminds me that I've finally worked out why you use Old Spice."

"No, you haven't," Mona said with a sigh.

"Yes, I have! As protection against rape. That's it, isn't it? After-shave that smells of testosterone. It chases them off as effectively as pepper spray. But has it occurred to you that it's chasing all the other men away as well, Mona?"

"I give up," Mona groaned.

"Yes, give up! Tell me!"

"It's because of my father."

"What?"

"He used Old Spice."

"Of course. Because you used to be *so* close. You miss him, poor—"

"I use it as a constant reminder of the most important thing he taught me."

Nora blinked. "Shaving?"

Mona laughed and picked up her glass. "Never giving up. *Never.*"

Nora tilted her head and gave her friend a serious look. "You *are* nervous, Mona. What is it? And why wouldn't you have taken that Skøyen piece? I mean, you *own* the vampirist murders."

"Because I've got bigger fish to fry." Mona moved her hands from the table as the waiter appeared again.

"I certainly hope so," Nora said, looking at the pathetic little fillet the waiter put down in front of her friend.

Mona prodded it with her fork. "And I'm nervous because I'm probably being watched."

"What do you mean?"

"I can't tell you, Nora. Or anyone else. Because that's the agreement, and for all I know we might be being bugged now."

"Bugged? You're kidding! And there was me saying that Harry Hole could—" Nora put her hand over her mouth.

Mona smiled. "That's unlikely to be used against you. The thing is, I'm looking at what might be the scoop of the century in crime reporting. Ever, in fact."

"You've got to tell me!"

Mona shook her head firmly. "What I *can* tell you is that I've got a pistol." She patted her handbag.

"Now you're scaring me, Mona! And what if they hear that you've got a pistol?"

"I want them to hear that. Then they'll know they can't mess with me."

Nora groaned in resignation. "But why do you have to do it alone, if it's dangerous?"

"Because that's when it becomes newspaper legend, my dear

Nora." Mona gave a big grin and raised her glass. "If this goes the way it should, I'll pay for lunch next time. And championship or no championship, we'll have champagne."

"Sorry I'm late," Harry said, closing the door to Tattoos & Piercings behind him.

"We're taking a look at what's on offer," Anders Wyller smiled. He was standing behind a table, leafing through a catalogue with a bow-legged man in a Vålerenga Football Club cap, a black Hüsker Dü T-shirt and a beard that Harry was pretty sure had been there before the always synchronised hipsters stopped shaving.

"Don't let me disturb you," Harry said, stopping by the door.

"As I was saying," the beard said, pointing at the catalogue, "those are only for decoration, you can't put them in your mouth. And the teeth aren't sharp either, apart from the canines."

"What about those?"

Harry looked round. There was no one else in the shop, and there would hardly have been room for anyone. Every square metre, not to mention cubic metre, had been used. The tattoo bench in the middle of the floor, T-shirts hanging from the ceiling. Racks of piercing jewellery and stands holding larger ornaments, skulls and chrome-covered metal models of comic-book characters. Any available wall space was covered with drawings and photographs of tattoos. In one of the photographs he recognised a Russian prison tattoo, a Makarov pistol, which told those in the know that its bearer had killed a police officer. And the indistinct lines could mean that it had been made the old way, using a guitar string fixed to a razor blade, the melted sole of a shoe and urine.

"Are these all your tattoos?" Harry wondered.

"No, none of them," the man replied. "They're from all over the place. Cool, aren't they?"

"We're nearly done," Anders said.

"Take all the time you n—" Harry stopped abruptly.

"Sorry I wasn't able to help," the beard said to Wyller. "What you describe sounds more like the sort of the thing you'd find in a shop for sex fetishists."

"Thanks, we've already looked into that."

"Right. Well, just say if there's anything else."

"There is."

They both turned to the tall policeman who was pointing at a picture towards the top of the wall. "Where did you get hold of that?"

The other two went over to join him.

"Ila Prison," the beard said. "It's one of the tattoos left by Rico Herrem, an inmate who was also a tattooist. He died in Pattaya in Thailand soon after he got out two or three years ago. Anthrax."

"Have you ever given anyone that tattoo?" Harry asked, feeling the screaming mouth in the demonic face draw his eyes to it.

"Never. No one's asked for it either. It's not exactly the sort of thing anyone would want to go around with."

"No one?"

"Not that I've seen. But now you mention it, there was a guy who worked here for a while who said he'd seen that tattoo. *Cin*, he called it. I only know that because *cin* and *seytan* are the only Turkish words I can still remember. *Cin* means demon."

"Did he say where he'd seen it?"

"No, and he moved back to Turkey. But if it's important I've probably got his phone number."

Harry and Wyller waited until the man returned from the back room with a handwritten note.

"I should warn you, he hardly speaks any English."

"How . . . ?"

"Sign language, my made-up Turkish and his kebab Norwegian. Which he's probably forgotten. I'd recommend using a translator."

"Thanks again," Harry said. "And I'm afraid we're going to have to take that drawing with us." He looked around for a chair to climb up on, only to see that Wyller had already put one in front of him.

Harry studied his smiling young colleague before climbing onto the chair.

"What do we do now?" Wyller asked when they were standing outside on Storgata and a tram rumbled past.

Harry put the drawing in the inside pocket of his jacket and looked up at the blue cross on the wall above them.

"Now we go to a bar."

He walked along the hospital corridor. Holding the bouquet of flowers up in front of him so that it covered part of his face. None of the people passing by, visitors or the ones in white, paid him any attention. His pulse was at its resting rate. When he was thirteen years old he fell off a ladder when he was trying to look at the neighbour's wife, hit his head on the cement terrace and lost consciousness. When he came round his mother had her ear to his chest and he smelt her scent, a scent of lavender. She said she thought he was dead because she couldn't hear his heart or find his pulse. It was hard to work out if that was relief or disappointment in her voice. But she had taken him to a young doctor, who only managed to find his pulse after a lot of effort, and said it was unusually low. That concussion often caused an increased heart rate. He was admitted and spent a week lying in a white bed, dreaming dazzlingly white dreams, like over-exposed photographs, the way life after death is depicted in films. Angel-white. Nothing in a hospital prepares you for all the blackness that awaits.

The blackness that awaited the woman lying in the room whose number he had found out.

The blackness that awaited the policeman with that look in his eyes when he found out what had happened.

The blackness that awaits us all.


Harry looked at the bottles on the shelves in front of the mirror, and the way the golden liquid inside them glowed warmly in the reflected light. Rakel was asleep. She was asleep now. Forty-five percent. Her chance of survival and the alcohol content of those bottles were roughly the same. Sleep. He could be there with her. He looked away. At Mehmet's mouth instead, the lips that were forming incomprehensible words. Harry had read somewhere that Turkish grammar was regarded as the third most difficult in the world. The phone he was holding belonged to Harry.

"*Sağ olun*," Mehmet said, and handed the phone back to Harry. "He says he saw the *cin* face on the chest of a man at a Turkish bath-house in Sagene, the Cagaloglu Hamam. He says he saw him there a few times, and that the last time was probably less than a year ago, just before he went back to Turkey. He says the man usually wore his bathrobe, even in the sauna. The only time he saw him without it was inside the *hararet*."

"*Hara*-what?"

"The steam room. The door opened, clearing the steam for a second or two, and that's when he caught a glimpse of him. He said you don't forget a tattoo like that, that it was like seeing *seytan* himself trying to break free."

"And you asked him about any distinguishing features?"

"Yes. He didn't notice the scars under his chin that you mentioned, or anything else come to that."

Harry nodded thoughtfully while Mehmet went to pour them more coffee.

"Stake out the bathhouse?" Wyller asked from the bar stool next to Harry's.

Harry shook his head. "We have no idea when or if he's going to show up, and if he does, we don't even know what Valentin looks like these days."

Mehmet came back and put their cups down on the counter in front of them.

"Thanks for your help, Mehmet," Harry said. "It would probably have taken us at least a day to get hold of an authorised Turkish interpreter."

Mehmet shrugged. "I feel I ought to help. After all, this was where Elise was before she got murdered."

"Hm." Harry looked down into his cup. "Anders?"

"Yes?" Anders Wyller seemed pleased, possibly because this was the first time he'd heard Harry use his first name.

"Can you go and get the car, and drive up to the door?"

"Yes, but it's only—"

"And I'll meet you outside."

Once Wyller had left Harry took a sip of coffee. "This is none of my business, but are you in trouble, Mehmet?"

"Trouble?"

"You have no criminal record, I checked. But the guy who was here and then vanished the moment he saw us arrive does. And even if he didn't stop to say hello, Danial Banks and I are old acquaintances. Has he got his claws into you?"

"What do you mean?"

"I mean that you've just opened a bar, and your tax history shows that you aren't sitting on a fortune. And Banks specialises in lending money to people like you."

"People like me?"

"People the banks won't touch. What he does is illegal, you know that? Usury, paragraph 295 of the Penal Code. You could report it, then you'd be free of him. Let me help you."

Mehmet looked at the blue-eyed policeman. Then he nodded. "You're right, Harry . . ."

"Good."

". . . it's none of your business. Sounds like your colleague's waiting for you."

He shut the door of the hospital room behind him. The blinds were down, letting only a little light filter into the room. He put the bouquet of flowers on the nightstand at the top end of the bed. He looked down at the sleeping woman. She seemed so alone, lying there like that. He closed the curtains. Sat down on the chair beside the bed, took a syringe from his jacket pocket and pulled the cap off the needle. Took hold of her arm. Gazed at the skin. Real skin. He loved real skin. He felt like kissing it, but knew he had to restrain himself. The plan. Stick to the plan. Then he stuck the point of the needle into the woman's arm. Felt it slip through the skin without any resistance.

"There, now," he whispered. "Now I'm going to take you from him. You're mine now. All mine."

He pushed the plunger and watched as the dark contents were forced out, injected into the woman. Filling her with blackness. And sleep.

"Police HQ?" Wyller said.

Harry looked at his watch. Two o'clock. He had arranged to meet Oleg at the hospital in an hour.

"Ullevål Hospital," he said.

"Are you unwell?"

"No."

Wyller waited, then when nothing more was forthcoming, he put the car into first gear and pulled away.

Harry looked out through the window while he wondered why he hadn't told anyone. He'd have to tell Katrine, for practical reasons. Anyone apart from her? No. Why should he?

"I downloaded Father John Misty yesterday," Wyller said.

"What for?"

"Because you recommended it."

"Did I? Must be good, then."

Nothing more was said until they were stuck in traffic, slowly creeping up Ullevålsveien past Sankt Olav Cathedral and Nordal Bruns gate.

"Stop at that bus stop," Harry said. "I can see someone I know."

Wyller braked and pulled in to the right, next to a shelter where some teenagers were waiting to catch the bus after school. Oslo Cathedral School, yes, that was the one she went to. She was standing slightly apart from the noisy crowd, with her hair hanging in front of her face. Without having any real idea what he was going to say, Harry lowered the window.

"Aurora!"

A twitch ran through the girl's long-legged frame, and she took off like a nervous antelope.

"Do you always have that effect on young girls?" Wyller asked, as Harry told him to drive on.

She's running in the opposite direction to the car, Harry thought, watching her in the wing mirror. She didn't even have to think. Because she'd thought this through in advance: that if you want to run from someone in a car, you run away from the direction the car is facing. But what that meant, he didn't know. Some sort of teenage angst, perhaps. Or a phase, as Ståle had called it.

The traffic grew lighter further along Ullevålsveien.

"I'll wait in the car," Anders said, after he pulled up in front of the entrance to Block 3 of the hospital.

"It might take a while," Harry said. "You wouldn't rather sit in the waiting room?"

He smiled and shook his head. "Bad memories of hospitals."

"Mm. Your mother?"

"How did you know that?"

Harry shrugged. "Had to be someone you were very close to. I lost my own mother in a hospital when I was a boy."

"Was that the doctors' fault as well?"

"No, she couldn't be saved. So I shouldered the guilt myself."

Wyller nodded wryly. "With my mother it was a self-appointed god in a white coat. That's why I won't set foot in there."

On his way in Harry noticed a man leaving, holding a bunch of flowers in front of his face, noticed because you expect to see people with flowers going into a hospital, not coming out. Oleg was sitting in the waiting area. They embraced as patients and visitors around them continued their subdued conversations and disengaged browsing through old magazines. Oleg was only a centimetre or so shorter than Harry. And Harry occasionally forgot that the lad had finally stopped growing now, and that he could have actually cashed in on their bet.

"Have they said anything else?" Oleg said. "About what it is, and whether it's dangerous?"

"No," Harry said. "But like I said, you shouldn't worry too much, they know what they're doing. She's been put in an *induced* coma, in a controlled way. OK?"

Oleg opened his mouth. Closed it again and nodded. And Harry saw it. That Oleg realised Harry was protecting him from the truth. And that he let him do it.

A nurse came over and told them they could go in and see her.

Harry went in first.

The blinds were down.

He went over to the bed. Looked down at the pale face. She looked like she was far away.

Far too far away.

"Is . . . is she breathing?"

Oleg. He was standing right behind Harry, the way he used to when he was little and they had to walk past one of Holmenkollen's many large dogs.

"Yes," Harry said, nodding towards the flashing machines.

They sat down on either side of the bed. And glanced at the twitching green line on the screen when they didn't think the other would notice.


Katrine looked out across the forest of hands.

The press conference had lasted barely fifteen minutes, and the impatience in the Parole Hall was already tangible. She wondered what had got them most worked up. The fact that there was nothing new on the police hunt for Valentin Gjertsen. Or that there was nothing new on Valentin Gjertsen's hunt for fresh victims. It had been forty-six hours since the last attack.

"I'm afraid it's going to be the same answers to the same questions," she said. "So if there aren't any new—"

"What's your reaction to the fact that you're now working on three murders rather than two?"

The question had been called out by a journalist at the back of the room.

Katrine saw unease spread through the room like ripples on water. She glanced at Bjørn Holm who was sitting in the front row, but he just shrugged in response. She leaned into the microphones.

"It's possible that there is information that hasn't reached me yet, so I'll have to get back to you about that."

Another voice: "The hospital has just released a statement. Penelope Rasch is dead."

Katrine hoped her face didn't betray the confusion she felt. Penelope Rasch's survival hadn't been in any doubt.

"We'll stop there and reconvene when we know more." Katrine gathered her papers and hurried away from the podium and out through the side door. "When *we* know more than *you*," she muttered to herself, and swore.

She marched down the corridor. What the hell had happened? Had something gone wrong with her treatment? She hoped so. Hoped there was a medical explanation, unforeseen complications, a sudden attack of something, even a mistake on the hospital's part. No, it wasn't possible, they'd placed Penelope in a secret room that only those closest to her knew the number of.

Bjørn came running up behind her. "I've just spoken to Ullevål. They say it was an unfamiliar poison, but which they wouldn't have been able to do anything about anyway."

"Poison? From the bite, or did it happen in the hospital?"

"Unclear—they say they'll know more tomorrow."

Bloody chaos. Katrine hated chaos. And where was Harry? Fuck, fuck.

"Take care not to stab those heels through the floor," Bjørn said quietly.


Harry had told Oleg that the doctors didn't know. About what was going to happen. About practical things that needed to be sorted out, even if there weren't many of those. Apart from that, silence hung heavy between them.

Harry looked at the time. Seven o'clock.

"You should go home," he said. "Grab something to eat and get some sleep. You've got college tomorrow."

"Only if I know you're going to be here," Oleg said. "We can't let her be alone."

"I'm going to be here until I get thrown out, which will be soon."

"But you'll stay until then? You're not going to go to work?"

"Work?"

"Yes. You're staying here now, you're not going on with . . . that case?"

"Of course not."

"I know how you get when you're working on a murder investigation."

"Do you?"

"I remember some of it. And Mum's told me."

Harry sighed. "I'm staying here now. I promise. The world will go on without me, but . . ." He fell silent, leaving the rest of the sentence hanging in the air between them: . . . *not without her.*

He took a deep breath.

"How are you feeling?"

Oleg shrugged. "I'm scared. And it hurts."

"I know. Go now, and come back tomorrow after college. I'll be here first thing in the morning."

"Harry?"

"Yes?"

"Is it going to be better tomorrow?"

Harry looked at him. The brown-eyed, black-haired boy didn't have one drop of Harry's blood in him, but it was still like looking in a mirror. "What do you think?"

Oleg shook his head, and Harry could see he was fighting back tears.

"Right," Harry said. "I sat here the way you are now with my mother when she was ill. Hour after hour, day in, day out. I was only a little boy, and it ate me up from inside."

Oleg wiped his eyes with the back of his hand and sniffed. "Do you wish you hadn't done it?"

Harry shook his head. "That's the weird thing. We couldn't talk much, she was too ill. She just lay there with a weak smile, and faded away a little bit at a time, like the colour from a photograph left out in the sun. It's simultaneously the worst and best memory from my childhood. Can you understand that?"

Oleg nodded slowly. "I think so."

They hugged each other goodbye.

"Dad . . ." Oleg whispered, and Harry felt a warm tear against his neck.

But he himself couldn't cry. Didn't want to cry. Forty-five percent, forty-five *wonderful* percentage points.

"I'm here, my boy," Harry said. In a steady voice. With a numb heart. He felt strong. He could manage this.

# 19

# Monday evening

Mona Daa had put her trainers on, but her footsteps still echoed between the containers. She had parked her little electric car by the gate and walked straight into the dark, empty container terminal, which was really a cemetery for defunct harbour equipment. The rows of containers were tombstones for dead and forgotten shipments, to recipients who had gone bankrupt or wouldn't acknowledge the consignment, from senders who no longer existed and couldn't accept returns. Now the goods were stuck in eternal transit here on Ormøya, in marked contrast to the redevelopment and gentrification of Bjørvika next to it. There, costly, luxurious buildings were rising up, one after the other, with the icy slopes of the Opera House as the jewel in the crown. Mona was convinced it would end up as a monument to the oil era, a Taj Mahal of social democracy.

Mona used the flashlight she had brought with her to find the way, with the help of the numbers and letters painted on the tarmac. She was wearing black leggings and a black tracksuit top. In one pocket she had pepper spray and a padlock, in the other the pistol, a 9mm Walther she had borrowed without permission from her father, who had served one year in the sanitation department of the military after his medical studies and never returned his gun.

And under the tracksuit top, beneath the transmitter belt, her heart was pounding faster and faster.

H23 was located between two rows of containers stacked three high.

And sure enough, there was a cage.

Its size suggested it had been used to transport something big. An elephant, maybe a giraffe or a hippo. The whole of one end of the cage could be swung open, but it was locked with a huge padlock that was brown with rust. In the middle of one of the long sides, though, was a small, unlocked door that Mona assumed was used by the people feeding the animals and cleaning the cage.

The hinges shrieked as she grabbed hold of the bars and pulled the door open. She looked around one last time. Presumably he was already here, hidden in the shadows or behind one of the containers, checking that she was alone, as agreed.

But there was no longer time for doubt and hesitation. She did the same thing she did when she was about to lift weights in competition, told herself the decision had been taken, that it was simple: the time for thinking was behind her, and action was all that remained. She got inside, took the padlock she had brought with her out of her pocket, and fastened it round the edge of the door and one of the bars. She locked it and put the key in her pocket.

The cage smelt of urine, but she couldn't tell if it was animal or human. She went and stood in the middle of the cage.

He could approach from right or left, towards one of the ends. She looked up. He could climb onto the stack of containers and talk to her from above. She switched on the recording function of her phone and put it down on the stinking iron floor. Then she pulled the left sleeve of her jacket up and saw that the time was 19:59. She did the same with the right sleeve. The pulse meter said 128.

"Hi, Katrine, it's me."

"Good. I've been trying to get hold of you—did you get my messages? Where are you?"

"At home."

"Penelope Rasch is dead."

"Complications. I saw it on *VG*'s website."

"And?"

"And I've had other things to think about."

"Really? Such as?"

"Rakel's in Ullevål."

"Shit. Is it serious?"

"Yes."

"Bloody hell, Harry. How bad?"

"Don't know, but I can't be part of the investigation any more. I'm going to be at the hospital from now on."

Pause.

"Katrine?"

"Yes? Yes, of course. I'm sorry, it's just a bit too much to take in all at once. Naturally, you have my full support and sympathy. But, bloody hell, Harry, have you got anyone there to talk to? Do you want me to—?"

"Thanks, Katrine, but you've got a man to catch. I'll disband my team, and you'll have to run with what you've got. Use Smith. His social skills are probably even worse than mine, but he's fearless and dares to think outside the box. And Anders Wyller is interesting. Give him a bit more responsibility and see what comes of it."

"I've been thinking of doing that. Call if you need anything, anything at all."

"Yep."

They ended the call and Harry stood up. Went over to the coffee machine, heard his own feet drag on the floor. He never used to drag his feet, never. He stood with the jug in his hand and looked around the empty kitchen. He'd forgotten where he'd left his mug. He put the jug down again, sat at the kitchen table and rang Mikael Bellman's number. He reached his voicemail. Which was just as well, he didn't have much to say.

"This is Hole. My wife's ill, so I'm leaving. This decision is final."

He remained seated and looked out through the window at the lights of the city.

Thought about that one-ton water buffalo standing there with a solitary lion hanging from its throat. The water buffalo was bleeding from its wounds, but it had a lot of blood, and if it could just shake the lion off, it could easily trample it underfoot or spear it on its horns. But time was running out, its windpipe was being squeezed and it needed air. And there were more lions on the way, the pride had caught the scent of blood.

Harry saw the lights, but thought they had never seemed so far away.

The engagement ring. Valentin had given her a ring, and had come back. Just like the Fiancé. Damn. He pushed it away. Time to switch his head off now. Turn the lights off, lock up and go home.

. . .

It was 20:14 when Mona heard a noise. It came from the darkness, which had grown more dense while she had been sitting inside the cage. She saw a movement. Something was approaching. She had been through the questions she had prepared and wondered what she was most frightened of: him coming, or not coming. But she was no longer in any doubt. She felt her pulse throbbing in her neck and clutched the pistol in her jacket pocket. She had practised firing it in her parents' basement, and from a distance of six metres she had hit what she'd been aiming at, a half-rotten raincoat hanging from a hook on the brick wall.

It came out of the darkness and into the light from a freight ship that was moored by the cement silos a few hundred metres away.

It was a dog.

It padded over to the cage and stared at her.

It looked like a stray. It didn't have a collar, anyway, and was so skinny and scabby that it was hard to imagine it belonging anywhere but here. It was the sort of dog little Mona with her cat allergy had always hoped would follow her home one day, and never leave her.

Mona met the dog's short-sighted stare, and imagined that she could see what it was thinking. *A human being in a cage.* And heard it laugh inside.

After looking at her for a while, the dog positioned itself parallel to the cage, lifted one back leg, and a stream of liquid hit the bars and floor inside.

Then it padded away and disappeared back into the darkness.

Without pricking its ears or sniffing the air.

And Mona realised.

There was no one coming.

She looked at the pulse meter. 119. And falling.

He wasn't here. So where was he?


Harry could see something in the darkness.

In the middle of the drive, beyond the light from the windows and by the steps, he could make out the shape of someone standing with their arms by their sides, motionless, as they stared at the kitchen window and Harry.

Harry lowered his head and looked down at his mug of coffee as if he hadn't seen the figure outside. His pistol was upstairs.

Should he run and get it?

On the other hand, if it really was the hunted man who was approaching the hunter, he didn't want to frighten him off.

Harry stood up, stretched, aware that he was easily visible in the well-lit kitchen. He went into the living room, which also had windows facing the driveway, picked up a book, before taking two rapid strides towards the front door, grabbing the garden shears Rakel had left next to her boots, yanking the door open and running down the steps.

The figure still didn't move.

Harry stopped.

Peered.

"Aurora?"


Harry rummaged through the kitchen cupboard. "Cardamom, cinnamon, camomile. Rakel has a lot of teas starting with 'c,' but seeing as I'm a coffee drinker I don't really know what to recommend."

"Cinnamon would be fine," Aurora said.

"Here," Harry said, handing her a box.

She took out a tea bag and Harry watched her as she dunked it in the mug of steaming water.

"You ran off from Police HQ the other day," he said.

"Yes," she said simply, pressing the tea bag with a teaspoon.

"And from the bus stop earlier today."

She didn't answer, her hair had fallen in front of her face.

He sat down, took a sip of coffee. Gave her the time she needed, didn't fill the silence with words that demanded answers.

"I didn't see it was you," she said eventually. "Well, I did see, but by then I was already scared, and it often takes a bit of time for your brain to tell your body that everything's fine. And in the meantime my body had already managed to run away."

"Mm. Is there someone you're afraid of?"

She nodded. "It's Dad."

Harry steeled himself, he didn't want to go on, didn't want to go there. But he had to.

"What's your dad done?"

Tears welled up in her eyes. "He raped me and said I must never tell anyone. Because then he would die . . ."

The nausea came so suddenly that Harry lost his breath for a moment, and bile burned in his throat when he swallowed. "Your dad said he would die?"

"No!" Her sudden, angry exclamation threw a short, hard echo off the walls of the kitchen.

"The man who raped me said he'd kill Dad if I ever told a soul. He said he'd nearly killed Dad once before, and that nothing would stop him next time."

Harry blinked. Tried to absorb the grim mixture of relief and shock. "You were raped?" he said, with feigned calmness.

She nodded, sniffed and wiped her eyes. "In the girls' toilet when we were playing in a handball tournament. It was the day you and Rakel got married. He did it, and then he left."

Harry felt like he was falling.

"Have you got somewhere I could get rid of this?" She raised a dripping, dangling tea bag above the cup.

Harry just held his hand out.

Aurora looked at him uncertainly before letting go of the tea bag. Harry clenched his fist, felt the water burn his skin and run out between his fingers. "Did he hurt you, besides . . . ?"

She shook her head. "He held me so tight that I got bruises. I told Mum they were from the match."

"You mean you've kept this to yourself right up to now? For three years?"

She nodded.

Harry felt that he was on the verge of getting up, going round the table and wrapping his arms round her. But a second thought had time to kick in, picking up on what Smith had said about closeness and intimacy.

"So why have you come to tell me about it now?"

"Because he's killing other people. I saw the drawing in the paper. It's him, it's the man with the funny eyes. You've got to help me, Uncle Harry. You've got to help me protect Dad."

He nodded, breathing with his mouth open.

Aurora tilted her head with a worried look on her face. "Uncle Harry?"

"Yes?"

"Are you crying?"

Harry could taste the salt of the first tear at the corner of his mouth. Damn.

"Sorry," he said in a thick voice. "How's the tea?"

Then Harry looked up and met her gaze. It had changed completely. As if something had opened it up. As if for the first time in a very long while she was looking *out* through those beautiful eyes of hers, not in, as she had done the last few times they had met.

Aurora stood up, pushed the mug away, and walked round the table. Leaned over Harry and wrapped her arms around him. "It's going to be OK," she said. "It's going to be OK."

Marte Ruud went over to the customer who had just walked in through the door of the otherwise empty Schrøder's Restaurant.

"Sorry, but we stopped serving beer half an hour ago, and we're closing in ten minutes."

"Give me a coffee," he said, and smiled. "I'll drink it quickly."

She went back to the kitchen. The cook had gone home over an hour ago, as had Rita. They usually only had one member of staff working this late on Monday evenings, and even though it was quiet, she was still a bit nervous because this was her first evening on her own. Rita would be coming back just after closing time to help with the till.

It didn't take more than a few seconds to boil enough water for a single cup in the kettle. She added freeze-dried coffee. Went back out and put the cup down in front of the man.

"Can I ask you something?" he said, looking at the steaming cup. "Seeing as it's just the two of us here."

"Yes," Marte said, even though she meant no. She just wanted him to drink the coffee and go, leaving her to lock the door and wait for Rita, so she could get home. Her first lecture started at quarter past eight tomorrow morning.

"Isn't this where that famous detective drinks? Harry Hole?"

Marte nodded. To be honest she hadn't actually heard of him before he showed up, a tall man with an ugly scar on his face. Then Rita had told her all about Harry Hole, in great detail.

"Where does he usually sit?"

"They say he sits over there," Marte said, pointing at the corner table by the window. "But he doesn't come as often as he used to."

"No, if he's going to catch that 'wretched pervert,' as he puts it, he probably hasn't got time to sit here. But this is still *his* place. If you understand me?"

Marte smiled and nodded, even though she wasn't sure that she did understand.

"What's your name?"

Marte hesitated, unsure if she liked the direction the conversation was taking. "We're closing in six minutes, so if you're going to have time to drink your coffee, maybe you . . ."

"Do you know why you have freckles, Marte?"

She froze. How did he know her name?

"You see, when you were little and had no freckles, you woke up one night. You'd been having a *kabuslar*, a nightmare. You were still frightened when you ran into your mother's bedroom so that she could tell you that monsters and ghosts didn't exist. But in her bedroom a naked blue-black man was sitting hunched up on your mother's chest. Long, pointed ears, blood running from the sides of his mouth. And as you just stood there staring, he puffed up his cheeks, and before you could get away he blew out all the blood he had in his mouth, covering your face and chest with tiny drops. And that blood, Marte, it never went away, no matter how hard you washed and scrubbed." The man blew on his coffee. "So that explains how you got freckles, but the question is, *why?* And the answer to that is as easy as it is unsatisfactory, Marte. Because you were in the wrong place at the wrong time. The world simply isn't very fair." He raised the cup to his lips, opened his mouth wide, and poured the still steaming black liquid into his mouth. She gasped in horror, short of breath, scared that something might be about to happen, without knowing what. And she didn't have time to see the spray from his mouth before the hot coffee hit her in the face.

Blinded, she turned round and slipped on the liquid, one knee hit the floor, but she got to her feet and rushed for the door, pushing a chair over to slow him down as she tried to blink the coffee away. She grabbed the door handle and tugged it. Locked. He'd put the latch on. She heard creaking footsteps behind her as she put her finger and thumb on the lock, but didn't have time to do more before she felt him grab hold of her belt and jerk her backwards. Marte tried to scream, but all she could get out were small whimpering sounds. Footsteps again. He was standing in front of her. She didn't want to look up, didn't want to look at him. She had never had a nightmare about any blue-black man when she was little, only one about a man with a dog's head. And she knew that if she looked up now, that was what she would see. So she kept her gaze lowered, staring at the pointed cowboy boots instead.

# 20

# Monday night, Tuesday morning

"Yes?"

"Harry?"

"Yes."

"I wasn't sure if this was your number. It's Rita. From Schrøder's. I know it's late, and I'm sorry to wake you."

"I wasn't asleep, Rita."

"I called the police, but they . . . well, they've been here, and now they've gone again."

"Try to calm down, Rita. What's happened?"

"It's Marte, the new girl you met the last time you were here."

Harry remembered her rolled-up shirtsleeves and slightly nervous eagerness. "Yes?"

"She's gone. I got here just before midnight to help her with the till, but there was no one here. The door wasn't locked, though. Marte's reliable, and we had an arrangement. She wouldn't just leave without locking up. She's not answering her phone and her boyfriend says she hasn't come home. The police checked the hospital, but nothing. And then the policewoman said it happens all the time, people disappearing in odd ways, then showing up again a few hours later with a perfectly reasonable explanation. She said I should call them if Marte hasn't shown up again within twelve hours."

"What they said is actually true, Rita, they're just following routine."

"Yes, but . . . hello?"

"I'm here, Rita."

"When I was cleaning up, getting ready to close I found that someone had written something on one of the tablecloths. It looks like lipstick, and it's exactly the shade of red that Marte uses."

"OK. So what does it say?"

"Nothing."

"Nothing?"

"No. It's just a single letter. A 'V.' And it's in your place."

Three o'clock in the morning.

A roar forced its way out between Harry's lips, echoing off bare cellar walls. Harry stared at the iron bar that was threatening to fall and crush him as his trembling arms held it up. Then, with one final effort, he thrust the weights away from him, and they clanked against each other as he let the bar rest in its cradle. He lay on the bench gasping for breath.

He closed his eyes. He had promised Oleg that he would be with Rakel. But he had to get back out there. Had to catch him. For Marte. For Aurora.

No.

It was too late. Too late for Aurora. Too late for Marte. So he had to do it for those who hadn't yet become victims, who could still be saved from Valentin.

Because it was for them, wasn't it?

Harry took hold of the bar, felt the metal against the calluses on his hands.

*Somewhere you can be useful.*

His grandfather had said that, that all you need is to be useful. When his grandmother had been giving birth to Harry's father, she had lost so much blood that the midwife had called the doctor. Grandfather, who had been told there was nothing he could do to help, couldn't bear to listen to Grandma's screams, so he walked out, harnessed the horse to the plough and started to plough one of the fields. He drove the horse on with his whip and cries loud enough to drown out those from the house, then started pushing the plough himself when his faithful old horse began to stumble in the harness. When the screaming had stopped and the doctor came out to tell him that both mother and child were going to survive, Grandfather fell to his knees, kissed the ground and thanked the God he didn't believe in.

That same night the horse collapsed in its stall and died.

Now Rakel was lying in bed. Silent. And he had to decide.

*Somewhere you can be useful.*

Harry lifted the bar from the cradle and lowered it to his chest. Took a deep breath. Tensed his muscles. And roared.

# Part II

# 21

# Tuesday morning

It was seven thirty. there was fine rain hanging in the air and Mehmet was about to cross the street when he noticed the man in front of Jealousy. He had made his hands into binoculars and was holding them against the window to see inside better. The first thing Mehmet thought was that Danial Banks was early asking for the next instalment, but as he got closer he realised that the man was taller, and blond. And it struck him that it must be one of the old, alcoholic customers who had come back, and hoped the bar still opened at seven o'clock in the morning.

But when the man turned to face the street again, sucking at the cigarette between his lips, he saw it was that policeman. Harry.

"Good morning," Mehmet said, getting his keys out. "Thirsty?"

"That too. But I've got an offer for you."

"What sort of offer?"

"The sort you can turn down."

"In that case I'm interested," Mehmet said, and let the policeman in. He followed, then locked the door. Switched the lights on from behind the counter.

"This is actually a good bar," Harry said, putting his elbows on the counter and breathing in deeply.

"Do you want to buy it?" Mehmet said drily, pouring water into a *cezve*, the special Turkish coffee pot.

"Yes," Harry said.

Mehmet laughed. "Make me an offer."

"Four hundred and thirty-five thousand."

Mehmet frowned. "Where did you get that number from?"

"From Danial Banks. I had a meeting with him this morning."

"This morning? But it's only . . ."

"I got up early. And so did he. That's to say, I had to wake him up and drag him out of bed."

Mehmet looked into the policeman's bloodshot eyes.

"Figuratively speaking," Harry said. "I know where he lives. I paid him a visit and made him an offer."

"What sort of offer?"

"The other sort. The sort you can't turn down."

"Meaning?"

"I bought the debt on the Jealousy Bar at face value in return for not setting Financial Crime on him for breaking paragraph 295 about usury."

"You're kidding?"

Harry shrugged. "It's possible that I'm exaggerating, it's possible that he could have turned it down. Because he was able to tell me that paragraph 295 was repealed a couple of years ago sadly. What's the world coming to when criminals keep up with changes to the law better than cops? Either way, the loan agreement with you didn't seem to be worth all the problems I promised to make for him else-where. So this document—" the detective put a handwritten sheet of paper on the bar—"confirms that Danial Banks has received his money, and that I, Harry Hole, am the proud owner of a debt of 435,000 kroner owed by Mehmet Kalak, with the Jealousy Bar, its contents and lease as collateral."

Mehmet read the few lines and shook his head. "Bloody hell. So you had almost half a million that you could give Banks there and then?"

"I worked as a debt collector in Hong Kong for a while. It was . . . well paid. So I built up a bit of capital. Banks received a cheque and a bank statement."

Mehmet laughed. "So you're going to be the one demanding extortionate repayments now, Harry?"

"Not if you agree to my offer."

"Which is?"

"That we turn the debt into working capital."

"You take over the bar?"

"I buy a share. You'd be my partner, and could buy me out when-ever you like."

"In return for what?"

"You go to a Turkish bathhouse while a friend of mine watches the bar."

"What?"

"I want you to sweat until you turn into a raisin at the Cagaloglu Hamam while you wait for Valentin Gjertsen to show up."

"Me? Why me?"

"Because Penelope Rasch died, and you and a fifteen-year-old girl are the only living people I'm aware of who know what Valentin Gjertsen looks like these days."

"I do . . . ?"

"You'll recognise him."

"What makes you think that?"

"I read the report. You said, quote: 'I didn't really look at him long enough or carefully enough to be able to describe him.'"

"Exactly."

"I had a colleague who could recognise every human face she had ever seen. She told me that the ability to differentiate and recognise a million faces is located in part of the brain called the fusiform gyrus, and that without that ability we would hardly have survived as a species. Can you describe the last customer who was in here yesterday?"

"Er . . . no."

"Yet you'd still recognise him in a fraction of a second if he walked in here now."

"Probably."

"That's what I'm counting on."

"You're staking 435,000 of your own money on that? What if I don't recognise him?"

Harry stuck his bottom lip out. "Then at least I'll own a bar."

At 7:45 Mona Daa shoved open the door to *VG*'s newsroom and rolled in. It had been a bad night. Even though she had gone straight to Gain from the container terminal, and exercised so hard that her entire body ached, she had hardly slept a wink. In the end she decided to raise it with the editor, without going into detail. Ask him if a source had the right to anonymity if they had completely deceived a journalist. In other words: could she go to the police with this now? Or would the smart response be to wait and see if he got in touch again? After all, there could be a good explanation for why he hadn't shown up.

"You look tired, Daa," the head of the newsroom said. "Party last night?"

"I wish," Mona said quietly, dropping her gym bag by her desk and switching her computer on.

"Of the more experimental variety, perhaps?"

"I wish," Mona repeated, more loudly. She looked up and saw a number of faces sticking up above computer screens around the open-plan office. Grinning, inquisitive faces.

"What?" she called out.

"Just stripping, or bestiality?" cried a deep voice that she didn't have time to identify before a couple of the girls burst out laughing uncontrollably.

"Check your email," the head of the newsroom said. "Some of us were copied in."

Mona turned cold. Felt a shiver of foreboding as she more hit than tapped her keyboard.

The sender was violentcrime@oslopol.no.

No text, just an image. Presumably taken with a light-sensitive camera, seeing as she hadn't noticed a flash. And probably a telephoto lens. In the foreground was the dog pissing on the cage, and there she was, in the middle of the cage, standing stiffly and staring like a wild animal. She'd been tricked. It wasn't the vampirist who had called her.


At 8:15 Smith, Wyller, Holm and Harry were gathered in the boiler room.

"We've got a disappearance that may be the work of the vampirist," Harry said. "Marte Ruud, twenty-four years old, disappeared from Schrøder's Restaurant last night, just before midnight. Katrine is briefing the investigative team at the moment."

"The crime-scene group are there," Bjørn Holm said. "Nothing so far. Apart from what you mentioned."

"Which is?" Wyller wondered.

"A 'V' written on a tablecloth with lipstick. The angle between the lines matches the one on Ewa Dolmen's door." He was interrupted by a steel guitar Harry recognised as Don Helms, playing the intro to Hank Williams's "Your Cheating Heart."

"Wow, we've got a signal," Bjørn Holm said, pulling his phone from his pocket. "Holm. What? I can't hear. Hang on."

Bjørn Holm vanished through the door out into the culvert.

"It looks like this kidnapping could be about me," Harry said. "That's my restaurant, my usual table."

"That's not good," Smith said, shaking his head. "He's lost his grip."

"Isn't it good that he's lost his grip?" Wyller asked. "Doesn't that mean he's going to be less careful?"

"That part might be good news," Smith said. "But now that he's experienced how it feels to have power and control, no one's going to be allowed to take that away from him. You're right, he's after you, Harry. And do you know why?"

"That article in *VG*," Wyller said.

"You called him a wretched pervert, who . . . what was it?"

"You were looking forward to slapping a pair of handcuffs on him," Wyller said.

"So you describe him as wretched and threaten to take his power and control away."

"Isabelle Skøyen called him that, not me, but it doesn't really matter now," Harry said, rubbing the back of his neck. "Do you think he's going to use the girl to get hold of me, Smith?"

Smith shook his head. "She's dead."

"How can you be so sure?"

"He doesn't want confrontation, he just wants to show you and everyone else that he's in control. That he can go to your place and take one of yours."

Harry stopped rubbing his neck. "One of *mine*?"

Smith didn't answer.

Bjørn Holm returned. "That was Ullevål. Just before Penelope Rasch died, a man came to reception and identified himself as someone she'd listed as a friend, a Roar Wiik, her former fiancé."

"The guy who gave her the engagement ring Valentin stole from her flat," Harry said.

"They contacted him to see if he'd noticed anything about her condition," Bjørn Holm said. "But Roar Wiik says he hasn't been to the hospital."

Silence spread round the boiler room.

"Not the fiancé . . ." Smith said. "So . . ."

The wheels of Harry's chair shrieked, but it was already empty and heading at speed towards the wall.

Harry himself was already at the door. "Wyller, with me!"

.   .   .

Harry ran.

The hospital corridor stretched out and seemed to grow, growing faster than he could run, like an expanding universe which light and even thought couldn't get through.

He only just managed to avoid running into a man who came out of a doorway clutching a drip stand with his hand.

*One of yours.*

Valentin had taken Aurora because she was Ståle Aune's daughter.

Marte Ruud because she worked at Harry's regular bar.

Penelope Rasch to show them that he could.

*One of yours.*

301.

Harry grabbed the pistol from his jacket pocket. A Glock 17 which had spent almost a year and a half lying untouched and locked away in a second-floor drawer. This morning he had taken it with him. Not because he imagined he would be using it, but because for the first time in four years he wasn't entirely sure that he *wouldn't* be using it.

He pushed the door open with his left hand as he pointed the pistol in front of him.

The room was empty. Had been emptied.

Rakel was gone. The bed was gone.

Harry gasped for air.

Went over to where the bed had been.

"Sorry, she's gone," a voice behind him said.

Harry spun round. Dr. Steffens was standing in the doorway with his hands in the pockets of his white coat. He raised an eyebrow when he caught sight of the pistol.

"Where is she?" Harry panted.

"I'll tell you if you put that away."

Harry lowered the pistol.

"Tests," Steffens said.

"Is she . . . is she OK?"

"Her condition is the same as before, stable but unstable. But she's going to survive the day, if that's what you're worrying about. Why the drama?"

"She needs to be watched."

"Right now she's being watched by five members of hospital staff."

"We'll be placing an armed police guard outside her door. Any objections?"

"No, but that isn't up to me. Are you worried the murderer will come here?"

"Yes."

"Because she's the wife of the man hunting him? We don't give out room numbers to anyone who isn't a relative."

"That didn't stop someone pretending to be Penelope Rasch's fiancé from getting hold of her room number."

"No?"

"I'll wait here until the officer is in place."

"In that case, maybe you'd like a cup of coffee."

"You don't have to—"

"No, but you need it. Just a moment, we've got some intriguingly bad coffee in the staffroom."

Steffens left the room and Harry looked around. The chairs he and Oleg had sat in were still where they had left them the day before, on either side of the bed that was no longer there. Harry sat down on one of them and stared at the grey floor. Felt his pulse slow. Even so, he still felt there wasn't enough air in the room. A strip of sunlight was falling through a gap in the curtains, reaching across the floor between the chairs, and he noticed a strand of fair hair curled on the floor. He picked it up. Could Valentin have been here looking for her, but got here too late? Harry swallowed. There was no reason to think about that now, she was safe.

Steffens came in and handed Harry a paper cup, took a sip of his own coffee and sat down on the other chair. The two men sat there opposite each other with a metre of empty space between them.

"Your boy was here," Steffens said.

"Oleg? He wasn't going to come until after college."

"He asked after you. He seemed upset that you'd left his mother on her own."

Harry nodded and drank some coffee.

"They often get angry and full of moral indignation at that age," Steffens said. "They shift the blame for anything that goes wrong onto their father, and the man they once wanted to become suddenly represents everything they *don't* want to become."

"Are you speaking from experience?"

"Of course, we do that all the time." Steffens's smile vanished as quickly as it had appeared.

"Hm. Can I ask a personal question, Steffens?"

"By all means."

"Does it end up positive?"

"Sorry?"

"The joy of saving lives minus the despair at losing people you *could* have saved."

Steffens looked Harry in the eye. Perhaps it was the situation, two men sitting opposite each other in a largely darkened room, that made it a natural question. Ships passing in the night. Steffens took his glasses off and ran his hands over his face as if to wipe the tiredness away. He shook his head. "No."

"But you still do it."

"It's a calling."

"Yes, I saw the crucifix in your office. You believe in callings."

"I think you do too, Hole. I've seen you. Maybe not a calling from God, but you still feel it all the same."

Harry looked down at his cup. Steffens was right about the coffee being intriguingly bad. "Does that mean you don't like your job?"

"I hate my job," the senior consultant smiled. "If it had been up to me, I'd have chosen to be a concert pianist."

"You're a good pianist?"

"That's the curse, isn't it? When you're not good at what you love, and good at something you hate."

Harry nodded. "That's the curse. We do jobs where we can be useful."

"And the lie is that there's a reward for someone who follows a calling."

"Perhaps sometimes the work in itself is reward enough."

"Only for the concert pianist who loves music, or the executioner who loves blood." Steffens pointed to the name badge on his white coat. "I was born and raised a Mormon in Salt Lake City, and I'm named after John Doyle Lee, a God-fearing, peace-loving man who in 1857 was ordered by the elders of his parish to massacre a group of ungodly immigrants who had strayed into their territory. He wrote about his torments in his diary, about the terrible calling that fate had dealt him, but that he simply had to accept it."

"The Mountain Meadows massacre."

"So, you know your history, Hole."

"I studied serial murders at the FBI, and we went through the most famous mass killings as well. I have to confess that I don't remember what happened to your namesake."

Steffens looked at his watch. "Hopefully his reward was waiting in heaven, because on earth everyone betrayed John Doyle Lee, including our spiritual leader, Brigham Young. John Doyle was sentenced to death. But my father still thought he had set an example worth following, abandoning the cheap love of your fellows in favour of following a calling you hate."

"Maybe he didn't hate it as much as he claimed."

"How do you mean?"

Harry shrugged. "An alcoholic hates and curses drink because it ruins his life. But at the same time it *is* his life."

"Interesting analogy." Steffens stood up, went over to the window and pulled the curtains open. "What about you, Hole? Is your calling still ruining your life, even though it is your life?"

Harry shaded his eyes and tried to look at Steffens, but was blinded by the sudden light. "Are you still a Mormon?"

"Are you still working on the case?"

"Looks like it."

"We don't have a choice, do we? I need to get back to work, Harry."

When Steffens had gone Harry called Gunnar Hagen's number.

"Hello, boss, I need a police guard at Ullevål Hospital," he said. "Immediately."

Wyller was standing where he had been told to, beside the bonnet of the car, which was parked untidily in front of the main entrance.

"I saw a police officer arrive," he said. "Everything OK?"

"We're putting a guard outside her door," Harry said, getting in the passenger seat.

Wyller tucked his pistol back in his holster and got in behind the wheel. "And Valentin?"

"God knows."

Harry took the strand of hair from his pocket. "This is probably just paranoia, but get Forensics to do an urgent analysis of this, just to rule out the possibility that it matches anything from the crime scenes, OK?"

They glided through the streets. It was like spooling back a slow-motion replay of their frantic drive twenty minutes earlier.

"Do Mormons actually use crucifixes?" Harry asked.

"No," Wyller said. "They believe the cross symbolises death and is heathen. They believe in the resurrection."

"Hm. So a Mormon with a crucifix on his wall would be like . . ."

"A Muslim with a drawing of Muhammad."

"Exactly." Harry turned the radio up. The White Stripes. "Blue Orchid." Guitars and drums. Sparseness. Clarity.

He turned it up even louder, without knowing what it was he was trying to drown out.


Hallstein Smith was twiddling his thumbs. He was alone in the boiler room, and without the others there wasn't a great deal he could do. He had completed his concise profile of the vampirist, and had surfed the Net reading the most recent articles about the vampirist murders. Then he had gone back and read what the media had written during the five days that had passed since the first murder. Hallstein Smith was wondering if he should make the most of the time to work on his PhD thesis when his phone rang.

"Hello?"

"Smith?" a woman's voice said. "This is Mona Daa from *VG*."

"Oh?"

"You sound surprised."

"Only because I didn't think we had any coverage down here."

"Speaking of coverage, can you confirm that the vampirist is probably responsible for the disappearance of a female member of staff from Schrøder's Restaurant last night?"

"Confirm? Me?"

"Yes, you work for the police now, don't you?"

"Yes, I suppose so, but I'm not in a position to say anything at all."

"Because you don't know or because you can't say?"

"Both, perhaps. If I were to say something, it would have to be something general. As an expert on vampirism, in other words."

"Great! Because I've got a podcast—"

"A what?"

"Radio. *VG* has its own radio station."

"Oh, OK."

"Could we invite you in to talk about the vampirist? In *general* terms, of course."

Hallstein Smith thought about it. "I'd have to get permission from the lead detective."

"Good, I'll wait to hear from you. On a different subject, Smith. I wrote that piece about you. Which I assume you were happy with. Seeing as it did indirectly get you to the centre of the action."

"Yes. Sure."

"In return, could you tell me who at Police HQ lured me out to the container terminal yesterday?"

"Lured you to do what?"

"Never mind. Have a good day."

Hallstein Smith was left staring at his phone. Container terminal? What was she talking about?

Truls Berntsen let his eyes roam across the rows of pictures of Megan Fox on his computer. It was almost frightening, the way she'd let herself go. Was it just the pictures or the fact that she'd turned thirty? Or knowing what childbirth must have done to the body that had defined perfection in the 2007 film *Transformers*? Or was it the fact that he himself had lost eight kilos of fat in the past two years, replacing them with four kilos of muscle and nine women fucked? Had that made his distant dreams of Megan Fox that bit less distant? The way one light year is less than two. Or was it simply the fact that in ten hours' time he would be sitting with Ulla Bellman, the only woman he had ever lusted after more than Megan Fox?

He heard someone clear their throat and looked up.

Katrine Bratt was standing there, leaning against the partition.

After Wyller had moved down to that laughable boys' club in the boiler room, Truls had been able to immerse himself fully in *The Shield*. He had now seen all the available seasons, and hoped Katrine Bratt wasn't about to do anything that spoiled his free time.

"Bellman wants to see you," she said.

"OK." Truls switched his computer off, stood up and walked past Katrine Bratt. So close that he would have smelt her perfume if she had been wearing any. He thought all women really ought to use a bit of perfume. Not as much as the ones who overdid it, the ones who suffered solvent damage, but a bit. Enough to set his imagination going about how they *really* smelt.

While he waited for the lift he had time to wonder what Mikael wanted. But his mind was blank.

It wasn't until he was standing in the Police Chief's office that he realised he'd been found out. When he saw Mikael's back over at the window, and heard him say, with no introduction: "You've let me down, Truls. Did the bitch approach you, or was it the other way round?"

It was like having a bucket of cold water tipped over him. What the hell had happened? Had Ulla broken down and confessed in a fit of guilty conscience? Or had Mikael pressurised her? And what the hell was he supposed to say now?

He cleared his throat. "She came to me, Mikael. She was the one who wanted it."

"Of course the bitch wanted it, they take whatever they can get. But the fact that she got it from you, my closest confidant, after all we've been through."

Truls almost couldn't believe that he was talking that way about his wife, the mother of his children.

"I didn't think I could say no to meeting up and having a chat, it wasn't supposed to go any further."

"But it did, didn't it?"

"Nothing's happened at all."

"Nothing at *all*? Do you not understand that you've told the murderer what we know and don't know? How much did she pay?"

Truls blinked. "Pay?" The penny dropped.

"I'm assuming Mona Daa didn't get the information for free? Tell me, and don't forget that I know you, Truls."

Truls Berntsen grinned. He was off the hook. And repeated: "Nothing's happened at all."

Mikael turned round, slammed his hand down on the desk and snarled: "Do you think we're idiots?"

Truls studied the way the patches on Mikael's face switched between white and red, as if the blood was sloshing back and forth inside. The patches had grown bigger over the years, like a snake shedding its skin.

"Let's hear what you think you know," Truls said, and sat down without asking.

Mikael looked at him in surprise. Then he sat down on his own chair. Because perhaps he had seen it in Truls's eyes. That he wasn't frightened. That if Truls was thrown overboard, he'd take Bellman with him. All the way down.

"What I know," Mikael said, "is that Katrine Bratt showed up in my office early this morning to tell me that because I'd asked her to keep a close eye on you, she'd asked one of her detectives to keep you under surveillance. You were evidently already suspected of being the source of the leaks, Truls."

"Who was the detective?"

"She didn't say, and I didn't ask."

Of course not, Truls thought. In case you find yourself in a tricky situation, where it would be useful to be able to deny all knowledge. Truls might not be the smartest guy in the world, but he wasn't as stupid as those around him thought, and he had gradually started to work out how Mikael and the others up at the top of the hierarchy reasoned.

"Bratt's detective was proactive," Mikael said. "He discovered that you'd been in telephone contact with Mona Daa at least twice in the past week."

A detective checking phone calls, Truls thought. Who had been in touch with telecoms companies. Anders Wyller. Little Truls wasn't stupid. Oh no.

"To confirm that you were Mona Daa's source, he called her. He pretended to be the vampirist, and to prove it he asked her to call her source to check a detail that only the perpetrator and the police could know."

"The smoothie mixer."

"So you admit it?"

"That Mona Daa called me, yes."

"Good. Because the detective woke Katrine Bratt last night to say he had a list of calls from the telecom company showing that Mona Daa called you right after he made his hoax call to her. This is going to be very hard to explain away, Truls."

Truls shrugged. "There's nothing to explain. Mona Daa called me, asked about a smoothie mixer, and naturally I refused to comment and referred her to the lead detective. The conversation lasted ten, maybe twenty seconds, as the list of calls no doubt confirms. Maybe Mona Daa already suspected that it was a bluff to try to uncover her source. So she called me instead of her source."

"According to the detective, she later went to the agreed location out in the container terminal to meet the vampirist. The detective even photographed the whole thing. So someone must have given her confirmation about the smoothie maker."

"Perhaps Mona Daa arranged to meet first, and *then* went to her source and got confirmation face-to-face. Police officers and journalists both know how easy it is to get hold of information showing who called who, and when."

"Speaking of which, you had two other telephone conversations with Mona Daa, one of which lasted several minutes."

"Check the list. Mona Daa called me, I've *never* called her. The fact that it takes a pit bull like Daa several minutes of banging on before she realises that she's not going to get anything, and that she still tries again later to lance the boil, is her problem. I have quite a bit of time during the day."

Truls leaned back in his chair. Folded his hands and looked at Mikael, who was sitting there nodding as if he was absorbing what Truls had said, thinking through possible holes that they might have missed. A little smile, a degree of warmth in those brown eyes, seemed to indicate that he had come to the conclusion that this *might* work, that they *might* be able to get Truls off the hook.

"Good," Mikael said. "But now that it turns out you aren't the leak, Truls, who could it be?"

Truls pouted his lips, the way his slightly plump French online date had taught him to do every time she asked him the complicated question "When are we going to meet again?"

"You tell me. No one wants to be seen talking to a journalist like Daa in a case like this. No, the only person I've seen doing that is Wyller. Hang on—unless I'm remembering wrong, he gave her a number she could call him on. Actually, yes, she told him where he could get hold of her too, at that gym, Gain."

Mikael Bellman looked at Truls. With a surprised little smile, like someone discovering after many years that their spouse can sing, has blue blood or a university degree.

"So what you're implying, Truls, is that our leak is probably someone who's new here." Bellman stroked his chin thoughtfully with his forefinger and thumb. "A natural assumption seeing as the problem of the leak has only recently emerged, one which doesn't—what's the word I'm looking for?—*reflect* the culture we've nurtured within the Oslo Police in recent years. But I don't suppose we shall ever know who it is or isn't, seeing as the journalist is legally obliged to protect the identity of her source."

Truls laughed his grunting laugh. "Good, Mikael."

Mikael nodded. Leaned forward and, before Truls had time to react, grabbed him by the shirt collar and pulled him towards him.

"How much did the bitch pay you, Beavis?"

# 22

# Tuesday afternoon

Mehmet pulled the bathrobe tighter around him. He stared at the screen of his phone and pretended not to see the men coming and going in the rudimentary changing room. The entrance fee to the Cagaloglu Hamam gave no time limit on how long you could spend in the baths. But obviously, if a man were to sit in a changing room for hours looking at other naked men, there was a risk he might become unpopular. That's why he kept moving about at regular intervals, between the the sauna and the perpetually fog-clouded steam room as well as the pools of varying temperatures, from steaming hot to cold. And there was a practical reason, too: the rooms were connected by a number of doors, so he risked not seeing everyone if he didn't move around. But right now the changing room was so cold that he wanted to get back into the warm. Mehmet looked at the time. Four o'clock. The Turkish tattooist thought he had seen the man with the demon tattoo at the baths early in the afternoon, and there probably wasn't anything to say that serial killers couldn't be creatures of habit too.

Harry Hole had explained that Mehmet was the perfect spy. Firstly, he was one of only two people who stood any chance of recognising Valentin Gjertsen's face. Secondly, as a Turk he wouldn't stand out in a bathhouse that was mostly frequented by his compatriots. Thirdly, because Valentin, according to Harry, would have spotted a police officer instantly. Besides, they had a mole at Crime Squad who was leaking everything to *VG* and God knows who else. So Harry and Mehmet were the only two people who knew about this operation. But the moment Mehmet let Harry know he had seen Valentin, it would take less than fifteen minutes before he was on the scene with armed police officers.

And in return, Harry had promised Mehmet that Øystein Eikeland was the perfect stand-in at the Jealousy Bar. A guy who had looked like an old scarecrow when he walked through the door, with the smell of a hard but enjoyable hippie lifestyle clinging to his shabby denim clothes. And when Mehmet asked if he'd stood behind a bar before, Eikeland had stuck a roll-up between his lips and sighed: "I've spent years in bars, lad. Standing, kneeling and lying down. Never on that side of the counter, though."

But Eikeland was Harry's trusted choice, so he just had to hope that nothing too bad happened. A week at most, Harry had said. Then he could go back to his bar. Harry had performed a little bow when he was given the key, on a key ring with a broken plastic heart, the logo of the Jealousy Bar, and told Mehmet that they needed to discuss the music. That there were people over thirty who don't get dandruff from new music, and that there was even hope for someone bogged down in the Bad Company swamp. The thought of that discussion alone was worth at least a week of tedium, Mehmet thought as he scrolled down *VG*'s website, even though he must have read the same headlines ten times now.

FAMOUS VAMPIRISTS IN HISTORY. And while he stared at the screen and waited for the rest of the article to load, something odd happened. It was as if he couldn't breathe for a moment. He looked up. The door to the baths swung shut. He looked around. The other three men in the changing room were the same ones as before. Someone had entered and walked through the room. Mehmet locked his phone in his locker, got up and followed.


The boilers in the next room were rumbling. Harry looked at the time. Five past four. He pushed his chair back, folded his hands behind his head and leaned against the brick wall. Smith, Bjørn and Wyller looked at him.

"It's been sixteen hours since Marte Ruud went missing," Harry said. "Anything new?"

"Hair," Bjørn Holm said. "The team at the scene found strands of hair by the main entrance at Schrøder's. They look like they could be a match for the hairs we got from Valentin Gjertsen off the handcuffs. They've been sent for analysis. Hair suggests a struggle, and also that he didn't clean up after himself this time. And that also means that there couldn't have been too much blood, so there's reason to hope that she was alive when they left."

"OK," Smith said. "There's a chance she's alive, and that he's using her as a cow."

"Cow?" Wyller asked.

The boiler room fell silent. Harry grimaced. "You mean he . . . he's *milking* her?"

"The body takes twenty-four hours to reproduce one percent of the body's red blood cells," Smith said. "At best, it might quench his thirst for blood for a while. At worst, it might mean that he's even more focused on regaining power and control. And that he's going to try again to find the people who've humiliated him. Which means you and yours, Harry."

"My wife is under police guard, round the clock, and I've left a message for my son telling him to be careful."

"So it's possible that he might attack men as well?" Wyller asked.

"Absolutely," Smith said.

Harry felt his trouser pocket vibrate. He pulled out his phone. "Yes?"

"It's Øystein. How do you make a daiquiri? I've got a difficult customer and Mehmet isn't answering."

"How should I know? Doesn't the customer know?"

"No."

"Something to do with rum and lime. Ever heard of Google?"

"Of course, I'm not an idiot. That's on the Internet, isn't it?"

"Try it, you might like it. I'm hanging up now." Harry ended the call. "Sorry. Anything else?"

"Witness statements from people in the vicinity of Schrøder's," Wyller said. "No one saw or heard anything. Odd, on such a busy street."

"It can be pretty deserted there around midnight on a Monday night," Harry said. "But getting someone, conscious or unconscious, away from there without being seen? Hardly. He might have been parked right outside."

"There's no vehicle registered to Valentin Gjertsen, and no vehicle was leased under that name yesterday," Wyller said.

Harry spun towards him.

Wyller looked back quizzically. "I know the chances of him using his real name are pretty much zero, but I checked anyway. Isn't that . . . ?"

"Yeah, that's absolutely fine," Harry said. "Send the photofit picture to the car-rental companies. And there's a twenty-four-hour Deli de Luca next to Schrøder's—"

"I was at the morning meeting of the investigative team and they've checked the security cameras there," Bjørn said. "Nothing."

"OK, anything else I should know about?"

"They're working in the U.S.A. to get access to the victims' IP addresses on Facebook using a subpoena rather than going via a court," Wyller said. "That means we wouldn't get the contents, but all the addresses of people they've sent and received messages to and from. It could be a matter of weeks rather than months."


Mehmet was standing outside the door of the *hararet*. He had seen the door close as he emerged into the baths from the changing room. And it was in the *hararet* that the man with the tattoo had been seen. Mehmet knew it wasn't very likely that Valentin would show up as soon as this, on the first day. Unless he came several times a week, of course. So why stand there hesitating?

Mehmet swallowed.

Then he pulled the door of the hararet open and went inside. The thick steam moved, swirled around, disappeared out through the door, opening a corridor into the room. And for a moment Mehmet found himself staring at the face of a man sitting on the second bench up. Then the corridor closed again and the face was gone. But Mehmet had seen enough.

It was him. The man who had come into the bar that evening.

Should he run out straight away or sit down for a while first? After all, the man had seen Mehmet staring at him, and if he walked out at once surely he'd get suspicious?

Mehmet stood where he was by the door.

If felt like the steam he was breathing in was making his airways tighter. He couldn't wait any longer, he had to get out. Mehmet nudged the door gently and slipped out. Ran across the slippery tiles with short, careful steps so as not to fall, and reached the changing room. He swore as he struggled with the code on his padlock. Four digits. 1683. The Battle of Vienna. The year when the Ottoman Empire ruled the world, or at least the part of the world that was worth ruling. When the empire couldn't expand any further, and the decline began. Defeat after defeat. Was that why he had picked that year, because it somehow reflected his own story, a story of having everything and losing it? Eventually he managed to open the lock. He grabbed his phone, tapped at it and held it to his ear. Stared at the door to the baths, which had swung shut again, every moment expecting the man to come rushing in and attack him.

"Yes?"

"He's here," Mehmet whispered.

"Sure?"

"Yes. In the *hararet*."

"Keep an eye on it, we'll be there in fifteen minutes."


"You've done *what*?" Bjørn Holm said, taking his foot off the clutch as the lights turned green on Hausmannsgate.

"I hired a civilian volunteer to watch the Turkish baths in Sagene," Harry said, looking in the wing mirror of Bjørn Holm's legendary 1970 Volvo Amazon. Originally white, later painted black, with a chequered rally stripe across the roof and boot. The car behind disappeared in a cloud of black exhaust fumes.

"Without asking us?" Bjørn blew his horn and overtook an Audi on the inside.

"It's not entirely by the book, so there was no reason to make any of you accomplices."

"There are fewer traffic lights if you take Maridalsveien," Wyller said from the backseat.

Bjørn changed into a lower gear and wrenched the car to the right. Harry felt the pressure of the three-point seat belt that Volvo had been the first to install, but they had no slack which meant you could hardly move.

"How are you doing, Smith?" Harry called over the roar of the engine. He wouldn't usually have brought an external adviser on an active operation like this, but at the last moment he decided to take Smith in case they found themselves in a hostage situation, when the psychologist's ability to read Valentin could come in handy. The way he had read Aurora. The way he had read Harry.

"A bit carsick, that's all," Smith smiled weakly. "What's that smell?"

"Old clutch, heater and adrenalin," Bjørn said.

"Listen up," Harry said. "We'll be there in two minutes, so I repeat: Smith, you stay in the car. Wyller and I will go in through the front door, Bjørn will watch the back door. You said you know where it is?"

"Yep," Bjørn said. "And your man is still online?"

Harry nodded and put his phone to his ear. They pulled up in front of an old brick building. Harry had looked at the plans. It was a former factory which now housed a printing firm, some offices, a recording studio and the hamam, and there was only one other door apart from the front entrance.

"Everyone loaded, safety off?" Harry asked, breathing out as he unfastened the tight seat belt. "We want him alive. But if that's not possible . . ." He looked up at the glinting windows on either side of the main entrance as he heard Bjørn recite in a low voice: "Police, warning shot, then shoot the bastard. Police, warning shot, then—"

"Let's go," Harry said.

They got out of the car, crossed the pavement and split up by the front entrance.

Harry and Wyller went up the three steps and in through a heavy door. The hallways inside smelt of ammonia and printers' ink. Two of the doors had shiny gilded signs with ornate writing: small, optimistic law firms that couldn't afford to rent in the city centre. On the third door was an unassuming sign saying CAGALOGLU HAMAM, so unassuming that it gave the impression they didn't want customers who didn't already know where it was.

Harry opened the door and walked in.

He found himself in a passageway with peeling paint on the walls and a simple desk, where a broad-shouldered man with dark stubble and a tracksuit was sitting and reading a magazine. If Harry hadn't known better, he would have thought he'd walked into a boxing club.

"Police," Wyller said, sticking his ID between the magazine and the man's face. "Sit completely still and don't warn anyone. This will be over in a couple of minutes."

Harry carried on down the passageway and saw two doors. One said CHANGING ROOM, the other HAMAM. He went into the baths, and heard Wyller follow close behind him.

There were three small pools laid out in a row. To their right were booths containing massage tables. To the left were two glass doors which Harry assumed led to the sauna and steam room, and a plain wooden door that he remembered from the plans as the door to the changing room. In the nearest pool two men looked up and stared at them. Mehmet was sitting on a bench by the wall, pretending to look at his phone. He hurried over to them and pointed towards the glass door with a misted plastic sign saying HARARET.

"Is he alone?" Harry asked quietly as he and Wyller each pulled out their Glocks. He heard frantic splashing from the pool behind him.

"No one's entered or left since I called you," Mehmet whispered.

Harry went over to the door and tried to look in, but saw nothing but impenetrable whiteness. He gestured to Wyller to cover the door. He took a deep breath and was about to go in when he changed his mind. The sound of shoes. Valentin's suspicions mustn't be aroused by the entrance of someone who wasn't barefoot. Harry pulled his shoes and socks off with his free hand. Then he pulled the door open and went in. The steam swirled around him. Like a bridal veil. Rakel. Harry didn't know where the thought had come from, and thrust it aside. And managed to catch a glimpse of a solitary figure on the wooden bench in front of him before he closed the door behind him and was enveloped in whiteness again. That and silence. Harry held his breath and listened for the other man's breathing. Had the man had time to see that the new arrival was fully clothed and holding a pistol? Was he scared? Was he scared the way Aurora had been scared when she saw his cowboy boots outside her toilet cubicle?

Harry raised his pistol and moved towards where he had seen the figure. And he could make out the shape of a seated man against the white. Harry squeezed the trigger until it resisted.

"Police," he said in a hoarse voice. "Don't move, or I'll shoot." And another thought struck him. That in a situation like this he would usually say *or we'll shoot*. It was simple psychology, it gave the impression that there were more of them, and increased the chances of the person surrendering immediately. So why had he said "I?" And now that his brain had accepted one question, others appeared: why was he on his own here, rather than the Delta team that specialised in this sort of job? Why had he *really* stationed Mehmet here in complete secrecy and not told anyone at all until after Mehmet had called?

Harry felt the slight resistance of the trigger against his index finger. So slight.

Two men in a room where no one else could see them.

Who would be able to deny that Valentin, who had already killed several people with just his bare hands and iron teeth, had attacked Harry, forcing Harry to shoot him in self-defence?

"*Vurma!*" the figure in front of him said, and raised his arms in the air.

Harry leaned closer.

The skinny man was naked. His eyes were wide with terror. And his chest was covered with grey hair, but was otherwise unblemished.

# 23

# Tuesday, late afternoon

"What the hell?!" Katrine Bratt yelled, throwing the eraser she'd picked up from her desk. It hit the wall just above Harry Hole's head where he was sitting slumped in a chair. "As if we didn't have enough problems, you manage to break pretty much every damn rule in the book, plus a couple of the country's laws for good measure. What were you *thinking*?"

Rakel, Harry thought, tipping backwards until his chair hit the wall. I was thinking about Rakel. And Aurora.

"What?"

"I was thinking that if there was a shortcut which meant we could bring Valentin Gjertsen in just one day earlier, it might save someone's life."

"Don't give me that, Harry! You know bloody well that isn't how it works. If everyone thought and acted—"

"You're right, I know that. And I know that Valentin Gjertsen came *very* close to being caught. He saw Mehmet, recognised him from the bar, realised what was going on and snuck out the back way while Mehmet was in the changing room phoning me. And I know that if it had been Valentin Gjertsen sitting in that steam room when we got there, you'd already have forgiven me and started praising proactive, creative police work. Exactly what you set up the boiler-room team for."

"You bastard!" Katrine snarled, and Harry saw her searching her desk for something else to throw at him. Fortunately she rejected the stapler and the sheaf of judicial correspondence from America relating to Facebook. "I did *not* give you licence to act like cowboys. I haven't seen a single newspaper that isn't running the raid at the baths as the lead on their website. Weapons in a peaceful bathhouse, innocent civilians in the firing line, a naked ninety-year-old threatened with a pistol. And *no* arrest! It's all just so . . ." She raised her hands and looked up at the ceiling, as if she were surrendering judgement to higher powers. ". . . amateurish!"

"Am I being fired?"

"Do you *want* to be fired?"

Harry saw her in front of him. Rakel, sleeping, her thin eyelids twitching, like Morse code from the land of coma. "Yes," he said. And he saw Aurora, the anxiety and pain in her eyes, the damage in there that could never be healed. "And no. Do you *want* to fire me?"

Katrine groaned, stood up and went over to the window. "Yes, I want to fire someone," she said with her back to him. "But not you."

"Mm."

"Mm," she mimicked.

"Do you feel like elaborating?"

"I'd like to fire Truls Berntsen."

"That goes without saying."

"Yes, but not for being useless and lazy. He's the one who's been leaking to *VG*."

"And how did you find that out?"

"Anders Wyller set a trap. He went a bit too far—I think perhaps there was a degree of payback as far as Mona Daa was concerned. Either way, we won't have any trouble from her if she's been paying a public official for information, seeing as she should have known that could lead to charges for corruption."

"So why haven't you fired Berntsen?"

"Guess," she said, going back to her desk.

"Mikael Bellman?"

Katrine threw a pencil, not at Harry but the closed door. "Bellman came in here, sat where you're sitting now, and said that Berntsen had convinced him of his innocence. And then he implied that it could have been Wyller himself who had been talking to *VG* and then tried to pin the blame on Berntsen. But that we couldn't prove anything yet, so it would be best to let it go and concentrate on catching Valentin, that was the only thing that mattered. What do you make of that?"

"Well, maybe Bellman's right, maybe it's best to delay washing our own dirty laundry until we've stopped wrestling in the gutter."

Katrine pulled a face. "Did you think of that one all by yourself?"

Harry extracted his packet of cigarettes. "Speaking of leaks. The papers are saying I was at the bathhouse, and that's OK, I got recognised. But no one apart from the boiler room and you know about Mehmet's role in this. And I'd rather keep it that way, just to be on the safe side."

Katrine nodded. "I actually raised that with Bellman and he agreed. He says we've got a lot to lose if it gets out that we're using civilians to do our work for us, that it makes us look desperate. He said that Mehmet and his role in this shouldn't be mentioned to anyone, including the investigative team. I think that makes sense, even if Truls is no longer allowed to take part in meetings."

"Really?"

Katrine raised one corner of her mouth. "He's been given his own office where he can file away reports about cases that are *nothing* to do with the vampirist murders."

"So you have fired him after all," Harry said, sticking a cigarette between his lips. His phone vibrated against his thigh. He pulled it out. A text from Dr. Steffens.

*Tests finished. Rakel's back in 301.*

"I need to go."

"Are you still with us, Harry?"

"I need to think about that."

Outside Police HQ Harry found his lighter in a hole in the lining of his jacket, and lit the cigarette. He looked at the people walking past him on the path. They seemed so calm, so untroubled. There was something very disconcerting about that. Where was he? Where the hell was Valentin?


"Hi," Harry said as he walked into room 301.

Oleg was sitting next to Rakel's bed, which was back in place. He looked up from the book he was reading but didn't respond.

Harry sat down on the other side of the bed. "Any news?"

Oleg leafed through the book.

"OK, listen," Harry said, taking his jacket off and hanging it on the back of his chair. "I know you think that when I'm not sitting here it means I care more about work than I do about her. That there are others who could solve the murders, but that she only has you and me."

"Isn't that true, then?" Oleg said, without looking up from the book.

"I'm of no use to her right now, Oleg. I can't save anyone in here, but out there I can make a difference. I can save lives."

Oleg closed his book and looked at Harry. "Good to hear that you're driven by philanthropy. Otherwise one might think it was something else."

"Something else?"

Oleg dropped the book in his bag. "A desire for glory. You know, all that Harry-Hole-is-back-to-save-the-day stuff."

"Do you think that's what it's about?"

Oleg shrugged. "The important thing is what you think. That you can convince yourself with that bullshit."

"Is that how you see me? A bullshitter?"

Oleg stood up. "Do you know why I always wanted to be like you? It wasn't because you were all that great. It was because I didn't have anyone else. You were the only man in the house. But now I can see you more clearly, I need to do all I can *not* to end up like you. Deprogramming initiated, Harry."

"Oleg . . ."

But he had already left the room.

Damn, damn.

Harry felt his phone buzz in his pocket and switched it off without looking at it. Listened to the machine. Someone had increased the volume so that it made a slightly delayed bleeping sound every time the green line jumped.

Like a clock counting down.

Counting down for her.

Counting down for someone out there.

What if Valentin was sitting looking at a clock right now, as he waited for the next one?

Harry started to pull out his phone. Then let go of it again.

The low, slanting light meant that when he put his broad hand on top of Rakel's thin one, blue veins cast shadows across the back of his hand. He tried not to count the bleeps.

By 806 he couldn't sit still any longer, and stood up and walked round the room. He went out, found a doctor who didn't want to go into any details but said that Rakel's condition was stable, and that they had discussed bringing her out of the coma.

"Sounds like good news," Harry said.

The doctor hesitated before replying. "We're only discussing it," he said. "There are arguments against it as well. Steffens is on duty tonight, you can talk to him when he gets here."

Harry found the cafeteria, got something to eat and went back to room 301. The police officer outside the door nodded.

It had got dark in the room and Harry lit the lamp on the table next to the bed. He tapped a cigarette out of the packet as he studied Rakel's eyelids. Her lips, which had become so dry. He tried to reconstruct the first time they met. He had been standing on the drive in front of her house, and she'd walked towards him, like a ballerina. After so many years, was he remembering it right? That first look. The first words. The first kiss. Maybe it was inevitable that you revised your memories, little by little, so that they eventually became a story, with the logic of a story, with weight and meaning. A story that said they had been on their way towards this all along, one that they repeated to each other, like a ritual, until they believed it. So when she disappeared, when the story of Rakel and Harry disappeared, what would he believe in then?

He lit the cigarette.

Inhaled, exhaled, saw the smoke swirl up towards the smoke alarm, dissipate.

Disappear. Alarm, he thought.

His hand slid into his pocket and grasped the cold, dormant phone. Damn, damn.

A calling, as Steffens had put it: what did that mean? When you take a job you hate because you know you're the best at it? *Somewhere you can be useful*. Like a self-effacing herd animal. Or was it like Oleg said, personal glory? Was he longing to be out there, shining, while she lay in here wasting away? OK, he'd never noticed any great sense of responsibility to society, and the recognition of colleagues or the public had never meant much. So what did that leave?

That left Valentin. That left the hunt.

There was a double knock, and the door slid open quietly. Bjørn Holm snuck in and sat down on the other chair.

"Smoking inside a hospital," he said. "A six-year sentence, I reckon."

"Two years," Harry said, passing the cigarette to Bjørn. "Do me a favour and be my accomplice?"

Bjørn nodded towards Rakel. "You're not worried she might get lung cancer?"

"Rakel loves passive smoking. She says she likes both the fact that it's free, and that my body has already absorbed most of the toxins before I blow the smoke out again. I act as a combination of wallet and cigarette filter for her."

Bjørn took a drag. "Your voicemail's switched off, so I figured you were here."

"Hm. For a forensics expert you've always been pretty good at deduction."

"Thanks. How's it going?"

"They're talking about bringing her out of the coma. I'm choosing to see that as good news. Something urgent?"

"No one we've spoken to from the bathhouse recognised Valentin from the photofit picture. The guy behind the desk said there were loads of people coming and going the whole time, but that he thought our man could be someone who usually shows up in a coat covering his bathrobe, with a cap pulled low, and that he always pays cash."

"So the payment doesn't leave any electronic record. Bathrobe on underneath, so there's no risk of anyone seeing the tattoo when he gets changed. How does he get from his home to the baths?"

"If he has a car, he must have had the car keys in the pocket of his bathrobe. Or bus money. Because there was absolutely nothing on the clothes we found in the changing room, not even fluff in the pockets. We can probably find some DNA on them, but they smelt of detergent. I reckon even his coat had been recently washed in a machine."

"That fits with the obsessive cleanliness at the crime scenes. The fact that he takes his keys and money into a steam sauna suggests he's ready for a quick escape."

"Yes. No witnesses who saw a man in a bathrobe on the streets of Sagene either, so he can't have caught the bus this time, at least."

"He had his car parked near the back door. It's no accident that he's managed to stay hidden for four years, he's smart." Harry rubbed the back of his neck. "OK. We chased him away. What now?"

"We're checking the security cameras in shops and petrol stations near the baths, looking for caps and maybe a bathrobe sticking out beneath a coat. By the way, I'm going to cut the coat open first thing tomorrow. There's a tiny hole in the lining of one pocket, and it's possible that something could have slipped in and got lost among the padding."

"He's avoiding security cameras."

"You think?"

"Yes. If we do see him, it will be because he wants to be seen."

"You're probably right." Bjørn Holm unbuttoned his parka. His pale forehead was damp with sweat.

Harry blew cigarette smoke towards Rakel. "What is it, Bjørn?"

"What do you mean?"

"You didn't have to come up here to give me that report."

Bjørn didn't answer. Harry waited. The machine bleeped and bleeped.

"It's Katrine," Bjørn said. "I don't understand. I saw from my call list that she tried to ring me last night, but when I called back she said her phone must have dialled me by accident."

"And?"

"At three o'clock in the morning? She doesn't sleep on *top* of her phone."

"So why didn't you ask her?"

"Because I didn't want to nag. She needs time. Space. She's a bit like you." Bjørn took the cigarette from Harry.

"Me?"

"A loner."

Harry snatched the cigarette back just as Bjørn was about to take a drag.

"You *are*," Bjørn protested.

"What do you want?"

"It's driving me mad, going round not knowing anything. So I was wondering . . ." Bjørn scratched his beard hard. "You and Katrine are close. Could you . . . ?"

"Check the lie of the land?"

"Something like that. I've *got* to get her back, Harry."

Harry stubbed the cigarette out on the leg of the chair. Looked at Rakel. "Sure. I'll talk to Katrine."

"But without her . . ."

". . . knowing it's come from you."

"Thanks," Bjørn said. "You're a good friend, Harry."

"Me?" Harry put the butt back in the cigarette packet. "I'm a loner."

When Bjørn had gone Harry closed his eyes. Listened to the machine. The countdown.

# 24

# Tuesday evening

His name was Olsen, and he ran Olsen's, but the place had been called that when he took it over twenty years ago. Some people thought it was an unlikely coincidence, but how unlikely is it when unlikely things happen all the time, every day, every single second? Because someone has to win the lottery, that much is obvious. Even so, the person who wins it not only thinks that it's unlikely, but that it's a miracle. For this reason, Olsen didn't believe in miracles. But this was a borderline case. Ulla Swart had just come in and sat down at Truls Berntsen's table, where he had already been sitting for twenty minutes. The miracle was that it was an arranged meeting. Because Olsen was in no doubt that it was an arranged meeting, he had spent over twenty years standing here watching nervous men unable to stand still, or sitting drumming their fingers, waiting for the girl of their dreams. The miracle was that when she was young Ulla Swart had been the most beautiful girl in the whole of Manglerud, and Truls Berntsen the biggest pile of shit and loser in the gang that hung out in Manglerud shopping centre and went to Olsen's. Truls, or Beavis, had been Mikael Bellman's shadow, and Mikael hadn't been top of the popularity lists either. But he had at least had his appearance and way with words on his side, and had managed to get the girl the hockey boys and bikers alike all drooled over. And then he went and became Chief of Police, so Mikael must have had something. Truls Berntsen, on the other hand: once a loser, always a loser.

Olsen went over to the table to take their order and try to hear what they were saying during this unlikely meeting.

"I got here a bit early," Truls said, nodding towards the almost empty glass of beer in front of him.

"I'm late," Ulla said, pulling her handbag over her head and unbuttoning her coat. "I almost didn't get away."

"Oh?" Truls took a small, quick sip of beer to hide how shaky he was.

"Yes, it . . . it's not easy, this, Truls." She smiled briefly. Noticed Olsen, who had sailed up behind her without a sound.

"I'll wait a while," she said, and he vanished.

Wait? Truls thought. Was she going to see how it went? Leave if she changed her mind? If he didn't live up to expectations? And what expectations were they, given that they had practically grown up together?

Ulla looked round. "God, the last time I was here was at that school reunion ten years ago, do you remember?"

"No," Truls said. "I didn't come."

She picked at the sleeves of her sweater.

"That case you're working on now is terrible. Shame you didn't catch him today. Mikael told me what happened."

"Yeah," Truls said. Mikael. So the first thing she did was bring him up, and hold him in front of her like a shield. Was she just nervous, or did she not know what she wanted? "What did he say about it?"

"That Harry Hole had used that bartender who saw the killer before the first murder. Mikael was very angry."

"The bartender at the Jealousy Bar?"

"I think so."

"Used him to do what?"

"To sit in that Turkish bathhouse and keep an eye out for the murderer. Didn't you know?"

"I've been working with . . . some other murder cases today."

"Oh. Well, it's nice to see you. I can't stay long, but—"

"Long enough for me to get another beer?"

He saw her hesitate. Damn.

"Is it the children?" he asked.

"What?"

"Are they ill?"

Truls saw Ulla's brief confusion before she grabbed the lifebelt he was offering her. Offering them both.

"The little one's a bit poorly." She shivered under her thick sweater, and looked as if she was trying to curl up inside as she looked around. Only three of the other tables were occupied, and Truls assumed she didn't know any of the other customers. She certainly looked a bit more relaxed after her scan. "Truls?"

"Yes."

"Can I ask you an odd question?"

"Of course."

"What is it you want?"

"Want?" He took another sip to gain himself a timeout. "Now, you mean?"

"I mean, what do you want for yourself? What does everyone want?"

I want to take off your clothes, fuck you and hear you scream for more, Truls thought. And after that, I want you to go to the fridge, get me a cold beer, then lie in my arms and say that you're giving it all up for me. The kids, Mikael, that fuck-off great house where I built the veranda, everything. All because I want to be with you, Truls Berntsen, because now, after this, it's impossible for me to go back to anyone but you, you, you. And then I want us to fuck some more.

"It's being liked, isn't it?"

Truls gulped. "Absolutely."

"Being liked by the people we like. Other people aren't as important, are they?"

Truls felt his face make an expression, but didn't know what it was supposed to mean.

Ulla leaned forward and lowered her voice. "And from time to time, when we think we aren't liked, when we get trampled on, we feel like trampling on them in return, don't we?"

"Yes," Truls said, nodding. "We feel like trampling on them in return."

"But that urge disappears as soon as we realise that we're liked after all. And you know what? This evening Mikael said he likes me. In passing, and not directly, but . . ." She bit her lower lip. That wonderful, blood-filled lower lip that Truls had been staring at since they were sixteen years old. "That's all it takes, Truls. Isn't that strange?"

"Very strange," Truls said, looking down into his empty glass. And wondering how to formulate what he was thinking. That sometimes someone saying they like you doesn't mean a damn thing. Especially when it's Mikael fucking Bellman saying it.

"I don't think I ought to make the little one wait any longer."

Truls looked up and saw Ulla peering at her watch with an expression of deep concern. "Of course not," he said.

"I hope we get longer next time."

Truls managed not to ask when that was going to be. He merely stood up, tried not to hug her longer than she hugged him. And sat down heavily on his chair when the door closed behind her. Felt rage building. Heavy, slow, painful, wonderful rage.

"Another beer?" Olsen had silently appeared again.

"Yes. Actually, no. I need to make a call. Does that still work?" He gestured towards the booth with the glass door where Mikael claimed to have fucked Stine Michaelsen during a student party when the place was so packed that no one could see what was going on below chest height. Least of all Ulla, who was standing in the queue at the bar to buy beer for them.

"Sure."

Truls went inside and looked up the number on his own mobile phone.

Tapped the payphone's shiny square buttons.

Waited. He had decided to wear a tight shirt to show off the fact that he had bigger pecs, bigger biceps and a narrower waist than Ulla probably remembered. But she had hardly looked at him. Truls puffed himself up and felt his shoulders touch both sides of the booth. It was even smaller than that fucking office they'd stuffed him in today.

Bellman. Bratt. Wyller. Hole. They could all burn in hell.

"Mona Daa."

"Berntsen. What will you pay to find out what really happened at the bathhouse today?"

"Have you got a teaser?"

"Yep. *Oslo Police risk life of innocent bartender to catch Valentin*."

"We can probably come to an arrangement."


He wiped the condensation from the bathroom mirror and looked at himself.

"Who are you?" he whispered. "Who are you?"

He closed his eyes. Opened them again.

"I'm Alexander Dreyer. But call me Alex."

From the living room behind him he heard insane laughter.

Something that sounded like a machine or a helicopter, and then the terrified screams that marked the transition between "Speak to Me" and "Breathe." It was those screams he had tried to conjure up, but none of them had wanted to scream like that.

The condensation was almost gone from the mirror. He was finally clean now. And he could see the tattoo. A lot of people, mostly women, had asked why he had chosen to have a demon engraved into the skin of his chest. As if he had chosen it. They knew nothing. Nothing about him.

"Who are you, Alex? I'm a claims manager at Storebrand. No, I don't want to talk about insurance, let's talk about you instead. What do you do, Tone? Would you like to scream for me while I slice your nipples off and eat them?"

He walked from the bathroom to the living room, and looked down at the picture lying on the desk, beside the white key. Tone. She had been on Tinder for two years, and lived on Professor Dahls gate. She worked in a horticultural nursery and wasn't all that attractive. And she was a bit plump. He would have preferred her to be thinner. Marte was thin. He liked Marte. Her freckles suited her. But Tone. He ran his hand across the red hilt of the revolver.

The plan hadn't changed, even though it had come close to falling apart today. He didn't recognise the guy who had come into the *hararet*, but it was obvious that the guy recognised him. His pupils had dilated, you could *see* his pulse rate rise, and he had stood paralysed in the thinner mist near the door before hurrying out. But not before the air was thick with the smell of his fear.

As usual, the car had been parked by the pavement less than a hundred metres from the back door that opened onto a little-used street. Obviously he had never been a regular at any bathhouse that didn't have an escape route of that sort. Or a bathhouse that wasn't clean. And he never went into a bathhouse without having his keys in the pocket of his bathrobe.

He wondered if he should shoot Tone after biting her. Just to create a bit of confusion. See what sort of headlines that led to. But that would be breaking the rules. And the other was already angry at him for breaking them with the waitress.

He pressed the revolver against his stomach to feel the shock of cold steel before putting it down. How close were the police? *VG* had said that the police were hoping that some sort of legal process would force Facebook to surrender addresses. But he didn't understand things like that, and wasn't bothered by them. It didn't trouble Alexander Dreyer or Valentin Gjertsen. His mother said she named him after Valentino, the first and greatest romantic lead in cinema history. So she only had herself to blame for giving him a name to live up to. At first it had been relatively risk-free. Because when you rape a girl before you're sixteen, and the lucky girl is past the age of consent, she's old enough to know that if the court concludes that it was consensual sex rather than rape, then *she* risks punishment for having sex with a minor. After you turn sixteen the risk of being reported is greater. Unless you rape the woman who named you Valentino. Mind you, was that really rape? When she'd started locking herself in her room, and he told her it was her or the girls in the neighbourhood, teachers, female relatives, or just random victims picked off the streets, and then she unlocked the door? The psychologists he had told that to hadn't believed him. Well, after a while they had believed him. All of them.

Pink Floyd moved on to "On the Run." Agitated drums, pulsing synthesisers, the sound of feet running, fleeing. Fleeing from the police. From Harry Hole's handcuffs. *Wretched pervert.*

He picked up the glass of lemonade from the table. Took a little sip, looked at it. Then he threw it at the wall. The glass shattered and the yellow liquid ran down the white wallpaper. He heard swearing from the neighbouring flat.

Then he went into the bedroom. Checked her ankles and wrists were securely tied to the bedposts. He looked down at the freckled waitress as she lay asleep in his bed. She was breathing evenly. The drug was working the way it should. Was she dreaming? About the blue-black man? Or was he the only one who did that? One of the psychologists had suggested that this recurring nightmare was a half-forgotten childhood memory, that it was his own father he had seen sitting on top of his mother. That was rubbish, obviously, he had never seen his father; according to his mother he had raped her once and then vanished. A bit like the Virgin Mary and the Holy Spirit. Which made him the Messiah. Why not? The one who would return in judgement.

He stroked Marte's cheek. It had been a long time since he'd had a real, live woman in his bed. And he definitely preferred Harry Hole's waitress to his own usual, dead Japanese girlfriend. So yes, it was a great shame that he was going to have to give her up. A shame that he couldn't follow the demon's instincts and had to listen to the other's voice instead, the voice of reason. The voice of reason had been angry. Its instructions detailed. A forest beside a deserted road to the north-east of the city.

He went back to the living room, sat down on the chair. The smooth leather felt good against his naked skin, which was still tingling with pain from the boiling hot shower. He switched on the new phone, into which he had already inserted the SIM card he had been given. Tinder and the *VG* app were next to each other. He clicked on *VG* first. Waited. Having to wait was part of the excitement. Was he still the lead story? He could understand the B-list celebrities who'd do anything to be seen. A singer preparing food with some clown of a television cook because—as she doubtless believed—she needed to *stay current*.

Harry Hole stared gloomily at him.

*Elise Hermansen's bartender exploited by police.*

He clicked on "Read more" below the picture. Scrolled down.

*Sources say that that bartender was stationed in a Turkish bathhouse to spy for the police . . .*

The guy in the *hararet*. Working for the police. For Harry Hole.

*. . . because he's the only person who can identify Valentin Gjertsen with any certainty.*

He stood up, felt the leather let go of his skin with a slurping sound, and went back to the bedroom.

He looked in the mirror. Who are you? Who are you? You're the only one. The *only* one who's seen and knows the face I'm looking at now.

There wasn't any name or picture of the man. And he hadn't looked at the bartender that evening in the Jealousy Bar. Because eye contact makes people remember. But now they had had eye contact. And he remembered. He ran his finger across the demon's face. The face that wanted to get out, that had to get out.

In the living room "On the Run" came to an end with the roar of an aeroplane and a madman's laughter, before the plane crashed in a violent, drawn-out explosion.

Valentin Gjertsen closed his eyes and saw the flames in his mind's eye.

"What are the risks in waking her?" Harry said, looking at the crucifix hanging above Dr. Steffens's head.

"There are various answers to that," Steffens said. "And one that's true."

"And that is?"

"That we don't know."

"Like you don't know what's wrong with her."

"Yes."

"Hm. What do you know, really?"

"If you're asking in general terms, we know quite a lot. But if people knew how much we *don't* know, they'd be scared, Harry. Needlessly scared. So we try to keep quiet about that."

"Really?"

"We say we're in the repair business, but we're actually in the consolation business."

"So why are you telling me this, Steffens? Why aren't you consoling me?"

"Because I'm pretty sure you know that consolation is an illusion. As a murder detective you're also selling something more than you say you are. You give people a feeling of comforting justice, of order and security. But there's no perfect, objective truth, and no true justice."

"Is she in any pain?"

"No."

Harry nodded. "Can I smoke in here?"

"In a doctor's office in a public hospital?"

"Sounds comforting, if smoking's as dangerous as they say."

Steffens smiled. "A nurse told me that the cleaner found ash on the floor under the bed in room 301. I'd rather you did that outside. How's your son dealing with this, by the way?"

Harry shrugged. "Upset. Scared. Angry."

"I saw him earlier. His name's Oleg, isn't it? Has he stayed in 301 because he doesn't want to be here?"

"He didn't want to come in with me. Or talk to me. He thinks I'm letting her down by continuing to work on the case while she's lying here."

Steffens nodded. "Young people have always had an enviable confidence in their own moral judgements. But he may have a point, in that increased efforts by the police aren't always the most effective way to fight crime."

"Meaning?"

"Do you know what made crime rates go down in the U.S.A. in the nineties?"

Harry shook his head, put his hands on the armrests and looked at the door.

"Think of it as a break from all the other things going on in your mind," Steffens said. "Guess."

"I don't know about guessing," Harry said. "It's generally accepted that it was Mayor Giuliani's zero-tolerance policy, and an increased police presence."

"And that's wrong. Because crime rates didn't just fall in New York, but right across the U.S.A. The answer is actually the more liberal abortion laws that were introduced in the 1970s." Steffens leaned back in his chair and paused, as if to let Harry think it through for himself. "Single, dissolute women having sex with men who vanish the next morning, or at least as soon as they realise she's pregnant. Pregnancies like that have been a conveyor belt producing criminal offspring for centuries. Children without fathers, without boundaries, without a mother with the money to give them an education or moral backbone or to teach them the ways of the Lord. These women would happily have taken their embryonic children's lives if they hadn't risked being punished for it. And then, in the 1970s, they got what they wanted. The U.S.A. harvested the fruits of the holocaust that was the result of liberal abortion laws fifteen, twenty years later."

"Hm. And what do the Mormons say about that? Unless you're not a Mormon?"

Steffens smiled and steepled his fingers. "I support the Church in much of what it says, Hole, but not in its opposition to abortion. In that instance I support the heathens. In the 1990s ordinary people could walk down the streets of American towns without having to be afraid of being robbed, raped and murdered. Because the man who would have murdered them had been scraped out of his mother's womb, Harry. But where I don't support liberal heathens is in their demands for so-called free abortions. A foetus's potential for good or evil will, twenty years later, benefit or damage a society so much that the decision to abort ought to be taken by that society, not by an irresponsible woman roaming the streets for someone to sleep with that night."

Harry looked at the time. "You're suggesting state-regulated abortion?"

"Not a pleasant job, obviously. So anyone doing it would naturally have to regard it as . . . well, as a calling."

"You're kidding, aren't you?"

Steffens held Harry's gaze for a few seconds. Then he smiled again. "Of course. I believe firmly in the inviolability of the individual."

Harry got to his feet. "I'm assuming I'll be informed of when you're going to wake her. Presumably it would be good for her to see a familiar face when she comes round?" "That's one consideration, Harry. And tell Oleg to look in if there's anything he wants to know."

Harry made his way to the main entrance of the hospital. Shivering outside in the cold, he took two drags on his cigarette, realised that it didn't taste of anything, stubbed it out and hurried back inside.

"How's it going, Antonsen?" he asked the police guard outside room 301.

"Fine, thanks," Antonsen said, looking up at him. "There's a picture of you in *VG*."

"Really?"

"Want to see?" Antonsen took out his smartphone.

"Not unless I look particularly good."

Antonsen chuckled. "Maybe you don't want to see it, then. I have to say, it looks like you're starting to lose it at Crime Squad. Pointing pistols at ninety-year-olds and using bartenders as spies."

Harry stopped abruptly with his hand on the door handle. "What was that last bit again?"

Antonsen held his phone out in front of him and squinted, evidently long-sighted. He managed to read "Barten—" before Harry snatched the phone from him.

Harry stared at the screen. "Fuck, fuck. Have you got a car, Antonsen?"

"No, I cycle. Oslo's so small, and you get a bit of exercise, so—"

Harry tossed the phone in Antonsen's lap and yanked open the door of room 301. Oleg looked up just long enough to see it was Harry before looking down at his book again.

"Oleg, you've got a car—you've got to drive me to Grünerløkka. Now."

Oleg snorted without raising his eyes. "Yeah, right."

"That wasn't a request, it was an order. Come on."

"An order?" His face contorted in fury. "You're not even my father. Thanks for that."

"You were right. You said grade trumps everything. Me, detective inspector, you, trainee police officer. So wipe your tears and shift your arse."

Oleg gawped at him, speechless.

Harry turned and hurried off along the corridor.

.  .  .

Mehmet Kalak had abandoned Coldplay and U2 and was trying out Ian Hunter on his clientele.

"All the Young Dudes" rang out from the speakers.

"Well?" Mehmet said.

"Not bad, but David Bowie did it better," the clientele said. Or, more accurately, Øystein Eikeland, who had taken up position on the other side of the bar since his job had come to an end. And seeing as they had the place to themselves, Mehmet turned the volume up.

"Doesn't make any difference how loud you crank Hunter up!" Øystein cried, and raised his daiquiri. It was his fifth. He claimed that because he had mixed them himself, they must therefore be counted as trial samples in conjunction with his apprenticeship as a bartender, and were an investment and thus tax-deductible. And because he was entitled to a staff discount, but intended to claim them back on his tax at full price, he was actually making a profit from his drinking.

"I wish I could stop now, but I should probably mix myself one more if I'm going to have enough to pay the rent," he sniffled.

"You make a better customer than a bartender," Mehmet said. "That's not to say that you're a useless bartender, just that you're the best customer I've had—"

"Thank you, dear Mehmet, I—"

"—and now you're going home."

"I am?"

"You are." To show that he meant it, Mehmet turned the music off.

Øystein opened his mouth, as if there was something he really wanted to say, something he assumed would form itself into words if he just opened his mouth, but that didn't happen. He tried again, then closed his mouth and merely nodded. He did up his taxi driver's jacket, slid off the bar stool, and walked rather unsteadily towards the door.

"No tip?" Mehmet called with a smile.

"Tips aren't tax-dec . . . deluct . . . are no good."

Mehmet picked up Øystein's glass, squirted some washing-up liquid in it and rinsed it under the tap. There hadn't been enough customers that evening to use the dishwasher. His phone lit up on the inside of the counter. It was Harry. And as he dried his hands to answer it, it struck him that there was something about the time. The time that had passed between Øystein opening the door and it closing again. It had taken slightly longer than usual. Someone had held the door open for a few seconds. He looked up.

"Quiet night?" the man standing at the bar asked.

Mehmet tried to breathe so he could answer. But couldn't.

"Quiet is good," Valentin Gjertsen said. Because it was him. The man from the steam room.

Mehmet silently reached his hand out towards his phone.

"Please, don't answer that, and I'll do you a favour."

Mehmet wouldn't have taken the offer if it hadn't been for the large revolver that was pointing right at him.

"Thanks, you'd only have regretted it." The man looked around. "A shame you don't have any customers. For you, I mean. It suits me fine, it means I've got your full attention. Well, I suppose I'd have had that anyway, because you're naturally curious about what I want. If I've come for a drink, or to kill you. Am I right?"

Mehmet nodded slowly.

"Yes, that's a reasonable concern seeing as you're the only person currently alive who can identify me. That's a fact, by the way? Even the plastic surgeon who . . . well, enough of that. Anyway, I'm going to do you a favour, seeing as you didn't take that call, and that business of shopping me to the police is no more than could be expected of a socially responsible person. Don't you think?"

Mehmet nodded again. And tried to fend off the unavoidable thought. That he was going to die. His brain tried desperately to find other possibilities, but just kept coming back to: you're going to die. But, as if in answer to his thoughts, there was a knock on the window over by the door. Mehmet looked past Valentin. A pair of hands and a familiar face were pressed against the glass, trying to peer inside. Come in, for God's sake, come in.

"Don't move," Valentin said calmly without turning round. His body was hiding the revolver, so the person at the window couldn't see it.

Why the hell didn't he just come in?

The answer came a moment later, with a loud banging on the door.

Valentin had locked the door when he came in.

The face was back at the window, and the man was waving his hands to get his attention, so he had evidently seen them inside.

"Don't move, just signal that you're closed," Valentin said. There was no trace of stress in his voice.

Mehmet stood still with his hands by his sides.

"Now, or I'll kill you."

"You're going to do that anyway."

"You can't know that with one hundred percent certainty. But if

you don't do as I say, I promise I'll kill you. And then the person outside. Look at me. I promise."

Mehmet looked at Valentin. Swallowed. Leaned slightly to one
side, into the light, so that the man outside the window could see him
more clearly, and shook his head.

The face was there for a couple of seconds. A wave, not all that
easy to see. Then Geir Sølle was gone.

Valentin watched in the mirror.

"There," he said. "Where were we? Oh yes, good and bad news.
The bad news is that the obvious thought that I'm here to kill you
is so obvious that . . . well, it's correct. In other words, we're now up
to one hundred percent certainty. I'm going to kill you." Valentin
looked at Mehmet with a sad expression. Then he burst out laughing.
"That's the longest face I've seen today! And of course I can understand that, but don't forget the good news. Which is that you get to
choose how you die. Here are the options, so listen carefully. Are
you with me? Good. Do you want to be shot in the head or have this
drainage tube stuck in your neck?" Valentin held up something that
looked like a large drinking straw made of metal, one end of which
was cut diagonally to form a sharp point.

Mehmet just stared at Valentin. The whole thing was so absurd
that he was starting to wonder if this was a dream he was about to
wake up from. Or was the man in front of him dreaming all of this?
But then Valentin jabbed the tube towards him and Mehmet automatically took a step back and hit the sink.

Valentin snapped: "Not the drainage tube, then?"

Mehmet nodded cautiously as he saw the sharpened metal point
glint in the light from the mirror shelf. Needles. That had always
been his greatest fear. Having things inserted into his body through
his skin. That was why he ran away from home and hid in the forest
as a child when they were going to vaccinate him.

"An agreement is an agreement, so no tube." Valentin put the
straw down on the bar and pulled a pair of black antique-looking
handcuffs from his pocket, all without the barrel of the revolver
moving an inch from Mehmet. "Pass one of them behind the metal
bar on the mirror unit, fasten them round your wrists, and lay your
head in the sink."

"I . . ."

Mehmet didn't see the blow coming. Just registered a crashing
sound in his head, an instant of blackness, and the fact that he was
facing a different direction when his vision returned. He realised he'd

been hit with the revolver and that the barrel was now pressed to his temple.

"The drainage tube," a voice whispered close to his ear. "Your choice."

Mehmet picked up the strange, heavy handcuffs and passed one behind the metal bar. He fastened them round his wrists. He felt something warm trickle down his nose and top lip. The sweet, metallic taste of blood.

"Tasty?" Valentin said in a high voice.

Mehmet looked up and met his gaze in the mirror.

"I can't stand it myself," Valentin smiled. "It tastes of iron and beatings. Yes, iron and beatings. Your own blood, fine, but other people's? And you can *taste* what they've been eating. Speaking of eating, does the condemned man have a last wish? Not that I'm thinking of serving a meal, I'm just curious."

Mehmet blinked. A last wish? The words found their way in, no more than that, but as if in a dream his mind couldn't help considering the answer. He hoped that the Jealousy Bar would one day be the coolest in Oslo. That Galatasaray would win the league. That Paul Rodgers's "Ready for Love" would be played at his funeral. What else? He tried, but couldn't think of anything. And felt sorrowful laughter welling up inside him.


Harry saw a figure hurrying away from the Jealousy Bar as he approached. The light from the big window fell across the pavement, but he couldn't hear any music from inside. He went over to the edge of the window and looked in. Saw the back of a figure behind the bar, but it was impossible to tell if it was Mehmet. It looked empty apart from that. Harry moved to the door and cautiously pushed the handle. Locked. The bar was open until midnight.

Harry pulled out the key ring with the broken plastic heart. Slowly inserted the key in the lock. Drew his Glock 17 with his right hand as he turned the key and opened the door with his left. He stepped inside, holding the pistol in front of him with both hands as he used his foot to make sure that the door closed gently behind him. But the sounds of the evening in Grünerløkka had drifted in, and the figure behind the bar straightened up and looked in the mirror.

"Police," Harry said. "Don't move."

"Harry Hole." The figure was wearing a peaked cap and the angle of the mirror meant Harry couldn't see his face, but he didn't need to. More than three years had passed since he had heard this high-pitched voice, but it was like yesterday.

"Valentin Gjertsen," Harry said, and heard the tremble in his own voice.

"At last we meet again, Harry. I've thought about you. Have you thought about me?"

"Where's Mehmet?"

"You're excited, you *have* thought about me." That high-pitched laugh. "Why? Because of my list of accomplishments? Or victims, as you call them. No, wait. It's obviously because of *your* list of accomplishments. I'm the one you never caught, aren't I?"

Harry didn't answer, just stood where he was by the door.

"It's unbearable, is that it? Good! That's why you're so good. You're like me, Harry, you can't bear it."

"I'm not like you, Valentin." Harry changed his grip on the pistol, aimed and wondered what was stopping him from going closer.

"No? You don't let yourself get distracted by any consideration of the people around you, do you? You keep your eyes on the prize, Harry. Look at yourself now. All you want is your trophy, no matter what the cost. Other people's lives, your own . . . If you're really honest, all of that comes second, doesn't it? You and me, we ought to sit down and get to know each other better, Harry. Because we don't meet many people like us."

"Shut up, Valentin. Stay where you are, put your hands up where I can see them, and tell me where Mehmet is."

"If Mehmet is the name of your spy, I shall have to move in order to show you. And then the situation we find ourselves in will also become much clearer."

Valentin Gjertsen took a step to one side. Mehmet was half standing, half hanging from his arms, which were tied to the metal bar that ran horizontally across the top of the mirror behind the bar. His head was bent forward, down into the sink, meaning that his long dark curls covered his face. Valentin was holding a long-barrelled revolver to the back of his head.

"Stay where you are, Harry. As you can see, we have an interesting balance of terror here. From where you're standing to here it's—what?—eight to ten metres? The chances of your first shot putting me out of action so that I don't have time to kill Mehmet are pretty slim, wouldn't you agree? But if I shoot Mehmet first, you'd be able to fire at me at least twice before I manage to turn the revolver on you. Worse odds for me. In other words, we've got a lose-lose situation here, so it really boils down to this, Harry: are you prepared to sacrifice your spy in order to catch me now? Or shall we save him and you can catch me later? What do you say?"

Harry looked at Valentin over the sights of his pistol. He was right. It was too dark and too great a distance for him to be sure of hitting Valentin with a headshot.

"I interpret your silence to mean that you agree with me, Harry. And because I believe I can hear police sirens in the distance, I presume we don't have much time."

Harry had considered telling them not to use sirens, but then they would have taken longer.

"Put your pistol down, Harry, and I'll walk out of here."

Harry shook his head. "You're here because he's seen your face, so you'll shoot him and me because now I've seen your face too."

"So come up with a suggestion within the next five seconds, otherwise I'll shoot him and gamble on you missing before I hit you."

"We maintain the balance of terror," Harry said. "But with matching disarmament."

"You're trying to drag things out, but the countdown has started. Four, three . . ."

"We both turn our guns at the same time and hold them by the barrel in our right hand, with the trigger and hilt visible."

"Two . . ."

"You head for the door along that wall there, while I head towards the bar past the booths on the other side of the room."

"One . . ."

"The distance between us will stay the same as it is now, and neither of us would be able to shoot the other before he had time to react."

The bar was silent. The sirens were closer. And if Oleg had done as he had been told—correction, ordered—he was still sitting in the car two blocks away and hadn't moved.

The light suddenly vanished, and Harry realised Valentin had turned the dimmer switch behind the bar. And when he turned towards Harry for the first time, it was too dark for Harry to see his face beneath the cap.

"We turn our guns on the count of three," Valentin said and raised his hand. "One, two . . . three."

Harry grasped the handle with his left hand, then the barrel with his right. He held his pistol in the air. Saw Valentin do the same. It looked like he was holding a flag in the children's procession on Constitution Day, with the characteristic red grip of a Ruger Redhawk sticking away from the long barrel of the revolver.

"There, you see," Valentin said. "Who but two men who truly understand each other could have done that? I like you, Harry. I *really* like you. So, now we start to move . . ."

Valentin walked towards the wall, while Harry moved towards the booths. It was so quiet that Harry could hear the creak of Valentin's boots as they each crept round the other in a semicircle, watching one another like two gladiators who knew that the first skirmish would mean death for at least one of them. Harry realised he'd reached the bar when he heard the low rumble of the fridge, the steady drip in the sink and the insect-like buzz from the stereo's amplifier. He felt around in the darkness without taking his eyes off the silhouette that stood out against the light from the window. Then he was behind the bar, heard the sounds from the street as the door opened, then footsteps running until they disappeared.

He pulled his phone from his pocket, put it to his ear.

"Did you hear?"

"I heard everything," Oleg replied. "I'll inform the patrol cars. Description?"

"Short black jacket, dark trousers, peaked cap with no logo, but he's bound to have got rid of that already. I didn't see his face. He ran left, towards Thorvald Meyers gate, so—"

"—he's heading for somewhere with a lot of people and traffic. I'll tell them."

Harry dropped his phone in his pocket and put his hand on Mehmet's shoulder. No reaction.

"Mehmet . . ."

He could no longer hear the fridge and amplifier. Only the steady dripping. He turned the dimmer switch up. He took hold of Mehmet's hair and gently lifted his head out of the sink. His face was pale. Too pale.

There was something sticking out of his neck.

It looked like a drinking straw made of metal.

Red drops were still dripping from the end, down into the sink, which was clogged with all the blood.

# 25

# Tuesday night

Katrine Bratt jumped out of the car and walked towards the cordon outside the Jealousy Bar. She spotted a man leaning against one of the police cars, smoking. The rotating blue light alternately lit up his ugly-handsome face and cast it into darkness. She shivered and walked over to him.

"It's cold," she said.

"Winter's coming," Harry said, blowing his cigarette smoke up so it was caught by the blue light.

"Emilia's coming."

"Mm, I'd forgotten that."

"They say the storm's going to hit Oslo tomorrow."

"Mm."

Katrine looked at him. She thought she had seen all the possible versions of Harry. But not this one. Not one so empty, crushed, resigned. She felt like stroking his cheek and giving him a hug. But she couldn't. There were so many reasons why she couldn't.

"What happened in there?"

"Valentin had a Ruger Redhawk, and made me believe I was negotiating for someone's life. But Mehmet was already dead by the time I got there. A metal tube inserted into his carotid artery. He'd been drained of blood like some damn fish. Just because he . . . because I . . ." Harry started to blink rapidly and stopped talking, and pretended to pick a strand of tobacco from his tongue.

Katrine didn't know what to say. So she said nothing. Instead she looked at the familiar black Volvo Amazon with the racing stripe that was parked on the other side of the street. Bjørn got out of it and Katrine felt her heart skip a beat when something-or-other Lien got out of the passenger side. What was Bjørn's boss doing here, out in the field? Had Bjørn offered her a romantic viewing of the many attractions of a murder scene? Damn. Bjørn had spotted them, and Katrine saw them adjust their course and head in their direction.

"I'm going in, we'll talk more later," she said, snuck under the cordon and hurried towards the door beneath the sign of a broken plastic heart.

"There you are," Bjørn said. "I've been trying to get hold of you."

"I've been . . ." Harry took a deep drag on his cigarette. ". . . a bit busy."

"This is Berna Lien, the new head of Krimteknisk. Berna, Harry Hole."

"I've heard a lot about you," the woman smiled.

"And I've heard nothing about you," Harry said. "Are you any good?"

She looked at Bjørn, uncertain. "Any good?"

"Valentin Gjertsen's good," Harry said. "I'm not good enough, so I'm just hoping there are other people here who are better, or else this bloodbath is just going to continue."

"I might have something," Bjørn said.

"Oh?"

"That's why I was trying to get hold of you. Valentin's jacket. When I cut it open I did actually find a couple of things in the lining. A ten-øre coin and two scraps of paper. Because the jacket's been washed all the ink was gone from the outside, but when I unfolded one of them there was some left inside. It's not much, but enough to see that it's a receipt from a cashpoint in Oslo City. Which fits the theory that he consistently avoids debit cards and pays cash. Sadly we can't see the card number, registration number or when the withdrawal was made, but parts of the date are visible."

"How much?"

"Enough to see that it's this year, August, and we've got enough of the last digit of the date to see that it could only be a 1."

"So, 1, 11, 21 and 31."

"Four possible days . . . I've been in touch with a woman at Nokas, which looks after DNB's cashpoint machines. She says they're allowed to store images from their security cameras for up to three months, so they'll have this withdrawal on film. It was made at one of the machines at Oslo Central Station, which is one the busiest in Norway. The official explanation is that it's because of all the shopping centres in the vicinity."

"But?"

"Everyone accepts cards these days. Except?"

"Mm. The drug dealers around the station and along the river."

"There are over two hundred transactions a day from the busiest machines," Bjørn said.

"Four days, so just under a thousand," Berna Lien said eagerly. Harry trod on the smouldering cigarette.

"We'll have the recordings first thing tomorrow, and with the efficient use of fast-forward and pause, we can check at least two faces per minute. In other words, seven or eight hours, probably less. Once we've identified Valentin, we just have to match the time of the recording to the time of the withdrawal in the cash machine's register."

"And hey presto, we've got Valentin Gjertsen's secret identity," Berna Lien said, evidently proud and excited on behalf of her department. "What do you think, Hole?"

"I think, fru Lien, that it's a shame the man who could have identified Valentin is lying in there with his head in the sink and no pulse." Harry buttoned his jacket. "But thanks for coming."

Berna Lien looked angrily from Harry to Bjørn, who cleared his throat unhappily. "As I understand it, you were face-to-face with Valentin," he said.

Harry shook his head. "I never saw his new face."

Bjørn nodded slowly without taking his eyes off Harry. "I see. That's a shame. A great shame."

"Mm." Harry looked down at the crushed cigarette butt in front of his shoe.

"OK. Well, we'll go inside and take a look."

"Have fun."

He watched them go. The press photographers had already gathered outside the cordon, and now the journalists were beginning to arrive as well. Perhaps they knew something, perhaps they didn't, perhaps they just didn't dare, but they left Harry alone.

Eight hours.

Eight hours as of tomorrow morning.

Within the space of another day, Valentin might have killed someone else.

Fuck.

"Bjørn!" Harry called, just as his colleague took hold of the door handle.

"Harry," Ståle Aune said, standing in the doorway. "Bjørn."

"Sorry to call so late," Harry said. "Can we come in?"

"Of course." Aune held the door open and Harry and Bjørn stepped into the Aune family home. A small woman, thinner than her husband but with exactly the same grey-coloured hair, darted out with quick, nimble steps. "Harry!" she sang. "I thought it was you, it's been *far* too long. How's Rakel, do they know any more?"

Harry shook his head and let Ingrid peck his cheek. "Coffee, or is it too late? Green tea?"

Bjørn and Harry replied yes please and no thanks simultaneously, and Ingrid disappeared into the kitchen.

They went into the living room and sat down on low armchairs. The walls were lined with bookcases, full of everything from travel guides and old atlases to poetry, graphic novels and heavy academic volumes. But mostly novels.

"You see I'm reading that book you gave me?" Ståle picked up the thin book that lay open, spine up, on the table beside his armchair, and showed it to Bjørn. "Édouard Levé. *Suicide*. Harry gave it to me for my sixtieth birthday. I suppose he thought it was time."

Bjørn and Harry laughed. Evidently not entirely convincingly, because Ståle frowned. "Is something wrong?"

Harry cleared his throat. "Valentin killed another person this evening."

"It pains me to hear that," Ståle said, and shook his head.

"And we have no reason to believe that he's going to stop."

"No. No, you haven't," the psychologist agreed.

"That's why we're here, and this is very hard for me, Ståle."

Ståle Aune sighed. "Hallstein Smith isn't working, and you want me to take over, is that it?"

"No. We need . . ." Harry fell silent when Ingrid came in and put the tea tray down on the coffee table between the silent men. "The sound of the oath of confidentiality," she said. "See you later, Harry. Give Oleg our love and tell him we're all thinking of Rakel."

"We need someone who can identify Valentin Gjertsen," Harry said when she'd gone. "And the last person alive who we know has seen him . . ."

Harry didn't intend it as a dramatic pause to increase the tension, but so that Ståle would get the fraction of a second his brain required to make the rapid, almost unconscious, yet horribly accurate deductions it was capable of. Not that it would make much difference. He was like a boxer in the process of being punched, but who gets a tenth of a second to shift his weight ever so slightly away from the punch instead of meeting it head-on.

". . . is Aurora."

In the silence that followed Harry could hear the rasping of the side of the book Ståle was still holding as it slid across his fingertips.

"What are you saying, Harry?"

"The day Rakel and I got married, while you and Ingrid were there, Valentin paid Aurora a visit at the handball tournament she was taking part in."

The book hit the carpet with a muffled thud. Ståle blinked uncomprehendingly. "She . . . he . . ."

Harry waited as he watched it sink in.

"Did he touch her? Did he hurt her?"

Harry held Ståle's gaze, but didn't answer. Saw him piece the information together. Saw him look at the previous three years in a new light. A light that provided answers.

"Yes," Ståle whispered, grimacing in pain. He took his glasses off. "Yes, of course he did. How blind I've been." He stared into space. "And how did you find this out?"

"Aurora came to see me yesterday and told me," Harry said.

Ståle Aune's eyes swung back to Harry as if in slow motion. "You . . . you've known since yesterday, and didn't say anything to me?"

"She made me promise."

Ståle Aune's voice didn't rise, it sank. "A fifteen-year-old girl who's been assaulted, whom you know perfectly well needs all the help she can get, and you chose to keep it secret?"

"Yes."

"But for God's sake, Harry, why?"

"Because Valentin threatened to kill you if she told anyone what had happened."

"Me?" Ståle let slip a sob. "Me? What does that matter? I'm way past sixty with a dodgy heart, Harry. She's a young girl with her whole life ahead of her!"

"You're the person she loves most in the whole world, and I made her a promise."

Ståle Aune put his glasses on, then raised a trembling finger towards Harry. "Yes, you made her a promise! And you kept that promise as long as it didn't mean anything to you! But now, now you see that you can use her to solve yet another Harry Hole case, that promise doesn't mean so much anymore."

Harry didn't protest.

"Get out, Harry! You're no friend of this house, and you're no longer welcome here."

"We're running out of time, Ståle."

"Out, now!" Ståle Aune had got up.

"We need her."

"I'll call the police. The *real* police."

Harry looked up at him. Saw that there was no point. That they'd have to wait, that this would have to run its course, that they could only hope Ståle Aune would see the bigger picture before morning.

He nodded. Levered himself out of the chair.

"We'll see ourselves out," he said.

Harry saw Ingrid's pale, silent face in the doorway as they passed the kitchen.

He put his shoes on in the hall and was about to leave when he heard a thin voice.

"Harry?"

He turned round and couldn't see where the voice had come from at first. Then, out of the darkness at the top of the stairs, she stepped into the light. She was wearing striped pyjamas that were far too big for her, possibly her father's, Harry thought.

"I'm sorry," Harry said. "I had to."

"I know," Aurora said. "It says on the Net that the man who died was called Mehmet. And I heard you."

At that moment Ståle came running out of the living room, waving his arms and with tears streaming from his eyes. "Aurora! You're not to—" His voice broke.

"Dad," Aurora said, sitting down calmly on the steps above them, "I want to help."

# 26

# Tuesday night

Mona daa was standing by the Monolith, watching Truls Berntsen hurry through the darkness. When they'd arranged to meet in Frognerparken she had suggested a few more discreet, less popular sculptures, seeing as the Monolith was visited by sightseers even at night. But when Truls Berntsen had said "What?" three times she had realised that the Monolith was the only one he was familiar with.

She pulled him round to the west side of the sculpture, away from the two couples who were looking at the view of the church spires to the east. She gave him the envelope containing the money, which he slipped inside his long Armani coat, which for some reason didn't look like an Armani coat on him.

"Anything new?" she asked.

"There won't be any more tip-offs," Truls said, glancing around.

"No?"

He looked at her, as if to check if she was joking. "The man was murdered, for fuck's sake."

"So you'd better offer something a bit less . . . *fatal* next time."

Truls Berntsen snorted. "Christ, you're even worse than me, the whole lot of you."

"Really? You gave us Mehmet's name, but we still chose not to reveal it or print his picture."

Truls shook his head. "Can you hear yourself, Daa? We just led Valentin straight to a guy who has only done two things wrong. Running a bar that Valentin's victim happened to visit, and agreeing to help the police."

"At least you're saying 'we.' Does that mean you've got a guilty conscience?"

"Do you think I'm some kind of psychopath, or what? Of course I think this is bad."

"I'm not going to answer that question. But yes, I agree that it's pretty bad. Does this mean that you're not going to be my source anymore?"

"If I say no, does that mean you won't protect my identity in future?"

"No," Mona said.

"Good. So you do have a conscience."

"Well," Mona said, "it's not so much that we care about the source than that we care what our colleagues would say if we blew a source. What are your colleagues saying, by the way?"

"Nothing. They've figured out that I'm the leak, so they've isolated me. I'm not allowed to take part in meetings or know anything about the investigation."

"No? I can feel myself losing interest in you, Truls."

Truls snorted. "You're cynical, but at least you're honest, Mona Daa."

"Thanks. I assume."

"OK, I might have one last tip-off. But this is about something else entirely."

"Fire away."

"Police Chief Mikael Bellman is fucking a high-profile woman."

"There's no money in tip-offs like that, Berntsen."

"OK, it's free, just print it anyway."

"The editor doesn't like infidelity stories, but if you've got evidence and are willing to stand by the story, I might be able to convince them. But in that case you'd be quoted, with your full name."

"With my name? That's suicide, you can see that, surely? I can tell you where they meet, you could send one of those hidden photographers."

Mona Daa laughed. "Sorry, it doesn't work like that."

"Doesn't it?"

"The press abroad do this sort of thing, but not us here in little Norway."

"Why not?"

"The official explanation is that we don't sink to that level."

"But?"

Mona shrugged her shoulders, shivering. "Because there aren't really any limits to how low we're actually prepared to go, my personal theory is that it's another example of everyone's-got-something-to-hide syndrome."

"Meaning?"

"Married editors are no less unfaithful than anyone else. If you reveal someone's infidelity, everyone in a small public arena like Norway's risks being caught in the blast. We can write about affairs in the great big 'abroad,' maybe refer to affairs abroad here at home if one public figure has said something careless about another. But investigative journalism into infidelity among people in positions of power?" Mona Daa shook her head.

Truls blew out scornfully through his nose. "So there's no way to make it public?"

"Is this something you think should be revealed because Bellman shouldn't be Police Chief?"

"What? No, maybe not that."

Mona nodded and looked up at the Monolith, and the remorseless struggle to reach the top that it depicted. "You must really hate him."

Truls didn't answer. He just looked rather surprised, as if that was something he hadn't thought about. And Mona wondered what was going on inside that pockmarked, not particularly attractive face, with its heavy jaw and beady eyes. She almost felt sorry for him. Almost.

"I'm going now, Berntsen. We'll be in touch."

"Will we?"

"Maybe not."

When Mona had walked some way into the park, she turned round and saw Truls Berntsen in the light of one of the lamps up by the Monolith. He had stuck his hands in his pockets, and was just standing there with his back hunched, looking for something. He seemed so incredibly alone standing there like that, as unmoving as the blocks of stone around him.

Harry stared at the ceiling. The ghosts hadn't come. Maybe they wouldn't be coming tonight. You never knew. But they had a new member. What would Mehmet look like when he came? Harry shut the thought out and listened to the silence. Holmenkollen was certainly quiet, there was no denying that. Too quiet. He preferred to hear the city outside. Like nighttime in the jungle, full of noises that could warn you in the darkness, tell you when something was coming and when it wasn't. Silence contained too little information. But that wasn't it. It was the fact that there was no one beside him in bed.

If he counted, then the number of nights he had shared a bed with anyone was in a clear minority. So why did he feel so alone, he, a man who had always sought out solitude and had never needed anyone else?

He rolled onto his side and tried shutting his eyes.

He didn't need anyone now either. He didn't need anyone. He didn't need *anyone*.

He just needed her.

A creaking sound. From the timber walls. Or a floorboard. Perhaps the storm was early. Or the ghosts late.

He turned onto the other side. Shut his eyes again.

The creaking was just outside the bedroom door.

He got up, walked over and opened it.

It was Mehmet. "I saw him, Harry." Where his eyes had been there were two black sockets that sparked and smoked.

Harry woke with a start.

His phone was purring like a cat on the bedside table next to him. "Yes?"

"This is Dr. Steffens."

Harry felt a sudden pain in his chest.

"It's about Rakel."

Of course it was about Rakel. And Harry knew that Steffens was only saying that to give him the seconds he needed to steel himself for the news.

"We can't bring her out of the coma."

"What?"

"She won't wake up."

"Is . . . will she . . . ?"

"We don't know, Harry. I know you must have an awful lot of questions, but so do we. I really can't tell you anything except that we're working as hard as we can here."

Harry bit the inside of his cheek to make sure this wasn't just the world premiere of a new nightmare. "OK, OK. Can I see her?"

"Not now, we've got her in intensive care. I'll call as soon as we know more. But it might take a while, Rakel is probably going to be in a coma for some time, so don't hold your breath, OK?"

Harry realised that Steffens was right: he wasn't breathing.

They hung up. Harry stared at the phone. *She won't wake up.* Of course not, she didn't want to, because who the hell wants to wake up? Harry got out of bed and went downstairs. Opened the kitchen cupboards. Nothing. Empty, empty. He rang for a taxi then went back upstairs to get dressed.

He saw the blue sign, read the name and braked. Pulled in to the side of the road and switched the engine off. Looked around. Forest and road. It reminded him of those anonymous, monotonous stretches of road in Finland, where you get the feeling that you're driving through a desert of trees. Where the trees stand like a silent wall on either side of the road and a body is as easy to hide as it would be to sink it in the sea. He waited until a car had passed. Checked the mirror. He couldn't see any lights now, either in front or behind. So he got out onto the road, walked round the car and opened the boot. She was so pale. Even her freckles were paler. And her frightened eyes looked big and black above the muzzle. He lifted her out, and had to help her stand up. He took hold of the handcuffs and led her across the road and over the ditch, towards the black wall of trees. He switched the flashlight on. Felt her trembling so much that the handcuffs were shaking.

"There, there, I'm not going to hurt you, darling," he said. And could feel that he meant it. He really didn't want to hurt her. Not anymore. And perhaps she knew that, perhaps she understood that he loved her. Perhaps she was trembling because she was only dressed in underwear and his Japanese girlfriend's negligee.

They headed into the trees, and it was like walking into a building. A different sort of silence settled, while at the same time new noises could be heard. Smaller but clearer, unidentifiable noises. A snapping sound, a sigh, a cry. The ground in the forest was soft, the carpet of pine needles gave a pleasant bounce as they moved forward with soundless steps, like a bridal couple in a church in a dream.

When he had counted to a hundred he stopped. Raised the flashlight and shone it around them. And the beam of light soon found what he was looking for. A tall, charred tree that had been split in two by lightning. He dragged her towards the tree. She didn't resist as he undid the handcuffs, pulled her arms around the tree and fastened the cuffs again. A lamb, he thought as he looked at her sitting there on her knees, hugging the tree. A sacrificial lamb. Because he wasn't the bridegroom: he was the father giving his child away at the altar.

He stroked her cheek one last time and turned to walk away when a voice rang out from among the trees.

"She's alive, Valentin."

He stopped, and instinctively pointed the flashlight in the direction of the sound.

"Put that away," said the voice in the darkness.

Valentin did as the voice said. "She wanted to live."

"But the bartender didn't?"

"He could identify me. I couldn't take the risk."

Valentin listened, but all he could hear was a low whistle from Marte's nostrils as she breathed.

"I'll clean up after you this one time," the voice said. "Have you got the revolver you were given?"

"Yes," Valentin said. Wasn't there something familiar about the voice?

"Put it down next to her and go. You'll get it back soon enough."

A thought struck Valentin. Draw the revolver, use the flashlight to find the other man, kill him. Kill the voice of reason, wipe out any trail that led to him, let the demon reign once more. The counter-argument was that Valentin might need him later.

"Where and when?" Valentin called. "We can't use the locker at the bathhouse anymore."

"Tomorrow. You'll be informed. Now that you've heard my voice anyway, I'll call."

Valentin pulled the revolver from its holster and put it down in front of the girl. Took one last look at her. Then he walked away.

When he got back in the car he hit his head twice against the wheel, hard. Then he started the car, indicated to pull out even though there were no other cars in sight, and calmly drove away.

"Stop over there," Harry told the taxi driver, pointing.

"It's three o'clock in the morning, and that bar looks very closed."

"It belongs to me."

Harry paid and got out. Where there had been febrile activity just a few hours ago, there was now no one in sight at all. The crime-scene investigators were finished, but there was white tape across the door. The tape was embossed with the Norwegian lion and the words POLICE. SEALED. DO NOT BREAK SEAL. TRANSGRESSION PUNISHABLE BY PENAL CODE 343. Harry inserted the key in the lock and turned it. The tape crackled as he pulled the door open and went inside.

They had left the lights beneath the mirror shelves on. Harry closed one eye and aimed his index finger at the bottles from where he stood by the door. Nine metres. What if he'd fired? What would things look like now? Impossible to know. It was what it was. Nothing to be done about it. Except forget about it, of course. His finger found the bottle of Jim Beam. It had been promoted and now had its own optic. The brothel lighting made the contents shimmer like gold. Harry walked across the room and went behind the bar, grabbed a glass and held it under the bottle. He filled it to the brim. Why fool himself?

He felt his muscles tense, all through his body, and wondered for a moment if he was going to throw up *before* the first mouthful. But he managed to hold on to both the contents of his stomach and the drink, until the third glass. Then he lurched for the sink, and before the yellow-green vomit hit the metal, he saw that the bottom was still red with congealed blood.

# 27

# Wednesday morning

It was five to eight, and in the boiler room the coffee machine had finished rattling for the second time that morning.

"What's happened to Harry?" Wyller wondered, looking at his watch again.

"Don't know," Bjørn Holm said. "We'll have to start without him." Smith and Wyller nodded.

"OK," Bjørn said. "Right now Aurora is sitting with her father in Nokas's head office looking at those recordings, along with someone from Nokas and a specialist in security cameras from the Street Crime Unit. If it goes according to plan, they should get through the four days' footage in eight hours at most. If the receipt we found really is from a withdrawal Valentin himself made, with a bit of luck we could have his new identity within four hours or so. But certainly before eight o'clock this evening."

"That's brilliant!" Smith exclaimed. "Isn't it?"

"Yes, but let's not count any chickens," Bjørn said. "Have you talked to Katrine, Anders?"

"Yes, and we've got authorisation to use Delta. They're ready to go."

"Delta, they're the ones with semi-automatics and gas masks and . . . er, that sort of thing?"

"You're starting to get the hang of it, Smith," Bjørn chuckled, and saw Wyller looking at his watch again. "Worried, Anders?"

"Maybe we should call Harry?"

"Go ahead."

Nine o'clock. Katrine had just dismissed the investigative team from the conference room. She was gathering her papers when she noticed the man standing in the doorway.

"Well, Smith?" she said. "Exciting day, eh? What are you lot up to down there?"

"Trying to get hold of Harry."

"Hasn't he shown up?"

"He's not answering his phone."

"He's probably sitting in the hospital, they're not allowed to have their phones on there. They say it can interfere with the machines and equipment, but that's supposed to be just as misleading as saying they can disrupt navigation systems on planes."

She realised that Smith wasn't listening and was looking past her.

She turned and saw that the picture from her laptop was still being projected onto the screen. A picture from the Jealousy Bar.

"I know," she said. "It's not pretty."

Smith shook his head like a sleepwalker, without taking his eyes off the screen.

"Are you OK, Smith?"

"No," he said slowly. "I'm not OK. I can't stand the sight of blood, I can't stand violence, and I don't know if can stand to see any more suffering. This individual . . . Valentin Gjertsen . . . I'm a psychologist, and I'm trying to relate to him as a professional case, but I think I might actually hate him."

"None of us is *that* professional, Smith. I wouldn't let a little hatred worry me. Doesn't it feel good to have someone to hate, as Harry says?"

"Harry says that?"

"Yes. Or Raga Rockers. Or . . . Was there something else?"

"I've spoken to Mona Daa at *VG.*"

"*There's* someone else we can hate. What did she want?"

"I was the one who called her."

Katrine stopped sorting her papers.

"I told her my conditions for agreeing to be interviewed about Valentin Gjertsen," Smith said. "That I'll talk about Valentin Gjertsen in general terms, and that I won't say a thing about the investigation. It's a so-called podcast, a sort of radio program that—"

"I know what a podcast is, Smith."

"So at least they can't misquote me. Whatever I say will actually be broadcast. Do I have your permission?"

Katrine considered. "My first question is: *why*?"

"Because people are scared. My wife is scared, my children are scared, the neighbours, the other parents at school are scared. And, as a researcher in this field, I have a responsibility to make them a bit less scared."

"Don't they have the right to be a bit scared?"

"Don't you read the papers, Katrine? The shops have run out of locks and alarm systems in the last week."

"Everyone's scared of what they don't understand."

"It's more than that. They're scared because they thought we were dealing with someone I initially assumed was purely a vampirist. A sick, confused individual who was attacking people as a consequence of profound personality disorders and paraphilias. But this monster is a cold, cynical, calculating fighter who's capable of making rational judgements, who runs when he needs to, like at the Turkish baths. And attacks when he can, like . . . like in that picture." Smith closed his eyes and turned his head away. "And I admit it, I'm scared as well. I lay awake all night wondering how these murders could have been committed by one and the same person. How is that possible? How could I have been so wrong? I don't understand it. But I *have* to understand it, no one's better placed than me to understand it, I'm the only person who can explain it and show them the monster. Because once they've seen the monster they'll understand, and their fear will become manageable. It won't disappear, but at least they'll feel they can take rational decisions, and that will make them safer."

Katrine put her hands on her hips. "Let's see if I understand you correctly. You don't really understand what Valentin Gjertsen is either, but you want to explain that to the public?"

"Yes."

"Lying, with the intention of calming the situation?"

"I think I'll manage the latter better than the former. Do I have your blessing?"

Katrine bit her bottom lip. "You're certainly right that you have a responsibility to inform as an expert, and obviously it would be good if people could be reassured. As long as you don't say anything about the investigation."

"Of course not."

"We can't have any more leaks. I'm the only person on this floor who knows what Aurora's doing right now, not even the Police Chief has been informed."

"My word of honour."


"Is that him? *Is* that him, Aurora?"

"Dad, you're nagging again."

"Aune, perhaps you and I should go and sit outside for a while, so they can look in peace."

"In peace? This is my daughter, Wyller, and she wants—"

"Do as he says, Dad. I'm OK."

"Oh. Sure?"

"Quite sure." Aurora turned to the woman from the bank and the man from the Street Crime Unit. "It's not him, move on."

Ståle Aune stood up, possibly a little too fast, perhaps that's why he felt giddy. Or perhaps because he hadn't got any sleep last night. Or eaten anything today. And had been looking at a screen for three hours without a break.

"You sit down on this sofa here, and I'll see if I can get us some coffee," Wyller said.

Ståle Aune just nodded.

Wyller walked off, leaving Ståle sitting there, looking at his daughter on the other side of the glass wall. She was gesturing at them to move on, stop, rewind. He couldn't remember the last time he had seen her this engaged in anything. Perhaps his initial response and anxiety had been an overreaction. Perhaps the worst was over, perhaps she had somehow managed to move on, while he and Ingrid had been blissfully unaware of what had happened.

And his young daughter had explained to him—the way a psychology lecturer would explain something to a new student—what an oath of confidentiality was. And that she had imposed one on Harry, and that Harry hadn't broken it until he realised that to do so could save people's lives—exactly the same way Ståle applied his own oath of confidentiality. And Aurora had survived, in spite of everything. Death. Ståle had been thinking about that recently. Not his own, but the fact that his daughter would also die one day. Why was that thought so unbearable? Maybe it would look different if he and Ingrid became grandparents, seeing as the human psyche is obviously as much a slave to biological imperatives as physical ones, and the impulse to pass on your own genes is presumably a precondition for the survival of the species. He had once asked Harry, long ago, if he didn't want a child that was biologically his own, but Harry had had his answer ready. He didn't have the happy gene, only the alcoholic one, and he didn't think anyone deserved to inherit that. It's possible that he had changed his mind, because the last few years had at least proved that Harry was capable of experiencing happiness. Ståle took his phone out. He was thinking about phoning Harry and telling him that. That he was a good person, a good friend, father and husband. OK, it sounded like an obituary, but Harry needed to hear it. That he had been wrong to believe that his compulsive attraction to hunting murderers was similar to his alcoholism. That it wasn't an act of escape, that what he was driven by, far more than Harry Hole the individualist was prepared to admit to himself, was the herding instinct. The *good* herding instinct. With morals and responsibility towards everyone. Harry would probably just laugh, but that's what Ståle wanted to tell his friend, if only he'd answer his damn phone.

Ståle saw Aurora straighten up, her muscles tense. Was it . . . ? But then she relaxed again and gestured with her hand that they should go on.

Ståle held the phone to his ear again. Answer, damn it!


"Successful at my career, sports and family life? Yes, maybe." Mikael Bellman looked round the table. "But first and foremost I'm just a simple guy from Manglerud."

He had been worried that the practised clichés would sound hollow, but Isabelle had been right: it only took a little bit of feeling to deliver even the most embarrassing banality with conviction.

"We're glad you found the time for this little chat, Bellman." The Party Secretary raised his napkin to his lips to indicate that lunch was over, and nodded to the two other representatives. "The process is under way and, as I said, we're extremely pleased that you've indicated that you're inclined to respond positively in the event of an offer being made."

Bellman nodded.

"By 'we,'" Isabelle Skøyen interjected, "you mean the Prime Minister as well, don't you?"

"We wouldn't have agreed to come here if it weren't for the positive attitude of the Prime Minister's office," the Party Secretary said.

At first they had invited Mikael to the Government Building for this conversation, but after consulting Isabelle, Mikael had countered by inviting them to neutral territory. Lunch, paid for by the Police Chief.

The Party Secretary looked at his watch. An Omega Seamaster, Bellman noted. Too heavy to be practical. And it made you a target for muggers in every Third World city. It stopped working if you left it off for longer than a day, so you had to wind and wind to reset the time, but if you forgot to tighten the screw afterwards and jumped in the pool, the clock was ruined and the repairs would cost more than four other high-quality watches. In short: he *really* needed to get that watch.

"But, as I mentioned, there are other people under consideration. Minister of Justice is one of the weightier ministerial appointments, and I can't deny that the path is slightly trickier for someone who hasn't risen through the political ranks."

Mikael made sure to get his timing spot on, and pushed back his chair and stood up at exactly the same time as the Party Secretary, and was first to hold out his hand and say "Let's talk soon." He was Chief of Police, damn it, and out of the two of them, it was him rather that this grey bureaucrat with the expensive watch who needed to get back to his responsible job fastest.

Once the representatives of the governing party had left, Mikael and Isabelle Skøyen sat down again. They had been given a private room in one of the new restaurants set among the apartment complexes at the far end of Sørenga. They had the Opera House and Ekebergsåsen behind them, and the new freshwater pool in front of them. The fjord was covered in choppy little waves, and the yachts hung crookedly out there like white commas. The latest weather forecasts predicted that the storm was going to hit Oslo before midnight.

"That went OK, didn't it?" Mikael asked, pouring the last of the Voss mineral water into their glasses.

"*If it weren't for the positive attitude from the Prime Minister's office,*" Isabelle mimicked, and wrinkled her nose.

"What's wrong with that?"

"That 'if it weren't for' is a modifier they haven't used before. And the fact that they're referring to the Prime Minister's office instead of the Prime Minister herself tells me they're distancing themselves."

"Why would they do that?"

"You heard what I did. A lunch where they mostly asked you about the vampirist case and how quickly you think he can be caught."

"Come on, Isabelle, that's what *everyone* in the city is talking about right now."

"They're asking because that's what everything depends on, Mikael."

"But—"

"They don't need you, your competence or ability to run a department, you do realise that, don't you?"

"Now you're exaggerating, but OK, yes—"

"They want your eyepatch, your hero status, popularity, success. Because that's what you've got and what this government lacks right now. Take that away and you're not worth anything to them. And, truth be told . . ." She pushed her glass away and stood up. ". . . not to me either."

Mikael smiled warily. "What?"

She took her short fur coat from the hat stand.

"I can't deal with losers, Mikael, you know that perfectly well. I went to the press and gave you the credit for saving the day by blowing the dust off Harry Hole. So far he's arrested a naked ninety-year-old and got an innocent bartender murdered. That doesn't just make you look like a loser, Mikael, it makes *me* look like one. I don't like that, and that's why I'm leaving you."

Mikael Bellman laughed. "Have you got your period, or what?"

"You used to know when that was due."

"OK," Mikael sighed. "Speak soon."

"I think you're interpreting 'leaving' a little too narrowly."

"Isabelle . . ."

"Goodbye. I liked what you said about your successful family life. Focus on that."

Mikael Bellman sat and watched the door close behind her.

He asked the waiter who looked in for the bill, and gazed out across the fjord again. It was said that the people who planned these apartments along the water's edge hadn't taken climate change and rising sea levels into account. He had actually thought about that when he and Ulla had their villa built, high up in Høyenhall: that they would be safe there, the sea couldn't drown them, invisible assailants couldn't sneak up on them, and no storm could blow the roof off. It would take more than that. He drank from his glass of water. Grimaced and looked at it. Voss. Why were people prepared to pay good money for something that tasted no better than what they could get from the tap? Not because they thought it tasted better, but because they thought *other* people thought it tasted better. So they ordered

Voss when they were out at restaurants with their far-too-boring trophy wives and far-too-heavy Omega Seamaster watches. Was that why he sometimes found himself longing for the old days? For Manglerud, and being drunk at Olsen's on a Saturday night, leaning over the bar and topping up his beer while Olsen looked the other way, dancing one last slow dance with Ulla as the first line of the Manglerud Stars and the Kawasaki 750 boys glared angrily at him, while he knew that he and Ulla would soon be leaving together, just the two of them, out into the night, walking down Plogveien towards the ice hall and Østensjøvannet, and there he would point out the stars and explain how they were going to get there.

Had they succeeded? Maybe, but it was like when he was a boy, when he was walking in the mountains with his father, when he was tired and thought they had finally reached the summit. Only to discover that beyond that summit lay one that was even higher.

Mikael Bellman closed his eyes.

It was just like that now. He was tired. Could he stop here? Lie down, feel the wind, the heather tickling him, sun-warmed rock against his skin. Say he was thinking of staying here. And he felt a peculiar urge to call Ulla and tell her just that. *We're staying here*.

And in response he felt his phone vibrate in his jacket pocket. Of course, it *had* to be Ulla.

"Yes?"

"This is Katrine Bratt."

"Right."

"I just wanted to inform you that we've found out the alias Valentin Gjertsen has been hiding behind."

"What?"

"He withdrew money at Oslo Central Station in August, and six minutes ago we managed to identify him from the recording made by the security camera. The card he used was issued to an Alexander Dreyer, born 1972."

"And?"

"And this Alexander Dreyer died in a car accident in 2010."

"Address? Have we got an address?"

"We have. Delta are on their way there now."

"Anything else?"

"Not yet, but I presume you'd like to be kept informed as things develop?"

"Yes. As things develop."

They hung up.

"Sorry." It was the waiter.

Bellman looked down at the bill. He tapped an amount that was far too high into the handheld card reader, and pressed Enter. Stood up and stormed out. Catching Gjertsen now would open all the doors.

His tiredness seemed to have blown away.


John D. Steffens turned the light on. The neon lights flickered for a few moments before the buzzing stabilised, casting a cold glow.

Oleg blinked and gasped. "Is that all blood?" His voice echoed around the room.

Steffens smiled as the metal door slid closed behind them. "Welcome to the Bloodbath."

Oleg shivered. The room was kept chilled, and the bluish light on the cracked white tiles only enhanced the feeling of being inside a fridge.

"How . . . how much is there?" Oleg asked as he followed Steffens between the rows of red blood bags, hanging four-deep from metal stands.

"Enough for us to be able to cope for a few days if Oslo were attacked by Lakotas," Steffens said, climbing down the steps into the pool.

"Lakotas?"

"You probably know them as Sioux," Steffens said, squeezing one of the bags, and Oleg saw the blood change colour, from dark to light. "It's a myth that the Native Americans the white man met were especially bloodthirsty. Except for the Lakotas."

"Really?" Oleg said. "What about the white man? Isn't blood-thirstiness pretty evenly divided between types of people?"

"I know that's what you learn at school now," Steffens said. "No one's better, no one's worse. But believe me, the Lakotas were both better and worse, they were the best fighters. The Apaches used to say that if Cheyenne or Blackfoot warriors came, they would send their young boys and old men to fight them. But if the Lakotas came, they didn't send anyone. They started to sing songs of death. And hoped for a quick end."

"Torture?"

"When the Lakotas burned their prisoners of war, they did it gradually, with small pieces of charcoal." Steffens carried on to where the blood bags were hanging more densely and there was less light. "And when the prisoners couldn't take any more, they were allowed a break with water and food, so that the torture could last a day or two. That food sometimes included chunks of their own flesh."

"Is that true?"

"Well, as true as any written history. One Lakota warrior called Moon Behind Cloud was famous for drinking every drop of blood from all the enemies he killed. That's clearly a historical exaggeration seeing as he killed a huge number of people and wouldn't have survived the excessive drinking. Human blood is poisonous in high doses."

"Is it?"

"You take in more iron than your body can get rid of. But he did drink someone's blood, I know that much." Steffens stopped beside one blood bag. "In 1871 my great-great-grandfather was found drained of blood in Moon Behind Cloud's Lakota camp in Utah, where he'd gone as a missionary. In my grandmother's diary she wrote that my great-great-grandmother thanked the Lord after the massacre of Lakotas at Wounded Knee in 1890. Speaking of mothers . . ."

"Yes?"

"This blood is your mother's. Well, it's mine now."

"I thought she was *receiving* blood?"

"Your mother has a very rare blood type, Oleg."

"Really? I thought she belonged to a fairly common blood group."

"Oh, blood's about so much more than *groups*, Oleg. Luckily hers is group A, so I can give her ordinary blood from here." He held his hands out. "Ordinary blood that her body will absorb, and then turn into the golden drops which are Rakel Fauke's blood. And speaking of Fauke, Oleg Fauke, I didn't just bring you here to give you a break from sitting at her bedside. I was thinking of asking you if I could take a blood sample to see if you produce the same blood as her?"

"Me?" Oleg thought about it. "Yes, why not, if it could help someone."

"It would help me, believe me. Are you ready?"

"Here? Now?"

Oleg met Dr. Steffens's gaze. Something made him hesitate, but he didn't quite know what.

"OK," Oleg said. "Help yourself."

"Great." Steffens put his hand in the right pocket of his white coat and took a step closer to Oleg. He frowned irritably when a cheerful tune rang out from his left pocket.

"I didn't think there was a signal down here," he muttered as he fished out his phone. Oleg saw the screen light up the doctor's face, reflecting off his glasses. "Hello, it looks like it's Police HQ." He put the phone to his ear. "Senior Consultant John Doyle Steffens."

Oleg heard the buzz of the other voice.

"No, Inspector Bratt, I haven't seen Harry Hole today, and I'm fairly sure he isn't here. This is hardly the only place where people have to switch their phones off, perhaps he's sitting on a plane?" Steffens looked at Oleg, who shrugged his shoulders. "'*We've found him?*' Yes, Bratt, I'll give him that message if he shows up. Who have you found, out of interest? . . . Thank you, I am aware of the oath of confidentiality, Bratt, but I thought it might be helpful to Hole if I didn't have to speak in code. So that he understands what you mean . . . OK, I'll just say '*We've found him*' to Hole when I see him. Have a good day, Bratt."

Steffens put his phone back in his pocket. Saw that Oleg had rolled up his shirtsleeve. He took him by the arm and led him to the steps of the pool. "Thanks, but I just saw on my phone that it's much later than I thought it was, and I've got a patient waiting. We'll have to take your blood another time, Fauke."

Sivert Falkeid, head of Delta, was sitting at the back of the rapid response unit's van, barking out concise orders as they lurched along Trondheimsveien. There was an eight-man team in the vehicle. Well, seven men and one woman. And she wasn't part of the response unit. No woman ever had been. The entry requirements to join Delta were in theory gender-neutral, but there hadn't been a single woman among that year's hundred or so applicants, and in the past there had only been five in total, the last of them in the previous millennium. And none of them had made it through the eye of the needle. But who knows, the woman sitting opposite him looked strong and determined, so perhaps she might stand a chance?

"So we don't know if this Dreyer is at home?" Sivert Falkeid said.

"Just so we're clear, this is Valentin Gjertsen, the vampirist."

"I'm kidding, Bratt," Falkeid smiled. "So he hasn't got a mobile phone we could use to pinpoint his location with?"

"He may well have, but none that's registered to Dreyer or Gjertsen. Is that a problem?"

Sivert Falkeid looked at her. They had downloaded plans from the Buildings Department of the City Council, and it looked promising. A 45-square-metre two-room apartment on the second floor, with no back door or cellar access directly from the flat. The plan was to send four men in through the front door, with two outside in case he jumped from the balcony.

"No problem," he said.

"Good," she said. "Go in silently?"

His smile widened. He liked her Bergen accent. "You're thinking we should cut a neat hole in the glass on the balcony and wipe our shoes politely before going in?"

"I was thinking that there's no reason to waste grenades and smoke when it's just one man who hopefully isn't going to be armed, and doesn't know we're coming. And quiet and drama-free gets higher marks for style, doesn't it?"

"Something like that," Falkeid said, checking the GPS and the road ahead of them. "But if we blast our way in, the risk of injury is lower, both for us and for him. Nine out of ten people are paralysed by the blast and light when we throw a grenade, no matter how tough they think they are. I think we've saved the lives of more suspects than we have our own people by using that tactic. Besides, we've got these shock grenades we'd like to use up before they reach their expiry date. And the lads are restless, they need a bit of rock 'n' roll. There've been too many ballads recently."

"You're joking, aren't you? You're not *really* that macho and childish?"

Falkeid grinned and shrugged.

"You know what?" Bratt had leaned closer, moistened her red lips and lowered her voice. "I kind of like that."

Falkeid laughed. He was happily married, but if he hadn't been, he wouldn't have turned down a dinner date with Katrine Bratt and a chance to look into those dark, dangerous eyes and listen to those rolling Bergen *rr*s that sounded like a growling beast of prey.

"One minute!" he said loudly, and the seven men lowered their visors in an almost perfectly synchronised movement.

"A Ruger Redhawk, was that what you said he had?"

"That's what Harry Hole said he had in the bar."

"Did you hear that, men?"

They nodded. The manufacturer claimed that the plastic in the new visors could stop a 9mm bullet heading for your face, but not one from the larger-calibre Redhawk. And Falkeid thought maybe that was just as well: a false sense of security seemed to have a debilitating effect.

"And if he resists?" Bratt said.

Falkeid cleared his throat. "Then we shoot him."

"Do you have to?"

"Someone will no doubt come up with an opinion with the benefit of hindsight, but we prefer to be wise in foresight, and shoot people who are contemplating shooting us. Knowing that that's OK plays an important role in our workplace satisfaction. Looks like we're here."

He was standing by the window. Noticed two greasy marks left by fingers on the glass. He had a view across the city, but couldn't see anything, just heard the sirens. No cause for alarm, you heard sirens all the time. People got caught in house fires, slipped on the bathroom floor, tortured their partners, and that's when you heard sirens. Irritating, nagging sirens telling people to get out of the way.

On the other side of the wall someone was having sex. In the middle of the working day. Infidelity. To spouses, to employers, probably both.

The sirens rose and fell over the buzzing sound of radio voices behind him. They were on their way, people with uniforms and authority, but without purpose or meaning. All they knew was that it was urgent, that if they didn't get there in time something terrible would happen.

The air-raid siren. Now, *there* was a siren that meant something. The sound of doomsday. A wonderful sound that could make your hair stand on end. Hearing that sound, looking at the time, seeing that it wasn't noon precisely and realising that it wasn't a test. That was when he would have bombed Oslo, twelve noon. Not a soul would have run for the shelters, they'd just have stood there, staring up at the sky in surprise and wondering what sort of weather it was. Or they'd have lain there fucking with a guilty conscience, unable to act any differently. Because we can't. We do what we have to because we are who we are. The idea of willpower allowing us to act differently from what's dictated by who we are, that's a misunderstanding. It's the opposite, the only thing willpower does is follow our nature, even when circumstances make that difficult. Raping a woman, breaking down or outsmarting her resistance, running from the police, taking revenge, hiding night and day, doesn't all this entail defying the obstacles in order to make love to this woman?

The sirens were further away now. The lovers had finished.

He tried to remember how it sounded, the alarm that meant *important message, listen to the radio.* Did they still use that one? When he was a boy there was one radio station, but which one should you listen to in order to hear that message, which must be incredibly important, yet not quite dramatic enough to mean that you had to run to the shelters. Maybe the plan made provision for them to take over all radio stations, for a voice to announce . . . what? That it was already too late. That the shelters were closed, because they couldn't save you, nothing could. That what mattered now was to gather your loved ones around you, say your goodbyes, and then die. Because he had learned this much. That many people organise their entire lives to facilitate one single goal: not to die alone. Few succeed, but the lengths people were prepared to go to because of this desperate fear of crossing that threshold without having someone to hold their hand. Ha. He'd held their hands. How many? Twenty? Thirty? And they hadn't looked any less terrified or alone as a result. Not even the ones he had loved. Now, they obviously hadn't had time to love him back, but they had been surrounded by love all the same. He thought about Marte Ruud. He should have treated her better, not let himself get dragged along. He hoped she was dead now, and that it had happened quickly and painlessly.

He heard the shower on the other side of the wall, and the radio voices on his phone.

". . . when the vampirist in some sections of academic literature is described as intelligent and showing no signs of mental illness or social pathology, that creates an impression that we are dealing with a strong and dangerous enemy. But the so-called 'Sacramento Vampire,' the vampirist Richard Chase, is probably a more typical comparison when it comes to Valentin Gjertsen's case. Both demonstrated mental disorders from an early age, bed-wetting, a fascination with fire, impotence. They were both diagnosed with paranoia and schizophrenia. Chase, admittedly, had taken the more common path of drinking animal blood. He also injected himself with chicken blood and made himself ill. Whereas Valentin as a boy was more interested in torturing cats. At his grandfather's farm, Valentin hid newborn kittens, he kept them in a secret cage so that he could torment them without any of the adults knowing. But both Valentin Gjertsen and Chase become obsessional after they carry out their first vampirist attack. Chase kills all seven of his victims within the space of just a few weeks. And, just like Gjertsen, he kills most of them in their own homes, he goes round Sacramento in December 1977 trying doors, and if they're open, he takes that as an invitation and goes in, as he explains later under questioning. One of his victims, Teresa Wallin, was three months pregnant, and when Chase found her home alone, he shot her three times and raped her corpse while stabbing her with a butcher's knife and drinking her blood. Sounds familiar, doesn't it?"

Yes, he thought. But what you daren't mention is that Richard *Trenton* Chase removed several of her internal organs, cut off one of her nipples, and collected dog shit from the backyard which he forced into her mouth. Or that he used one victim's penis as a straw to drink the blood of another of his victims.

"And the similarities don't end there. Just like Chase, Valentin Gjertsen is coming to the end of the road. I can't see him killing more people now."

"What makes you so sure of that, herr Smith? You're working with the police, have you got any specific leads?"

"What makes me so sure has nothing to do with the investigation, which I naturally can't comment on, either directly or indirectly."

"So why?"

He heard Smith take a deep breath. He could see the absentminded psychologist in front of him, sitting there taking notes. Eagerly asking about childhood, bed-wetting, early sexual experiences, the forest he set light to, and particularly the cat-fishing, as he called it, which involved getting his grandfather's fishing rod, throwing the line over the beam in the barn, attaching the hook under the chin of one of the kittens, winding the line back until it was hanging in midair, then watching the kitten's hopeless attempts to climb up and free itself.

"Because Valentin Gjertsen isn't anything special, apart from being extremely evil. He's not stupid, but he's not particularly intelligent. He hasn't achieved anything special. Creating something requires imagination, vision, but destruction requires nothing, only blindness. What's saved Gjertsen from being caught in the past few days isn't skill, but pure luck. Until he is caught, which will be soon, naturally Valentin Gjertsen remains a dangerous man to get too close to, the way you should watch out for dogs that are frothing at the mouth. But a dog with rabies is dying, and, despite all his evil, Valentin Gjertsen is—to use Harry Hole's vernacular—just a wretched pervert who's now so out of control that he's going to make a big mistake very soon."

"So you want to reassure Oslo's inhabitants by . . ."

He heard a sound and switched the podcast off. Listened. It was the sound of shuffling feet right outside the door. Someone concentrating on something.

. . .

Four men dressed in Delta's dark uniform were standing at Alexander Dreyer's door. Katrine Bratt was watching from the corridor, twenty metres away.

One of the men was holding a one-and-a-half-metre battering ram shaped like a giant tube of Pringles with two handles on it.

It was impossible to tell the four of them apart behind their helmets and visors. But she assumed that the man holding up three gloved fingers was Sivert Falkeid.

During the silent countdown she could hear music from the flat. Pink Floyd? She hated Pink Floyd. No, that wasn't true, she just felt deeply suspicious of people who liked Pink Floyd. Bjørn had said he only liked one Pink Floyd track, then had pulled out an album with a picture of something that looked like a hairy ear on it, said it was from before they became big, and played an ordinary blues track with a howling dog on it. The sort of thing they use on television programs that have run out of ideas. Bjørn had said he gave any track featuring a bit of decent bottleneck guitar a full amnesty, and the fact that this one featured double bass drums, rough vocals and tributes to dark powers and rotting corpses—just the way Katrine liked it— was also a plus. She missed Bjørn. And now, as Falkeid lowered his last finger to form a clenched fist, and as they swung the battering ram that was about to smash in the door of the man who in the past seven days had murdered at least four, and probably five, people, she thought about the man she had left.

The lock shattered and the door was smashed in. The third man threw a flash grenade and Katrine Bratt covered her ears. The Delta men cast shadows across the corridor in the light from the flat that Katrine registered a fraction of a second before the two explosions that followed.

Three of the men disappeared inside with their MP5s against their shoulders, the fourth stood outside with his weapon trained on the doorway.

She took her hands away from her ears.

The grenade had knocked out Pink Floyd.

"Clear!" Falkeid's voice.

The police officer outside turned to Katrine and nodded.

She took a deep breath and walked towards the door.

Went inside the flat. There was still smoke in the air from the grenade, but surprisingly little smell.

Hall. Living room. Kitchen. The first thing that struck her was that it looked so normal. As if a perfectly ordinary, clean, tidy person lived there. Who made food, drank coffee, watched television, listened to music. No meat hooks hanging from the ceiling, no bloodstains on the wallpaper, no newspaper cuttings about murders and pictures of the victims on the walls.

And the thought hit her. That Aurora had been wrong.

She looked in through the open bathroom door. It was empty, no shower curtain, no toiletries except one object on the shelf below the mirror. She went in. It wasn't a toiletry. The metal was stained with black paint and red-brown rust. The iron teeth were closed, forming a zigzag pattern.

"Bratt!"

"Yes?" Katrine went into the living room.

"In here." Falkeid's voice was coming from the bedroom. It sounded calm, measured. As if something was over. Katrine stepped across the threshold and avoided touching the door frame, as if she was already aware that this was a crime scene. The wardrobe door was open, and the Delta men were standing on either side of the double bed with their semi-automatics aimed at the naked body that was lying on top of it, its lifeless eyes staring up at the ceiling. It was giving off a smell that she couldn't place at first, so she leaned a bit closer. Lavender.

Katrine pulled her phone out, rang a number and got an answer immediately.

"Have you got him?" Bjørn Holm sounded out of breath.

"No," she said. "But there's a woman's body here."

"Dead?"

"Not living, anyway."

"Damn. Is it Marte Ruud? Hang on, what do you mean, 'not living'?"

"Not dead, not alive."

"What . . . ?"

"It's a sex doll."

"A what?"

"A fuck doll. An expensive one, from the looks of it, made in Japan, very lifelike. At first I thought it was a person. Alexander Dreyer *is* Valentin, at least, the iron teeth are here. So we'll have to wait and see if he shows up. Heard anything from Harry?"

"No."

Katrine's gaze fell on a coat hanger and a pair of underpants that were lying on the floor in front of the wardrobe. "I don't like it, Bjørn. He wasn't at the hospital either."

"No one likes it. Shall we put out an alert?"

"For Harry? What would be the point of that?"

"You're right. Listen, don't disturb things too much, there could be evidence of Marte Ruud there."

"OK, but I have a feeling that any evidence has been cleaned up. Judging by the flat, Harry was right, Valentin is extremely clean and tidy." Her eyes went back to the coat hanger and underpants. "Mind you . . ."

"What?" Bjørn said.

"Fuck," Katrine said.

"Which means?"

"He threw some clothes in a bag in a hurry and grabbed his toiletries from the bathroom. Valentin knew we were coming . . ."


Valentin opened the door. And saw who had been shuffling about outside. The cleaner, who had been bent over holding the key card to the door of his hotel room, straightened up.

"Oh, sorry," she smiled. "I didn't know the room was occupied."

"I'll take those," he said, and took the towels from her hand. "And could you please clean again?"

"Sorry?"

"I'm not happy with the cleaning. There are finger marks on the window. Please clean the room again, let's say in an hour?"

Her surprised face disappeared behind the door as he closed it.

He put the towels on the coffee table, sat down in the armchair and opened his bag.

The sirens had fallen silent. If it was them he had heard, perhaps they were inside his flat now, it wasn't more than a couple of kilometres up to Sinsen, as the crow flies. It had already been half an hour since the other man had called to say that the police knew where he was and what name he was using, that he had to get out. Valentin had packed only the most important things, and left the car there seeing as they had the name it was registered under.

He took the folder out of the bag and leafed through it. Looked at the pictures, addresses. And he realised that for the first time in a very long while, he didn't know what to do.

He heard the psychologist's voice inside his ear.

"*. . . just a wretched pervert who's now so out of control that he's going to make a big mistake very soon.*"

Valentin Gjertsen stood up and undressed. Picked up the towels and went into the bathroom. Turned on the hot water in the shower. Stood in front of the mirror, waiting for the water to get scalding hot as he watched the condensation spread across the mirror. He looked at the tattoo. Heard his phone start to ring and knew it was him. Reason. Salvation. With new instructions, new orders. Should he ignore it? Was it time to cut the umbilical cord, the lifeline? Time to break free entirely?

He filled his lungs. And screamed.

# 28

# Wednesday afternoon

"Sex dolls are nothing new," Smith said, looking down at the plastic and silicon woman on the bed. "When the Dutch ruled the seven seas, the sailors used to take a sort of doll-like vagina with them, sewn out of leather. It was so common that the Chinese called it a 'Dutch wife.'"

"Really?" Katrine asked, watching the white-clad angels of the forensics team as they examined the bedroom. "So they spoke English?"

Smith laughed. "Got me. The articles in academic journals are in English. In Japan there are brothels containing nothing but sex dolls. The most expensive ones are heated, so they stay at body temperature, they have skeletons which mean you can bend their arms and legs into natural and unnatural positions, and they have automatic lubrication of—"

"Thank you, I think that's enough," Katrine said.

"Of course, sorry."

"Did Bjørn tell you why he was staying in the boiler room?"

Smith shook his head.

"He and Lien had things to do," Wyller said.

"Berna Lien? *Things to do*?"

"He just said that as long as this wasn't assumed to be a murder scene, he'd leave it to the others."

"Things to do," Katrine muttered as she walked out of the bedroom with the other two hot on her heels. Out of the flat, out to the car park in front of the apartment blocks. They stopped behind the blue Honda where two forensics experts were examining the boot. They had found the keys in the flat, and it had been confirmed that the car was registered to Alexander Dreyer. The sky above them was steel grey, and on the far side of Torshovdalen's billowing grass-covered slopes Katrine could see the wind grabbing the treetops. The latest forecast said that Emilia was only a matter of hours away.

"Smart of him not to take the car," Wyller said.

"Yep," Katrine said.

"What do you mean?" Smith asked.

"The toll stations, car parks and traffic cameras," Wyller said. "You can run number-plate recognition software on video recordings, it only take seconds."

"Brave new world," Katrine said.

"*O brave new world, that has such people in it,*" Smith said.

Katrine turned to the psychologist. "Can you imagine where someone like Valentin might go if he ran?"

"No."

"No, as in 'no idea'?"

Smith pushed his glasses further up his nose. "No, as in 'I can't imagine him running.'"

"Why not?"

"Because he's angry."

Katrine shivered. "You didn't exactly make him less angry if he heard your podcast with Daa."

"No," Smith sighed. "Maybe I went too far. Again. Fortunately we've got decent locks and security cameras after the break-in in the barn. But maybe . . ."

"Maybe what?"

"Maybe we'd feel safer if I had a weapon, a pistol or something."

"Regulations don't permit us to give you a police weapon without a licence and weapons training."

"Emergency armament," Wyller said.

Katrine looked at him. Perhaps the criteria for emergency armament had been met, perhaps not. But she could see the headlines after Smith had been shot and it emerged that he had requested emergency armament and had been turned down. "Can you help Hallstein get issued with a pistol?"

"Yes."

"OK. I've told Skarre to check trains, boats, flights, hotels and boarding houses. We'll have to hope that Valentin doesn't have the paperwork to support other identities apart from Alexander Dreyer." Katrine looked up at the sky. She had once had a boyfriend who was keen on paragliding, and he had told her that even if there was no wind on the ground, the air just a couple of hundred metres up could break the speed limit on a motorway. Dreyer. Dutch wife. *Things to do*? Pistol. Angry.

"And Harry wasn't at home?" she said.

Wyller shook his head. "I rang the doorbell, walked round the house, looked in all the windows."

"Time to talk to Oleg," she said. "He must have keys."

"I'll get on to it."

She sighed. "If you don't find Harry there, it might be an idea to get Telenor to try and locate his phone."

One of the white-clad forensics guys came over to her.

"There's blood in the boot," he said.

"Much?"

"Yes. And this." He held up a large transparent plastic evidence bag. Inside was a white blouse. Torn. Bloody. With lace on it, the way customers had described the blouse Marte Ruud had been wearing the night she went missing.

# 29

# Wednesday evening

Harry opened his eyes and stared into the darkness.

Where was he? What had happened? How long had he been unconscious? His head felt like someone had hit it with an iron bar. His pulse was throbbing against his eardrums in a monotonous rhythm. All he could remember was that he was locked in. And as far as he could work out, he was lying on a floor covered in cold tiles. Cold like the inside of a fridge. He was lying in something wet, sticky. He raised his hand and stared at it. Was that blood?

Then, slowly, it dawned on Harry that it wasn't his pulse throbbing against his eardrums.

It was a bass guitar.

Kaiser Chiefs? Probably. It was definitely one of those hip English bands that he'd actually forgotten. Not that Kaiser Chiefs were bad, but they weren't exceptional and had therefore ended up in the grey soup of things he had heard more than a year ago but less than twenty: they just hadn't stuck. While he could remember every note and lyric from the very worst songs from the 1980s, the period between then and now was a blank. Just like the period between yesterday and now. Nothing. Just that insistent bass. Or his heartbeat. Or someone banging on the door.

Harry opened his eyes again. He smelt his hand, hoping it wasn't blood, piss or vomit.

The bass started to play out of time with the song.

It was the door.

"Closed!" Harry shouted. And regretted it when it felt like his head was going to explode.

The track ended and the Smiths took over. And Harry realised he must have plugged his own phone into the stereo when he got sick of Bad Company. "There is a Light That Never Goes Out." If only it would. But the hammering on the door merely continued. Harry put his hands over his ears. But when the track reached the last part with nothing but strings, he heard a voice shouting his name. And because it could hardly be someone who had found out that the new owner of the Jealousy Bar was called Harry, and because he recognised the voice, he grabbed hold of the edge of the counter and heaved himself up. First to his knees. Then a forward-leaning posture, which in spite of everything had to qualify as standing, seeing as the soles of his shoes were planted on the sticky floor. He saw the two empty Jim Beam bottles lying on their sides with their mouths over the edge of the counter, and realised that he had lain there marinating in his own bourbon whiskey.

He saw her face outside the window. It looked like she was alone.

He ran one stiff index finger across his throat to indicate that the bar was closed, but she gave him a long stiff finger in return and started banging on the window instead.

And because the noise sounded like a hammer on the already battered parts of his brain, Harry decided that he may as well open the door. He let go of the counter, took a step. And fell over. Both his feet had fallen asleep—how was that possible? He got up again, and with the help of the tables and chairs he staggered to the door.

"Bloody hell," Katrine groaned when he opened the door. "You're drunk!"

"Possibly," Harry said. "But I wish I was drunker."

"We've been looking for you, you bloody idiot! Have you been here all this time?"

"I don't know what 'all this time' is, but there are two empty bottles on the bar. Let's hope I took *my* time and enjoyed it."

"We've been calling and calling."

"Mm. Must have put my phone on flight mode. Do you like the playlist? Listen. This angry lady is Martha Wainwright. 'Bloody Mother Fucking Arsehole.' Remind you of anyone?"

"Fucking hell, Harry, what are you thinking?"

"I don't know about thinking. I am—as you can see—in flight mode."

She grabbed hold of the collar of his jacket. "People are being murdered out there, Harry. And you're standing here trying to be funny?"

"I try to be funny every fucking day, Katrine. And you know what? It doesn't make people any better, or any worse. And it doesn't seem to have any effect on the number of murders either."

"Harry, Harry . . ."

He swayed, and it dawned on him that she had grabbed his collar primarily to stop him falling over.

"We missed him, Harry. We need you."

"OK. Just let me have a drink first."

"Harry!"

"Your voice is very . . . loud . . ."

"We're going now. I've got a car waiting outside."

"My bar is having a happy hour, and I'm not ready for work, Katrine."

"You're not going to work, you're going home to sober up. Oleg's waiting for you."

"Oleg?"

"We got him to unlock the house up in Holmenkollen. He was so scared of what he was going to find that he made Bjørn go in first."

Harry closed his eyes. Shit, shit. "I can't, Katrine."

"You can't what?"

"Call Oleg and say I'm OK, tell him to go back to his mother instead."

"He seemed pretty determined to wait there until you arrived, Harry."

"I can't let him see me like this. And I'm no use to you. Sorry, this isn't up for discussion." He took hold of the door. "Now go."

"Go? And leave you here?"

"I'll be OK. Only soft drinks from now on. Maybe a bit of Coldplay."

Katrine shook her head. "You're coming home."

"I'm *not* going home."

"Not your home."

# 30

# Wednesday night

There was one hour left until midnight, Olsen's was packed with fully grown adults, and from the speakers Gerry Rafferty and his saxophone were blowing the ponytails of the people standing closest to them.

"The sounds of the eighties," Liz cried.

"I think this is from the seventies," Ulla said.

"Yeah, but it didn't reach Manglerud until the eighties."

They laughed. Ulla saw Liz shake her head towards a man who looked questioningly at her as he passed their table.

"This is actually the second time I've been here in a week," Ulla said.

"Oh? Was it this much fun last time?"

Ulla shook her head. "Nothing's as much fun as going out with you. Time passes, but you haven't changed."

"No," Liz said, tilting her head and studying her friend. "But you have."

"Really? Have I lost myself?"

"No, and that's actually quite annoying. But you don't smile anymore."

"Don't I?"

"You smile, but you don't *smile*. Not like Ulla from Manglerud."

Ulla tilted her head. "We moved."

"Yes, you got a husband and children and villa. But that's a poor exchange for *the smile*, Ulla. What happened?"

"Yes, what happened?" She smiled at Liz and drank. Then looked around. The average age was roughly the same as them, but she couldn't see any familiar faces. Manglerud had grown, people had moved in, moved on. Some had died, some had just disappeared. And some were sitting at home. Dead *and* disappeared.

"Would it be mean of me to guess?" Liz wondered.

"Guess away."

Rafferty had finished his verse and Liz had to shout to drown out the saxophone blasting out again. "Mikael Bellman from Manglerud. He took your smile."

"That *is* actually pretty mean, Liz."

"Yes, but it's true, isn't it?"

Ulla raised her glass of wine again. "Yes, I suppose it is."

"Is he being unfaithful?"

"Liz!"

"It's hardly a secret . . ."

"What isn't a secret?"

"That Mikael likes the ladies. Come on, Ulla, you're not that naive."

Ulla sighed. "Maybe not. But what am I supposed to do?"

"The same as me," Liz said, taking the bottle of white wine from the ice bucket and topping up both their glasses. "Give them a taste of their own medicine. Cheers!"

Ulla could feel that she ought to switch to water. "I tried, but I just couldn't do it."

"Try again!"

"What good would it do?"

"You only work that out after you've done it. Nothing fixes a shaky sex life at home like a really bad one-night stand."

Ulla laughed. "It's not the sex, Liz."

"What is it, then?"

"It's . . . I'm . . . jealous."

"Ulla Swart jealous? It's not possible to be that beautiful *and* jealous."

"Well, I am," Ulla protested. "And it hurts. A lot. I want payback."

"Of course you want payback, sister! Shaft him where it hurts . . . I mean . . ." Wine sprayed as they burst out laughing.

"Liz, you're drunk!"

"I'm drunk and happy, Mrs. Police Chief's Wife. Whereas you're drunk and unhappy. Call him!"

"Call Mikael? Now?"

"Not Mikael, you idiot! Ring the lucky guy who's going to get some pussy tonight."

"What? No, Liz!"

"Yes, do it! Call him now!" Liz pointed at the phone booth by the wall. "Call him from in there, then he'll be able to hear! Actually, calling from in there would be *very* appropriate."

"Appropriate?" Ulla laughed, and looked at her watch. She was going to have to go home soon. "Why?"

"Why? Bloody hell, Ulla! Because that was where Mikael fucked Stine Michaelsen that time, wasn't it?!"


"What is it?" Harry asked. The room was spinning around him.

"Camomile tea," Katrine said.

"The music," Harry said, feeling the woollen sweater he had been lent scratch his skin. His own clothes were hanging up to dry in the bathroom, and despite the door being closed he could still smell the cloying stench of strong spirits. So his senses were working, even if the room was spinning.

"Beach House. Haven't you heard them before?"

"I don't know," Harry said. "That's the problem. Things are starting to slip away from me." He could feel the coarse weave of the bedspread beneath him, which covered the whole of the low, almost two-metre-wide bed that was the only item of furniture in the room apart from a desk and chair, and a good old-fashioned stereo cabinet with a single candle on top of it. Harry presumed both the sweater and stereo belonged to Bjørn Holm. The music sounded like it was floating round the room. Harry had felt this way a few times before: when he had been on the brink of alcohol poisoning and was on his way back to the surface again, passing through all the same stages on the way up that he had been through on the way down.

"I suppose that's just the way it is," Katrine said. "We start off having everything, and then lose it, piece by piece. Strength. Youth. Future. People we like . . ."

Harry tried to remember what it was Bjørn had wanted him to say to Katrine, but it slipped away. Rakel. Oleg. And just as he felt tears welling up, they were suppressed by rage. Of course we lose them, everyone we try to hold on to, the fates disdain us, make us small, pathetic. When we cry for people we've lost, it's not out of sympathy, because of course we know that they're free from pain at last. But still we cry. We cry because we're alone again. We cry out of self-pity.

"Where are you, Harry?"

He felt her hand on his forehead. A sudden gust of wind made the window rattle. Outside in the street came the sound of something hitting the ground. The storm. It was on its way now.

"I'm here," he said.

The room was spinning. He could sense the warmth not only from her hand, but from the whole of her as they lay there just half a metre apart.

"I want to die first," he said.

"What?"

"I don't want to lose them. They can lose me instead. Let *them* see how it feels for once."

Her laughter was so gentle. "Now you're stealing my lines, Harry."

"Am I?"

"When I was in the hospital . . ."

"Yes?" Harry closed his eyes when her hand slipped to the back of his neck, squeezed gently and sent little jolts up into his brain.

"They kept changing the diagnosis. Manic depressive, borderline, bipolar. But there was one word that was in all the reports. Suicidal."

"Hm.

"But it passes."

"Yes," Harry said. "And then it comes back. Doesn't it?"

She laughed again. "Nothing's forever, life is by definition temporary and always changing. It's horrible, but that's also what makes it bearable."

"This too shall pass."

"Let's hope so. You know what, Harry? We're the same, you and I. We're made for loneliness. We're drawn to loneliness."

"By getting rid of the people we love, you mean?"

"Is that what we do?"

"I don't know. I just know that when I'm walking on the wafer-thin ice of happiness, I'm terrified, so terrified that I wish it was over, that I was already in the water."

"And that's why we run from those we love," Katrine said. "Alcohol. Work. Casual sex."

Something we can be useful for, Harry thought. While they bleed to death.

"We can't save them," she said, in answer to his thoughts. "And they can't save us. Only we can save ourselves."

Harry felt the mattress move and knew she had turned towards him, he could feel her warm breath on his face.

"You had it in your life, Harry, you had the only person you loved. At least the two of you had that. And I don't know which of you I've been most jealous of."

What was it that was making him so sensitive? Had he taken E or acid? And, if so, where had he got hold of it? He had no idea, the last twenty-four hours were a big blank.

"They say you shouldn't meet trouble halfway," she said. "But when you know that trouble is all that lies ahead of you, meeting it halfway is the only airbag you've got. And the best way to fend it off is to live each day like it was your last. Don't you think?"

Beach House. He remembered this track. "Wishes." It really was something special. And he remembered Rakel's pale face on the white pillow, in the light yet simultaneously in the dark, out of focus, close, yet distant, a face in the dark water, pressed against the underside of the ice. And he remembered Valentin's words. *You're like me, Harry, you can't bear it.*

"What would you do, Harry? If you knew you were about to die?"

"I don't know."

"Would you—?"

"I said I don't know."

"What don't you know?" she whispered.

"If I would have fucked you."

In the silence that followed he heard the scraping sound of metal being blown across the tarmac by the wind.

"Just feel," she whispered. "We're dying."

Harry stopped breathing. Yes, he thought. I'm dying. And then felt that she had stopped breathing too.


Hallstein Smith heard the wind whistling in the gutters outside and felt the draught right through the wall. Even though they had insulated the walls as well as they could, it was and would remain a barn. Emilia. He had heard of a novel that was published during the war about a storm called Maria, and that that was the reason why hurricanes were given girls' names. But that changed after the idea of gender equality became widespread in the seventies and people insisted that these catastrophic disasters should have boys' names as well. He looked at the smiling face above the Skype icon on the big computer screen. The voice was running slightly ahead of the lips: "I think I have what I need, thank you so much for being with us, Mr. Smith.

At what for you must be very late, no? Here in LA it's nearly 3 p.m. What time is it in Sweden?"

"Norway. Almost midnight." Hallstein Smith smiled. "No problem, I'm just glad the press finally realise that vampirism is real, and are interested in it."

They ended the conversation, and Smith opened his inbox again.

Thirteen unopened emails, but he could see from the senders and subject lines that they were requests for interviews and invitations to give lectures. He hadn't opened the one from *Psychology Today* either. Because he knew it wasn't urgent. Because he wanted to save it. Savour it.

He looked at the time. He had put the kids to bed at half past eight, then had a cup of tea at the kitchen table with May, as usual, going through their day, sharing its small joys and venting its small frustrations. In the past few days he had naturally had more to tell her than vice versa, but he had made sure that the smaller but no less important aspects of the home got as much attention as his own activities. Because what he said was true: "I talk too much, and you can read all about this wretched vampirist in the papers, darling." He looked out of the window, could just make out the corner of the farmhouse where they were all lying asleep now, all his loved ones. The wall creaked. The moon was slipping in and out of the clouds, scudding faster and faster across the sky, and the bare branches of the dead oak out in the field were waving as if it wanted to warn them that something was coming, that destruction and more death were on the way.

He opened an email inviting him to give a keynote speech at a psychology conference in Lyon. The same conference that had rejected his abstract last year. In his head he composed a reply in which he thanked them, said it was an honour to be asked, but that he had to prioritise more important conferences and therefore had to say no on this occasion, but that they were welcome to try again another time. Then he chuckled and shook his head. There was no reason to get too full of himself, this sudden interest in vampirism would vanish again when the attacks stopped. He accepted the invitation, aware that he could have asked for more in terms of travel, accommodation and fee, but couldn't be bothered. He was getting what he needed, he just wanted them to *listen* to him, to join him on this journey into the labyrinths of the human psyche, recognise his work, so that together they could *understand* and contribute to making people's lives better. That was all. He looked at the time. Three minutes to twelve. He heard a sound. It could have been the wind, obviously. He clicked the icon to bring up the security cameras on his screen. The first image he saw was from the camera by the gate. The gate was open.


Truls cleared his throat.

She had called. Ulla had called.

He put the washing-up in the dishwasher, rinsed the two wine-glasses, he still had the bottle he had bought just in case before that evening when they had met at Olsen's. He folded the empty pizza boxes and tried to push them down into the bin bag, but it split. Damn. He tucked them out of sight behind the bucket and mop in the cupboard. Music. What did she like? He tried to think back. He could hear something inside his head, but he wasn't sure what it was. Something about barricades. Duran Duran? It was something a bit like a-ha, anyway. And he had a-ha's first album. Candles. Damn. He'd had women here before, but on those occasions the mood hadn't been so important.

Olsen's was located right in the middle of things, so even if there was a storm on the way it wouldn't be hard to get a taxi on a Wednesday evening, so she could be here any moment, which meant he couldn't have a shower, he'd have to make do with washing his cock and armpits. Or armpits and cock, in that order. Fuck, he was stressed! He had been planning a quiet evening with Megan Fox in her prime, and then Ulla had called and asked if it was OK for her to pay a little visit. What did she mean by *little* visit? That she was going to bail on him like last time? T-shirt. The one from Thailand, with "Same Same, But Different?" Maybe she wouldn't find it funny. And maybe Thailand would make her think of venereal disease. How about the Armani shirt from MBK in Bangkok? No, the synthetic fabric would make him sweat, as well as letting on that it was a cheap copy. Truls pulled on a white T-shirt of unknown origin and hurried into the bathroom. He saw that the toilet needed another go with the brush. But first things first . . .

Truls was standing at the basin with his cock in his hand when the doorbell rang.


Katrine stared at her buzzing phone.

It was almost midnight, the wind had gained in strength in just the past few minutes, and the gusts were now making howling, groaning, slamming sounds outside, but Harry was fast asleep.

She answered.

"This is Hallstein Smith." His whispering voice sounded upset.

"So I see. What is it?"

"He's here."

"What?"

"I think it's Valentin."

"What are you saying?"

"Someone's opened the gate, and I . . . oh God, I can hear the door of the barn. What should I do?"

"Don't do anything . . . Try . . . Can you hide?"

"No. I can see him on the camera outside. Dear God, it's him." Smith sounded like he was crying. "What should I do?"

"Fuck, let me think," Katrine groaned.

The phone was snatched from her hand.

"Smith? This is Harry, I'm with you. Have you locked the office door? OK, do that now, and switch the light off. Nice and calmly." Hallstein Smith stared at the computer screen. "OK, I've locked the door and turned the light out," he whispered.

"Can you see him?"

"No. Yes, now I see him." Hallstein saw a figure enter the end of the passageway. He stumbled on the scales, regained his balance, and carried on past the stalls, towards the camera. As the man passed beneath one of the lights, his face was illuminated.

"Oh God, it's him, Harry. It's Valentin."

"Stay calm."

"But . . . he's unlocked the door, he's got keys, Harry. Maybe he's got the office key as well."

"Is there a window in there?"

"Yes, but it's too small and too high up the wall."

"Anything heavy you can hit him with?"

"No. I . . . I've got the pistol, though."

"You've got a pistol?"

"Yes, it's in the drawer. But I haven't had time to test it."

"Breathe, Smith. What does it look like?"

"Er, it's black. At Police HQ they said it's a Glock something-or-other."

"Glock 17. Is the magazine inserted?"

"Yes. And it's loaded, they said. But I can't see a safety catch."

"That's OK, it's in the trigger, so you just have to squeeze the trigger to fire."

Smith pressed the phone to his mouth and whispered as quietly as he could. "I can hear keys in the lock."

"How far away is the door?"

"Two metres."

"Stand up and hold the pistol with both hands. Remember, you're in darkness and he's got the light behind him, he won't be able to see you clearly. If he's unarmed, you shout 'Police, down on your knees.' If you see a weapon you shoot three times. Three times. Understood?"

"Yes."

The door in front of Smith opened.

And there he stood, silhouetted against the light of the barn behind him. Hallstein Smith gasped for the air that felt like it was being sucked out of the room as the man raised his hand. Valentin Gjertsen.


Katrine jumped. She had heard the bang from the phone, even though Harry was holding it tightly to his ear.

"Smith?" Harry cried. "Smith, are you there?"

No reply.

"Smith!"

"Valentin's shot him!" Katrine groaned.

"No," Harry said.

"No? You told him to fire three times, and he's not answering!"

"That was a Glock, not a Ruger."

"But why . . . ?" Katrine stopped when she heard a voice on the phone. She stared at the look of intense concentration on Harry's face. Tried in vain to work out who he was listening to, if it was Smith or the voice she had only heard in recordings of old interviews, the high voice that had given her nightmares. Who right now was telling Harry what he was thinking of doing to . . .

"OK," Harry said. "You've picked up his revolver? . . . Good, put it in the drawer and stay sitting where you can see him properly. If he's lying in the doorway, just leave him there. Is he moving? . . . OK, no . . . No, no first aid. If he's only wounded, he'll be waiting for you to move closer. If he's dead, it's too late. And if he's somewhere in between, then that's his bad luck, because you're just going to sit there and watch. Understood, Smith? Good. We'll be there in half an hour, I'll call you when we're in the car. Don't take your eyes off him, and call your wife and tell them to stay in the house, and say that we're on our way."

Katrine took the phone, as Harry slipped out of bed and vanished into the bathroom. She thought he was saying something to her before she realised he was throwing up.


Truls's hands were sweating so much he could feel it right through the legs of his trousers.

Ulla was drunk. Even so, she was sitting at the very edge of the sofa and holding the beer bottle he had given her in front of her like a defensive weapon.

"Imagine, this is the first time I've been in your home," she said, slurring slightly. "And we've know each other . . . how many years?"

"Since we were fifteen," Truls said, who at that precise moment wasn't capable of any complicated mental arithmetic.

She smiled to herself and nodded, or rather, her head just fell forward.

Truls coughed. "It's getting really windy out there now. This Emilia . . ."

"Truls?"

"Yes?"

"Could you imagine fucking me?"

He swallowed.

She giggled without looking up. "Truls, I hope that pause doesn't mean—"

"Of course I can," Truls said.

"Good," she said. "Good." She lifted her head and gazed at him with unfocused eyes. "Good." Her head was swaying on her slender neck. As if it were full of something heavy. A heavy mood. Heavy thoughts. This was his chance. The opening he had been dreaming of, but never imagined he would get: he had been granted permission to fuck Ulla Swart.

"Have you got a bedroom so we can get it done?"

He looked at her. Nodded. She smiled, but she didn't look happy. To hell with that. Fuck happy—Ulla Swart was horny, and that was what mattered now. Truls was about to reach out and stroke her cheek, but his hand wouldn't obey him.

"Is something wrong, Truls?"

"Wrong? No, how could there be?"

"You look so . . ."

He waited. But nothing more came.

"So what?" he prompted.

"So lost." Instead of his hand, it was hers, it was hers stroking his cheek. "Poor, poor Truls."

He was about to knock her hand away. Knock away the hand of Ulla Swart, who after all these years had reached out to touch him without contempt or disgust. What the hell was wrong with him? The woman wanted to get fucked, plain and simple, and that was a job he could manage, he'd never had any trouble getting it up. All he had to do now was get them up from this sofa, out into the bedroom, off with their clothes and then slip the salmon in. She could scream and groan and whine, he wasn't going to stop before she—

"Are you crying, Truls?"

Crying? She was obviously so drunk she was seeing things.

He saw her pull her hand back and press it to her lips.

"Real salt tears," she said. "Are you upset about something?"

And now Truls felt it. Felt the hot tears running down his cheeks. Felt his nose start to run as well. Felt the pressure in his throat as if he was trying to swallow something that was too big, something that would smother him or make him burst.

"Is it me?" she asked.

Truls shook his head, unable to speak.

"Is it . . . Mikael?"

It was such an idiotic question that he almost got angry. Of course it wasn't Mikael. Why the hell would it be Mikael? The man who was supposed to be his best friend, but who, ever since they were boys, had taken every opportunity to tease him in front of the others, only to shove him out in front when they were threatened with a beating. And who later, when they were both in the police, got Beavis to do all the shitty jobs that had to be done so that Mikael Bellman could get where he was today. Why would Truls sit here crying about something like that, over a friendship that had been nothing more than two outsiders who had been forced together, in which one of them had become a success and the other a pathetic loser? Like hell! So what was it, then? Why was it that when the loser had the chance to make up lost ground and fuck his wife, he started crying like an old woman? Now Truls could see tears in Ulla's eyes too. Ulla Swart. Truls Berntsen. Mikael Bellman. It had been the three of them. And the rest of Manglerud could go to hell. Because they had no one. Only each other.

She took a handkerchief out of her bag and gently wiped beneath her eyes. "Do you want me to go?" she sniffed.

"I . . ." Truls didn't recognise his own voice. "Damned if I know, Ulla."

"Me too," she laughed, looked at the makeup stains on the hand-kerchief and put it back in her bag. "Forgive me, Truls. This was probably a bad idea. I'll go now."

He nodded. "Another time," he said. "In another life."

"Nail on the head," she said, and stood up.

Truls was left standing in the hall after the door closed behind her, listening to the sound of her steps echoing in the stairwell, gradually getting fainter. He heard the door open far below. Close. She was gone. Completely gone.

He felt . . . yes, what did he feel? Relief. But also a despair that was almost unbearable, like a physical pain in his chest and stomach which made him think for a moment of the gun in the cupboard in the bedroom, and the fact that he *could* actually be free right here, right now. Then he sank to his knees and rested his forehead on the doormat. And laughed. A grunting laugh that wouldn't stop, and just got louder and louder. Hell, it was a wonderful life!


Hallstein Smith's heart was still racing.

He was doing what Harry had said, keeping his eyes and pistol trained on the motionless man lying in the doorway. He felt nausea rising as he saw the pool of blood spreading towards him across the floor. He mustn't throw up, he mustn't lose his concentration now. Harry had told him to fire three times. Should he put another two bullets in him? No, he was dead.

He rang May's number with trembling fingers. She answered immediately.

"Hallstein?"

"I thought you were asleep," he said.

"I'm sitting in bed with the children. They can't sleep because of the storm."

"Of course. Listen, the police are going to be arriving soon. Blue lights and maybe sirens, so don't be scared."

"Scared of what?" she asked, and he heard the tremble in her voice. "What's going on, Hallstein? We heard a bang. Was that the wind, or something else?"

"May, don't worry. Everything's fine . . ."

"I can hear from your voice that everything isn't fine, Hallstein! The kids are sitting here crying!"

"I . . . I'll come in and explain."

Katrine steered the car down the narrow gravel road that wound between the fields and patches of woodland.

Harry put his phone in his pocket. "Smith went into the farmhouse to be with his family."

"It must be OK, then," Katrine said.

Harry didn't respond.

The wind was increasing in strength. In the patches of forest she had to watch out for broken branches and other debris in the road, and out in the open she had to hold the wheel tight as gusts of wind grabbed at the car.

Harry's phone rang again as Katrine turned into the open gate to Smith's property.

"We're here now," Harry said into his phone. "When you arrive, cordon off the area but don't touch anything until Forensics get here."

Katrine stopped in front of the barn and jumped out.

"Lead the way," Harry said, following her through the barn door. She heard Harry swear as she turned right towards the office.

"Sorry, forgot to warn you about the scales," Katrine said.

"It's not that," Harry said. "I can see blood on the floor here."

Katrine stopped in front of the open door to the office. Stared at the pool of blood on the floor. Shit. There was no Valentin there.

"Keep an eye on the Smiths," Harry said behind her.

"What . . . ?"

She turned round in time to see Harry disappear off to the left and out through the door.

A gust of wind grabbed Harry as he switched on the light on his phone and aimed it at the ground. He regained his balance. The blood stood out against the pale grey gravel. He followed the thin trail of drops that indicated which direction Valentin had fled in. The wind was on his back. Towards the farmhouse.

No . . .

Harry drew his Glock. He hadn't taken the time to check if Valentin's revolver was in the drawer in the office, so he had to work from the assumption that Valentin was armed.

The trail was gone.

Harry swung his phone around and breathed out in relief when he saw that the blood led away from the track, away from the house. Out across the dry yellow grass, towards the field. Here too the trail of blood was easy to follow. The wind had to be up at full gale force now, and Harry felt the first drops of rain hit his cheek like projectiles. When it really started, it would wash away the trail of blood in a matter of seconds.

Valentin closed his eyes and opened his mouth to the wind. As if it could blow new life into him. Life. Why did everything only reach its full value just as it was in the process of being lost? Her. Freedom. And now life.

Life, draining out of him. He could feel the cooling blood filling his shoes. He hated blood. It was the other one who loved blood. The other, the man he had entered into a pact with. And when had he realised that it wasn't he who was the devil, but the other, the blood-man? That it was he, Valentin Gjertsen, who had sold and lost his soul? Valentin Gjertsen lifted his face towards the sky and laughed. The storm was here. The demon was free.

Harry ran with the Glock in one hand, his phone in the other.

Across the open ground. Downhill, with the wind behind him. Valentin was injured, and would have taken the easiest possible path to get as much distance between himself and those he knew would soon be coming after him. Harry felt the jolts from his feet transmit themselves to his head, felt his stomach want to turn itself inside out again, and swallowed to keep the vomit down. Thought about a forest track. Thought about a guy in new Under Armour gear ahead of him on the path. And ran.

He was getting close to the forest and slowed down. He knew he would have to face the wind when he changed direction.

There was a small, dilapidated shack in among the trees. Rotten planks, corrugated-iron roof. For tools, maybe, or somewhere the animals could shelter from the rain.

Harry shone his phone towards the shack. He couldn't hear anything but the storm, it was dark and he would hardly have been able to smell blood on a warm day with the wind in the right direction.

All the same, he *knew* that Valentin was here. The way he just *knew* things at regular intervals, and kept getting them wrong.

He shone the light down at the ground again. There was less of a gap between the drops of blood. Valentin had slowed down here too. Because he wanted to evaluate the situation. Or because he was exhausted. Because he *had* to stop. And the blood—which had led in a straight line so far—turned off here. Towards the shack. He hadn't been mistaken.

Harry set off towards the patch of woodland to the right of the shack. He ran in among the trees before he stopped, switched off the light on his phone, raised his Glock and walked in an arc so he could approach the shack from the other side. He lay down and snaked across the ground.

He had the wind in his face now, which lowered the chance of Valentin hearing him. It was carrying sounds towards him, and Harry could hear police sirens in the distance, rising and falling between the gusts.

Harry crept over a fallen tree. A silent flash of lightning. And there, a silhouette standing out against the shack. It was him. He was sitting between two trees with his back to Harry, only five or six metres ahead of him.

Harry aimed his pistol at the figure.

"Valentin!"

His cry was partially drowned out by a delayed rumble of thunder, but he saw the figure before him stiffen.

"I've got you in my sights, Valentin. Put your gun down."

It was as if the wind suddenly eased. And Harry heard another sound. High-pitched. Laughter.

"Harry. You came out to play again."

"You shouldn't give up until the game turns in your favour. Put the gun down."

"You found me. How did you know I'd be sitting outside the shack and not inside?"

"Because I know you, Valentin. You thought I'd look in the most obvious place first, so you sat down outside where you could dispatch one last soul."

"Fellow travellers." Valentin coughed wetly. "We're twin souls, so our souls ought to be in the same place, Harry."

"Put the gun down now, or I'll shoot."

"I often think about my mother, Harry. Do you?"

Harry saw the back of Valentin's head rock back and forth in the darkness. It was suddenly lit up by another flash of light. More raindrops. Big and heavy this time, not torn by the wind. They were in the eye of the storm.

"I think of her because she's the only person I've ever hated more than myself, Harry. I'm trying to lay waste to more than she did, but I don't know if that's possible. She destroyed me."

"And more isn't possible? Where's Marte Ruud?"

"No, more isn't possible. Because I'm unique, Harry. You and I, we aren't like them. We're unique."

"Sorry to disappoint you, Valentin, but I'm not unique. Where is she?"

"Two bits of bad news, Harry. One. You can forget the little red-haired girl. Two. Yes, you *are* unique." More laughter. "It's not a nice thought, is it? You take refuge in normality, in the averageness of the herd, and think you'll find a sense of belonging there, something that's your true self. But the real you is sitting here now, Harry. Wondering whether or not you're going to kill me. And you use these girls, Aurora, Marte, to fuel your delicious hatred. Because now it's your turn to decide if someone should live or die, and you're enjoying it. You're *enjoying* being God. You've dreamt of being me. You've been waiting for your turn to be a vampire. You recognise the thirst—just admit it, Harry. And one day you too will drink."

"I'm not you," Harry said, and swallowed. He heard the roaring in his head. Felt a fresh gust of wind. A new, shattered raindrop against the hand that was holding the pistol. That was that. They would soon be out of the calm eye.

"You're like me," Valentin said. "And that's why you're also being fooled. You and me, we think we're clever bastards, but we all get fooled in the end, Harry."

"Not—"

Valentin spun round and Harry had time to see the long barrel point towards him before he squeezed the trigger of the Glock. Once, twice. Another flash lit up the forest and Harry saw Valentin's body: just like the lightning, it was frozen in a jagged shape against the sky. His eyes were bulging, his mouth was open, and the front of his shirt dyed red with blood. In his right hand he was holding a broken branch which was pointing at Harry. Then he fell.

Harry got to his feet and went over to Valentin, who was on his knees with his torso slumped against one of the trees, staring into space. He was dead.

Harry aimed the pistol at Valentin's chest and fired again. A crack of thunder swallowed the sound of the shot.

Three shots.

Not because it made any sense, but because that was what music was like, that was how the story went. There should be three.

Something was approaching; it sounded like thundering hooves against the ground, pushing the air ahead of it and making the trees bend.

Then came the rain.

# 31

# Wednesday night

Harry was sitting at Smith's kitchen table with a cup of tea in his hands and a towel around his neck. Rainwater was dripping onto the floor from his clothes. The wind was still howling and the rain was hammering against the windowpanes, making the police cars outside in the yard look like distorted UFOs with their revolving blue lights. It was as if all the water had slowed down slightly in the air currents. Moon. It smelt of moon.

Harry concluded that Hallstein Smith—who was sitting opposite him—was still in shock. His pupils were dilated, his expression apathetic.

"You're quite sure . . ."

"Yes, he's completely dead now, Hallstein," Harry said. "But it's by no means certain that I'd be alive now if you hadn't taken his revolver with you when you left him."

"I don't know why I did that, I thought he was dead," Smith whispered in a metallic, robotic voice, and stared down at the table where he had laid the long-barrelled revolver beside the pistol he had wounded Valentin with. "I thought I hit him in the middle of the chest."

"You did," Harry said. Moon. That was what the astronauts had reported. That the moon smelt of burnt gunpowder. The smell was partly coming from the pistol Harry was carrying inside his jacket, but mostly from the Glock on the table. Harry picked up Valentin's red revolver. Sniffed the barrel. That too smelt of powder, but not as much. Katrine came into the kitchen with rain dripping from her black hair. "The crime-scene team are down with Gjertsen now."

She looked at the revolver.

"It's been fired," Harry said.

"No, no," Smith whispered, mechanically shaking his head. "He only pointed it at me."

"Not now," Harry said, looking at Katrine. "The smell of powder hangs around for days."

"Marte Ruud?" Katrine said. "Do you think . . . ?"

"I shot first." Smith raised his glassy eyes. "I shot Valentin. And now he's dead."

Harry leaned forward and put a hand on his shoulder. "And that's why you're alive, Hallstein."

Smith nodded slowly.

Harry signalled to Katrine with his eyes that she should look after Hallstein, and stood up. "I'm going down to the barn."

"No further than that," Katrine said. "They're going to want to talk to you."

Harry ran from the farmhouse down to the barn, but all the same he was soaked again by the time he reached the office. He sat down at the desk and let his eyes roam around the room. He stopped at the drawing of the man with bat's wings. It radiated more loneliness than any actual eeriness. Possibly because it seemed so familiar. Harry closed his eyes.

He needed a drink. He thrust the thought aside and opened his eyes again. The picture on the computer screen in front of him was split in two, one window for each security camera. Using the mouse, he moved the cursor over to the clock, wound back to the minutes before midnight, which was roughly the time Smith had called. After twenty seconds or so a shape slid into shot in front of the gate. Valentin. He came from the left. From the main road. Bus? Taxi? He had a white key ready, unlocked the gate and sneaked in. The gate closed behind him, but the latch didn't click. Fifteen to twenty seconds later Harry saw Valentin on the other image with the empty stalls and scales. Valentin came close to losing his balance on the metal weighing platform, and the dial behind him whirred and showed that this monster who had killed so many people, some of them with his bare hands, weighed just seventy-four kilos, twenty-one kilos less than Harry. Then Valentin walked towards the camera, it was as if he was staring straight into the lens, yet still didn't see it. Before he disappeared from view Harry saw him put his hand into his deep coat pocket. All Harry could see in the picture now was the empty stalls, the scales and the top part of Valentin's shadow. Harry reconstructed those seconds, he remembered every word of his phone conversation with Hallstein Smith. The rest of the day and the hours at Katrine's were completely gone, but those seconds had been riveted into place. It had always been like that, whenever he drank his private brain took on a Teflon coating, while his police brain retained its layer of adhesive, as if one part *wanted* to forget and the other *had* to remember. Internal Investigations were going to have to transcribe a very long interview report if they wanted to include all the details he could remember.

Harry saw the edge of the door come into shot as Valentin opened it, then his shadow lifted one arm, then let it fall.

Harry speeded up the replay.

He saw Hallstein from the back as he shuffled past the stalls and went out.

And a minute later Valentin dragged himself out the same way. Harry slowed the video down. Valentin was leaning against the stalls, looked like he might collapse at any moment. But he kept going, metre by metre. He stood on the scales, swaying. The dial showed he was one and a half kilos lighter than when he had arrived. Harry glanced at the pool of blood on the floor behind the computer screen, before watching as Valentin struggled to get the door open. And that was where Harry could *feel* the will to survive. Unless it was just fear of getting caught? And it occurred to Harry that this film clip was inevitably going to be leaked at some point, and would end up being a hit on YouTube.

Bjørn Holm's pale face appeared in the doorway. "So this is where it started." He walked in, and Harry was once again fascinated that this otherwise not particularly elegant forensics expert became a ballet dancer the moment he entered a crime scene. Bjørn crouched down beside the pool of blood. "They're taking him away now."

"Mm."

"Four entry wounds, Harry. How many of them are from . . . ?"

"Three," Harry said. "Hallstein only shot once."

Bjørn Holm grimaced. "He shot an armed man, Harry. Have you thought about what you're going to say to Internal Investigations about your shots?"

Harry shrugged. "The truth, of course. That it was dark and Valentin was holding a branch in an attempt to fool me into thinking he was armed. He knew he was finished, and he *wanted* me to shoot him, Bjørn."

"All the same. Three shots in the chest of an unarmed man . . ."

Harry nodded.

Bjørn took a deep breath, looked over his shoulder and lowered his voice. "But of course it's dark, raining hard, a full-blown storm down in those woods. And if I were to go down there now and have a look on my own, there's always a chance I might find a pistol hidden where Valentin was lying."

The two of them looked at each other as the wind made the walls creak.

Harry saw Bjørn Holm's cheek flush red. And knew what that had cost him. Knew that he was standing there offering Harry more than he actually owned. He was offering him everything he held dear. Their shared values, their moral code. His, their, soul.

"Thank you," Harry said. "Thank you, my friend, but I have to say no."

Bjørn Holm blinked twice. Swallowed. Breathed out in a long, shivering wheeze, and gave a brief, out-of-place chuckle of relief.

"I'd better get back," he said, standing up.

"Go on," Harry said.

Bjørn Holm stood in front of him, hesitating. As if he wanted to say something, or take a step forward and give him a hug. Harry leaned over towards the computer screen again. "We'll talk soon, Bjørn."

On the screen he watched the forensics expert's hunched shoulders as he made his way outside.

Harry slammed his fist down on the keyboard. A drink. Fuck, fuck! Just one drink.

His eyes settled on the bat-man.

What was it Hallstein had said? *He knew. He knew where I was.*

# 32

# Wednesday night

Mikael Bellman stood with his arms folded, wondering if Oslo Police District had ever held a press conference at two o'clock in the morning before. He was leaning against the wall to the left of the podium, looking out across the room, which contained a mixture of night editors and other newsroom staff, journalists who were probably supposed to be covering the ravages of Emilia and sleepy reporters who had been dragged out of bed. Mona Daa had arrived wearing gym clothes under her raincoat, and looked wide awake.

Up on the podium, beside head of Crime Squad Gunnar Hagen, Katrine Bratt was talking through the details of the raid on Valentin Gjertsen's flat in Sinsen and the subsequent drama out at Hallstein Smith's farm. Camera flashes kept going off, and Bellman knew that even if he wasn't sitting up there, the occasional camera was still being aimed at him, so he tried to settle his face into the expression Isabelle had recommended when he called her on the way here. Serious, but with the inner satisfaction of the victor. "Remember that people are dead," Isabelle had said. "So no grinning or obvious celebration. Think of yourself as General Eisenhower after D-Day, you bear the leader's responsibility for both the victory and the tragedy."

Bellman stifled a yawn. Ulla had woken him when she got home from her girls' night out in the city. He couldn't recall having seen her drunk since they were young. Speaking of drunk: Harry Hole was standing next to him, and if Bellman hadn't known better he would have sworn that the former detective was inebriated. He looked more exhausted than any of the reporters, and that was booze he could smell on his wet clothes, wasn't it?

A Rogaland dialect cut through the room. "I appreciate that you don't want to go public with the name of the officer who shot and killed Valentin Gjertsen, but surely you can tell us if Valentin was armed, or shot back?"

"Like I said, we want to wait until we're in full command of the facts before making the details public," Katrine said, then pointed at Mona Daa who was waving her hand.

"But you're willing and able to tell us the details surrounding Hallstein Smith's involvement?"

"Yes," Katrine said. "We have all the details on that point because we have a recording of the incident, and were talking to Smith on the phone as it happened."

"So you said, but who was he talking to?"

"Me." She paused. "And Harry Hole."

Mona Daa tilted her head. "So you and Harry Hole were here in Police HQ when it happened?"

Mikael Bellman saw Katrine glance at Gunnar Hagen as if to ask for help, but the head of Crime Squad appeared not to notice what she wanted. Nor did Bellman.

"We don't want to go into the working methods of the police in too much detail at present," Hagen said. "Out of consideration for both loss of evidence and our tactics in future cases."

Mona Daa and the rest of the room seemed content with this, but Bellman could see that Hagen didn't know what he was hiding.

"It's late, and all of us have work to do," Hagen said, looking at the time. "The next press conference will be at twelve noon, hopefully we'll have more for you then. In the meantime, have a good night. We can all sleep a bit more soundly now."

The blitz of camera flashes intensified as Hagen and Bratt stood up. Some of the photographers turned their lenses on Bellman, and when some of the people standing up came between Bellman and the cameras, he took a step forward so the photographers could get an unimpeded view.

"Hold on, Harry," Bellman said, without looking round or changing his Eisenhower expression. Once the cascade of flashes had stopped, he turned towards Harry Hole, who was standing there with his arms folded.

"I'm not going to throw you to the wolves," Bellman said. "You did your job, you shot a dangerous serial killer." He put one hand on Harry's shoulder. "And we look after our own. OK?"

The taller policeman looked pointedly at the hand on his shoulder and Bellman removed it. Harry's voice was hoarser than usual. "Enjoy your victory, Bellman. I'm being questioned first thing in the morning, so goodnight."

Bellman watched Harry Hole as he made his way towards the exit, with his legs wide apart and his knees bent, like a sailor on deck in a rough sea.

Bellman had already conferred with Isabelle, and they had agreed that if this success wasn't to leave a nasty aftertaste, it would be best if Internal Investigations concluded that there was little or nothing to criticise Hole for. Exactly how they were going to help Internal Investigations to reach this conclusion was as yet unclear, seeing as they couldn't be bribed directly. But obviously any thinking person was receptive to a bit of common sense. And as far as the press and general public were concerned, Isabelle believed that it had become almost a matter of routine in recent years that mass murders ended with the perpetrator being killed by the police, and that the press and general public had more or less tacitly accepted that this was how society dealt with this sort of case—quickly and efficiently, in a way that appealed to ordinary people's sense of justice and without the spiralling costs associated with court proceedings in big murder cases.

Bellman looked for Katrine Bratt, aware that the pair of them together would make a good subject for the photographers. But she was already gone.

"Gunnar!" he called, loudly enough for a couple of photographers to turn round. The head of Crime Squad stopped in the doorway and came over to him.

"Look serious," Bellman whispered, and held out his hand. "Congratulations," he said loudly.


Harry was standing beneath one of the street lamps on Borggata, trying to light a cigarette in Emilia's dying gasps. He was freezing, his teeth were chattering, and he could feel the cigarette bobbing up and down between his lips.

He glanced up at the entrance of Police HQ, where the reporters and journalists were still coming out. Perhaps they were just as tired as him and for that reason weren't talking noisily among themselves the way they usually did, but were heading down the road towards Grønlandsleiret as a silent, sluggish mass. Or perhaps they could feel it too. The emptiness. The emptiness that comes when a case is solved, when you reach the end of the road and realise that there's no road left. No more field to plough. But your wife is still in the house, with the doctor and midwife, and there's still nothing you can do. Nowhere you can be useful.

"What are you waiting for?"

Harry turned. It was Bjørn.

"Katrine," Harry said. "She said she'd drive me home. She's getting the car from the garage, so if you need a lift as well . . ."

Bjørn shook his head. "Have you spoken to Katrine about what we talked about?"

Harry nodded and made a fresh attempt to light his cigarette.

"Is that a 'Yes'?" Bjørn wondered.

"No," Harry said. "I haven't asked her where you stand."

"You haven't?"

Harry closed his eyes for a moment. Perhaps he had. Either way, he couldn't remember the answer.

"I'm just asking because I was thinking that if the two of you were together around midnight, somewhere that wasn't Police HQ, then maybe you weren't just talking about work."

Harry cupped his hand round the cigarette and lighter as he looked at Bjørn. His childlike, pale blue eyes were bulging out more than usual.

"I can't remember anything but work stuff, Bjørn."

Bjørn Holm looked at the ground and stamped his feet. As if to get his circulation going. As if he couldn't move from the spot.

"I'll let you know, Bjørn."

Bjørn Holm nodded without looking up, then turned and walked off.

Harry watched him go. With a feeling that Bjørn had seen something, something he himself hadn't spotted. There! Lit, at last!

A car pulled up beside him.

Harry sighed, tossed the cigarette on the ground, opened the door and got in.

"What were you two talking about?" Katrine asked, looking at Bjørn as she drove towards the nocturnal calm of Grønlandsleiret.

"Did we have sex?" Harry asked.

"What?"

"I don't remember a thing from earlier this evening. We didn't fuck?"

Katrine didn't answer, apparently concentrating on stopping exactly on the white line in front of a red traffic light. Harry waited.

The light turned green.

"No," Katrine said, putting her foot down and easing off the clutch. "We didn't have sex."

"Good," Harry said, and let out a low whistle.

"You were too drunk."

"What?"

"You were too drunk. You fell asleep."

Harry closed his eyes. "Shit."

"Yes, that's what I thought."

"Not like that. Rakel's in a coma. While I—"

"While you're doing your best to join her there. Forget it, Harry, worse things have happened."

On the radio a dry voice announced that Valentin Gjertsen, the so-called vampirist, had been shot and killed at midnight. And that Oslo had experienced and survived its first tropical storm. Katrine and Harry drove in silence through Majorstua and Vinderen, towards Holmenkollen.

"What are your thoughts about Bjørn these days?" Harry asked. "Any possibility of you giving him another chance?"

"Did he tell you to ask?"

Harry didn't answer.

"I thought he had something going on with what's-her-name Lien."

"I don't know anything about that. OK, fine. You can let me out here."

"Don't you want me to drive you all the way to the house?"

"You'd only wake Oleg. This is great. Thanks." Harry opened the door, but didn't move.

"Yes?"

"Mm. Nothing." He got out.


Harry watched the rear lights of the car vanish, then walked up the drive towards the house.

It sat there, looming even darker than the darkness. No lights. No breathing.

He unlocked and opened the door.

Saw Oleg's shoes but couldn't hear anything.

He took his clothes off in the laundry room, put them in the basket. Went up to the bedroom, got out some clean clothes. He knew he wasn't going to be able to sleep, so he went down to the kitchen. Put some coffee on and looked out of the window.

Thinking. Then he pushed his thoughts aside and poured the coffee, knowing he wasn't going to drink it. He could go off to the Jealousy Bar, but he didn't feel like drinking alcohol either. But he would do. Later.

His thoughts returned.

There were only two of them.

And they were the simplest and the loudest.

One said that if Rakel didn't survive, he would follow her, walk the same path.

The other was that if she did survive, he would leave her. Because she deserved better and because she shouldn't have to be the one to leave.

A third thought appeared.

Harry rested his head in his hands.

The thought of whether he wanted her to survive or not.

Damn, damn.

And then a fourth thought.

What Valentin had said out in the forest.

*We all get fooled in the end, Harry.*

He must have meant that it was Harry who had fooled him. Or did he mean other people? That someone else had fooled Valentin?

*That's why you're also being fooled.*

He had said that just before he fooled Harry into thinking he was pointing a gun at him, but perhaps that wasn't what he meant. Perhaps it was about more than that.

He started when he felt a hand on the back of his neck.

Turned and looked up.

Oleg was standing behind his chair.

"I didn't hear you come in," Harry tried to say, but his voice couldn't seem to settle.

"You were asleep."

"Asleep?" Harry pushed himself up from the table. "No, I was just sitting and—"

"You were asleep, Dad," Oleg interrupted with a little smile.

Harry blinked away the fog. Looked around. Put his hand out and felt the coffee cup. It was cold. "Bloody hell."

"I've been doing some thinking," Oleg said, pulling out the chair next to Harry and sitting down.

Harry smacked his lips, loosened the saliva in his mouth.

"And you're right."

"Am I?" Harry took a sip of the cold coffee to take away the taste of stale bile.

"Yes. You have a responsibility that stretches beyond those closest to you. You have to be there for people who aren't so close. And I have no right to demand that you let them all down. The fact that murder cases are like a drug to you doesn't change that."

"Hm. And you came to this conclusion all on your own?"

"Yes. With a bit of help from Helga." Oleg looked down at his hands. "She's better than me at seeing things from other angles. And I didn't mean what I said, about not wanting to be like you."

Harry put his hand on Oleg's shoulder. Saw that he was wearing Harry's old Elvis Costello T-shirt to sleep in. "My boy?"

"Yes?"

"Promise me that you won't be like me. That's all I ask of you."

Oleg nodded. "One other thing," he said.

"Yes?"

"Steffens called. It's Mum."

It felt like an iron claw was squeezing Harry's heart, and he stopped breathing.

"She's woken up."

# 33

# Thursday morning

"Yes?"

"Anders Wyller?"

"Yes."

"Good morning, I'm calling from the Forensic Medical Institute."

"Good morning."

"It's about that strand of hair you sent for analysis."

"Oh?"

"Did you get the printout I sent you?"

"Yes."

"Well, that isn't the full analysis, but as you can see there's a link between the DNA in the hair and one of the DNA profiles we registered in the vampirist case. To be more precise, DNA profile 201."

"Yes, I saw that."

"I don't know who 201 is, but we do at least know that it isn't Valentin Gjertsen. But seeing as it's a partial match and I haven't heard anything from you, I just wanted to make sure you'd got the results. Because I'm assuming you want us to complete the analysis?"

"No, thanks."

"No? But—"

"The case is solved, and you've got a lot of other work to be getting on with. By the way, was that printout sent to anyone else but me?"

"No, I can't see that there was any request to that effect. Do you want—?"

"No, there's no need. You can close the case. Thanks for your help."

# Part III

# 34

# Saturday daytime

Masa Kanagawa used the tongs to lift the red-hot iron from the oven. He put it on the anvil and started to beat it with one of the smaller hammers. The hammer was the traditional Japanese design, with a head that stuck out at the front in a sort of gallows shape. Masa had taken over the little smithy from his father and grandfather, but like plenty of the other smiths in Wakayama he had found it a struggle to make ends meet. The steel industry, which had long been the backbone of the city's economy, had moved to China, and Masa had had to concentrate on niche products. Such as the *katana*, a samurai sword that was particularly popular in the U.S.A., and which he produced to order for private customers all over the world. Japanese law dictated that a sword-smith needed a licence, must have served a five-year apprenticeship, and was only permitted to produce two long swords per month, all of which had to be registered with the authorities. Masa was just a simple smith, who made good swords for a fraction of the price charged by the licenced smiths, but he knew he could get caught, so kept a low profile. He neither knew nor wanted to know what his clients used the swords for, but he hoped it was for exercise, for decoration or collecting. All he knew was that it helped feed him and his family, and enabled him to keep the little smithy running. But he had told his son that he ought to find a different profession, that he ought to study, that being a smith was too hard and the rewards too meagre. His son had followed his father's advice, but it cost money to keep him at university, so Masa accepted whatever commissions he was offered. Such as this one, to make a replica of a set of iron teeth from the Heian period. It was for a client in Norway, and this was the second time he had ordered the same thing. The first time was six months ago. Masa Kanagawa didn't know the client's name, he just had the address of a post office box. But that was fine, the goods had been paid for in advance and the price Masa had asked for was high. Not just because it was complicated work, making the little teeth to match the design the customer had sent him, but because it felt wrong. Masa couldn't explain why it felt more wrong than forging a sword, but when he looked at the iron teeth they made him shudder. And as he drove home along Highway 370, the singing road where the carefully designed and constructed ridges in the surface created a tune as the tires rolled over them, he no longer heard it as beautiful, soothing choral music. He heard a warning, a deep rumble that grew and grew until it became a scream. A scream like a demon's.

Harry woke up. He lit a cigarette and reflected. What sort of awakening was this? This wasn't waking up to work. It was Saturday, his first lecture after the winter break wasn't until Monday, and Øystein was looking after the bar today.

It wasn't waking up alone. Rakel was lying by his side. During the first few weeks after she came home from hospital, whenever he lay and looked at her sleeping he had been terrified that she wouldn't wake up, that the mysterious "it" that the doctors hadn't identified was going to come back.

"People can't cope with doubt," Steffens had said. "People like to believe that you and I know, Harry. The accused is guilty, the diagnosis is definite. Admitting that we have doubts is taken as an admission of our own inadequacy, not an indication of the complexity of the mystery or the limitations of our profession. But the truth is that we will never know for certain what was wrong with Rakel. Her mast cell count was slightly elevated, so at first I thought it was a rare blood disease. But all the signs are gone and there's a lot to suggest that it was some sort of poison. In which case you don't have to worry about it recurring. Just like these vampirist murders, wouldn't you say?"

"But we *know* who killed those women."

"You're right. Bad analogy."

As the weeks passed, the gaps between him thinking about Rakel having a relapse grew longer.

As did the gaps between him thinking there had been another vampirist killing every time the phone rang.

So it wasn't waking up full of angst.

He had had a few of those after Valentin Gjertsen died. Oddly enough, not while Internal Investigations were interviewing him, before eventually concluding that Harry couldn't be blamed for firing in an uncertain situation with a dangerous murderer who had himself provoked the response. It was only after, then, that Valentin and Marte Ruud started to haunt him in his dreams. And it was her, not him, who whispered in his ear. *That's why you're also being fooled.* He had told himself that it was other people's responsibility to find her now. And as the weeks turned to months, their visits had become less frequent. It helped that he had got back into his daily routine at Police College and at home, and that he wasn't touching alcohol.

And now, at last, he was where he ought to be. Because this was the fifth sort. Waking up content. He would copy and paste yet another day, with his serotonin level exactly where it should be.

Harry crept out of bed as quietly as he could, pulled on some trousers and went downstairs, inserted Rakel's favourite capsule into the espresso machine, switched it on and went out onto the steps. He felt the snow sting pleasantly under his bare feet as he breathed in the winter air. The white-clad city was still in darkness, but a new day was blushing off to the east.

*Aftenposten* was saying that the future looked brighter than the news might make us think. That in spite of the increasingly detailed picture the media were painting of murders, wars and atrocities, recently published research showed that the number of people being murdered was at a historic low, and sinking. Yes, one day murder might even become extinct. Mikael Bellman, whose appointment as Justice Minister was going to be confirmed next week, according to *Aftenposten*, had commented that there was obviously nothing wrong with setting ambitious targets, but that his personal target wasn't a perfect society, but a *better* one. Harry couldn't help smiling. Isabelle Skøyen was a talented prompt. Harry looked again to the sentence about murder one day becoming extinct. Why was this long-term claim triggering the anxiety he had to admit he had—in spite of his own contentment—felt for the past month, possibly longer? Murder. He had made it his life's work to fight murderers. But if he succeeded, if they all disappeared, wouldn't he disappear with them? Had he not buried a part of himself with Valentin? Was that why Harry had found himself standing by Valentin Gjertsen's grave just a few days ago? Or was there some other reason? What Steffens had said about not being able to cope with doubt. Was it the lack of answers that was nagging at him? Damn it, Rakel was better, Valentin was gone, time to let go now.

The snow creaked.

"Nice winter break, Harry?"

"We survived, fru Syvertsen. I see you haven't had enough skiing, though."

"Skiing weather is skiing weather," she said, jutting her hip out. Her ski suit looked like it had been painted on her. She was holding her cross-country skis, no doubt as light as helium, in one hand as if they were chopsticks.

"You don't fancy coming for a quick circuit, Harry? We could sprint to Tryvann while everyone's asleep." She smiled, the light from the lamp above them reflecting off her lips, some sort of cream to fend off the cold. "Nice and . . . slippery."

"I haven't got any skis," Harry smiled back.

She laughed. "You're kidding? You're Norwegian and you haven't got a pair of skis?"

"Treason, I know." Harry glanced down at the paper. Looked at the date. 4 March.

"I seem to remember that you didn't have a Christmas tree either."

"Shocking, isn't it? Someone should report us."

"You know what, Harry? Sometimes I envy you."

Harry looked up.

"You don't care, you just break all the rules. I sometimes wish I could be that frivolous."

Harry laughed. "With that kind of smooth talk I don't doubt that you get both a bit of friction and a nice slippery ride, fru Syvertsen."

"What?"

"Have a good ski!" Harry saluted her with the folded newspaper and walked back to the house.

He looked at the picture of the one-eyed Mikael Bellman. Maybe that was why his gaze looked so unflinching. It was the look of a man who appeared certain that he knew the truth. The look of a priest. A look that could convert people.

*The truth is that we will never know for certain.*

*We all get fooled in the end, Harry.*

Did it show? Did his doubt show?

Rakel was sitting at the kitchen table pouring coffee for both of them.

"Up already?" he said, kissing her on the head. Her hair smelt faintly of vanilla and sleep-Rakel, his favourite smell.

"Steffens just called," she said, squeezing his hand.

"What did he want so early?"

"He was just wondering how things were going. He's called Oleg in for a follow-up after that blood sample he took before Christmas. He says there's nothing to worry about, but he wants to see if there could be a genetic link that might explain 'it.'"

*It.* She, he and Oleg had hugged each other more after Rakel came home from hospital. Talked more. Planned less. Had just been together. Then, as if someone had thrown a stone in the water, the surface went back to the way it had been before. Ice. But even so, it felt like something was moving down there in the abyss beneath him.

"Nothing to worry about," Harry repeated, as much to himself as her. "But it worried you anyway?"

She shrugged. "Have you thought any more about the bar?"

Harry sat and took a sip of his instant coffee. "When I was there yesterday I thought I'm obviously going to have to sell it. I don't know anything about running a bar, and it doesn't feel like much of a calling, serving youngsters with potentially unlucky genes."

"But . . ."

Harry pulled on his fleece jacket. "Øystein loves working there. And he's staying off the stock, I know that. Easy, unlimited access seems to make some people pull themselves together. And it is actually paying its way."

"Hardly surprising, when it can boast two vampirist murders, one near shootout and Harry Hole behind the bar."

"Hm. No, I think it's just that Oleg's idea of musical themes is working. Tonight, for instance, it's nothing but the most stylish ladies over fifty. Lucinda Williams, Emmylou Harris, Patti Smith, Chrissie Hynde . . ."

"Before my time, darling."

"Tomorrow it's jazz from the sixties, and the funny thing is that the same people who come to the punk evenings will show up for that too. We do one Paul Rodgers night a week in Mehmet's honour. Øystein says we ought to have a music quiz. And—"

"Harry?"

"Yes?"

"It sounds like you're planning to hold on to the Jealousy."

"Does it?" Harry scratched his head. "Damn. I haven't got time for that. A couple of daft sods like me and Øystein."

Rakel laughed.

"Unless . . ." Harry said.

"Unless?"

Harry didn't answer, just smiled.

"No, no, forget it!" Rakel said. "I've got enough on my hands unless I—"

"Just one day a week. You don't work on Fridays. A bit of accounting and some other paperwork. You could have some shares, be chairman of the board."

"Chairwoman."

"Deal."

She batted his outstretched hand away. "No."

"Think about it."

"OK, I'll think about it before I say no. Shall we go back up to bed?"

"Tired?"

". . . No." She looked at him over her coffee cup with half-closed eyes. "I could imagine helping myself to some of what I see fru Syvertsen can't have."

"Hm. So you've been spying. Well, after you, chairwoman."

Harry glanced at the front of the paper again. 4 March. The day of his release. He followed her to the stairs. Passed the mirror without looking in it.


Svein Finne, "the Fiancé," walked into Vår Frelsers Cemetery. It was daybreak, and there was no one about. Only an hour earlier he had walked out through the gate of Ila Prison a free man, and this was his first errand. Against the white snow the small, black, rounded headstones looked like dots on a sheet of paper. He walked along the icy path, taking cautious steps. He was an old man now, and he hadn't walked on ice for many years. He stopped in front of a particularly small headstone, just neutral initials—VG—beneath the cross.

Valentin Gjertsen.

No words of remembrance. Of course. No one wanted to remember. And no flowers.

Svein Finne took out the feather he had in his coat pocket, knelt down and stuck it in the snow in front of the headstone. In the Cherokee tribe they used to place an eagle's feather in the coffins of their dead. He had avoided contact with Valentin when they had both been in Ila. Not for the same reason as the other inmates, whom Valentin scared the life out of. But because Svein Finne didn't want the young man to recognise him. Because he would, sooner or later. It had taken Svein one single glance on the day Valentin arrived in Ila. He had his mother's narrow shoulders and high-pitched voice, just as he remembered her from their engagement. She was one of the ones who had tried to get an abortion while Svein was busy elsewhere, so he had forced his way in and lived there to watch over his offspring. She had lain beside him, trembling and sobbing every night until she gave birth to the boy in a magnificent bloodbath there in the room, and he had cut the umbilical cord with his own knife. His thirteenth child, his seventh son. But it wasn't when Svein learned the name of the new inmate that he was one hundred percent certain. It was when he was told the details of what this Valentin had been convicted of.

Svein Finne got to his feet again.

The dead were dead.

And the living would soon be dead.

He took a deep breath. The man had contacted him. And had woken the thirst inside him, the thirst he'd thought the years had cured him of.

Svein Finne looked at the sky. The sun would soon be up. And the city would wake, rub its eyes, shake off the nightmare of the murderer who had rampaged last autumn. Smile and see that the sun was shining on them, blissfully unaware of what was coming. Something that would make the autumn look like a tame prelude. Like father, like son. Like son, like father.

The policeman. Harry Hole. He was out there somewhere.

Svein Finne turned and began to walk. His steps were longer, faster, more sure.

There was so much to do.


Truls Berntsen was sitting on the sixth floor, watching the red glow of the sun try to force its way over Ekebergsåsen. In December Katrine Bratt had moved him from the doghouse to an office with a window. Which was nice. But he was still archiving reports and incoming material about closed or cold cases. So the reason why he got there so early had to be that at minus twelve degrees, it was warmer in the office than in his flat. Or that he was having trouble sleeping these days.

In recent weeks most of the material that needed archiving had naturally enough been late tip-offs and unnecessary witness statements relating to the vampirist murders. Someone claiming to have seen Valentin Gjertsen, probably someone who also thought Elvis was still alive. It didn't matter that the DNA test of the corpse had provided incontrovertible evidence that it really *had* been Valentin Gjertsen that Harry Hole had killed, because for some people facts were just minor irritants that got in the way of their obsessions.

*Got in the way of their obsessions.* Truls Berntsen didn't know why the sentence stuck, it was just something he had thought rather than said out loud.

He picked up the next envelope from the pile. Like the others, it had been opened and its contents listed by another officer. This one featured the Facebook logo, a stamp that showed it had been sent by special delivery, and an archiving order attached with a paper clip, on which it said "Vampirist Case" beside the case number, and Magnus Skarre's name and signature next to the word *case manager.*

Truls Berntsen took out the contents. On top was a letter in English. Truls didn't understand all of it, but enough to recognise that it referred to a court disclosure order, and that the enclosed material was printouts of the Facebook accounts of all the murder victims in the vampirist case, plus the still missing Marte Ruud. He leafed through the pages and noticed that some of them were stuck together, so he guessed that Skarre hadn't looked through everything. Fine, the case had been solved and the perpetrator would never find himself in the dock. But obviously Truls would dearly love to catch that bastard Skarre with his trousers down. He checked the names of the people the victims had been in contact with. Looked rather optimistically for Facebook messages to or from Valentin Gjertsen or Alexander Dreyer which he could accuse Skarre of having missed. He scanned page after page, only stopping to check senders and recipients. He sighed when he got to the end. No mistakes there. The only names he had recognised apart from the victims had been a couple that he and Wyller had dismissed because they had been in touch with the victims by phone. And it was surely only natural that some of the same people who had been in touch by phone, such as Ewa Dolmen and that Lenny Hell, had also been in contact on Facebook.

Truls put the documents back in the envelope, stood up and went over to the filing cabinet. He pulled out the top drawer. Let go of it. He liked the way it glided out, with a sigh, like a goods train. Until he stopped the drawer with one hand.

Looked at the envelope.

Dolmen, not Hermansen.

He hunted through the drawer until he found the file containing the interviews from the phone list, then took it and the envelope back to the desk. He leafed through the printouts until he found the name again. Lenny Hell. Truls remembered the name because it had made him think of Lemmy, even if the guy he had spoken to over the phone had sounded more like a terrified bastard with that tremble in his voice that so many people—regardless of how innocent they were—got when they found out it was the police calling them. So, Lenny Hell had been in touch with Ewa Dolmen on Facebook. Victim number two.

Truls opened the file of interviews. Found the report of his own brief conversation with Lenny Hell. And his conversation with the owner of Åneby Pizza & Grill. And a note he didn't understand, in which Wyller reported that Nittedal Police Station had vouched for both Lenny and the owner of the pizzeria, confirming that Lenny had been in the restaurant at the time of Elise Hermansen's murder.

Elise Hermansen. Victim number one.

They had questioned Lenny because he had called Elise Hermansen several times. And he had been in touch with Ewa Dolmen on Facebook. *There* was the mistake. Magnus Skarre's mistake. And, possibly, Lenny Hell's mistake. Unless it was just a coincidence. Single men and women of a similar age seeking each other within the same geographic area of what was after all a fairly sparsely populated country. There were more improbable coincidences. And the case was closed, there was nothing to consider. Not *really*. But on the other hand . . . The papers were still writing about the vampirist. In the U.S.A., Valentin Gjertsen had acquired an obscure little fan club, and someone had bought the book and film rights to his life story from his estate. It may not have been on the front pages any more, but it could be again. Truls Berntsen got his phone out. Found Mona Daa's number. Looked at it. Then he stood up, grabbed his coat and walked towards the lift.

Mona Daa screwed up her eyes and pushed with her arms as she curled the dumbbells up towards her chest. She imagined she was unfurling her wings and flying away from here with her arms outstretched. Across Frognerparken, across Oslo. That she could see everything. Absolutely everything.

And she was showing them.

She had seen a documentary about her favourite photographer,

Don McCullin, who became known as a humanitarian war reporter because he showed the worst aspects of humanity in order to encourage reflection and soul-searching, not for cheap thrills. She couldn't say the same of herself. And it had struck her that there was one word that hadn't been mentioned in the one-sided hagiography of the documentary. Ambition. McCullin became the best, and he must have met thousands of admirers in between his battles, quite literally. Young colleagues who wanted to be like him, who had heard the myth about the photographer who stayed with the soldiers in Hue during the Tet Offensive, and the anecdotes from Beirut, Biafra, Congo, Cyprus. Here was a photographer who achieved what human beings thirsted for most, recognition and acclaim, yet not a word about how it could make a man put himself through the very worst trials, take risks he would otherwise never have dreamed of. And—potentially—commit similar offences to the ones he was documenting, all to take the perfect picture, get the groundbreaking story.

Mona had agreed to sit in a cage and wait for the vampirist. Without telling the police and potentially saving people's lives. It would have been easy to sound the alarm, even if she did think she was being watched. A note slipped discreetly across the table to Nora. But she had—like Nora's sexual fantasy of allowing herself to be raped by Harry Hole—made it feel like she was obliged to go through with it. Of course she had wanted it. The recognition, the acclaim, seeing the admiration in younger colleagues' eyes when she was giving her acceptance speech for the Journalism Award, humbly saying that she was just a lucky, hard-working girl from a small town in the north. Before going on, slightly less humbly, to talk about her childhood, the bullying, and revenge and ambition. Yes, she would talk out loud about ambition, she wouldn't be afraid to tell it how it was. And she wanted to fly. Fly.

"You need a bit more resistance."

It had got harder to lift the weights. She opened her eyes and saw two hands pushing down gently on the weights. The person was standing immediately behind her, so that in the big mirror in front of her she looked like some sort of four-armed Ganesh.

"Come on, two more," the voice whispered in her ear. She recognised it. The police officer's. And now she looked up and saw his face above hers. He was smiling. Blue eyes below a white fringe. White teeth. Anders Wyller.

"What are you doing here?" she said, forgetting to push with her arms, but feeling herself fly anyway.

. . .

"What are you doing here?" Øystein Eikeland asked, putting a half-litre of beer on the counter in front of the customer.

"Huh?"

"Not you, him there," Øystein said, gesturing over his shoulder with his thumb towards the tall man with the crew cut who had just walked behind the bar and was filling the *cezve* with coffee and water.

"Can't deal with any more instant coffee," Harry said.

"Can't deal with any more time off," Øystein said. "Can't deal with being away from your beloved bar. Hear what this is?"

Harry stopped to listen to the rapid, rhythmic music. "Not until she starts singing, no."

"She doesn't, that what's so great," Øystein said. "It's Taylor Swift, '1989.'"

Harry nodded. He remembered that Swift or her record company hadn't wanted to put the album on Spotify, so instead they'd released a version with no singing.

"Didn't we agree that today's singers were only going to be women over fifty?" Harry said.

"Didn't you hear what I said?" Øystein said. "She's not *singing*."

Harry gave up any idea of arguing against the logic of that. "People are here early today."

"Alligator sausage," Øystein said, pointing at the long, smoked sausages hanging above the bar. "The first week was because it was weird, but now the same people are back wanting more. Maybe we should change the name to Alligator Joe's, Everglades, or—"

"Jealousy is fine."

"OK, OK, just trying to be proactive here. Someone's going to nick that idea, though."

"We'll have had another one by then."

Harry put the *cezve* on the hotplate and turned round just as a familiar figure came in through the door.

Harry folded his arms as the man stamped his boots and glared across the room.

"Something wrong?" Øystein wondered.

"Don't think so," Harry said. "Make sure the coffee doesn't boil."

"You and that Turkish not-boiling thing."

Harry walked round the bar and went over to the man, who had unbuttoned his coat. Heat was steaming off him.

"Hole," he said.

"Berntsen," Harry said.

"I've got something for you."

"Why?"

Truls Berntsen grunt-laughed. "Don't you want to know *what* it is?"

"Only if I'm happy with the answer to the first question."

Harry saw Truls Berntsen attempt an indifferent smirk, but fail and swallow instead. And the blush on his scarred face could of course be the result of the transition from the cold outside.

"You're a bastard, Hole, but you did save my life that time."

"Don't make me regret it. Out with it."

Berntsen pulled the document file from the inside pocket of his coat. "Lemmy—I mean Lenny Hell. You'll see that he was in touch with both Elise Hermansen and Ewa Dolmen."

"Really?" Harry looked at the yellow folder, held together by a rubber band, Truls Berntsen was holding towards him. "Why haven't you gone to Bratt with this?"

"Because she—unlike you—has to think about her career and would have had to take this to Mikael."

"And?"

"Mikael's taking over as Justice Minister next week. He doesn't want any blots on his copybook."

Harry looked at Truls Berntsen. He had long since figured out that Berntsen wasn't as stupid as he might appear. "You mean he doesn't want this case dragged out again?"

Berntsen shrugged. "The vampirist case came close to sticking a serious spoke in Mikael's wheel. Then it turned into one of his greatest successes instead. So no, he doesn't want to spoil that image."

"Hm. You're giving these documents to me because you're worried that otherwise they'll end up in a drawer in the Police Chief's office?"

"I'm worried they'll end up in the paper shredder, Hole."

"OK. But you still haven't answered my question. Why?"

"Didn't you hear? The paper shredder."

"Why do *you*, Truls Berntsen, care about that? And no bullshit, I know who and what you are."

Truls grunted something.

Harry waited.

Truls glanced at him, looked away, stamped his feet as if there was more snow on them. "I don't know," he said eventually. "It's true, I don't know. I thought maybe it would be good if Magnus Skarre got a bloody nose for not noticing the link between the phones and Facebook, but it's not that either. I don't think. I think I just want . . . no, fuck it, I don't know." He coughed. "But if you don't want it, I'll put it back in the filing cabinet and it can rot in there, same difference to me."

Harry wiped the condensation from the window and watched Truls Berntsen as he walked out of the door and crossed the street, head bowed, in the sharp winter light. Was he mistaken, or had Truls Berntsen just shown symptoms of the partially benign illness known as police?

"What's that you've got there?" Øystein asked when Harry walked back behind the bar.

"Police porn," Harry said, putting the yellow folder on the counter. "Printouts and transcripts."

"The vampirist case? Hasn't that been solved?"

"Yes, there are just a few loose ends, formalities. Can't you hear that the coffee's boiling?"

"Can't you hear that Taylor Swift isn't singing?"

Harry opened his mouth to say something, but instead heard himself laughing. He loved this guy. Loved this bar. He poured the spoiled coffee into two cups and tapped along on the folder to the beat of "Welcome to Some Pork." As he glanced at the pages he thought that Rakel was bound to say yes, if he just sat quiet as a mouse and gave her some time.

His eyes stopped.

It was as if the ice creaked beneath him.

His heart began to beat faster. *We all get fooled in the end, Harry.*

"What is it?" Øystein asked.

"What's what?"

"You look like you've . . . well . . ."

"Seen a ghost?" Harry asked, and reread it to make sure.

"No," Øystein said.

"No?"

"No, you look more like you've . . . woken up."

Harry looked up from the files and looked at Øystein. And felt it. His anxiety. It was gone.


"It's sixty," Harry warned. "And icy."

Oleg eased off the accelerator slightly. "Why don't you drive, seeing as you've got a car and a driving licence?"

"Because you and Rakel are better drivers," Harry said, squinting against the sharp sunlight reflecting off the low snow- and tree-covered hillsides. A sign announced that they were four kilometres from Åneby.

"Mum could have driven, then?"

"I thought it might be useful for you to see a sheriff's office. You could end up being sent somewhere like this one day, you know."

Oleg braked behind a tractor that was throwing up snow as its chains sang against the tarmac. "I'm heading for Crime Squad, not the countryside."

"Oslo is almost the countryside, it's only half an hour away."

"I've applied to the FBI course in Chicago."

Harry smiled. "If you're that ambitious, a couple of years in a sheriff's office shouldn't scare you. Take a left here."

"Jimmy," said the burly, cheery-looking man standing in front of the door of Nittedal sheriff's office, which was located next door to social services and the job centre, in the sort of plain modern building that provided public services all over Norway. His fresh suntan made Harry assume he'd spent his winter break in the Canary Islands, even if his thoughts of "Lanzagrotty" were based on a prejudiced assumption about where people from Nittedal with first names ending in "y" went on holiday.

Harry shook his hand. "Thanks for taking the time to talk to us on a Saturday, Jimmy. This is Oleg, he's a student at Police College."

"Looks like a future sheriff," Jimmy said, looking the tall young man up and down. "I consider it an honour that Harry Hole himself would want to visit us. So I'm afraid you're the ones wasting your time here, not me."

"Oh?"

"You said on the phone that you couldn't get any answer from Lenny Hell, so I did a quick check while you were on your way. Turns out he went off to Thailand just after that interview with you."

"Turns out?"

"Yes, before he left he told his neighbours and regular clients that he might be gone a while. So presumably he's got a Thai number now, even if none of the people I spoke to know what it is. They don't know where he's staying out there either."

"A loner, maybe?"

"You can safely say that."

"Family?"

"Single. Only child. He never left home, and since his parents died he's lived up in the Pig House on his own."

"Pig House?"

"That's just what we call it here in town. The Hell family worked with pigs for generations, did quite well out of it, and a hundred years ago they built a rather striking three-storey house up there. The Pig House." The sheriff chuckled. "Doesn't do to get ideas above your station, eh?"

"Hm. So what do you think Lenny Hell is doing in Thailand for so long?"

"Well, what do people like Lenny do in Thailand?"

"I don't know Lenny," Harry said.

"Nice guy," the sheriff said. "Smart too, an IT engineer. Works from home, freelance, we sometimes call him in when we get computer trouble. No drugs, nothing stupid. No money problems either, as far as I know. But he's never quite got to grips with the whole women thing."

"What does that mean?"

Jimmy looked at the smoke from their breath as it hung in the air. "Bit cold out here, guys. Shall we go inside and get some coffee?"

"I reckon Lenny's on the lookout for a Thai bride," Jimmy said as he poured filter coffee into two white social services mugs and his own Lillestrøm Sportsklubb mug. "He couldn't cope with the competition here at home."

"No?"

"No. Like I said, Lenny's something of a lone wolf, he keeps to himself and doesn't say much, and he's not much of a babe magnet to start with. And he has trouble controlling his jealousy. As far I know, he's never hurt a fly—or a woman—but there was one incident when a woman called us, saying that Lenny had become a bit intense after their first date."

"Stalking?"

"That's what it's called these days, yes. Lenny had evidently sent her a load of text messages and flowers, even though she'd said she wasn't interested in taking it any further. He'd be standing there waiting when she finished work. She made it very clear that she never wanted to see him again, and so she didn't. But instead she told us she started to feel that things in her flat had been moved while she was at work. So she called us."

"She thought he'd been in her flat?"

"I talked to Lenny, but he denied it. And we never heard any more about it after that."

"Does Lenny Hell have a 3D printer?"

"A what?"

"A machine that can be used to copy keys."

"No idea, but like I said, he's an IT engineer."

"How jealous is he?" Oleg asked, and the other two turned towards him.

"On a scale of one to ten?" Jimmy asked. Harry couldn't tell if he was being sarcastic.

"I'm just wondering if it could be morbid jealousy?" Oleg asked, glancing uncertainly at Harry.

"What's the lad talking about, Hole?" Jimmy took an audible slurp from his canary-yellow mug. "Is he asking if Lenny's killed anyone?"

"OK. Like I said on the phone, we're just tidying up a few loose ends from the vampirist case, and Lenny did talk to two of the victims."

"And this Valentin guy killed them," Jimmy said. "Or is there some doubt about that now?"

"No doubt," Harry said. "As I said, I just wanted to talk to Lenny Hell about those conversations. See if I could find out anything we didn't already know. I saw on the map that his address is only a few kilometres from here, so I was thinking we could head up there and knock on the door. Get it out of the way."

The sheriff stroked the emblem on his mug with a large hand. "It said in the paper that you're a lecturer these days, not a detective."

"I suppose I'm like Lenny, a freelancer."

Jimmy folded his arms, and his left sleeve slid up to reveal a faded tattoo of a naked woman. "OK, Hole. As you'll appreciate, not much happens in Nittedal sheriff's district, and thank God for that. So when you called, I didn't just make a few phone calls, and I also took a drive up to Lenny's house. Or rather, I drove as far as I could. The Pig House is at the end of a forest road, and once you've passed the last neighbour there's still a kilometre and a half to go. And the snow is half a metre deep, just as high as it is at the side of the road, with no sign of tracks made by either wheels or shoes. Only elk and foxes. And maybe the odd wolf. You get my meaning? There hasn't been anyone there for weeks, Hole. If you want to get hold of Lenny, you'll have to buy a plane ticket to Thailand. Pattaya's popular with men who are after Thai ladies, or so I've heard."

"Snowmobile," Harry said.

"What?"

"If I come back tomorrow with a warrant, can you organise a snowmobile?"

Harry realised that the sheriff's good humour had run out. Presumably he had imagined sharing a nice cup of coffee while he proved to the cops from the big city that they knew what effective police work was out in the countryside too. Instead they were making fun of his judgements and asking him to put a vehicle at their disposal, like he was some sort of supplies manager.

"You don't need a snowmobile for a kilometre and a half," Jimmy said, rubbing the tip of his suntanned nose, which had begun to peel. "Use skis, Hole."

"I haven't got any skis. A snowmobile, and someone to drive it."

The silence that followed seemed to last an eternity.

"I saw that the youngster was driving." Jimmy tilted his head. "No driving licence, Hole?"

"Yes, but I killed a police officer once when I was driving." Harry picked up his mug and emptied it. "I'd prefer to avoid that happening again. Thanks for the coffee, and see you tomorrow."

"So what was that?" Oleg said as they were waiting at the junction indicating to pull out onto the main road. "A local sheriff volunteers to help on a Saturday, and you start giving him the runaround?"

"Did I do that?"

"Yes!"

"Mm. Indicate left instead."

"Oslo's right."

"According to the satnav, Åneby Pizza & Grill is two minutes away if we turn left."

The owner of Åneby Pizza & Grill, who had introduced himself as Tommy, wiped his fingers on his apron as he looked carefully at the picture Harry was holding in front of him.

"Maybe, but I don't remember what Lenny's friend looked like, I just remember that he was here, and that he had company on the night that woman got killed in Oslo. Lenny's a lone wolf, always on his own, doesn't come here much. That's why I remembered that evening when you called back in the autumn."

"The man in the picture's name is Alexander, or Valentin. Did you hear Lenny call him either of those names when they were talking?"

"I don't remember hearing them talk at all. And I was out front alone that night, my wife was in the kitchen."

"When did they leave?"

"Couldn't say. They shared a Knut Special XXL with pepperoni and ham."

"You remember that?"

Tommy grinned and tapped a finger to his temple. "Order a pizza and come back in three months' time and ask me what it was. I'll give you the same discount that the police station gets. All the pizza bases are low-carb, with nuts."

"Tempting, but I've got my boy waiting in the car. Thanks for your help."

"Don't mention it."

Oleg set off into the early dusk.

They were both silent, immersed in their own thoughts.

Harry was doing calculations. Valentin could easily have eaten a pizza with Lenny and then got back to Oslo in time to kill Elise Hermansen.

A lorry passed them going so fast that the car shook.

Oleg cleared his throat. "How are you going to get hold of a warrant?"

"Mm?"

"To start with, you don't work at Crime Squad. And you don't have any legal basis for the warrant."

"No?"

"Not if I've understood the course correctly."

"Let's hear it," Harry smiled.

Oleg slowed down slightly. "There's incontrovertible proof that Valentin killed a number of women. Lenny Hell met these women by coincidence. That on its own isn't enough to give the police the right to break into Lenny Hell's house while he's on holiday in Thailand."

"Agreed, it would be difficult to get a search warrant on those grounds. So let's drive to Grini."

"Grini?"

"I was thinking of having a chat with Hallstein Smith."

"Helga and I are making dinner together tonight."

"To be more precise, a chat about morbid jealousy. Dinner, you say? I understand, I'll find my own way out to Grini."

"Grini's almost on the way, so OK."

"Go and make dinner, it might take a while with Smith."

"Too late, you've already said I can come along." Oleg sped up, pulled out and overtook a tractor, and put the lights on full beam.

They drove for a while in silence.

"Sixty," Harry said, typing on his phone.

"And icy," Oleg said, easing off the accelerator slightly.

"Wyller?" Harry said. "Harry Hole. I hope you're sitting at home and feeling bored on a Saturday afternoon. Oh? Then you'll have to explain to the lovely lady, whoever she is, that you need to help a washed-up but legendary detective check a few things."


"Morbid jealousy," Hallstein Smith said, looking keenly at the guests who had just arrived. "It's an interesting subject. But have you really come all this way to talk about that? Isn't this more Ståle Aune's specialty?"

Oleg nodded and looked like he agreed.

"I wanted to talk to you, seeing as you've got doubts," Harry said.

"Doubts?"

"You said something that night Valentin was here. You said he knew."

"Knew what?"

"You didn't say."

"I was in shock, I probably said all sorts of things."

"No, for once you said relatively little, Smith."

"Did you hear that, May?" Hallstein Smith laughed at the slight figure who was pouring tea for them.

She smiled and nodded, then went off into the living room with the teapot and one cup.

"I said 'he knew,' and you interpreted that to mean I doubted something?" Smith asked.

"It sounded like something inexplicable," Harry said. "Something you couldn't quite understand how Valentin could know. Am I wrong?"

"I don't know, Harry. When it comes to my own subconscious, you can probably answer as well as me, maybe better. Why do you ask?"

"Because a man has popped up. Well, he's actually gone off to Thailand in something of a hurry. But I asked Wyller to check. And the person in question isn't on any passenger lists during the period when he's supposed to have gone. And during the past three months there hasn't been any activity on this individual's bank or credit cards, either in Thailand or anywhere else. And, almost as interestingly, Wyller found his name on our list of people who have bought 3D printers in the past year."

Smith looked at Harry. Then he turned and looked out through the kitchen window. The snow lay like a soft, sparkling blanket over the field in the darkness outside. "Valentin knew where my office was. That's what I meant by 'he *knew*.'"

"Your address, you mean?"

"No, I mean the fact that he walked straight from the gate to the barn. He didn't just know that my office was there, he also knew that I was usually there in the middle of the night."

"Maybe he saw light from the window?"

"You can't see any light in that window from the gate. Come with me, I want to show you something."

They headed down to the barn, unlocked the door and went into the office, where Smith turned on his computer.

"I've got all the security footage here, I just need to find it," Smith said, and started tapping.

"Cool drawing," Oleg said, nodding at the bat-man on the wall. "Grim."

"Alfred Kubin," Smith said. "*Der Vampyr*. My father had a book of Kubin's drawings. I used to sit at home and look at it while other kids went to the cinema to watch bad horror films. But sadly May won't let me have any of Kubin's pictures in the house, she says they give her nightmares. And speaking of nightmares, here's the footage of Valentin."

Smith pointed and Harry and Oleg leaned over his shoulders.

"Here he is coming into the barn. You see, he's not hesitating, he knows exactly where he's going. How? The therapy sessions I had with Valentin weren't here, but in a rented office in the city centre."

"You're saying someone must have given him instructions in advance?"

"I'm saying someone *could* have given Valentin Gjertsen instructions. That's been the problem with this case right from the start. Vampirists don't have the capacity for planning that these murders demonstrate."

"Hm. We didn't find a 3D printer in Valentin's flat. Someone else *could* have made the copies of the keys for him. Someone who had previously made copies of keys for himself, to let himself into the homes of women who had dumped him. Who had rejected him. Who had gone on to meet other men."

"Bigger men," Smith said.

"Jealousy," Harry said. "Morbid jealousy. But in a man who's never hurt a fly."

"And when a man isn't capable of hurting anyone, he needs someone to act for him. Someone who can do the things he can't."

"A murderer," Smith said, nodding slowly.

"Someone who's prepared to kill for the sake of killing. Valentin Gjertsen. So we have one man who plans, and another who acts. The agent and the artist."

"Bloody hell," Smith said, rubbing his cheeks with his hands. "Now my dissertation is actually starting to make sense."

"In what way?"

"I was in Lyon recently, giving a lecture about the vampirist murders, and even if my colleagues have been enthusiastic as far as my pioneering work goes, I keep having to point out that there's something missing that stops it from qualifying as truly groundbreaking, and that is that these murders don't fit the general profile of a vampirist that I've come up with."

"Which is?"

"An individual with schizophrenia and aspects of paranoia who, as a result of their overwhelming thirst for blood, kills whoever happens to be closest to them, an individual who can't commit murders that require a lot of planning and patience. But this vampirist's murders point more towards an engineering personality."

"A brain," Harry said. "Who approaches Valentin, who has had to put a stop to his activities because he can't move freely without being caught by the police. The brain offers Valentin the keys to the flats of single women. Pictures, information about their routines, when they come and go, everything Valentin needs to get them without having to expose himself. How could he turn down an offer like that?"

"A perfect symbiosis," Smith said.

Oleg cleared his throat.

"Yes?" Harry said.

"The police spent years trying to find Valentin. How did Lenny find him?"

"Good question," Harry said. "They didn't get to know each other in prison, anyway. Lenny's past is as clean as a priest's dog collar."

"What did you say?" Smith asked.

"A dog collar."

"No, the name."

"Lenny Hell," Harry repeated. "What about it?"

Hallstein Smith didn't answer, just stared at Harry with his mouth open.

"Bloody hell," Harry said calmly.

"Bloody hell, what?" Oleg said.

"Patients," Harry said. "With the same psychologist. Valentin Gjertsen and Lenny Hell met each other in the waiting room. Is that it, Hallstein? Come on, the risk of further murders outranks the oath of confidentiality."

"Yes, it's true that Lenny Hell was a patient of mine a while ago. And he used to come here, and he knew about my habit of working in the barn at night. But he and Valentin couldn't have met here, because Valentin's sessions with me took place in the city."

Harry pushed himself forward on his chair. "But is it possible that Lenny Hell is a morbidly jealous individual who worked with Valentin Gjertsen to kill women who had dumped him?"

Hallstein Smith rubbed his chin thoughtfully with two fingers. Nodded.

Harry leaned back in his chair. Looked at the computer screen, and the frozen image of the injured Valentin making his way out of the barn. The arrow on the scale, which had read 74.7 kilos when he arrived, now read 73.2 kilos. Which meant that he had left one and a half kilos of blood on the office floor. It was all just basic math, and the calculation worked now. Valentin Gjertsen plus Lenny Hell. And the answer was two.

"So the case has to be reopened," Oleg said.

"That's not going to happen," Gunnar Hagen said, looking at his watch.

"Why not?" Harry said, signalling to Rita for the bill.

The head of Crime Squad sighed. "Because the case has been solved, Harry, and because what you're presenting me with feels too much like a conspiracy theory. Random coincidences, such as this Lenny Hell being in touch with two of the victims, and psychological guesswork based on the fact that it *looks* like Valentin knows that he ought to turn right? That's the sort of thing journalists and authors use to conclude that Kennedy was shot by the CIA and the real Paul McCartney is dead. The vampirist case is still high profile, and we'd be making high-profile clowns of ourselves if we reopened the case on that sort of evidence."

"Is that what's worrying you, boss? Looking like a clown?"

Gunnar Hagen smiled. "You always used to call me 'boss' in a way that made me feel like a clown, Harry. Because everyone knew that you were really the boss. But that was fine, I could accept that, you were given free rein to make fun of us because you got results. But the lid's already on this case. And it's been screwed down very tightly."

"Mikael Bellman," Harry said. "He doesn't want anyone to spoil his image before he becomes Minister of Justice."

Hagen shrugged. "Thanks for inviting me for coffee late on a Saturday evening, Harry. How's everything at home?"

"Fine," Harry said. "Rakel's fit and strong. Oleg's making dinner with his girlfriend. How about you?"

"Oh, fine, too. Katrine and Bjørn have just bought themselves a house, but you probably know that."

"No, I didn't know."

"They had that little break, of course, but now they've decided to go for it. Katrine's pregnant."

"Really?"

"Yes, due in June. The world moves on."

"For some," Harry said, handing a 200-krone note to Rita, who started counting out his change. "Not for others. Here at Schrøder's things are standing still."

"So I see," Gunnar Hagen said. "I didn't think cash was legal tender any more."

"That's not what I meant. Thanks, Rita."

Hagen waited until the waitress had gone. "So that's why you wanted to meet here? To remind me. Did you think I'd have forgotten?"

"No, I didn't," Harry said. "But until we know what happened to Marte Ruud, this case isn't solved. Not for her family, not for the people who work here, not for me. And not for you either, I can tell. And you know that if Mikael Bellman has screwed the lid on so tightly that it can't be opened, then I'm going to smash the glass."

"Harry . . ."

"Look, all I need is a search warrant and authorisation from you to investigate this single loose end. I promise to stop after that. Just this one favour, Gunnar. Then I'll stop."

Hagen raised one bushy eyebrow. "*Gunnar?*"

Harry shrugged. "You said it yourself, you're not my boss anymore. Come on, you've always been on the side of good, thorough police work, Gunnar."

"You know that sounds like flattery, Harry?"

"So?"

Hagen let out a deep sigh. "I'm not making any promises, but I'll think about it. OK?" The head of Crime Squad stood up and buttoned his coat. "I remember some advice I was given when I first started working on cases, Harry. That if you want to survive, you have to learn when to let go."

"I'm sure that's good advice," Harry said, lifting his coffee cup to his lips and looking up at Hagen. "If you think survival's so bloody important."

# 35

# Sunday morning

"There they are," Harry said to Hallstein Smith, who braked and stopped the car in front of the two men who were standing in the middle of the forest track, arms folded.

"Brr," Smith said, sticking his hands in the pockets of his multi-coloured blazer. "You're right, I should have worn more clothes."

"Take this," Harry said, pulling off his black woolly hat with its embroidered skull and crossbones and the name "St. Pauli" underneath.

"Thanks," Smith said, pulling it down over his ears.

"Good morning, Hole," the sheriff said. Behind him, where the track was no longer driveable, stood two snowmobiles.

"Good morning," Harry said, taking off his sunglasses. The sunlight reflecting off the snow stung his eyes. "And thanks for agreeing to help at such short notice. This is Hallstein Smith."

"You don't have to thank us for doing our job," the sheriff said, and nodded towards a man who was dressed the same way as him, in blue-and-white overalls that made them look like overgrown toddlers. "Artur, can you take the guy in the blazer?"

Harry looked on as the snowmobile carrying Smith and the police officer disappeared along the track. The noise cut through the cold, clear air like a chainsaw.

Jimmy straddled the oblong seat of the snowmobile and coughed before turning the ignition key. "If you'll permit the local sheriff to drive a snowmobile?"

Harry put his sunglasses back on and got on behind him.

Their conversation the previous evening had been short.

"*Jimmy.*"

"Harry Hole here. I've got what I need—can you arrange snowmobiles, and show us the way to the house tomorrow morning?"

"*Oh.*"

"There'll be two of us."

"*How the hell did you get—?*"

"Half eleven?"

Pause.

"*OK.*"

The snowmobile followed the trail left by the first one. In the scattered community below them in the valley the sunlight glinted off windows and the church spire. The temperature fell rapidly when they entered dense pine forest that shut out the sun, and plummeted when they headed into a depression in the landscape where the ice-covered river ran.

The journey only took three or four minutes, but Harry's teeth were still chattering when they stopped next to Smith and the officer beside an overgrown, ice-covered fence. In front of them was a wrought-iron gate, cemented in snow.

"And there you have the Pig House," the sheriff said.

Thirty metres from the gate a large, ramshackle, elaborate three-storey house loomed up, guarded by tall pines on all sides. If the planks lining the walls had ever been painted, the paint was now all gone, and the house was varying shades of grey and silver. The curtains behind the windows looked like they were made of rough sheets and canvas.

"Dark place to build a house," Harry said.

"Three floors of old-school Gothic," Smith said. "That must break building regulations here, doesn't it?"

"The Hell family broke all sorts of regulations," the sheriff said. "But never the law."

"Hm. Could I ask you to bring some tools, Sheriff?"

"Artur, have you got the crowbar? Come on, let's get this over with."

Harry got off the snowmobile and sank into the snow halfway up his thighs, but he managed to reach the gate and climb over. The other three followed.

There was a covered veranda along the front of the house. It faced south, so perhaps the house got a bit of sunlight in the middle of the day in the summer. Why else would you have a veranda? As a place where the midges could drain you of blood? Harry went over to the door and tried to see something behind the frosted glass before pressing the rust-red button of an old-fashioned doorbell.

It worked, at least, because a bell rang deep inside the house.

The other three came and stood beside him as Harry rang the bell again.

"If he was home he'd have been standing in the doorway waiting for us," the sheriff said. "You can hear those snowmobiles from two kilometres away, and the road only leads here."

Harry tried again.

"Lenny Hell can't hear that in Thailand," the sheriff said. "My family are waiting to go skiing, so let's get this glass smashed, Artur."

The policeman swung the crowbar and the window beside the door shattered crisply. He pulled one of his gloves off, stuck his hand through and fumbled for a while with a look of concentration before Harry heard the sound of a lock turning.

"After you," Jimmy said, opening the door and holding his hand out.

Harry stepped inside.

It seemed uninhabited, that was the first thing that struck him. Maybe it was the lack of modern comforts that made him think of the houses of famous people that had been turned into museums. Like the time when he was fourteen and his parents took him and Sis to Moscow, where they visited the house where Fyodor Dostoevsky once lived. It had been the most soulless house Harry had ever seen, which may go some way to explaining why *Crime and Punishment* came as such a shock when he read it three years later.

Harry walked through the hall and into the large living room. He pressed the light switch on the wall but nothing happened. The daylight filtering in through the greyish-white curtains, though, was enough for him to see the steam from his own breath, and the few pieces of old-fashioned furniture scattered randomly around the room, as if matching tables and chairs had been split up after an acrimonious inheritance dispute. He could see heavy paintings hanging crookedly on the walls, probably as a result of changes in temperature. And he could see that Lenny Hell wasn't in Thailand.

Soulless.

Lenny Hell—or at least someone who resembled the picture Harry had seen of Lenny Hell—was sitting in a wing-backed chair in the same majestic posture in which Harry's grandfather used to fall asleep when he was sufficiently drunk. With the difference that his right foot was slightly raised from the floor, and his lower right arm was hovering a few centimetres above the arm of the chair. In other words, the body had tipped slightly to its left after rigor mortis had set in. And that was a long time ago. Five months, perhaps.

The head made Harry think of an Easter egg. Brittle, dry, empty of content. It looked as if the head had shrunk, forcing the mouth open and revealing the dry, grey gums holding the teeth. There was a black hole in his forehead, bloodless seeing as Lenny Hell was sitting with his head tilted backwards, gawping and staring stiffly at the ceiling.

When Harry went round the chair he saw that the bolt had gone right through the tall chair-back. A black metal object, the shape of a pocket torch, was lying on the floor beside the chair. He recognised it. When Harry was about ten years old his grandfather decided it would do the boy good to see where the pork ribs for Christmas dinner came from, and took him with him behind the barn where he placed a contraption he called the slaughtering mask, even though it wasn't a mask, over the forehead of Helga, the big sow. Then he pressed something, there was a sharp bang, and Helga jerked as if taken by surprise and fell to the ground. Then he had drained her of blood, but what Harry remembered most was the smell of powder and the way Helga's legs started to twitch after a while. His grandfather had explained that that was how the body worked, that Helga was long since dead, but Harry had nightmares about twitching pigs' legs for a ages afterwards.

The floorboards behind Harry creaked and he heard breathing that quickly became very heavy.

"Lenny Hell?" Harry asked without turning round.

The sheriff had to clear his throat twice before he managed to say "Yes."

"Don't come any closer," Harry said, crouching down and looking round the room.

It wasn't speaking to him. This crime scene was silent. Possibly because it was too old, possibly because it wasn't a crime scene, but a room in which the man who lived there had decided he didn't want to live any more.

Harry took his phone out and called Bjørn Holm.

"I've got a dead body in Åneby, in Nittedal. A man called Artur is going to call and tell you where to meet him."

Harry hung up and went out into the kitchen. He tried the light switch, but this one didn't work either. It was tidy, though there was a plate with stiff, mould-covered sauce on it in the sink. There was a dam of ice in front of the fridge.

Harry went out into the hall.

"See if you can find the fuse box," he said to Artur.

"The electricity may have been cut off," the sheriff said.

"The doorbell worked," Harry said, then went up the stairs that curved away from the hall.

On the first floor he looked in three bedrooms. They had all been carefully cleaned, but in one the covers were folded back and there were clothes hanging over the chair.

On the second floor he went into a room that had evidently functioned as an office. There were books and files on the shelves and, in front of the window, on one of the rectangular tables, stood a computer with three large screens. Harry turned round. On the table by the door was a box, maybe seventy-five centimetres square, with a black metal frame and glass sides, with a small white plastic key on a frame inside. A 3D printer.

There was the sound of bells ringing in the distance. Harry went over to the window. From there he could see the church, presumably they were ringing the bells for the Sunday service. The Hell house was taller than it was wide, like a tower in the middle of the forest, as if they had wanted a place where they could see but without being seen. His eyes landed on a folder on the table in front of him. The name on the front of it. He opened it and read the first page. Then he looked up at the identical folders on the bookcase. He went over to the top of the stairs.

"Smith!"

"Yes?"

"Come up here!"

When the psychologist stepped into the room thirty seconds later, he didn't immediately go over to the desk where Harry was leafing through the folder, but stopped in the doorway with a surprised expression on his face.

"Recognise them?" Harry asked.

"Yes." Smith went over to the bookcase and pulled out one of the folders. "They're mine. These are my records. The ones that were stolen."

"This too, I presume," Harry said, holding up the folder so that Hallstein Smith could read the label.

"Alexander Dreyer. That's my handwriting, yes."

"I don't understand all the terminology here, but I can see that Dreyer was obsessed with *Dark Side of the Moon*. And women. And blood. You wrote that he might go on to develop vampirism and noted that if this happened you would have to consider breaking your oath of confidentiality and telling the police about your concerns."

"Like I said, Dreyer stopped coming to see me."

Harry heard the sound of a door being opened and looked out of the window, just in time to see the policeman stick his head over the railing of the veranda and throw up in the snow.

"Where did they go to look for the fuse box?"

"The cellar," Smith said.

"Wait here," Harry said.

He went downstairs. There was a light on in the hall now, and the door to the cellar was open. He crouched down as he descended the narrow, dark cellar steps but still managed to hit his head on something and felt the skin break. The edge of a water pipe. Then he felt the solid floor beneath his feet, and saw a single lightbulb outside a storeroom, where Jimmy was standing with his hands hanging limply by his sides, staring in.

Harry walked towards him. The cold in the living room had hidden the smell, even though the corpse showed signs of decomposition. But it was damp down here, and even if it did get cold, it was never as far below zero as above ground. And as Harry approached, he realised that what he had thought was the smell of rotten potatoes was actually another body.

"Jimmy," he said quietly, and the sheriff started and turned round. His eyes were wide open and he had a little cut on his forehead that made Harry jump before he realised it was the result of another encounter with the water pipe above the stairs.

The sheriff stepped aside and Harry looked in the storeroom.

It was a cage. Three metres by two. Iron mesh, and a door with an open padlock on it. But it wasn't holding anyone captive now. Because whatever had been in that empty shell had long since departed. Soulless, again. But Harry could see why the young policeman had reacted so strongly.

Even if the level of decay indicated that she had been dead a long time, the mice and rats hadn't been able to reach the naked woman who was hanging from the mesh roof of the cage. And the fact that the body was intact meant that Harry could see in detail what had been done to her. Knives. Mostly knives. Harry had seen so many, mutilated in so many different ways. You might think that would harden you. And it did. You got used to seeing the results of random violence, of vicious fights, fatal and efficient stabbings, of ritual madness. But it didn't prepare you for this. For a type of mutilation where you could see what it was trying to achieve. The physical pain and desperate terror of the victim when she realised what was in the process of happening. The sexual pleasure and creative satisfaction of the murderer. The shock, the helpless desolation of those who found the body. Had the murderer got what he wanted here?

The sheriff began to cough behind him.

"Not here," Harry said. "Go outside."

He heard the sheriff's stumbling steps behind him as he opened the door to the cage and went inside. The girl hanging there was thin and her skin as white as the snow outside, with red marks on it. Not blood. Freckles. And a black hole at the top of her stomach, from a bullet.

Harry doubted she had escaped her suffering by hanging herself. The cause of death could of course have been the bullet hole in her stomach, but the shot could also have been fired in frustration after she was dead, when she no longer worked, the way children go on destroying a broken toy.

Harry brushed aside the red hair hanging in front of her face. No doubt at all. The girl's face expressed nothing. Fortunately. When, before too long, her ghost came to him at night, Harry would rather it did so with a blank expression on its face.

"W-who's that?"

Harry turned round. Hallstein Smith still had the St. Pauli hat pulled down to his eyes as if he was freezing, but Harry doubted that his trembling was caused by the cold.

"It's Marte Ruud."

# 36

# Sunday evening

Harry sat with his head in his hands, listening to the voices and heavy steps from the floor above. They were in the living room. The kitchen. The hall. Setting up cordons, placing little white flags, taking photographs.

Then he forced himself to raise his head and look again.

He had explained to the sheriff that they mustn't cut Marte Ruud down until the crime-scene investigators had been. Of course, you could tell yourself that she had bled to death in the boot of Valentin's car, there had been enough of her blood there for that. But there was a mattress on the floor in the left-hand side of the cage that told a different story. It was black, had over time become saturated with the sort of thing the human body rids itself of. And immediately above the mattress, attached to the mesh, hung a pair of handcuffs.

There was the sound of footsteps on the stairs. A familiar voice cursed loudly, then Bjørn Holm appeared, with a bleeding cut on his forehead. He stopped next to Harry and looked at the cage before turning towards him. "Now I understand why our two colleagues have identical wounds on their heads. You too, I see. But none of you felt like telling me, eh?" He turned quickly and called towards the stairs: "Look out for the water p—"

"Ow!" a muffled voice exclaimed.

"Why would anyone build a set of stairs so that you *have* to hit your head on—?"

"You don't want to look at her," Harry said quietly.

"What?"

"I don't want to either, Bjørn. I've been here almost an hour, and it doesn't get any damn easier."

"So why are you sitting here?"

Harry stood up. "She's been alone for so long. I thought . . ." Harry heard the telltale vibrato in his voice. He walked quickly towards the stairs and nodded to the forensics officer who was standing there rubbing his forehead.

The sheriff was in the hall talking on his phone.

"Smith?" Harry asked.

The sheriff pointed upstairs.

Hallstein Smith was sitting in front of the computer reading the folder with Alexander Dreyer's name on it when Harry walked in.

He looked up. "Down there, Harry, that's Alexander Dreyer's work."

"Let's call him Valentin. Are you sure?"

"It's all in my own notes. The cuts. He described it to me, told me his fantasies about torturing and then killing a woman. He described it as if he were planning a work of art."

"And you still didn't tell the police?"

"I thought about it, of course, but if we were to report all the grotesque crimes our clients commit in their imaginations, then neither we nor the police would do much else, Harry." Smith put his head in his hands. "Just think of all the lives that could have been saved if I'd only . . ."

"Don't be too hard on yourself, Hallstein, it isn't even clear that the police would have done anything. Anyway, it's possible that Lenny Hell used your stolen notes to copy Valentin's fantasy."

"That's not impossible. Not very likely, but not impossible." Smith scratched his head. "But I still don't understand how Hell knew that by stealing my notes, he would find a murderer he could work with."

"You do talk quite a lot."

"What?"

"Think about it, Smith. How likely is it that in your conversations with Lenny Hell about morbid jealousy you mentioned that you had other patients who fantasised about murder?"

"I'm sure I did that, I always try to explain to my patients that they aren't alone in their thoughts, in order to calm and normalise—" Smith fell silent and put his hand to his mouth. "Dear God, you mean that I . . . that my big mouth is responsible?"

Harry shook his head. "We can find a hundred ways to blame ourselves, Hallstein. During my years as a detective, at least a dozen people have been killed because I haven't managed to catch a serial killer as quickly as I should have. But if you're going to survive, you have to learn to let go."

"You're right." Smith laughed hollowly. "But I'm pretty sure the psychologist is supposed to say that, not the cop."

"Go home to your family, eat Sunday dinner and forget this for a while. Tord will be here soon to go through the computer, so we'll see what he can find."

"OK." Smith stood up, pulled off the woolly hat and gave it to Harry.

"Keep it," Harry said. "And if anyone asks, you'll remember why we came out here today, won't you?"

"Of course," Smith said, pulling the hat back on. And it struck Harry that there was something unintentionally comic but also ominous about the St. Pauli skull above the psychologist's jovial features.


"*Without* a search warrant, Harry!" Gunnar Hagen was shouting so loud that Harry had to hold the phone away from his ear, and Tord, who was sitting in front of Hell's computer, looked up.

"You went to the address and broke in without permission! I said no, loudly and clearly!"

"*I* didn't break in, boss." Harry looked out through the window at the valley. Darkness had started to fall and lights were going on. "The local sheriff did that. I just rang the doorbell."

"I've spoken to him, and he says he had a very clear impression that you had a warrant to search the house."

"I just said I had what I needed. And I did."

"Which was?"

"Hallstein Smith is Lenny Hell's psychologist. He was perfectly entitled to visit a patient he was concerned about. And in light of what has emerged regarding Hell's connection to two murder victims, Smith believed there were grounds for concern. He asked me to accompany him, because of my police background, in case Lenny Hell turned violent."

"And Smith will back this up, I suppose?"

"Of course, boss. We can't mess about with this sort of psychologist–patient thing."

Harry heard Gunnar Hagen manage the tricky feat of laughing while spitting with rage. "You deceived the sheriff, Harry. And you know that any evidence could be disregarded by a court if they find out—"

"Stop going on about it and shut up, Gunnar."

There was a brief pause. "What did you just say?"

"I asked you, in a very friendly way, to shut up," Harry said. "Because there's nothing to find out, the way we got in is perfectly correct. And there's no one to stand trial. They're all dead, Gunnar. The only thing that's happened today is that we've found out what happened to Marte Ruud. And that Valentin Gjertsen wasn't alone. I can't see how either you or Bellman could come out of this badly."

"I don't care about—"

"Yes, you do, so here's the text for the Police Chief's next press release: *The police have worked tirelessly to locate Marte Ruud, and that persistence has now paid off. And we damn well believe that Marte's family and the whole of fucking Norway deserve that.* Have you written that down? Lenny Hell in no way detracts from the Police Chief's success with Valentin, boss. This is a bonus. So relax and enjoy your steak." Harry put his phone in his trouser pocket. Rubbed his face. "What have you got, Tord?"

The IT expert looked up. "Email correspondence. It confirms what you're saying. When Lenny Hell first contacts Alexander Dreyer, he tells Dreyer that he's got hold of his address from Smith's patient archive, which he's stolen. Then Hell gets straight to the point and suggests a collaboration."

"Does he use the word 'murder'?"

"Yes."

"Good. Go on."

"A couple of days pass before Dreyer, or rather Valentin, replies. He writes that he had to check that the patient archive really had been stolen, and that this wasn't just the police setting a trap for him. Then he goes on to say that he's open to suggestions."

Harry looked over Tord's shoulder. Shivered when he saw the words on the screen.

*My friend, I'm open to attractive suggestions.*

Tord scrolled down and continued: "Lenny Hell writes that they should only ever contact each other by email, and that under no circumstances should Valentin try to find out who he is. He asks Valentin to suggest a place where Hell can supply him with keys to the women's flats, as well as any additional instructions, but without the two of them meeting. Valentin suggests the changing room of the Cagaloglu Hamam . . ."

"The Turkish bathhouse."

"Four days before Elise Hermansen is murdered, Hell writes that the key to her flat and some extra instructions are inside one of the lockers in the changing room, that there's one padlock with a fleck of blue paint on it. And that the code to the lock is 0999."

"Hm. Hell wasn't just directing Valentin, he was steering him by remote control. What else does it say?"

"It's similar for Ewa Dolmen and Penelope Rasch. But there are no instructions about killing Marte Ruud. Quite the contrary. Let's see . . . Here it is. The day after Marte Ruud went missing Hell writes: *I know it was you who took that girl from Harry Hole's favourite haunt, Alexander. That's not part of our plan. I'm guessing you still have her in your flat. The girl will lead the police to you, Alexander. We need to act quickly. Bring the girl and I'll make sure she disappears. Drive to map reference 60.148083, 10.777245, it's a desolate stretch of road with very little traffic at night. Be there at 01.00 tonight, stop at the sign saying Hadeland 1km. Walk exactly one hundred metres straight into the forest to your right, lay her down by the big burnt tree, and leave.*"

Harry looked at the screen and tapped the coordinates into Google Maps on his phone. "That's only a few kilometres from here. Anything else?"

"No, that was the last email."

"Really?"

"Well, I haven't found anything else on this computer yet. Maybe they *were* in touch by phone."

"Hm. Let me know if you find anything else."

"Will do."

Harry went back downstairs.

Bjørn Holm was standing in the hall talking to one of the forensics officers.

"One little detail," Harry said. "Take DNA samples from that water pipe."

"What?"

"The first time anyone goes down there, they hit that water pipe. Skin and blood. It's basically a big guestbook."

"OK."

Harry walked towards the front door. Then stopped and turned back.

"Congratulations, by the way. Hagen told me yesterday."

Bjørn looked at him blankly. Harry made a round gesture over his stomach.

"Oh, that." Bjørn Holm smiled. "Thanks."

Harry went outside and breathed in deeply as the winter darkness and cold embraced him. It felt cleansing. He headed for the black wall of pine trees. They were using the two snowmobiles as shuttles between the house and the ploughed part of the road, and Harry was pretty sure he could get transport from there. But right now there was no one here. He found the compacted trail made by the snow-mobiles, made sure he wasn't going to fall through, and started to walk. The house had disappeared into the darkness behind him when a noise made him stop. He listened.

Church bells. Now?

He didn't know if they were ringing for a funeral or christen-ing, only that the sound made him shudder. And at that moment he saw something in the dense darkness ahead of him. A pair of yellow, glowing eyes, moving. Animal's eyes. Hyena's eyes. And a low growl that grew in strength. It was getting closer fast.

Harry raised his hand in front of him but was still blinded by the headlights of the snowmobile as it stopped ahead of him.

"Where are you heading?" a voice asked from behind the light.

Harry took his phone out, opened the app and gave it to the snow-mobile driver. "There."

60.148083, 10.777245.

There was forest on either side of the main road. No cars. A blue sign.

Harry found the tree precisely one hundred metres into the forest from the sign.

He waded over to the charred, splintered black trunk, where the snow wasn't as deep as elsewhere. He crouched down and saw a paler scar in the wood, lit up by the lights of the snowmobile. Rope. A chain, perhaps. Which meant that Marte Ruud had been alive at that point.

"They were here," he said, looking round. "Valentin and Lenny, there were both here. Perhaps they met?"

The trees stared back at him in silence, like reluctant witnesses.

Harry went back to the snowmobile and sat behind the police officer.

"You'll need to bring forensics back here so they can get hold of anything that's left."

The officer half turned round. "Where are you going?"

"Back to the city with the bad news."

"You know Marte Ruud's family have already been informed?"

"Mm. But not her family at Schrøder's."

From inside the forest a bird shrieked a lone warning, far too late.

# 37

# Wednesday afternoon

Harry moved the half-metre-high pile of written answers so that he could see the two boys who had sat down in front of his desk better.

"Well, I've read your answers regarding the case of the devil's star," he said. "And obviously you deserve praise for spending your free time on a task I set the final-year students . . ."

"But?" Oleg said.

"No but."

"No, because our answers were better than any of theirs, weren't they?" Jesus had folded his hands behind his head, over his long black plait.

"No," Harry said.

"No? Which of theirs was better?"

"Ann Grimset's group, if I remember rightly."

"What?" Oleg said. "They didn't even get the prime suspect right!"

"That's correct, they actually declared that they didn't have a prime suspect at all. And, based on the information that was made available, that was the correct conclusion. You identified the right person, but that's because you couldn't help yourselves and googled to find out who the real culprit was twelve years ago. As a result, you got hung up working to a template and drew several mistaken conclusions so that you could end up with the right result."

"So you set a task that has no solution?" Oleg said.

"Not using the information provided," Harry said. "A taste of the future, if you really want to become detectives."

"So what should we do, then?"

"Look for fresh information," Harry said. "Or put what you already know together in a different way. Often the solution is hidden in the information you already have."

"What about the vampirist case?" Jesus asked.

"Some fresh information. And some that was already there."

"Did you see what *VG* said today?" Oleg asked. "That Lenny Hell instructed Valentin Gjertsen to kill women Hell was jealous about. Just like in *Othello*."

"Mm. I seem to remember you saying that the motive for murder in *Othello* wasn't primarily jealousy, but ambition."

"Othello *syndrome*, then. By the way, it wasn't Mona Daa who wrote it. It's funny, but I haven't seen anything written by her in ages."

"Who's Mona Daa?" Jesus asked.

"The only crime reporter who got the whole picture," Oleg said. "A strange girl from up north. Goes to the gym in the middle of the night and wears Old Spice. So, tell us, Harry!"

Harry looked at the two eager faces in front of him. Tried to remember if he'd been that keen on the course when he was at Police College. Hardly. He was usually hungover and couldn't wait to get drunk again. These two were better. He cleared his throat. "OK. In that case, this is a lecture, and I must remind you that as police students you are under an oath of confidentiality. Understood?"

The pair of them nodded and leaned forward.

Harry leaned back. He wanted a smoke, and knew that cigarette outside on the steps was going to taste good.

"We've been through Hell's computer, and it's all there," he said. "Plans of action, notes, information about the victims, information about Valentin Gjertsen, alias Alexander Dreyer, about Hallstein Smith, about me—"

"About *you*?" Jesus said.

"Let him go on," Oleg said.

"Hell wrote a manual about how to take impressions of the house keys of these women. He had discovered that on a Tinder date, eight out of ten women leave their bag at the table when they go to the toilet, and that most of them keep their keys in the little zipped compartment inside the bag. And that it takes on average fifteen seconds to make a wax impression of three keys, both sides, and that it's easier to photograph the keys, but that for some types of keys a photograph isn't enough to make a sufficiently accurate 3D file from which to produce copies using the 3D printer.

"Does that mean he *knew* he was going to feel jealous about them as early as the first date?" Jesus asked.

"In some cases, maybe," Harry said. "All he wrote was that when it was so simple, there was no reason *not* to make sure he had access to their homes."

"Creepy," Jesus whispered.

"What made him pick Valentin, and how did he find him?" Oleg asked.

"Everything he needed was in the patient records he'd stolen from Smith. It said there that Alexander Dreyer was a man with such intense and detailed vampiristic fantasies of killing that Smith was considering trying to get him sectioned. The argument against was that Dreyer demonstrated a high degree of self-control, and lived such a well-ordered life. I assume that it was this combination of a desire to kill and self-control that made him the perfect candidate for Hell."

"But what did Hell have to offer Valentin Gjertsen?" Jesus asked. "Money?"

"Blood," Harry said. "Young, warm blood from female victims who couldn't be linked to Alexander Dreyer."

"Murders in which there's no obvious motive, and where the murderer hasn't previously been in contact with the victims, are the worst ones to solve," Oleg said, as Jesus nodded. Harry recognised the quote from one of his own lectures.

"Mm. The most important thing for Valentin was to keep his alias, Alexander Dreyer, away from the case. Together with his new face, it was that name which meant he was able to move about in public without being caught. He was less concerned about it coming out that Valentin Gjertsen was behind the murders. And of course in the end he was unable to resist the temptation to signal to us that he was the man behind the murders."

"To us," Oleg said. "Or to you?"

Harry shrugged. "Either way, it didn't actually get us any closer to the man we'd been searching for all these years. He was able to just carry on following Hell's directions, carry on killing. And it could be done safely, because Hell's replica keys meant that Valentin could let himself into his victims' homes."

"A perfect symbiosis," Oleg said.

"Like the hyena and the vulture," Jesus whispered. "The vulture shows the hyena where to go by hovering over the wounded prey, and the hyena kills it. Food for both of them."

"So Valentin kills Elise Hermansen, Ewa Dolmen and Penelope Rasch," Oleg said. "But Marte Ruud? Did Lenny Hell know her?"

"No, that was Valentin's own work. And that was directed at me. He'd read in the papers that I had called him a wretched pervert, so he took someone who was close to me."

"Just because you called him a pervert?" Jesus wrinkled his nose.

"Narcissists love being loved," Harry said. "Or hated. Other people's fear confirms and inflates their self-image. What they find insulting is to be ignored or belittled."

"The same thing happened when Smith insulted Valentin in the podcast," Oleg said. "Valentin saw red and set off at once to his farm to kill him. Do you think Valentin became psychotic? I mean, he'd managed to control himself for so long, and the first murders were cold, calculated acts. Whereas Smith and Marte Ruud were spontaneous reactions."

"Maybe," Harry said. "Or maybe he was just full of the self-confidence serial killers often get when their first murders are successful, making them think they can walk on water."

"But why did Lenny Hell commit suicide?" Jesus asked.

"Well," Harry said. "Suggestions?"

"Isn't it obvious?" Oleg said. "Lenny had planned the murder of women who had let him down and therefore deserved it, but now he was standing there with Marte Ruud's and Mehmet Kalak's blood on his hands. Two innocent people who had nothing to do with this. His conscience woke up. He couldn't live with what he had caused to happen."

"Nope," Jesus said. "Lenny planned to kill himself right from the start, once the whole thing was over. These were the three women he wanted to kill, Elise, Ewa and Penelope."

"I doubt that," Harry said. "There were more women mentioned in Hell's notes, and other replica keys."

"OK, what if he didn't kill himself?" Oleg said. "What if Valentin murdered him? They could have fallen out about the murders of Mehmet and Marte. Seeing as Lenny saw them as innocent victims. So maybe Lenny wanted to turn himself in to the police, and Valentin found out about that."

"Unless Valentin just got fed up with Lenny," Jesus said. "It's not that unusual for hyenas to eat a vulture if it gets too close."

"The only fingerprints on the bolt gun are Lenny Hell's," Harry said. "Obviously it's possible that Valentin killed Lenny and tried to make it look like suicide. But why go to the trouble? The police have enough evidence against Valentin to put him away for life. And if Valentin was concerned about covering his tracks, he wouldn't have left Marte Ruud in the cellar, or the computer and files that proved that he and Hell were working together upstairs."

"OK," Jesus said. "I agree with Oleg about the first part. Lenny Hell realised what he had allowed to happen and decided he couldn't live with himself."

"You should never underestimate the first thing you think," Harry said. "That's usually based on more information than you're actually aware of. And the simplest solution is often the right one."

"But there's one thing I don't understand," Oleg said. "Lenny and Valentin didn't want to be seen together, fine. But why such a complicated system of handing things over? Couldn't they just have met in one of their homes?"

Harry shook his head. "It was important to Lenny to keep his identity hidden from Valentin, seeing as the risk of Valentin being arrested was still pretty high."

Jesus nodded. "And he was worried that Valentin would lead the police to him in order to get a reduced sentence."

"And Valentin definitely didn't want to let Lenny know where he lived," Harry said. "One of the reasons Valentin was able to stay hidden for so long was that he was very careful about that."

"So the case is solved, no loose ends," Oleg said. "Hell committed suicide and Valentin kidnapped Marte Ruud. But have you got evidence to show that he was the one who killed her?"

"Crime Squad thinks so."

"Because?"

"Because they found Valentin's DNA at Schrøder's, and Marte's blood in the boot of his car, and because they found the bullet she was shot in the stomach with. It had drilled its way into the brick wall in Hell's cellar, and the angle in comparison to the position of the body showed that she was shot before she was hanged. The bullet came from the same Ruger Redhawk revolver Valentin had with him when he was planning to shoot Smith."

"But you don't agree," Oleg said.

Harry raised an eyebrow. "Don't I?"

"When you say 'Crime Squad thinks so,' that means you think otherwise."

"Hm."

"So what do you think?" Oleg asked.

Harry ran one hand over his face. "I'm not sure it's all that important who put her out of her misery. Because in this instance that's exactly what it was. An act of deliverance. The mattress in the cage was teeming with DNA. Blood, sweat, semen, vomit. Some hers, some Lenny Hell's."

"Oh God," Jesus said. "You mean Hell abused her too?"

"There could even have been more of them."

"More than Valentin and Hell?"

"There's a water pipe above the stairs to the cellar. It's impossible not to hit it if you don't know it's there. So I asked Bjørn Holm, our senior criminal forensics officer, to send me a list of everyone whose DNA was found on that pipe. Anything too old degrades, but he found seven unique profiles. As usual, we'd taken DNA samples from everyone working at the scene, and found matches for the local sheriff, his colleague, Bjørn, Smith and me, plus another member of crime-scene unit we didn't manage to warn in time. But we couldn't identify the seventh profile."

"So it wasn't Valentin Gjertsen or Lenny Hell?"

"No. All we know is that it's a man, and he isn't related to Lenny Hell."

"Could have been someone working there?" Oleg said. "An electrician, a plumber, someone like that?"

"True," Harry said, and his gaze fell on the copy of *Dagbladet* that lay open in front of him, and a portrait of Bellman, who was about to take over as Justice Minister. He read the caption again: "*I'm particularly pleased that the persistence and tireless work of the police enabled us to find Marte Ruud. The family and the police both deserved that. And that makes it easier for me to leave my post as Police Chief.*"

"I have to go now, guys."

They left Police College together and just as they were about to go their separate ways in front of Chateau Neuf Harry remembered the invitation.

"Hallstein's finished his vampirist dissertation, and the disputation is on Friday. We've been invited."

"Disputation?"

"Oral exam with all your family and friends dressed up to the nines in the room," Jesus said. "Hard not to screw up."

"Your mum and I are going," Harry said. "I don't know if you feel like it, or have time? Ståle's one of his opponents."

"Wow!" Oleg said. "Hope it's not too early. I'm going to Ullevål on Friday."

Harry frowned. "What for?"

"It's just Dr. Steffens, he wants another blood sample. He says he's researching a rare blood disorder called systemic mastocytosis, and that if that's what Mum had, then her blood repaired itself."

"Mastocytosis?"

"It's caused by a genetic defect called c-kit mutation. It's not hereditary, but Steffens is hoping that the substance in the blood that may help to repair it might be. So he wants some of my blood to compare it to Mum's."

"So that's the genetic link your mother was talking about?"

"Steffens says he still thinks it was a case of poisoning, and that this is a shot in the dark. But that most big discoveries are just that. Shots in the dark."

"He's right about that. The disputation is at two o'clock. There's a reception afterwards you can go to if you like, but I'll probably skip that."

"I'm sure you will," Oleg smiled, and turned to Jesus. "Harry doesn't like people, you see."

"I do like people," Harry said. "I just don't like being *with* them. Particularly not when there's a lot of them at the same time." He looked at his watch. "Speaking of which."


"Sorry I'm late, private tutorial," Harry said, slipping behind the bar.

Øystein groaned as he put two glasses of beer down on the counter, spilling them as he did so. "Harry, we've *got* to get more people in here."

Harry peered at the crowd filling the bar. "I think there are too many already."

"I mean on this side of the counter, you idiot."

"The idiot was joking. Do you know anyone with good taste in music?"

"Tresko."

"Who isn't autistic."

"No." Øystein poured the next beer and gestured to Harry to take payment.

"OK, let's think about it. So Hallstein looked in?" Harry pointed at the St. Pauli hat that had been pulled down over a glass next to the Galatasaray banner.

"Yes, he said thanks for the loan. He had a few foreign journalists with him, to show them the place where it all began. He's having one of those doctor's things the day after tomorrow."

"Disputation." Harry handed the customer his card back and thanked him.

"Yeah. There was another guy who came over to them—Smith introduced him to the others as a colleague from Crime Squad."

"Oh?" Harry said, taking the next order from a man with a hipster beard and a Cage the Elephant T-shirt. "What did he look like?"

"Teeth," Øystein said, pointing to his own row of brown pegs.

"Not Truls Berntsen, surely?"

"Don't know his name, but I've seen him here several times. Usually sits in that booth over there. Usually comes on his own."

"Bound to be Truls Berntsen."

"The women are all over him."

"Can't be Truls Berntsen."

"But he still goes home alone. Weird bloke."

"Because he doesn't take a woman home?"

"Would *you* trust someone who turns down free cunt?"

The bearded hipster raised an eyebrow. Harry shrugged, put the beers in front of him, went over to the mirror and pulled on the St. Pauli hat. He was about to turn round again when he froze. He stood and looked at himself in the mirror, at the skull on his forehead.

"Harry?"

"Mm."

"Can you give me a hand here? Two mojitos with Sprite Light."

Harry nodded slowly. Then he took the hat off, went round the bar and hurried for the door.

"Harry!"

"Call Tresko."


"Yes?"

"Sorry to call so late, I thought maybe the Forensic Medical Institute was closed for the night."

"We're supposed to be closed, but this is just how it is when you work in a place with a systemic lack of capacity. And you're calling on the internal number that only the police are supposed to use."

"Yes, this is Harry Hole, I'm an inspector at—"

"I know it's you, Harry. This is Paula, and you're not an inspector anywhere."

"Oh, it's you. OK, I'm working on the vampirist case, that's why I'm calling. I want you to check those matches you got for the samples from the water pipe."

"I wasn't the person who did them, but let me look. But I should tell you that, apart from Valentin Gjertsen, I don't have the names of the DNA profiles in the vampirist case, just numbers."

"That's OK, I've got lists of names and numbers from all the crime scenes in front of me, so go ahead."

Harry ticked them off as Paula read off the DNA profiles that matched. The sheriff, the local officer, Hole, Smith, Holm and his colleague from Forensics. And finally the seventh person.

"Still no match there, then?" Harry said.

"No."

"What about the rest of Hell's house, was any other DNA found that matched Valentin's profile?"

"Let's see . . . No, it doesn't look like it."

"Nothing on the mattress, the body, nothing to connect—?"

"Nope."

"OK, Paula. Thanks."

"Speaking of connections, did you ever find out what was going on with that strand of hair?"

"Strand of hair?"

"Yes, last autumn. Wyller brought me a strand of hair and said it was something you wanted to have analysed. He probably thought it would get rushed through if he dropped your name."

"And was it?"

"Of course, Harry—you know all the girls here have a soft spot for you."

"Isn't that the sort of thing you say to very old men?"

Paula laughed. "That's what happens when you get married, Harry. Voluntary castration."

"Hm. I found that strand of hair on the floor of the room my wife was in at Ullevål Hospital, it was probably just paranoia."

"I see. I assumed it couldn't have been important seeing as Wyller told me to forget it. Were you worried your wife had a lover?"

"Not really. Not until you just planted the idea, anyway."

"You men are so naive."

"That's how we survive."

"But you're not, are you? We're taking over the planet, if you hadn't noticed."

"Well, you're working in the middle of the night, and that's bloody weird. Goodnight, Paula."

"Goodnight."

"Hang on, Paula. Forget what?"

"What?"

"What did Wyller tell you to forget?"

"The connection."

"Between what?"

"Between the strand of hair and one of the DNA profiles from the vampirist case."

"Really? Which one?"

"I don't know, like I said, we only have the numbers. We don't even know if they're suspects or police officers working at the scene."

Harry said nothing for a few moments. "Have you got the number?" he eventually asked.

"Good evening," the older paramedic said as he came into the staffroom in A&E.

"Good evening, Hansen," said the only other person in the room as he pumped black coffee from the flask into his cup.

"Your police friend just called."

Senior Consultant John Doyle Steffens turned round and raised an eyebrow. "Have I got friends in the police?"

"He mentioned you, anyway. A Harry Hole."

"What did he want?"

"He sent us a picture of a pool of blood and asked us to estimate how much it was. He said you'd done that based on a picture of a crime scene, and assumed that those of us who attend accidents are trained to do the same. I had to disappoint him."

"Interesting," Steffens said, and picked a hair off his shoulder. He didn't regard his increasing hair loss as a sign that he was fading, but rather the reverse, that he was blossoming, mobilising, getting rid of things he had no use for. "Why didn't he get in touch with me directly?"

"Probably didn't think a senior consultant would be working in the middle of the night. And it sounded urgent."

"I see. Did he say what it was about?"

"Just something he was working on, he said."

"Have you got the picture?"

"Here." The paramedic pulled out his phone and showed the doctor the message. Steffens glanced at the picture of a pool of blood on a wooden floor. There was a ruler beside the pool.

"One and a half litres," Steffens said. "Fairly precisely. You can call and tell him." He took a sip of his coffee. "A lecturer working in the middle of the night, what is the world coming to?"

The paramedic chuckled. "The same could be said of you, Steffens."

"What?" the senior consultant said, making way for the other man in front of the flask.

"Every other night, Steffens. What are you really doing here?"

"Taking care of patients who are badly injured."

"I know that, but why? You've got a full-time job as senior consultant of haematology, but you still take extra shifts here in A&E. That's not exactly common."

"Who wants common? It's mostly a desire to be where you can be most useful, isn't it?"

"So you've got no family who'd rather you stayed at home?"

"No, but I've got colleagues whose families would rather they didn't stay at home."

"Ha! But you're wearing a wedding ring."

"And you've got blood on your sleeve, Hansen. Have you just brought in someone who was bleeding?"

"Yes. Divorced?"

"Widowed." Steffens drank some more coffee. "Who's the patient? Woman, man, young, old?"

"Woman in her thirties. Why?"

"Just wondered. Where is she now?"


"Yes?" Bjørn Holm whispered.

"Harry. Had you gone to bed?"

"It's two o'clock in the morning, what do you think?"

"There was around a litre and a half of Valentin's blood on the office floor."

"What?"

"It's basic mathematics. He weighed too much."

Harry heard the bed creak, then bedclothes brushing the phone before he heard Bjørn's whispered voice again. "What are you talking about?"

"You can see it on the scales in the security camera footage when Valentin is leaving. He only weighs one and a half kilos less than when he arrived."

"One and a half litres of blood weighs one and a half kilos, Harry."

"I know that. Even so, we're still short of evidence. Once we've got it I'll explain. And you're not to tell a soul about this, OK? Not even the person lying next to you."

"She's asleep."

"So I can hear."

Bjørn laughed. "She's snoring for two."

"Can we meet at eight o'clock, in the boiler room?"

"I guess. Are Smith and Wyller coming too?"

"We'll be seeing Smith at his disputation on Friday."

"And Wyller?"

"Just you and me, Bjørn. And I want you to bring Hell's computer and Valentin's revolver."

# 38

# Thursday morning

"Up and about early, Bjørn," said the older officer behind the counter of the evidence store.

"Morning, Jens. I'd like to sign out something from the vampirist case."

"Yes, that's back under the spotlight, isn't it? Crime Squad was here getting stuff yesterday, I'm pretty sure it's on shelf G. But let's see what the bastard machine thinks . . ." He tapped at the keyboard as if it were red hot, and looked across the screen. ". . . let's see . . . bloody thing's frozen again . . ." He looked up at Bjørn with a resigned and rather helpless expression. "What do you say, Bjørn, wasn't it better when we could just look in a folder and find out exactly wh—?"

"Who was here from Crime Squad?" Bjørn Holm asked, trying to hide his impatience.

"What's his name again? The one with the teeth."

"Truls Berntsen?"

"No, no, the one with the *nice* teeth. The new guy."


"Anders Wyller," Bjørn said.

"Mm," Harry said, leaning back in his chair in the boiler room. "And he signed out Valentin's Redhawk?"

"Plus the iron teeth and handcuffs."

"And Jens didn't say what Wyller wanted them for?"

"No, he didn't know. I've tried calling Wyller in the office, but they said he's taken some time owing so I called his mobile."

"And?"

"No answer. Probably asleep, but I can try again now."

"No," Harry said.

"No?"

Harry closed his eyes. "*We all get fooled in the end*," he whispered.

"What?"

"Nothing. Let's go and wake Wyller. Can you call the unit and find out where he lives?"

Thirty seconds later Bjørn put the phone back on the desk and repeated the name of the street in a clear voice.

"You're kidding," Harry said.


Bjørn Holm turned the Volvo Amazon into the quiet street and drove down between the banks of snow where the cars seemed to have gone into hibernation for the winter.

"Here it is," Harry said, leaning forward and looking up at the four-storey building. There was some graffiti on the pale blue wall between the second and third floors.

"Sofies gate 5," Bjørn said. "And to think that you used to live here . . ."

"In another life," Harry said. "Wait here."

Harry got out, went up the two steps to the door and looked at the names beside the doorbells. Some of the old names had changed. Wyller's name was further down than where his had once stood. He pressed the buzzer. Waited. Pressed again. Nothing. He was about to press it a third time when the door opened and a young woman hurried out. Harry caught the door before it closed and slipped inside.

The stairwell smelt the same as it used to. A mixture of Norwegian and Pakistani food, and the cloying smell of old fru Sennheim on the first floor. Harry listened. Silence. Then he crept up the stairs, instinctively avoiding the sixth step, which he knew creaked.

He stopped outside the door on the first landing.

There was no light behind the frosted glass.

Harry knocked. Looked at the lock. Knew it wouldn't take much to break in. A plastic card and a hard shove. He thought about it. Being the person who broke in. And felt his heart beat faster, and his breath misted the glass in front of him. That tantalising excitement, was that what Valentin had felt when he opened the doors of his victims' flats?

Harry knocked again. He waited, then gave up and turned to leave. At that moment he heard footsteps behind the door. He turned round. Saw a shadow through the frosted glass. The door opened.

Anders Wyller was wearing jeans, but his chest was bare and he hadn't shaved. But he didn't look like he'd just woken up. On the contrary, his pupils were big and dark, his forehead wet with sweat. Harry noticed something red on his shoulder—a cut? There was some blood, anyway.

"Harry," Wyller said. "What are you doing here?" His voice sounded different from the usual high, boyish pitch. "And how did you get in?"

Harry cleared his throat. "We need the serial number of Valentin's revolver. I rang the bell."

"And?"

"And you didn't answer. I thought maybe you were asleep, so I came in anyway. I actually used to live in this building, on the fourth floor, so I know the doorbells aren't very loud."

"Yes," Wyller said, stretching as he let out a yawn.

"So," Harry said. "Have you got it?"

"Got what?"

"The Redhawk. The revolver."

"Oh, that. Yes. The serial number? Hang on, I'll go and get it."

Wyller pulled the door to, and Harry saw him disappear across the hall through the glass. The flats all had the same layout, so he knew that was where the bedroom was. The figure headed back towards the front door, then turned left into the living room.

Harry pulled the door open. There was a smell—perfume? He saw that the bedroom door was closed. That was what Wyller had done, he had closed the door. Harry looked automatically for clothes or shoes in the hall that could tell him something, but there was nothing there. He looked at the bedroom door and listened. Then he took three long, silent strides and was inside the living room. Anders Wyller hadn't heard him as he knelt in front of the coffee table with his back to Harry, writing on a notepad. Next to the pad was a plate with a slice of pizza on it. Pepperoni. And the big revolver with the red butt. But Harry couldn't see the handcuffs or iron teeth.

There was an empty cage in one corner of the living room. The sort people keep rabbits in. Hang on, though. Harry remembered the meeting where Skarre had pressured Wyller about the leak to *VG*, when Wyller said he had told *VG* that he had a cat. So where was the cat? And did you keep cats in cages? Harry's gaze moved on to the end wall, where there was a narrow bookcase containing a few textbooks from Police College, including Bjerknes and Hoff Johansen's *Investigative Methods*. But there were some that weren't on the syllabus, like Ressler, Burgess and Douglas's *Sexual Homicide—Patterns and Motives*, a book about serial killings that he had referred to in recent lectures because it contained information about the FBI's newly established ViCAP unit. Harry looked at the other shelves. There were what looked like family photographs, two adults and Anders Wyller as a young boy. There were more books on the shelf below: *Haematology at a Glance*, Atul B. Mehta, A. Victor Hoffbrand. And *Basic Haematology* by John D. Steffens. A young man who was interested in blood disorders? Why not? Harry moved closer and looked more carefully at the family photograph. The boy looked happy. The parents less so. "Why did you sign out Valentin's things?" Harry said, and saw Wyller's back stiffen. "Katrine Bratt didn't ask you to. Physical evidence isn't the sort of thing you normally take home with you, even if the case has been solved."

Wyller turned round and Harry saw his eyes dart automatically to the right. Towards the bedroom.

"I'm a detective with Crime Squad and you're a lecturer at Police College, Harry, so strictly speaking I should be asking you what you want the serial number for."

Harry looked at Wyller. Realised that he wasn't going to get an answer. "The serial number was never checked in order to trace its original owner. And that could hardly have been Valentin Gjertsen, seeing as he didn't exactly have a firearms licence, to put it mildly."

"Is that important?"

"Don't you think it is?"

Wyller shrugged his bare shoulders. "As far as we know, the revolver was never used to kill anyone, not even Marte Ruud, because the post-mortem showed she was dead before she was shot. We've got the ballistic data for the revolver, and it doesn't match any of the other cases in our database. So no, I don't think it's important to check the serial number, not while there are other things crying out for our attention."

"I see," Harry said. "Well, maybe this lecturer can make himself useful by seeing where the serial number leads."

"Of course," Wyller said, tearing the sheet from the notepad and giving it to Harry.

"Thanks," Harry said, looking at the blood on his shoulder.

Wyller followed him to the door, and when Harry turned round on the landing he saw that Wyller had spread himself out in the doorway, the way bouncers do.

"Just out of curiosity," Harry said. "That cage in the living room, what do you keep in it?"

Wyller blinked a couple of times. "Nothing," he said. Then he quietly closed the door.


"Did you find him?" Bjørn asked as he pulled out into the road.

"Yes," Harry said, tearing a page out of his own notebook. "And here's the serial number. Ruger's an American company, can you check with the ATF?"

"You don't seriously think they'll be able to trace that revolver?"

"Why not?"

"Because the Americans are pretty halfhearted when it comes to registering the owners of firearms. And there are more than three hundred million weapons in the U.S.A. More guns than people, in other words."

"Frightening."

"What is frightening," Bjørn Holm said, putting his foot down harder on the accelerator to get a controlled slide as they turned to go down the hill towards Pilestredet, "is that even the ones who aren't criminals and say they've got guns for self-defence use their guns to shoot the wrong people. There was an article in the *Los Angeles Times* saying that in 2012 more than twice as many people were killed in accidental shootings as in self-defence. And almost forty times as many shot themselves. And that's *before* you even start to look at the statistics for murder."

"You read the *Los Angeles Times*?"

"Well, mostly because Robert Hilburn used to write about music in it. Have you read his biography of Johnny Cash?"

"Nope. Hilburn—is he the one who wrote about the Sex Pistols' tour of the U.S.A.?"

"Yep."

They stopped at a red light in front of Blitz, once the bridgehead of punk in Norway, where you could still see the occasional Mohawk. Bjørn Holm grinned at Harry. He was happy now. Happy about becoming a father, happy the vampirist case was over, happy to be able to slide a car that smelt of the 1970s and talk about music that was almost as old.

"It would be great if you could let me have an answer before twelve o'clock, Bjørn."

"If I'm not mistaken, the ATF is based in Washington DC, where it's the middle of the night."

"They've got an office with Interpol in The Hague, try there."

"OK. Did you find out why Wyller had signed out those things?"

Harry stared at the traffic light. "No. Have you got Lenny Hell's computer?"

"Tord's got it, he should be waiting for us in the boiler room."

"Good." Harry tried impatiently to stare the red light green.

"Harry?"

"Yes?"

"Did it ever occur to you that it looked as if Valentin had left his flat very quickly, just before Katrine and Delta got there? As if someone had warned him?"

"No," Harry lied.

The light turned green.


Tord was pointing and explaining things to Harry as the coffee machine spluttered and groaned behind them.

"Here are Lenny Hell's emails to Valentin before the murders of Elise, Ewa and Penelope."

The emails were short. Just the victim's name, address and a date. The date of the murder. And they all ended with the same line. *Instructions and keys in agreed location. Instructions to be burned after reading.*

"They don't say much," Tord said. "But enough."

"Hm."

"What?"

"Why do the instructions have to be burned?"

"Isn't it obvious? There were things in them that could lead people to Lenny."

"But he didn't delete the emails from his computer. Is that because he knew that IT experts like you could reconstruct the correspondence anyway?"

Tord shook his head. "Nowadays it isn't that simple. Not if both sender and recipient delete the emails thoroughly."

"Lenny would have known how to delete emails thoroughly. So why didn't he?"

Tord shrugged his broad shoulders. "Because he knew that by the time we had his computer, the game would already be up."

Harry nodded slowly. "Maybe Lenny knew that from the start. That one day the war he was waging from his bunker would be lost. And that it would then be time for a bullet to the head."

"Maybe." Tord looked at his watch. "Was there anything else?"

"Do you know what stylometry is?"

"Yes. The analysis of variations in writing style. There was a lot of research into stylometry after the Enron scandal. Several hundred thousand emails were made public so that researchers could see if they could identify their senders. They got a hit rate of between eighty and ninety percent."

After Tord had left Harry rang the number of *VG*'s crime desk.

"Harry Hole. Can I speak to Mona Daa?"

"Long time, Harry." Harry recognised the voice of one of the older crime reporters. "You could have done, but Mona vanished a few days ago."

"Vanished?"

"We got a text saying she was taking a few days off and that her phone would be switched off. Probably a good move, that girl's worked bloody hard over the past year, but the editor was pissed off she didn't ask, just sent that short message and pretty much disappeared. Kids these day, eh, Harry? Anything I can help you with?"

"No, thanks," Harry said, and hung up. He looked at his phone for a moment before slipping it into his pocket.


By quarter past eleven Bjørn Holm had got hold of the name of the man who had imported the Ruger Redhawk into Norway, a sailor from Farsund. And at half past eleven Harry spoke to his daughter on the phone. She remembered the Redhawk because she had dropped the heavy revolver, which weighed more than a kilo, on her father's big toe when she was little. But she couldn't say where it had gone.

"Dad moved to Oslo when he retired, to be closer to us children. But he was ill towards the end, and did a lot of peculiar things. He started giving away lots of his possessions, as we discovered afterwards when we were trying to sort out his will. I never saw the revolver again, so he could have given it away."

"But you don't know who to?"

"No."

"You said he was ill. I presume that was what led to his death?"

"No, he died of pneumonia. It was fast and relatively painless, thank goodness."

"I see. So what was the other illness, and who was his doctor?"

"That was just it, we realised he wasn't very well, but Dad always thought of himself as a big, strong sailor. I suppose he thought it was embarrassing, so he kept it secret, both what was wrong with him and who he saw about it. It wasn't until his funeral that I heard about it from an old friend he'd confided in."

"Would that friend know who your father's doctor was, do you think?"

"Hardly, Dad just mentioned the illness, no details."

"And what was the illness?"

Harry wrote it down. Looked at the word. A rather lonely Greek term among all the Latin names in the world of medicine.

"Thanks," he said.

# 39

# Thursday night

"I'm sure," Harry said into the darkness of the bedroom.

"Motive?" Rakel said, curling up beside him.

"Othello. Oleg was right. First and foremost, it's not about jealousy. It's about ambition."

"Are you still talking about Othello? Are you sure you don't want to close the window, it's supposed to be minus fifteen tonight."

"No."

"You're not sure if the window should be closed, but you're quite sure who the architect behind the vampirist murders is?"

"Yes."

"You're just missing that silly little thing called evidence."

"Yes." Harry pulled her closer to him. "That's why I need a confession."

"So ask Katrine Bratt to call him in for questioning."

"Like I said, Bellman won't let anyone touch the case."

"So what are you going to do?"

Harry stared at the ceiling. Felt the heat of her body. Would that be enough? Should they close the window?

"I'm going to question him myself. Without him knowing that that's what's going on."

"Just let me remind you, as a lawyer, that an informal confession to you, one to one, has zero value."

"So we'll have to make sure I'm not the only one who hears it, then."

Ståle Aune rolled over in bed and picked up the phone. Saw who was calling and pressed the button to answer. "Yes?"

"I thought you'd be asleep." Harry's gruff voice.

"And you still called?"

"You've got to help me with something."

"Still *you* rather than *us*?"

"Still humanity. Do you remember we talked about *Zen and the Art of Motorcycle Maintenance*?"

"Yes."

"I need you to set a monkey trap during Hallstein's disputation."

"Really? You, me, Hallstein and who else?"

Ståle Aune heard Harry take a deep breath.

"A doctor."

"And this is a person you've managed to link to the case?"

"More or less."

Ståle felt the hairs on his arms stand up. "Meaning?"

"Meaning that I found a hair in Rakel's room, and in a fit of paranoia I sent it for analysis. It turned out that there was nothing suspicious about the fact that it was there, because it came from this doctor. But then it turned out that the DNA profile of the hair ties him to the scenes of the vampirist murders."

"What?"

"And that there's a link between this doctor and a young detective who's been among us the whole time."

"What are you saying? You've got *proof* that this doctor and the detective are involved in the vampirist murders?"

"No," Harry sighed.

"No? Explain."

When Ståle Aune hung up twenty minutes later, he listened to the silence in the house. The calm. Everyone was asleep. But he knew he wasn't going to get any more sleep.

# 40

# Friday morning

Wenche Syvertsen looked out across Frognerparken as she used the step machine. One of her friends had advised her against it, saying it made your backside bigger. She evidently hadn't understood the point: Wenche *wanted* a bigger backside. Wenche had read online that exercise only gave you a more muscular backside rather than one that was bigger and more perfectly formed, and that the solution was oestrogen supplements, eating more, or—simplest of all—implants. But Wenche had ruled out the last, because one of her principles was keeping her body natural, and she had never—*never*—submitted to the knife. Apart from getting her bust fixed, of course, but that didn't count. And she was a woman of principle. That was why she had never been unfaithful to herr Syvertsen, in spite of all the offers she got, particularly in gyms like this. It was often young men, who took her for a cougar on the prowl. But Wenche had always preferred men who were more mature. Not as old as the wrinkled, battered old man on the cycle beside her, but like her neighbour. Harry Hole. Men who were inferior to her intellectually and in terms of maturity were actually a turnoff, she needed men who could stimulate her, entertain her, spiritually as well as in material terms. It really was that simple, there was no point pretending otherwise. And herr Syvertsen had done a good job of the last of these. But Harry was unavailable, apparently. And then there was that business of her principles, too. Besides, herr Syvertsen had become unreasonably jealous and had threatened to interfere with her privileges and lifestyle on the few occasions he had found out that she had been unfaithful. Which of course was *before* she had established the principle of *not* being unfaithful.

"Why isn't a beautiful woman like you married?"

The words sounded like they were being ground out, and Wenche turned to face the old man on the bicycle. He smiled at her. His face was thin, with wrinkles like deep valleys, big lips and long, thick, greasy hair. He was thin, but broad-shouldered. A bit like Mick Jagger. Apart from his red bandanna and truck driver's moustache.

Wenche smiled and raised her ringless right hand. "Married. But I take it off when I exercise."

"Shame," the old man smiled. "Because I'm not married, and I could have offered a b-betrothal on the spot."

He raised his own right hand. Wenche started. She thought for a moment that she was seeing things. Was that really a big *hole*, right through his hand?


"Oleg Fauke is here," the voice said over the intercom.

"Send him in," John D. Steffens said, pushing his chair away from his desk and looking out of the window at the laboratory building, the department of transfusion medicine. He had already seen young Fauke get out of the little Japanese car that was still in the car park with its engine running. Another young man was sitting behind the wheel, presumably with the heater at full blast. It was a sparklingly cold, sunny day. For many people it was a paradox that a cloudless sky in July promised heat but cold in January. Because many people couldn't be bothered to understand the basics of physics, meteorology and the nature of the world. It no longer irritated Steffens that people thought that cold was a thing, and didn't understand that it was merely the absence of heat. Cold was the natural, dominant state. Heat the exception. The way murder and cruelty were natural, logical, and mercy an anomaly, a result of the human herd's intricate way of promoting the survival of the species. Because mercy stopped there, within the species, and it was humanity's boundless cruelty towards other species that allowed it to survive. For instance, the growth of human beings as a species meant that meat wasn't just hunted, but *produced*. The very words, *meat production*, the very idea! People kept animals in cages, stripping them of all their happiness and pleasure in life, inseminating them so that they involuntarily produced milk and tender young flesh, took their offspring away as soon as they were born, while the mothers bellowed with pain, and then made them pregnant again as soon as possible. People got furious if certain species were eaten, dogs, whales, dolphins, cats. But mercy, for unfathomable reasons, stopped there. The far more intelligent pigs could and would be humiliated and eaten, and we had been doing it for so long human beings no longer even thought about the calculated cruelty that was part and parcel of modern food production. Brainwashing!

Steffens stared at the closed door that would soon be opening. Wondered if they would ever understand. That morality—which some people imagine is God-given and eternal—is as malleable and learned as our ideas of beauty, our enemies, our fashion trends. It seemed unlikely. And as a result, it was hardly surprising that humanity was unable to understand and accept radical research projects which went against their own engrained thoughts. Unable to understand that it was as logical and necessary as it was cruel.

The door opened.

"Good morning, Oleg. Come in, have a seat."

"Thanks." The young man sat down. "Before you take the sample, can I ask you for a favour?"

"A favour?" Steffens pulled on a pair of white rubber gloves. "You know that my research could benefit you, your mother and the whole of your future family?"

"And I know that research is more important to you than a slightly longer life is to me."

Steffens smiled. "Wise words for such a young man."

"I'm asking on my father's behalf if you could spare two hours to attend and give a professional opinion during a friend's disputation. Harry would very much appreciate it."

"A disputation? By all means, it would be an honour."

"The only problem is . . ." Oleg said, then cleared his throat, "that it starts now, or soon, and we'd need to go as soon as you've got your blood sample."

"Now?" Steffens looked down at the diary that lay open in front of him. "I'm afraid I have a meeting which—"

"He'd *really* appreciate it," Oleg said.

Steffens looked at the young man as he rubbed his chin thoughtfully. "You mean . . . your blood in exchange for my time?"

"Something like that," Oleg said.

Steffens leaned back in his office chair and clasped his hands together in front of his mouth. "Just tell me one thing, Oleg. What is it that leads you to have such a close relationship to Harry Hole? After all, he isn't your biological father."

"You tell me," Oleg said.

"Answer that and give me your blood, and I'll go with you to this disputation."

Oleg thought. "I almost said that it's because he's honest. That in spite of the fact that he isn't the best father in the world or anything like that, I can trust what he says. But I don't think that's the most important thing."

"So what is the most important thing?"

"That we hate the same groups."

"That you what?"

"Music. We don't like the same music, but we hate the same stuff." Oleg pulled his padded jacket off and rolled up his sleeve. "Ready?"

# 41

# Friday afternoon

Rakel looked up at Harry as they walked arm in arm across Universitetsplassen towards the Domus Academica, one of three buildings belonging to the University of Oslo in the centre of the city. She had persuaded him to wear the smart shoes she had bought him in London, even though he had said they were too slippery for this sort of weather.

"You ought to wear a suit more often," she said.

"And the council should grit more often," Harry said, pretending to slip again.

She laughed and held him tight. Felt the hard yellow file he had folded and stuffed into his inside pocket. "Isn't that Bjørn Holm's car, and a *very* illegal piece of parking?"

They passed the black Volvo Amazon, which was parked right in front of the steps.

"Police authorisation behind the windscreen," Harry said. "Clear case of misuse."

"It's because of Katrine," Rakel smiled. "He's just worried she'll fall."

There was a buzz of voices in the vestibule outside the Gamle festsal auditorium. Rakel looked for familiar faces. It was mostly professional colleagues and family. But there was someone she recognised at the other end of the room, Truls Berntsen. He evidently hadn't understood that a suit was the correct attire for a disputation. Rakel forged a path for herself and Harry over to Katrine and Bjørn.

"Congratulations, you two!" Rakel said, and hugged them both.

"Thanks!" Katrine beamed, stroking her bulging stomach.

"When . . . ?"

"In June."

"June," Rakel repeated, and saw Katrine's smile twitch.

Rakel leaned forward, put a hand on Katrine's arm and whispered: "Don't think about it, it'll be fine."

Rakel saw Katrine look at her as if in shock.

"Epidural," Rakel said. "They're brilliant things. They get rid of any pain just like that!"

Katrine blinked twice. Then she laughed. "Do you know, I've never been to a disputation before. I had no idea it was so formal until I saw Bjørn putting on his finest bootlace tie. What actually happens?"

"Oh, it's fairly straightforward really," Rakel said. "We go into the auditorium first, stand as the chair of the defence, the candidate and the two opponents come in. Smith is probably pretty tense even if he's already had to give an examination lecture to them either yesterday or this morning. He's probably most worried that Ståle Aune's going to be awkward, but there can't be much chance of that."

"No?" Bjørn Holm said. "But Aune's said he doesn't believe in vampirism."

"Ståle believes in serious scholarship," Rakel said. "The opponents are supposed to be critical, and get to the heart of the subject of the dissertation, but they have to stay within the bounds of the subject and the premise of the occasion, not ride their own hobbyhorses."

"Wow, you've done your homework!" Katrine said as Rakel took a deep breath.

Rakel nodded and went on. "The opponents have three-quarters of an hour each, and between them brief questions from the hall are permitted, known as *ex auditorio*, but that doesn't usually happen. After that there's the disputation dinner, paid for by the candidate, but we're not invited to that. Which Harry thinks is a great shame."

Katrine turned towards Harry. "Is that true?"

Harry shrugged. "Who doesn't like a bit of meat and gravy and dozing off to half-hour speeches made by the relatives of someone you really don't know that well?"

People started to move around them, and a few cameras flashed.

"The next Justice Minister," Katrine said.

It was as if the waters parted before Mikael and Ulla Bellman as they walked in, arm in arm. They were smiling, but Rakel didn't think that Ulla was really *smiling*. Perhaps she wasn't the smiling type. Or perhaps Ulla Bellman had been that beautiful, bashful girl who had learned that an exaggerated smile only led to more unwanted attention, and that a chilly exterior made life easier. If that was the case, Rakel couldn't help wondering what she was going to make of life as the wife of a cabinet minister.

Mikael Bellman stopped next to them when a question was yelled out and a microphone stuck in front of his face.

"Oh, I'm just here to celebrate one of the men who contributed to us solving the vampirist case," he said in English. "Dr. Smith is the one you should be talking to today, not me." But Bellman did as he was asked and posed happily as the photographers called out their requests.

"International press," Bjørn said.

"Vampirism is hot," Katrine said, looking at the crowd. "All the crime reporters are here."

"Except Mona Daa," Harry said as he looked around.

"And everyone from the boiler room," Katrine said, "except Anders Wyller. Do you know where he is?"

The others shook their heads.

"He called me this morning," Katrine said. "Asked if he could have a chat with me on his own."

"What about?" Bjørn wondered.

"God knows. Ah, there he is!"

Anders Wyller had appeared at the far side of the crowd. He looked breathless and red-faced as he took his scarf off. At that moment the doors to the auditorium opened.

"Right, we need to get seats," Katrine said, and hurried towards the door. "Make way, pregnant woman coming through!"

"She's so pretty," Rakel whispered, sticking her hand under Harry's arm and leaning against his shoulder. "I've always wondered if you and she ever had a thing."

"A *thing*?"

"Just a little one. When we weren't together, for instance."

" 'Fraid not," Harry said gloomily.

"Afraid not? Meaning?"

"Meaning sometimes I regret not making more use of our little gaps."

"I'm not joking, Harry."

"Nor am I."

. . .

Hallstein Smith opened the door to the imposing room a crack and peered in. Looked at the chandelier hanging above the crowd filling all the seats in the auditorium. There were even people standing in the gallery. Once this room had housed Norway's national assembly, and now he—little Hallstein—was going to stand at the podium and defend his research, and be awarded the title of doctor! He looked at May, who was sitting in the front row, nervous, but as proud as a mother hen. He looked at his foreign colleagues who had come even though he had warned them that the disputation would be in Norwegian; he looked at the journalists, at Bellman, who was sitting with his wife in the front row, right in the middle. At Harry, Bjørn and Katrine, his new friends in the police, who had played such a part in his dissertation about vampirism, in which the case of Valentin Gjertsen had obviously become one of the central planks. And even if the image of Valentin had changed dramatically in light of the events of recent days, they had only strengthened his conclusions about the vampiristic personality. Because of course Hallstein had pointed out that vampirists primarily act on instinct, and are driven by their desires and impulses—so the revelation that Lenny Hell had been the mastermind behind the well-planned murders had come in the nick of time.

"Let's get started," the chairman said, picking a speck of dust from his academic gown.

Hallstein took a deep breath and walked in. The audience rose to its feet.

Smith and the two opponents sat down, while the chairman explained how the disputation was going to proceed. Then he gave the floor to Hallstein.

The first opponent, Ståle Aune, leaned forward and whispered good luck.

Hallstein walked up to the podium, and looked out across the auditorium. Felt silence descend. The examination lecture that morning had gone well. Well? It had been fantastic! He couldn't help noting that the adjudication committee had seemed happy, and even Ståle Aune had nodded appreciatively at his best points.

Now he was going to give a shorter version of the lecture, twenty minutes maximum. He began to speak, and soon got the same feeling he had had that morning, and departed from the script he had in front of him. His thoughts became words instantly, and it was as if he could see himself from outside, could see the audience, could see the expressions on their faces, hanging on his every word, their senses entirely focused on him, Hallstein Smith, professor of vampirism.

Obviously there was no such thing yet, but he was going to change that, and today marked the start. He was approaching his conclusion. "During my brief time in the independent investigative group led by Harry Hole, I managed to learn many things. One of them was that the central question in any murder case is 'Why?' But that that doesn't help if you can't also answer 'How?'" Hallstein went over to the table next to the podium, on which lay three objects covered by a felt cloth. He took hold of one end of the cloth and waited. A bit of theatre was forgivable.

"This is how," he declared, and pulled the cloth away.

A gasp ran through the audience as they saw the large revolver, the grotesque handcuffs, and the black iron teeth.

He pointed at the revolver. "One tool to threaten and compel."

At the handcuffs. "One to control, incapacitate, imprison."

The iron teeth. "And one to get to the source, to gain access to the blood, to conduct the ritual."

He looked up. "Thank you to Detective Anders Wyller for letting me borrow these objects so that I could illustrate my point. Because this is more than three 'hows.' It is also a 'why.' But how is it a 'why'?"

Scattered, knowing laughter.

"Because all the tools are old. Unnecessarily old, one might say. The vampirist has gone to the trouble of obtaining copies of artefacts from specific time periods. And that underlines what I say in my dissertation about the importance of ritual, and the fact that drinking blood can be traced back to a time when there were gods who needed to be worshipped and placated, and the currency for that was blood."

He pointed at the revolver. "This marks a link to America, two hundred years ago, when there were Native American tribes that drank their enemies' blood in the belief that they would absorb their power." He pointed at the handcuffs. "This is a link to the Middle Ages, when witches and sorcerers had to be caught, exorcised and ritually burned." He pointed at the teeth. "And these are a link to the ancient world, when sacrifices and human bloodletting were a common way of appeasing the gods. Just as I with my answers today . . ." He gestured towards the chair and two opponents. ". . . hope to appease these gods."

The laughter was more relaxed this time.

"Thank you."

The applause was, as far as Hallstein Smith could judge, thunderous.

Ståle Aune stood up, adjusted his spotted bow tie, stuck his stomach out and marched up to the podium.

"Dear candidate, you have based your doctoral dissertation on case studies, and what I am wondering is how you were able to draw the conclusion you did given that your main example—Valentin Gjertsen—didn't support your conclusions. That is, until Lenny Hell's role was uncovered."

Hallstein Smith cleared his throat. "Within psychology, there is more scope for interpretation than in most other sciences, and naturally it was tempting to interpret Valentin Gjertsen's behaviour within the frame of the typical vampirist I had already described. But, as a researcher, I have to be honest. Until a few days ago, Valentin Gjertsen didn't entirely fit my theory. And even if it is the case that the map and the terrain are never identical in psychology, I have to admit that that was frustrating. It is hard to take any pleasure from the tragedy of Lenny Hell. But if nothing else, his case reinforces the theory of this dissertation, and therefore provides an even clearer illustration and more precise understanding of the vampirist. Hopefully this can help prevent future tragedies by enabling the vampirist to be caught earlier." Hallstein cleared his throat. "I must thank the adjudication committee, who had already devoted so much time to studying my original dissertation, for permitting me to incorporate the changes made possible by the discovery of Hell's role in the case, and which therefore made everything fall into place . . ."

When the chair discreetly signalled to the first opponent that his time was up, Hallstein felt that only five minutes had passed, not forty-five. It had gone like a dream!

And when the chair went up to the podium to say that there would now be an interval in which questions could be submitted *ex auditorio*, Hallstein could hardly wait to show them this fantastic piece of work which, in all its grimness, was still about the greatest and most beautiful thing of all: the human mind.

Hallstein used the break to mingle in the vestibule, to talk to people who weren't invited to the dinner. He saw Harry Hole standing with a dark-haired woman, and made his way over to them.

"Harry!" he said, shaking the policeman's hand, which was as hard and cold as marble. "This must be Rakel."

"It is," Harry said.

Hallstein shook her hand as he saw Harry look at his watch, then over at the door.

"Are we expecting someone?"

"Yes," Harry said. "And here he is at last."

Hallstein saw two people coming through the door at the other end of the room. A tall, dark young man, and a man in his fifties with fair hair and thin, rectangular, frameless glasses. It struck him that the young man looked like Rakel, but there was also something familiar about the other man.

"Where have I seen that man in the glasses?" Hallstein wondered.

"I don't know. He's a haematologist, John D. Steffens."

"And what's he doing here?"

Hallstein saw Harry take a deep breath. "He's here to put an end to this story. He just doesn't know it yet."

At that moment the chair rang a bell and announced in a booming voice that it was time to go back into the auditorium.


John D. Steffens was making his way between two rows of seats with Oleg Fauke behind him. Steffens glanced around the room, trying to locate Harry Hole. And felt his heart stop when he caught sight of the fair-haired young man in the back row. At the same moment Anders caught sight of him, and Steffens saw the fear in the young man's face. Steffens turned to Oleg to say he had forgotten a meeting and had to leave.

"I know," Oleg said, and showed no sign of moving out of the way. Steffens noted that the boy was almost as tall as his pseudo-father, Hole. "But we're going to let this run its course now, Steffens."

The boy gently put his hand on Steffens's shoulder, but it still felt to the senior consultant that he was being pushed onto the chair behind him. Steffens sat and felt his pulse slow down. Dignity. Yes, dignity. Oleg Fauke knew. Which meant that Harry knew. And hadn't given him any chance to escape. And it was obvious from Anders's reaction that he hadn't known about this either. They had been fooled. Fooled into being here together. What now?


Katrine Bratt sat down between Harry and Bjørn just as the chair began to speak up at the podium.

"The candidate has received a question *ex auditorio*. Harry Hole, please go ahead."

Katrine looked at Harry in surprise as he stood up. "Thank you."

She could see the looks of surprise on other people's faces too, some of them with a smile on their lips, as if they were expecting a joke. Even Hallstein Smith seemed amused as he took over at the podium.

"Congratulations," Harry said. "You're very close to achieving your goal, and I must also thank you for your contribution to solving the vampirist case."

"I should be thanking you," Smith said with a small bow.

"Yes, maybe," Harry said. "Because of course we found the person who was pulling the strings and directing Valentin. And, as Aune pointed out, your entire dissertation is based upon that. So you were lucky there."

"I was."

"But there are a couple of other things I think we'd all like answers to."

"I'll do my best, Harry."

"I remember when I saw the recording of Valentin entering your barn. He knew exactly where he was going, but he didn't know about the scales inside the door. He marched in, unconcerned, convinced he had firm ground under his feet. And he almost lost his balance. Why does that happen?"

"We take some things for granted," Smith said. "In psychology we call it rationalising, which basically means that we simplify things. Without rationalisation, the world would be unmanageable, our brains would become overloaded by all the uncertainties we have to deal with."

"That would also explain why we go down a flight of cellar steps without concern, without thinking that we might hit our heads on a water pipe."

"Exactly."

"But after we've done it once, we remember—or at least most of us do—the next time. That's why Katrine Bratt takes care when she walks across those scales in your barn on only her second visit. So it's no mystery that we found blood and skin on that water pipe in Hell's cellar belonging to you and me, but not from Lenny Hell. He must have learned to duck as long ago as . . . well, when he was a child. Otherwise we would have found Hell's DNA, because DNA can often be traced years after it ends up on something like that water pipe."

"I'm sure that's correct, Harry."

"I'll come back to that, but let me first deal with something that *is* a mystery."

Katrine sat up in her chair. She didn't yet know what was going on, but she knew Harry, could feel the vibration of the inaudible, low-frequency growl that lay beneath his voice.

"When Valentin Gjertsen goes into your barn at midnight, he weights 74.7 kilos," Harry said. "But when he leaves, he weighs 73.2 kilos, according to the security camera footage. Exactly one and a half kilos lighter." Harry gestured with his hand. "The obvious explanation is, of course, that the weight difference is the result of the blood he lost in your office."

Katrine heard the chairman's discreet but impatient cough.

"But then I realised something," Harry said. "We'd forgotten the revolver! The one Valentin had brought with him, and which was still in the office when he left. A Ruger Redhawk weighs around 1.2 kilos. So, for the sums to add up, Valentin had only lost 0.3 kilos of blood . . ."

"Hole," the chairman said. "If there is a question to the candidate here . . ."

"First a question to an expert in blood," Harry said, and turned to face the audience. "Senior Consultant John Steffens, you're a haematologist, and you happened to be on duty when Penelope Rasch was taken to hospital . . ."


John Steffens felt sweat break out on his forehead when all eyes turned to look at him. Just as they had looked at him when he had been on the witness stand explaining how his wife had died. How she had been stabbed, how she had literally bled to death in his arms. All eyes, then as now. Anders's eyes, then as now.

He swallowed.

"Yes, I was."

"You demonstrated then that you have a good eye for estimating blood quantities. Based on a photograph from the crime scene, you estimated the amount of blood she had lost at one and a half litres."

"Yes."

Harry took a photograph out of his jacket pocket and held it up. "And based on this picture from Hallstein Smith's office, which was shown to you by one of the paramedics, you estimated the amount of blood here also to be one and a half litres. In other words, one and a half kilos. Is that correct?"

Steffens swallowed. Knew that Anders was staring at him from behind. "That's correct. Give or take a decilitre or two."

"Just to be clear, is it possible for someone to get to their feet and escape even if they've lost a litre and a half of blood?"

"It differs from individual to individual, but yes, if the person has the physique and determination."

"Which brings me to my very simple question," Harry said.

Steffens felt a bead of sweat trickle down his forehead.

Harry turned back to the podium.

"How come, Smith?"


Katrine gasped. The silence that followed felt like a physical weight in the room.

"I'll have to pass on that, Harry, I don't know," Smith said. "I hope that doesn't mean that my doctorate is at risk, but in my defence I would like to point out that this question is outside the frame of my dissertation." He smiled, but garnered no laughter this time. "But it's within the parameters of the police investigation, so perhaps you ought to answer that yourself, Harry?"

"Very well," Harry said, and took a deep breath.

No, Katrine thought, and held her breath.

"Valentin Gjertsen didn't have a revolver on him when he arrived. It was already in your office."

"What?" Smith's laughter sounded like the cry of a lone bird in the auditorium. "How on earth could it have got there?"

"You took it there," Harry said.

"Me? I've got nothing to do with that revolver."

"It was your revolver, Smith."

"Mine? I've never owned a revolver in my life, you only have to check the firearms register."

"In which this revolver is registered to a sailor from Farsund. Whom you treated. For schizophrenia."

"A sailor? What are you talking about, Harry? You said yourself that Valentin threatened you with the revolver in the bar, when he killed Mehmet Kalak."

"You got it back after that."

A wave of anxiety spread around the auditorium, and there was a sound of low muttering and chairs being moved.

The chairman stood up, and looked like a cockerel spreading his feathers as he raised his gowned arms to appeal for calm. "Sorry, herr Hole, but this is a disputation. If you have information for the police, might I suggest that you address it to the correct authorities and not bring it into the world of academe."

"Herr Chairman, opponents," Harry said, "is it not of fundamental importance to the examination of this doctoral thesis if it is based upon a misinterpreted case study? Isn't that the sort of thing that's supposed to be illuminated in a disputation?"

"Herr Hole—" the chairman began, with thunder in his voice.

"—is right," Ståle Aune said from the front row. "My dear chairman, as a member of the adjudication committee, I am very interested to hear what herr Hole wishes to say to the candidate."

The chairman looked at Aune. Then at Harry. And finally at Smith, before sitting down again.

"Well, then," Harry said. "I would like to ask the candidate if he held Lenny Hell hostage in his own house, and if it was him rather than Hell who was directing Valentin Gjertsen?"

An almost inaudible gasp ran round the auditorium, followed by a silence so complete that it seemed to suck all the air out of the room.

Smith shook his head in disbelief. "This is a joke, isn't it, Harry? This is something you've cooked up in the boiler room to liven up the disputation, and now—"

"I suggest you answer, Hallstein."

Perhaps it was the use of his first name that made Smith realise that Harry was serious. Katrine at least thought she saw something sink in as he stood there at the podium.

"Harry," he said quietly, "I had *never* been in Hell's house before Sunday, when you took me there."

"Yes, you had," Harry said. "You were very careful to get rid of the evidence from anywhere you might have left fingerprints and DNA. But there was one place you forgot. The water pipe."

"The water pipe? We all left our DNA on that damn water pipe on Sunday, Harry!"

"Not you."

"Yes, me too! Ask Bjørn Holm, he's sitting right there!"

"What Bjørn Holm can confirm is that your DNA was found on the water pipe, not that it got there on Sunday. Because on Sunday you came down to the cellar when I was already there. Silently, I didn't hear you come, if you remember? Silently, because you didn't hit your head on the water pipe. You ducked. Because your brain remembered."

"This is laughable, Harry. I hit that water pipe on Sunday, you just didn't hear it."

"Perhaps because you were wearing this, which cushioned the blow . . ." Harry pulled a black woollen hat from his pocket and put it on his head. On the front of the hat was a skull, and Katrine read the name St. Pauli. "But how can someone leave DNA, in the form of skin or blood or hair, when they're wearing this pulled down over their forehead?"

Hallstein blinked hard.

"The candidate isn't answering," Harry said. "So let me answer for him. Hallstein Smith walked into that water pipe the first time he was there, which was a long time ago, before the vampirist set to work."

In the silence that followed, Hallstein Smith's low chuckle was the only sound.

"Before I say anything," Smith said, "I think we should give former detective Harry Hole a generous round of applause for this fantastic story."

Smith started to clap his hands, and a few others joined in before the applause died out.

"But for this to be more than just a story, it requires the same thing as a doctoral thesis," Smith said. "Evidence! And you have none, Harry. Your entire deduction is based upon two highly dubious assumptions. That some very old scales in a barn show exactly the right weight of a person who stands on it for barely a second, scales that I can tell you have a tendency to stick. And that because I was wearing a woollen hat I couldn't have left DNA on the water pipe on Sunday. A hat that I can tell you I took off when I was going down those steps before I hit my head on the water pipe, and put on again seeing as it was colder down in the cellar. The fact that I have no scar on my forehead now is because I heal quickly. My wife can also confirm that I had a mark on my forehead when I returned home."

Katrine saw the woman in the homemade, drab-coloured dress look at her husband with dark eyes in a blank face, as if she were suffering shock after a grenade explosion.

"Isn't that so, May?"

The woman's mouth opened and closed. Then she nodded slowly.

"You see, Harry?" Smith tilted his head and looked at Harry with an expression of sad sympathy. "You see how easy it is to blow holes in your theory?"

"Well," Harry said. "I respect your wife's loyalty, but I'm afraid the DNA evidence is indisputable. The analysis from the Forensic Medical Institute not only proves that the organic matter matches your DNA profile, but also that it's more than two months old, so couldn't possibly have ended up there on Sunday."

Katrine started in her chair and looked at Bjørn. He shook his head almost imperceptibly.

"As a result, Smith, it isn't a theory that you were in Hell's cellar sometime last autumn. It is a fact. Just as it's a fact that you had the Ruger revolver in your possession, and that it was in your office when you shot the unarmed Valentin Gjertsen. Besides, we also have stylo-metrical analysis."

Katrine looked at the battered yellow folder Harry had pulled out of the inside pocket of his jacket. "A computer program that compares word choices, sentence structure, textual style and punctuation to identify the author. It was stylometry that gave fresh life to the debate about which of his plays Shakespeare actually wrote. The success rate for identifying the correct author is between eighty and ninety percent. In other words, not high enough for it to count as evidence. But the success rate for ruling out a particular author, such as Shake-speare, is 99.9 percent. Our IT expert, Tord Gren, used the program to compare the emails that were sent to Valentin with thousands of Lenny Hell's earlier emails to other people. The conclusion is . . ." Harry passed the file to Katrine. ". . . that Lenny Hell didn't write the instructions which Valentin Gjertsen received by email."

Smith looked at Harry. His fringe had fallen forward over his sweating brow.

"We'll discuss this further in a police interview," Harry said. "But this is a disputation. And you still have the chance to give the adju-dication committee an explanation that will stop them refusing to award your doctorate. Isn't that right, Aune?"

Ståle Aune cleared his throat. "That's right. Ideally, science is blind to the morality of the age, and this wouldn't be the first doctor-ate to have been achieved by morally questionable or even directly illegal methods. What we on the adjudication committee need to know before we can approve the dissertation is whether or not there was anyone actually steering Valentin. If that isn't the case, I can't see how this thesis can be accepted by the adjudication committee."

"Thank you," Harry said. "So what do you say, Smith? Would you like to explain this to the adjudication committee here and now, before we arrest you?"

Hallstein Smith looked at Harry. His panting was the only sound that could be heard, as if he were the only person in the auditorium who was still breathing. A lone flashbulb went off.

A bloodshot disputation chairman leaned towards Ståle and whispered in a hiss:

"Holy Jeremiah, Aune, what's going on here?"

"Do you know what a monkey trap is?" Ståle Aune asked, then settled back in his chair and folded his arms.

Hallstein Smith's head jerked, as if he'd been given an electric shock. He laughed as he raised his arm and pointed at the ceiling. "What have I got to lose, Harry?"

Harry didn't answer.

"Yes, Valentin was steered. By me. Of course I wrote those emails. But the most important thing isn't who was behind them, the scientific point is that Valentin was a genuine vampirist, as my research demonstrates, and nothing you've said invalidates my results. And if I had to adjust the circumstances to re-create laboratory conditions, that's no more than researchers have always done. Is it?" He looked around the audience. "But when it comes down to it, I'm not choosing what he does, he is. And six human lives isn't an unreasonable price to pay for what this—" Smith tapped his printed and bound thesis with his forefinger—"can save humanity from in future, in terms of murder and suffering. The signs and profiles are all laid out here. Valentin Gjertsen was the one who drank their blood, who killed them, not me. I just made it easier for him. When you just for once have the good fortune to encounter a real vampirist, you have a duty to make the most of it, you can't let short-sighted moralistic attitudes stop you. You have to look at the bigger picture, consider what's best for humanity. Just ask Oppenheimer, ask Mao, ask the thousands of lab rats with cancer."

"So you killed Lenny Hell and shot Marte Ruud for our sakes?" Harry said.

"Yes, yes! Sacrifices on the altar of research!"

"The way you're sacrificing yourself and your own humanity? To *benefit* humanity?"

"Exactly, yes!"

"So they didn't die in order that you, Hallstein Smith, could be vindicated? So that the monkey could sit on the throne, get his name in the history books? Because that's what's been driving you all along, isn't it?"

"I have shown you what a vampirist is, and what one is capable of! Don't I deserve to be thanked for that?"

"Well," Harry said, "first and foremost, you've demonstrated what a humiliated man is capable of."

Hallstein Smith's head jerked again. His mouth opened and closed. But nothing more came out.

"We've heard enough." The chair stood up. "This disputation is at an end. And can I ask any police officers present to arrest—?"

Hallstein Smith moved surprisingly quickly. With two rapid steps he reached the table and snatched up the revolver, then took a long stride towards the audience and aimed the revolver at the forehead of the nearest person.

"Get up!" he snarled. "And the rest of you remain seated!"

Katrine saw a blonde woman stand up. Smith turned her round so that she was standing in front of him like a shield. It was Ulla Bellman. Her mouth was open and she was looking in mute despair at a man in the front row. Katrine could only see the back of Mikael Bellman's head and had no idea what his face was expressing, only that he was sitting there as if frozen to the spot. There was a whimpering sound. It came from May Smith. She was leaning sideways slightly in her chair.

"Let go of her."

Katrine turned towards the gruff voice. It was Truls Berntsen. He had stood up from his chair in the back row and was walking down the steps.

"Stop, Berntsen," Smith screamed. "Or I'll shoot her and then you!"

But Truls Berntsen didn't stop. In profile his jaw looked even heavier than usual, but his new muscles were also visible under his thick sweater. He reached the front, turned and walked along the front row, straight towards Smith and Ulla Bellman.

"One step closer—"

"Shoot me first, Smith, otherwise you won't have time."

"As you wish."

Berntsen snorted. "You fucking civilian, you wouldn't d—"

Katrine felt sudden pressure against her ears, as if she were sitting in a plane that was rapidly losing altitude. It took a moment for her to realise that it was the blast from the heavy revolver.

Truls Berntsen had stopped and was standing there, swaying. His

his mouth was open, his eyes bulging. Katrine saw the hole in his sweater, waited for the blood. And then it came. It was as if Truls was making one last effort to stay upright as he looked directly at Ulla Bellman. Then he fell backwards.

Somewhere in the room a woman screamed.

"No one move," Smith shouted, backing towards the exit with Ulla Bellman in front of him. "If I see a single one of you stand up, I'll shoot her."

Of course it was a bluff. And of course no one was going to take the risk that it wasn't.

"The keys to the Amazon," Harry whispered. He was still standing. He held his hand out towards Bjørn, who took a moment to react before putting the car keys in his hand.

"Hallstein!" Harry called, and started to move along the row. "Your car is parked in the university's visitors' car park, and right now it's being examined by Forensics. I've got the keys to a car that's parked right in front of this building, and I'm a better hostage for you."

"Because?" Smith replied, still backing away.

"Because I'll stay calm, and because you have a conscience."

Smith stopped. Looked thoughtfully at Harry for a few seconds.

"Go over there and put the handcuffs on," he said, nodding towards the table.

Harry emerged from the row of seats, went past Truls, who was lying motionless on the floor, and stopped at the table with his back to Smith and the rest of the room.

"So that I can see!" Smith yelled.

Harry turned towards him and held his hands up so that he could see that they were held by the replica handcuffs with the chain between them.

"Come here!"

Harry walked towards him.

"One minute!"

Katrine saw Smith use his free hand to grab Harry, who was taller, by his shoulder, then turn him round and steer him out through the door, which he left ajar.

Ulla Bellman looked at the half-open door before she turned to her husband. Katrine saw Bellman beckon her to him. And Ulla started to walk towards him. With short, unsteady steps, as if she was walking on thin ice. But when she reached Truls Berntsen she sank to her knees. She rested her head against his bloody sweater. And in the silence of the auditorium the single painful sob that Ulla emitted sounded louder than the blast of the revolver.

Harry felt the barrel of the revolver against his back as he walked ahead of Smith. Damn, damn! He had been planning this in detail since yesterday, thinking through different scenarios, but he hadn't seen this coming.

Harry shoved the door open, and the cold winter air hit him in the face. Universitetsplassen was deserted, bathing in winter sunshine in front of them. The black paint of Bjørn's Volvo Amazon glinted in the light.

"Walk!"

Harry went down the steps out onto the open ground. With his second step his feet vanished from under him and he fell sideways without being able to brace his fall. Pain shot down his arm and back as his shoulder struck the icy ground.

"Up!" Smith hissed, grabbing the chain of the handcuffs and dragging him to his feet.

Harry used the momentum Smith had given him, aware that he was unlikely to get a better chance. He thrust his head forward as soon as he was standing, and headbutted Smith, who stumbled, took two steps back and fell down. Harry took a step closer to follow through, but Smith was lying on his back with both hands clutching the revolver, which was pointing straight at Harry.

"Come on, Harry. I'm used to this, I ended up lying on the ground during every other break time at school. So come on!"

Harry stared down the barrel of the revolver. He had hit Smith's nose, and a flash of white bone was visible through the broken skin. A trickle of blood ran down the side of one nostril.

"I know what you're thinking, Harry," Smith laughed. *"He didn't manage to kill Valentin from two and a half metres away.* So come on, then! Or unlock the car."

Harry's brain did the necessary calculations. Then he turned round, slowly opened the driver's door and heard Smith get to his feet. Harry got in and took his time inserting the key in the ignition.

"I'll drive," Smith said. "Move."

Harry did as he said, moving slowly and clumsily across the gearstick to the passenger seat.

"Then slip your feet over the handcuffs."

Harry looked at him.

"I don't want the chain round my neck while I'm driving," Smith said, and raised the revolver. "It's your bad luck if you've been skipping yoga classes. And I can see that you're trying to delay us. You have five seconds, starting now. Four . . ."

Harry leaned back, as far as the rigid seat would let him, held his chained hands out in front of him and bent his knees.

"Three, two . . ."

With difficulty Harry managed to tuck his smartly polished shoes through the chain of the handcuffs.

Smith got in, leaned across Harry. Pulled the old-fashioned seat belt across his chest and waist, fastened it, then tightened it with a hard tug so that Harry was literally strapped to the back of the seat. He fished Harry's mobile from his jacket pocket. He fastened his own seat belt and turned the key. He revved the engine and wrestled with the gearstick. He figured the clutch out and reversed in a semi-circle. Rolled down the window and threw Harry's phone out, followed by his own.

They pulled out onto Karl Johans gate, turning right so that the Palace filled their field of vision. Green at the lights. They turned left, roundabout, another green, past the Concert House. Aker Brygge. The traffic was flowing smoothly. Far too smoothly, Harry thought. The further he and Smith managed to get before Katrine alerted the patrol cars and police helicopter, the larger the area they would have to cover, and the more roadblocks they would need to set up.

Smith looked out across the fjord. "Oslo rarely looks more beautiful than it does on days like this, does it?"

His voice sounded nasal, and was accompanied by a faint whistle. His nose was probably broken.

"A silent travelling companion," Smith said. "Well, you've done enough talking for today."

Harry looked at the motorway ahead of them. Katrine couldn't use their mobile phones to track them, but as long as Smith kept to the main roads there was still hope that they might be found quickly. From a helicopter, a car with a rally check across the roof and boot would be easy to distinguish from the others.

"He came to see me, calling himself Alexander Dreyer, and wanting to talk about Pink Floyd and the voices he was hearing," Smith said, shaking his head. "But as you noticed, I'm good at reading people, and I soon realised that this was no ordinary person, but an extremely rare type of psychopath. So I used what he told me about his sexual preferences to check with colleagues who are experts in questions of morality and eventually figured out who I was dealing with. And what his dilemma was. That he was desperate to follow his hunting instinct, but that one single mistake, one faint suspicion, one silly little detail might give him away and put the police on to Alexander Dreyer. Are you following this, Harry?" Smith cast a quick glance at him. "That if he was going to hunt again, it had to be in the knowledge that he was absolutely safe. He was perfect, a man with no options, it was just a matter of putting a leash on him and opening the cage and he'd eat—and drink—everything he was offered. But I couldn't present myself as the person offering this, I needed a fictional puppet master, a lightning conductor to whom the trail would lead if Valentin was caught and confessed. Someone who would end up being uncovered at some point, regardless, to show that the terrain matched the map, who confirmed the theory in my dissertation of the impulsive, childishly chaotic vampirist. And Lenny Hell was the hermit who lived in an isolated house and never had any visitors. But one day he received a surprise visit from his psychologist. A psychologist with something on his head that made him look like a chickenhawk, and a big red revolver in his hand. Caw, caw, caw!" Smith laughed loudly. "You should have seen Lenny's face when he realised he was my slave! First I got him to take my patient records up to his office. Then we found a cage that the family had used to transport pigs, and we carried it down to the cellar. That must have been when I hit my head on that damn water pipe. We put a mattress inside for Lenny before I chained him up using handcuffs. And there he sat. I didn't actually have any use for Lenny once I'd pumped him for details of all the women he'd stalked, got copies of the keys to their flats, and the password so I could email Valentin from Lenny's computer. But I still had to wait before staging his suicide. If Valentin got caught or ended up dead and the police were led to Hell too soon, I had to make sure he had a watertight alibi for the first murder. Because of course I knew they'd check his alibi seeing as he'd been in contact with Elise Hermansen by phone. So I took Lenny to that local pizzeria at the time when I had instructed Valentin to kill Elise, and made sure people saw him. In fact I was so busy concentrating on holding that bolt gun against Lenny under the table that I didn't notice there were nuts in the pizza bases until it was too late." More laughter. "As a result of that, Lenny had to spend a lot of time on his own in that cage. I had to laugh when you found Lenny Hell's sperm on the mattress and concluded that he had abused Marte Ruud there."

They passed Bygdøy. Snarøya. Harry was counting the seconds automatically. Ten minutes since they had driven away from Universitetsplassen. He looked up at the empty blue sky.

"Marte Ruud was never assaulted. I shot her as soon as I brought her from the forest down into the cellar. Valentin had wrecked her, so it was an act of mercy to put her down." Smith turned towards him. "I hope you appreciate that, Harry. Harry? Do you think I talk too much, Harry?"

They were approaching Høvikodden. The Oslo Fjord appeared again to their left. Harry calculated. The police might have time to set up a roadblock at Asker, they'd be there in ten minutes.

"Can you imagine what a gift it was to me when you asked me to join the investigation, Harry? I was so surprised that I said no at first. Before I realised that if I was sitting there getting hold of all the information, I could warn Valentin when you were getting so close that he could no longer carry on. *My* vampirist was going to outshine Kürten, Haigh and Chase and become the greatest of them all. But I still didn't know that his hamam was under surveillance until we were sitting in this car on the way there. And I was starting to lose control of Valentin—he killed that bartender, and kidnapped Marte Ruud. Luckily I found out that Alexander Dreyer had been identified at that cashpoint machine in time to be able to warn him to get out of his flat. By that point Valentin had worked out that it was me, his former psychologist, who was pulling the strings, but so what? The identity of the person who was in the boat with him didn't make any difference. But I knew that the net was closing in. That it was time for the grand finale I had been planning for a while. I had got him to leave the flat and book into the Plaza Hotel, which obviously wasn't somewhere he could stay for long, but I was at least able to send him an envelope containing copies of the keys to the barn and office, and instructions telling him to hide until midnight, when everyone had gone to bed. Naturally I couldn't rule out that he might have started to suspect something, but what alternative did he have now that his cover was blown? He simply had to gamble that I could be trusted. And you have to give me credit for the way that was set up, Harry. Calling you and Katrine so that I had witnesses on the phone, as well as the security camera footage. Yes, of course it could be regarded as a cold-blooded liquidation, fabricating the story of the heroic researcher who had upset the serial killer with his public statements, and then killed him in self-defence. Yes, I accept that it meant that a perfectly ordinary disputation was attended by international media, and that fourteen companies have bought the rights to publish my thesis. But in the end it comes down to research, scholarship. It's progress, Harry. And it's possible that the road to hell is paved with good intentions, but it's also the road to an enlightened, humane future."

Oleg turned the ignition key.

"A&E at Ullevål!" the young blond detective shouted from the backseat, where he was sitting with Truls Berntsen's head in his lap. They were both soaked with Berntsen's blood. "Foot on the floor and sirens on!"

Oleg was about to release the clutch when the back door was yanked open.

"No!" the detective shouted furiously.

"Move, Anders!" It was Steffens. He pushed his way in, forcing the young detective to move to the other side.

"Hold his legs up," Steffens barked, now holding Berntsen's head. "So he gets—"

"Blood to his heart and brain," Anders said.

Oleg released the clutch and they pulled away from the car park, out onto the road between a clanging tram and an angry taxi.

"How's it looking?"

"See for yourself," Anders snarled. "Unconscious, weak pulse, but he's breathing. As you can see, the bullet hit him in the right hemithorax."

"That's not the problem," Steffens said. "The big problem's at the back. Help me turn him over." Oleg glanced in the rear-view mirror. Saw them turn Truls Berntsen onto his side and tear his sweater and shirt off. He concentrated on the road again, used his horn to get past a lorry, accelerated as he crossed a junction on red.

"Oh, fuck," Anders groaned.

"Yes, it's a big hole," Steffens said. "The bullet probably blew part of his rib out. He's going to bleed out before we get to Ullevål unless . . ."

"Unless . . . ?"

Oleg heard Steffens take a deep breath. "Unless we do a better job than I did with your mother. Use the backs of your hands on either side of the wound—like that—and press them together. Just close the wound as well as you can, there's no other way."

"My hands are just sliding."

"Tear off some of his shirt and use that to get more friction."

Oleg heard Anders breathing heavily. He glanced in the rear-view mirror again. Saw that Steffens had put one finger on Berntsen's chest while he tapped it with another finger.

"I'm trying percussion, but I'm too cramped to be able to put my ear alongside," Steffens said. "Can you manage to . . . ?"

Anders leaned forward without taking his hands away from the wound. Put his head to Berntsen's chest. "Very muffled," he said. "No air. Do you think . . . ?"

"Yes, I'm afraid it's a haemothorax," his father said. "The pleural cavity's filling with blood, and his lungs will soon collapse. Oleg . . ."

"I hear you," Oleg said, and put his foot down.


Katrine was standing in the middle of Universitetsplassen with her phone pressed to her ear, looking up at the empty, cloudless sky. It wasn't yet visible, but she had requisitioned the police helicopter from Gardermoen with orders to scan the E6 motorway as it approached Oslo from the north.

"No, there are no mobile phones we can track," she called over the noise of sirens approaching from different parts of the city and merging together. "Nothing registered by the toll stations. We're setting up roadblocks on the southbound E6 and E18. I'll let you know as soon as we've got anything."

"OK," Falkeid said at the other end. "We're on standby."

Katrine ended the call. Another one came through.

"Asker Police, on the E18," the voice said. "We've stopped an articulated lorry here and are positioning it across the road just after the slip road to Asker, and are filtering the traffic off there and back onto the motorway after the roundabout. A black 1970s Amazon with rally stripes?"

"Yes."

"So we're talking the world's worst choice of getaway vehicle?"

"Let's hope so. Keep me informed."

Bjørn jogged over. "Oleg and that doctor are driving Berntsen to Ullevål," he panted. "Wyller's gone with them."

"What are his chances, do you think?"

"I only have experience of dead bodies."

"OK, did Berntsen look like one?"

Bjørn Holm shrugged. "He was still bleeding, and at least that means he isn't completely empty yet."

"And Rakel?"

"She's sitting in the auditorium with Bellman's wife, she's really cut up about it. Bellman himself had to rush off to manage the operation from somewhere he could get an overview of the situation, he said."

"Overview?" Katrine snorted. "The only place we've got any sort of overview is *here*!"

"I know, but take it easy, darling, we don't want the little one to get stressed, do we?"

"Bloody hell, Bjørn." She squeezed her phone. "Why couldn't you have told me what Harry was planning?"

"Because I didn't know."

"You didn't know? You must have known something if he's brought Forensics in to examine Smith's car."

"He hasn't, that was a bluff. Like that bit about the dating of the DNA found on the water pipe."

"What?"

"The Forensic Medical Institute can't determine how old DNA is. What Harry said about them having found out that Smith's DNA was more than two months old, that was a complete lie."

Katrine looked at Bjørn. Put her hand in her bag and pulled out the yellow document folder Harry had given her. She opened it. Three sheets of A4. All blank.

"A bluff," Bjørn said. "For stylometry to be able to reveal anything with any degree of accuracy, the text has to be at least five thousand characters long. Those short emails that were sent to Valentin reveal nothing about the identity of their author."

"Harry had nothing," Katrine whispered.

"Not a damn thing!" Bjørn said. "He was just going for a confession."

"Damn him!" Katrine pressed her phone to her forehead, not quite sure if she wanted to warm it up or cool it down. "So why didn't he say anything? Christ, we could have had armed police outside."

"Because he couldn't say anything."

The answer came from Ståle Aune, who had walked over and stopped beside them.

"Why not?"

"Simple," Ståle said. "If he'd informed anyone in the police of what he was planning, and the police hadn't already intervened, then what happened in the auditorium would de facto have been a police interview. A police interview way outside the rules, in which the person being questioned wasn't informed of his rights, and in which the interviewer lied intentionally in order to mislead. And then none of what Smith said today could have been used in a trial. But as it is now . . ."

Katrine Bratt blinked. Then she nodded slowly. "As it is, Harry Hole, lecturer and private citizen took part in a disputation in which Smith spoke out of his own volition and in the presence of witnesses. Did you know about this, Ståle?"

Ståle Aune nodded. "Harry called me yesterday. He told me all the things that were pointing to Hallstein Smith. But he had no proof. So he explained his plan to use the disputation to set a monkey trap, with my help. And using Dr. Steffens as an expert witness."

"And how did you reply?"

"I said Hallstein Smith, 'the Monkey,' had walked into that sort of trap once before, and was hardly likely to do so again."

"But?"

"But Harry used my own words against me by referring to Aune's Thesis."

"Human beings are notorious," Bjørn said. "They make the same mistakes over and over again."

"Precisely," Aune nodded. "And Smith had apparently told Harry in the lift at Police HQ that he'd rather have his doctorate than a long life."

"And he walked straight into the monkey trap, of course, the idiot," Katrine groaned.

"He lived up to his nickname, yes."

"Not Smith, I'm talking about Harry."

Aune nodded. "I'm going back to the auditorium—Bellman's wife needs help."

"I'll come with you to secure the crime scene," Bjørn said.

"Crime scene?" Katrine asked.

"Berntsen."

"Oh, yes. Yes."

When the men had left her she looked up at the sky. Where had that helicopter got to?

"Damn you," she muttered. "Damn you, Harry Hole."

"Is it his fault?"

Katrine turned round.

Mona Daa was standing there. "I don't want to disturb you," she said. "I'm not actually working at the moment, but I saw it online so

I came down. If you want to use *VG* to say anything, to send Smith a message or anything . . . ?"

"Thanks, Daa, I'll let you know."

"OK." Mona Daa turned on her heel and started to leave, walking her penguin walk.

"I was actually surprised not to see you at the disputation," Katrine said.

Mona Daa stopped.

"You've been *VG*'s lead reporter on the vampirist case from the start," Katrine said.

"So Anders hasn't spoken to you."

Something about the way Mona Daa used Anders Wyller's first name, so naturally, made Katrine raise an eyebrow. "Spoken to me?"

"Yes. Anders and me, we . . ."

"You're kidding?" Katrine said.

Mona Daa laughed. "No. I realise that there are certain practical issues, purely professionally, but no, I'm not joking."

"And when did you . . . ?"

"Now, really. We've both got a few days off, and have been spending them in claustrophobically close proximity in Anders's little flat, to find out if we'd make a good match. We thought it made sense to know before we told anyone."

"So no one knows about it?"

"Not until Harry very nearly caught us red-handed with a surprise visit. Anders reckons Harry realised. And I know he tried to get hold of me at *VG*. I'm assuming that was to confirm his suspicions."

"He's pretty good at suspicions," Katrine said, looking up at the sky for the helicopter.

"I know."


Harry listened to the faint whistling sound as Smith breathed in and out. Then he noticed something odd out on the fjord. A dog that looked like it was walking on water. Meltwater. Seeping up through cracks in the ice even though it was below freezing.

"I've been accused of seeing vampirism simply because I *want* it to exist," Smith said. "But now it's been proven, once and for all, and soon the whole world will know what Professor Smith's vampirism is, regardless of what happens to me. And Valentin isn't the only one, there'll be more. More opportunities to keep the world focused on vampirism. I promise you, they've already been recruited. You asked me once if recognition meant more than life. Of course it does. Recognition is eternal life. And you're going to get eternal life too, Harry. As the man who almost caught Hallstein Smith, the man they once called the Monkey. *Do* you think I talk too much?"

They were approaching IKEA. They'd be at Asker in five minutes. Smith wouldn't react if there was a bit of a queue, the traffic often built up there.

"Denmark," Smith said. "Spring comes earlier there."

Denmark? Was Smith turning psychotic? Harry heard a dry clicking sound. The car was indicating. No, no, he was turning off the main road! Harry saw a sign with the name Nesøya on it.

"There's enough meltwater for me to be able to get out to the edge of the ice, wouldn't you say? A super-light aluminium boat with just one man on board won't sit too deep."

Boat. Harry clenched his teeth and swore silently. The boathouse. The boathouse Smith had said had formed part of his wife's inheritance. That was where they were going.

"The Skagerrak is 130 nautical miles across. Average speed, twenty knots. How long would that take, Harry, seeing as you're so good at math?" Smith laughed. "I've already worked it out. On a calculator. Six and a half hours. And from there you can get all the way across Denmark by bus, that won't take long. Then Copenhagen. Nørrebro. Red Square. Sit on a bench, hold up a bus ticket and wait for the travel agent. What do you think about Uruguay? A nice little country. It's a good thing I've already cleared the road all the way to the boatshed, and made enough space inside for a car. Otherwise these stripes on the roof would have been easy to spot from a helicopter, wouldn't they?"

Harry closed his eyes. Smith had had his escape route planned for a while. Just in case. And there was only one reason why he was telling Harry about it now. Because Harry wasn't going to get the chance to tell anyone else.

"Turn left up ahead," Steffens said from the backseat. "Block 17."

Oleg turned and felt the wheels lose their grip on the ice before regaining it again.

He had a feeling there was a speed limit in the hospital grounds, but was well aware that time and blood were both running out for Berntsen.

He braked in front of the entrance, where two men in yellow paramedics' tunics were waiting with a trolley. With practised movements they lifted Berntsen out of the back seat and up onto the trolley.

"He's got no pulse," Steffens said. "Straight into the hybrid room. The crash team—"

"Already in place," the older paramedic said.

Oleg and Anders followed the trolley and Steffens through two sets of doors to a room where a team of six people in caps, plastic glasses and silver-grey tunics were standing waiting.

"Thanks," a woman said, and made a gesture that Oleg interpreted as meaning that he and Anders could go no further. The trolley, Steffens and the team disappeared behind two wide doors that swung shut behind them.

"I knew you worked at Crime Squad," Oleg said when everything was quiet again. "But I didn't know you'd studied medicine."

"I haven't," Anders said, looking at the closed doors.

"No? It sounded like it in the car."

"I read a few medical books on my own when I was at college, but I never studied medicine properly."

"Why not? Grades?"

"I had the grades."

"But?" Oleg didn't know if he was asking because he was interested, or to keep his mind off what was happening to Harry.

Anders looked down at his bloody hands. "I suppose it was the same for me as it is for you."

"Me?"

"I wanted to be like my father."

"And?"

Anders shrugged. "Then I didn't want that anymore."

"You wanted to join the police instead?"

"At least then I could have saved her."

"Her?"

"My mother. Or people in the same situation. Or so I thought."

"How did she die?"

Anders shrugged again. "Our house got broken into, and it turned into a hostage situation. My father and I just stood there and watched. Dad got hysterical, and the burglar stabbed my mother and got away. Dad ran around like a headless chicken, shouting at me not to touch her while he looked for a pair of scissors." Wyller swallowed. "My father, the senior consultant, was looking for a pair of scissors while I stood there and watched her bleed to death. I talked to a few doctors afterwards, and found out that she could have been saved if we'd only done what needed to be done straight away. My father's a haematologist, the state's invested millions into teaching him everything there is to know about blood. Yet he still didn't manage to do the simple things that were needed to stop it draining out of her. If a jury had known how much he knows about saving lives, they'd have convicted him of manslaughter."

"So your father made a mistake. Making mistakes is human."

"Even so, he sits there in his office and thinks he's better than other people just because he can say he's a senior consultant." Anders's voice started to tremble. "A policeman with average qualifications and a week-long course in close combat could have overpowered that burglar before he stabbed her."

"But he didn't make a mistake today," Oleg said. "Steffens is your father, isn't he?"

Anders nodded. "When it comes to saving the life of a corrupt, lazy piece of shit like Berntsen, of course he doesn't make mistakes."

Oleg looked at his watch. Pulled out his phone. No message from his mum. He put it back. She'd told him there was nothing he could do to help Harry. But that he could help Truls Berntsen.

"It's none of my business," Oleg said. "But have you ever asked your father how much he's given up? How many years of hard work he's devoted to learning everything there is to learn about blood, and how many people that work has saved?"

Anders shook his bowed head.

"No?" Oleg said.

"I don't talk to him."

"Not at all?"

Anders shrugged. "I moved. Changed my name."

"Is Wyller your mother's name?"

"Yes."

They saw a man dressed in silver rush into the hybrid room before the doors closed again.

Oleg cleared his throat. "Like I said, it's none of my business. But don't you think you're being hard on him?"

Anders raised his head. Looked Oleg in the eye. "You're right," he said, nodding slowly. "It's none of your business." Then he got up and walked towards the exit.

"Where are you going?" Oleg asked.

"Back to the university. Will you take me? If not, I'll catch the bus."

Oleg stood up and followed him. "There are enough cooks there.

But there's a police officer here who might be about to die." He caught up with Anders and put his hand on his shoulder. "And as a fellow police officer, right now you're his next of kin. So you can't leave. He needs you."

When he turned Anders round he saw that the young detective's eyes were wet.

"They both need you," Oleg said.


Harry needed to do something. Fast.

Smith had turned off the main road and was driving carefully down a narrow forest road with banks of snow on both sides. Between them and the frozen water was a red-painted boathouse with a white wooden plank across its double doors. He could see two houses, one on either side of the road, but they were partially hidden by trees and rocks, and were so far away that there was no way he could alert anyone there by shouting for help. Harry took a deep breath and felt his top lip with his tongue; it tasted metallic. He could feel sweat running under his shirt, even though he was freezing. He tried to think. Think the way Smith was thinking. A small, open boat all the way to Denmark. It was obviously perfectly possible, yet still so daring that no one in the police would consider it as a likely escape route. And what about him—how was Smith thinking of solving that problem? Harry tried to shut out the voice that was desperately hoping he would be spared. And the comfortably apathetic voice telling him everything was lost, and that fighting against the inevitable would only mean more pain. Instead he listened to the cold, logical voice. Which said that Harry no longer had any value as a hostage and would only hold Smith back in the boat. Smith wasn't scared of using the gun, he'd already shot Valentin and a police officer. And it was likely to happen in here, before they got out of the car, because that would muffle the noise best.

Harry tried to lean forward, but the fixed, three-pointed belt was pinning him to the seat. And the handcuffs were pressing against the small of his back and rubbing through the skin of his wrists.

There was a hundred metres to go to the boathouse.

Harry bellowed. A guttural, rattling sound that came from the depths of his stomach. Then he rocked from side to side and hit his head against the side window. It cracked and a white rosette appeared in the glass. He roared as he butted it again. The rosette grew larger. A third time. A piece of glass fell out.

"Shut up or I'll shoot you now!" Smith shouted, and aimed the revolver at Harry's head while he kept one eye on the road.

Harry bit.

Felt the pain of the pressure on his gums, felt the metallic taste that had been there ever since he had stood in front of the table in the auditorium with his back to Smith and quickly picked up the iron teeth and put them in his mouth before putting the handcuffs on. How strangely easily the sharp teeth sank into Hallstein Smith's wrist. Smith's scream filled the car and Harry felt the revolver hit his left knee before falling to the floor between his feet. Harry tensed his neck muscles and pulled Smith's arm to the right. Smith let go of the wheel and punched Harry in the head, but his own seat belt prevented him from reaching properly. Harry opened his mouth, heard a gurgling sound, and bit again. His mouth filled with warm blood. Perhaps he had hit the artery, perhaps not. He swallowed. It was thick, like drinking brown sauce, and tasted sickeningly sweet.

Smith grabbed hold of the wheel again with his left hand. Harry had been expecting him to brake, but instead he accelerated.

The Amazon spun on the ice before racing off down the slope. The plank across the boathouse snapped like a matchstick when it was struck by more than a ton of vintage Swedish car, and the doors were torn off their hinges.

Harry was thrown forward in his seat belt as the car slammed into the back of a twelve-foot metal boat that was forced into the doors at the end of the boathouse facing the water.

He noticed that the car key had snapped in the ignition before the engine died. Then he felt an intense pain in his teeth and mouth as Smith tried to pull his arm free. But he knew he had to hold on. Not that he was doing much damage. Even though he had punctured the artery, it was—as every self-harmer knew—so thin at that point in the wrist that it could take hours for Smith to bleed to death. Smith jerked his arm again, but more weakly this time. Harry caught a glimpse of his face out of the corner of his eye. Smith was pale. If he couldn't stand the sight of blood, maybe Harry could get him to faint? Harry clamped his jaws together as hard as he could.

"I see that I'm bleeding, Harry." Smith's voice was weak but calm. "Did you know that when Peter Kürten, the 'Vampire of Düsseldorf' was about to be executed, he asked Dr. Karl Berg a question? He asked if Berg thought Kürten would have time to hear his own blood squirt from his decapitated neck before he lost consciousness. And if so, that pleasure would triumph over all other pleasure. But

I'm afraid this isn't enough to count as an execution, and it's only the start of my pleasure."

With a quick movement Smith released his seat belt with his left hand, and leaned over Harry, putting his head in his lap as he reached down to the floor. His hand fumbled over the rubber mat, but couldn't find the revolver. He leaned further, then turned his head towards Harry as he pushed his arm deeper under the seat. Harry saw a broad smile spread across Smith's lips. He had found the revolver. Harry lifted his foot and stamped down hard with it. He felt the lump of metal and Smith's hand through the thin sole of his shoe.

Smith groaned and looked up at him. "Move your foot, Harry. Otherwise I'll fetch the slaughter knife and use that instead. Do you hear? Move y—"

Harry loosened his bite and tensed his stomach muscles. *"Assh you woosh."*

He raised both legs with a jerk, using the taut seat belt to help him as he forced his knees, and Smith's head, up towards his chest.

Smith felt the revolver come free beneath Harry's shoe, but as he was lifted up by Harry's knees he lost his grip on it. He had to reach his arm further down, and managed to touch the hilt with two fingers just as Harry let go of his right arm. All he had to do was pick up the revolver and turn it round to point at Harry. Then Smith realised what was happening, and he saw Harry's mouth open again, saw the glint of metal, saw him lean down towards him, felt warm breath on his neck. It was as if icicles were drilling through his skin. His scream was cut short as Harry's jaws locked around his larynx. Then Harry's foot came down again and stamped on his hand and the revolver.

Smith tried to hit Harry with his right hand, but the angle was too tight for him to get any force in the blow. Harry hadn't bitten through his carotid artery, because then the jet of blood would have hit the roof, but he was blocking his airway, and Smith could already feel the pressure in his head building. But he still didn't want to let go of the revolver. He had always been like that, the boy who never let go. The monkey. The monkey. But he had to get some air, otherwise his head was going to burst.

Hallstein Smith let go of the revolver, he could grab it again later. He raised his right hand and hit Harry on the side of his head. Then with his left hand, across Harry's ear. Then again with his right, Harry's eye, and he felt his wedding ring tear the policeman's eyebrow. He felt his rage rise at the sight of the other man's blood, it was like petrol on a fire, felt himself gain new strength, and let loose. Fight. Keep fighting.

"So what do I do?" Mikael Bellman said as he stared out across the fjord.

"To begin with, I can't actually believe you've done what you have," Isabelle Skøyen said, walking up and down behind him.

"It happened so fast," Mikael said, focusing on his own reflection. "I didn't have time to think."

"Oh, you had time to think," Isabelle said. "You just didn't have time to think long enough. You had time to think that he'd shoot you if you tried to intervene, but not that the entire media would shoot you if you *didn't* intervene."

"I was unarmed, he had a revolver, and it wouldn't even have occurred to anyone that intervention was an option if Truls Berntsen, the idiot, hadn't got it into his head that this was a good time to play the hero." Bellman shook his head. "But then the poor bastard has always been head over heels in love with Ulla."

Isabelle groaned. "Truls couldn't have done any more damage to your career if he'd tried. The first thing people are going to think, whether or not it's fair, is cowardice."

"Hold it there!" Mikael snapped. "I wasn't the only one who didn't intervene, there were police officers there who—"

"She's your wife, Mikael. You were sitting next to her in the front row, and even if you're at the end of your tenure, you are still Chief of Police. You're supposed to be their leader. And now you're supposed to become Minister of Justice—"

"So you think I should have got myself shot? Because Smith did actually shoot. And Truls *didn't* rescue Ulla! Doesn't that prove that I, as Police Chief, made the correct judgement while Constable Berntsen, acting on his own initiative, got it badly wrong? In fact he actually put Ulla's life in danger."

"Obviously that's how we're going to have to try to present this, but all I can say is that it's going to be difficult."

"And what's so damn difficult about it?"

"Harry Hole. That he volunteered himself as hostage and you didn't."

Mikael threw his arms out. "Isabelle, it was Harry Hole who provoked the whole situation. By unmasking Smith as the puppet master he practically forced Smith to grab that revolver, which was just sitting there in front of him. By offering himself as a hostage, Harry Hole was merely taking responsibility for something that was his fault anyway."

"Yes, but we feel first and reason afterwards. We see a man who doesn't intervene to rescue his wife, and we feel contempt. Then along comes what we think is cold, objective reflection, but is actually us trying to find new information to justify what we felt initially. It may be the contempt of stupid, unreflective people, Mikael, but I'm pretty sure that's what people are going to feel."

"Why?"

She didn't answer.

He looked her in the eye.

"OK," he said. "Because you're feeling that contempt now?"

Mikael Bellman saw Isabelle Skøyen's impressive nostrils flare as she took a deep breath. "You are so many things," she said. "You have so many qualities that have brought you to where you are."

"And?"

"And one of them is your ability to know when to take cover and let others take the blow, when cowardice will pay off. It's just that this time you forgot that you had an audience—and not just the usual audience, but the worst possible audience."

Mikael Bellman nodded. Journalists from both home and abroad. He and Isabelle had a lot of work ahead of them. He picked up a pair of East German binoculars from her windowsill, presumably a gift from a male admirer. Pointed them at the fjord. He had seen something out there.

"What do you think would be the best outcome for us?" he asked.

"I beg your pardon?" Isabelle said. In spite of the fact that she had grown up in the country, or perhaps precisely because of that, she still spoke like the upper classes of western Oslo used to, without it sounding odd. Mikael had tried, and it hadn't worked. Growing up in the east of the city had caused irreparable damage.

"For Truls to die, or for him to survive?" He adjusted the focus on the binoculars. It took him a moment to hear her laughter.

"And that's another of those qualities," she said. "You can switch off all emotion when the situation demands it. This is going to damage you, but you'll survive."

"Dead would be best, wouldn't it? Then it would be beyond question that he took the wrong decision, and that I was right. And then he won't be able to give any interviews, and the whole thing will have a limited shelf life."

He felt her hand on his belt buckle as her voice whispered right next to his ear: "So you'd like the next text to your phone to tell you that your best friend is dead?"

It was a dog. Far out on the fjord. Where on earth was it going?

The next thought came automatically.

And it was a new thought. A thought that had basically never before occurred to Police Chief and soon-to-be Justice Minister Mikael Bellman at any point in his forty-year life.

Where on earth are we going?


Harry had a high-pitched buzzing in his ear, and his own blood on one eye. And the blows were still coming. He no longer felt any pain, only that the car was getting colder and the darkness deeper.

But he wasn't letting go. He had let go so many times before. Had given in to pain, fear, a death wish. But he had also given in to a primitive, egocentric survival instinct that had shouted down any longing for a painless nothingness, sleep, darkness. And that was why he was here. Still here. And this time he wasn't letting go.

His jaw muscles ached so badly that his whole body was shaking. And the blows were still coming. But he didn't let go. Seventy kilos of pressure. If he had managed to get a firmer grip of the neck, he could have stemmed the flow of blood to the brain, and Smith would have lost consciousness fairly quickly. By only stopping the supply of air, that could take several minutes. Another blow to his temple. Harry felt his own consciousness waver. No! He jerked in the seat. Clenched his teeth tighter. Stick it out, stick it out. Lion. Water buffalo. Harry counted as he breathed through his nose. One hundred. The blows kept coming, but weren't the gaps between them longer, weren't they a bit less forceful? Smith's fingers closed over his face and tried to push Harry away. Then gave up. Let go of him. Was Smith's brain finally so starved of oxygen that he had stopped functioning? Harry felt relief, swallowed some more of Smith's blood, and at that moment the thought struck him. Valentin's prediction. *You've been waiting for your turn to be a vampire. And one day you too will drink.* Perhaps it was that thought, a gap in his concentration, but at that instant Harry felt the revolver move under the sole of his shoe, and realised that he had eased the pressure without noticing. That Smith had stopped punching him in order to reach for the gun. And that he had succeeded.

Katrine stopped in the doorway to the auditorium.

The room was empty apart from the two women who were sitting in the front row with their arms round each other.

She looked at them. An odd couple. Rakel and Ulla. The wives of sworn enemies. Was it the case that women found it easier to seek comfort in one another than men? Katrine didn't know. So-called sisterhood had never interested her.

She went over to them. Ulla Bellman's shoulders were shaking, but her sobbing was soundless.

Rakel looked up at Katrine with a questioning look.

"We haven't heard anything," Katrine said.

"OK," Rakel said. "But he'll be OK."

It occurred to Katrine that that was her line, not Rakel's. Rakel Fauke. Dark-haired, strong, with soft brown eyes. Katrine had always felt jealous. Not because she wanted the other woman's life or to be Harry's woman. Harry might be able to make a woman giddy and happy for a while, but in the long term he created sorrow, despair, destruction. For the long term you ought to have a Bjørn Holm. Yet even so she envied Rakel Fauke. She envied her for being the one Harry Hole wanted.

"Sorry." Ståle Aune had come in. "I've got hold of a room where we can have a talk."

Ulla Bellman nodded, still sniffing, then stood up and left the room with Aune.

"Emergency psychiatry?" Katrine asked.

"Yes," Rakel said. "And the weird thing is that it works."

"Does it?"

"I've been there. How are you holding up?"

"*Me?*"

"Yes. All this responsibility. Pregnant. And you're close to Harry as well."

Katrine stroked her stomach. And was struck by a strange thought, or at least one she had never had before. How close they were, birth and death. It was as if one foretold the other, as if life's never-ending game of musical chairs demanded a death before granting new life.

"Do you know if it's a boy or a girl?"

Katrine shook her head.

"Names?"

"Bjørn's suggested Hank," Katrine said. "After Hank Williams."

"Of course. So he thinks it's going to be a boy?"

"Regardless of sex."

They laughed. And it didn't feel absurd. They were laughing and talking about a life that was about to start, instead of impending death. Because life was magical and death trivial.

"I've got to go, but I'll let you know as soon as we hear anything," Katrine said.

Rakel nodded. "I'll stay here, but just say if there's anything I can do to help."

Katrine hesitated, then made her mind up. Stroked her stomach again. "I sometimes worry that I'm going to lose it."

"That's natural."

"And then I wonder what would be left of me afterwards. If I'd be able to go on."

"You would," Rakel said firmly.

"You have to promise that you'd do the same," Katrine said. "You say that Harry will be OK, and hope is important, but I also think it's right that I tell you that I've spoken to the Delta group, and their evaluation is that the hostage taker—Hallstein Smith—probably won't . . . well, the most common . . ."

"Thanks," Rakel said, taking Katrine's hand. "I love Harry, but if I lose him now, I promise to carry on."

"And Oleg, how would he . . . ?"

Katrine saw the pain in Rakel's eyes and instantly regretted saying it. Saw Rakel try to say something, but she failed and ended up shrugging her shoulders instead.

When she went outside again she heard a chopping sound and looked up. The sunlight shimmered off the body of the helicopter up in the sky.

John D. Steffens pushed open the door of A&E and breathed in the cold air. Then he went over to the older paramedic who was leaning against the wall, letting the sunlight warm his face as he smoked, slowly, visibly enjoying it with his eyes closed.

"Well, Hansen?" Steffens said, leaning against the wall alongside him.

"Good winter," the paramedic said, without opening his eyes.

"Could I . . . ?"

The paramedic took out his packet of cigarettes and held it out.

Steffens took a cigarette and the lighter.

"Is he going to make it?"

"We'll see," Steffens said. "We managed to get some blood back into him, but the bullet's still in his body."

"How many lives do you think you have to save, Steffens?"

"What?"

"You worked the night shift, and you're still here. As usual. So how many have you seen ahead of you, how many do you have to save in order to do good?"

"I don't quite know what you're talking about now, Hansen."

"Your wife. The one you didn't save."

Steffens didn't answer, just inhaled.

"I checked up on you."

"What for?"

"Because I'm worried about you. And because I know what it's like. I lost my wife too. But all the overtime, all the lives saved, won't bring her back. But you know that, don't you? And one day you'll make a mistake, because you're tired, and you'll have another life on your conscience."

"Will I?" Steffens said, and yawned. "Do you know a haematologist who's better than me in A&E?"

Steffens heard the paramedic's footsteps move away.

Closed his eyes.

Sleep.

He wished he could.

It had been 2,154 days. Not since Ina, his wife and Anders's mother, died—that was 2,912 days ago. But since he last saw Anders. During the initial period after Ina's death there had at least been sporadic phone calls, even if Anders was furious and blamed him. On good grounds. Anders moved, fled, put as much distance between them as he could. By giving up his plans to study medicine, for instance, and studying to become a police officer instead. During one of their irregular, ill-tempered phone conversations Anders had said he'd rather be like one of his lecturers, a former murder detective, Harry Hole, whom Anders evidently worshipped the way he used to worship his own father. He had tried to see Anders at his various addresses, at Police College, but had been rejected. He had more or less ended up stalking his own son. In an attempt to make him realise that they each lost her a little less if they didn't lose each other. That together they could keep a part of her alive. But Anders hadn't been willing to listen.

So when Rakel Fauke had come for an examination and Steffens realised she was Harry Hole's wife, he had naturally been very curious. What did this Harry Hole have that made him so able to influence Anders? Could he teach him something he could use to approach Anders again? And then he had discovered that the stepson, Oleg, reacted just like Anders had when he realised that Harry Hole couldn't save his mother. It was the same, endless paternal betrayal.

Sleep.

It had been a shock, seeing Anders today. His first crazy thought was that they had been tricked, that Oleg and Harry had arranged some sort of reconciliation meeting.

Sleep now.

It was getting darker, and a chill fell across his face. A cloud passing in front of the sun? John D. Steffens opened his eyes. There was a figure standing in front of him, surrounded by a halo from the sun shining immediately behind.

John D. Steffens blinked. The halo was stinging his eyes. He had to clear his throat before he got any sound out. "Anders?"

"Berntsen's going to make it." Pause. "They're saying it's thanks to you."


Clas Hafslund was sitting in his winter garden, looking out across the fjord, where the ice had this peculiar layer of perfectly still water on top of it, making it look like a vast mirror. He had put down his newspaper, which once again was printing page after page about that vampirist case. Surely they had to get tired of it soon? Out here in Nesøya they didn't have monsters like that, thank goodness. Everything was nice and peaceful, all year round. Even if right at the moment he could hear the irritating sound of a helicopter somewhere, probably an accident on the E18. Clas Hafslund jumped when he heard a sudden bang.

The sound waves rolled across the fjord.

A gun.

It sounded like it had come from one of the neighbouring properties. Hagen's, or Reinertsen's. The two businessmen had spent years arguing about whether the boundary between them ran to the left or the right of an oak tree that was hundreds of years old. In an interview with the local paper, Reinertsen had said that even if the dispute might appear comical because it concerned just a few square metres on the edge of what were otherwise very large plots of land, it wasn't a petty matter, but about the principle of ownership itself. And he was certain that Nesøya's homeowners would agree that this was a principle which was every citizen's duty to fight for. Because there could be no doubt that the tree belonged to his, Reinertsen's, land, you only had to look at the coat of arms of the family he had bought the estate from. It featured a large oak, and anyone could see that it was a copy of the one at the heart of the dispute. Reinertsen went on to declare that sitting and looking at the mighty tree warmed the very depths of his soul (here the journalist noted that Reinertsen would have had to sit on the roof of his house in order to see it), knowing that it was *his*. The day after the interview was printed, Hagen had chopped the tree down and used it to fuel his stove, and told the newspaper that it had warmed not only his soul but his toes as well. And that Reinertsen from now on would have to enjoy the sight of the smoke from his chimney, because whenever he lit his stove over the course of the next few years, it would be with nothing but the wood from the oak. Provocative, of course, but even if the bang had undoubtedly come from a gun, Clas Hafslund found it hard to believe that Reinertsen had just shot Hagen because of a damn tree.

Hafslund saw movement down by the old boathouse that lay approximately 150 metres away from both his and Hagen's and Reinertsen's properties. It was a man. In a suit. He was wading out onto the ice, pulling an aluminium boat behind him. Clas blinked. The man stumbled and sank to his knees in the icy water. Then the kneeling man turned towards Clas Hafslund's house as if he could feel that he was being watched. The man's face was black. A refugee? Had they reached Nesøya now? Affronted, he reached for the binoculars on the shelf behind him and trained them on the man. No. He wasn't black. The man's face was covered with blood. Now he put both hands on the side of the boat and pulled himself to his feet again. And stumbled on. Taking the rope again, he dragged the boat behind him. And Clas Hafslund, who was by no means a religious man, thought that he was seeing Jesus. Jesus, walking on water. Jesus dragging his cross to Calvary. Jesus who had risen from the dead in order to pay a visit to Clas Hafslund and the whole of Nesøya. Jesus with a big revolver in his hand.

Sivert Falkeid was sitting at the front of the inflatable boat with the wind in his face and Nesøya in sight. He looked at his watch one last time. It was precisely thirteen minutes since he and Delta had received the message and immediately linked it to the hostage situation.

"A call reporting shots being fired in Nesøya."

Their response time was acceptable. They would be there before the emergency vehicles that had also been sent to Nesøya. But either way, it went without saying that a bullet travelled faster.

He could see the aluminium boat and the outline of the water's edge where the ice started.

"Now," he said, and moved back in the boat to the others, so that the bow of the boat lifted and they could use their speed to slide across the ice on the meltwater.

The officer steering the boat pulled the propeller out of the water.

The boat lurched as it hit the edge of the ice, and Falkeid heard it scrape the bottom of the boat, but they had enough speed to carry them far enough onto the ice for them to be able to walk on it.

Hopefully.

Sivert Falkeid climbed over the side and tentatively put one foot down on the ice. The meltwater reached just above his ankle.

"Give me twenty metres before you follow," he said. "Ten metres apart."

Falkeid started to splash towards the aluminium boat. He estimated the distance to be three hundred metres. It looked abandoned, but the report had said that the man they assumed had fired the shot had dragged it out of the boatshed belonging to Hallstein Smith.

"The ice is holding," he whispered into his radio.

Everyone in Delta had been equipped with ice picks on a cord attached to the chest of their uniform, so that they could pull themselves out if they went through the ice. And that cord had just tangled itself around the barrel of Falkeid's semi-automatic, and he had to look down to free his weapon.

And he therefore heard the shot without having any chance of seeing anything that might indicate where it had come from. He instinctively threw himself down in the water.

There was another shot. And now he saw a little puff of smoke rise from the aluminium boat.

"Shots from the boat," he heard in his earpiece. "We've all got it in our sights. Awaiting orders to blast it to hell."

They had been informed that Smith was armed with a revolver. Naturally the risk of him managing to hit Falkeid from more than two hundred metres away was fairly slim, but that was still the situation. Sivert Falkeid lay there breathing as the numbingly cold meltwater soaked through his clothes and covered his skin. It wasn't his job to work out what it would cost the state to spare the life of this serial killer. Cost in the form of trials, prison guards, the daily rate at a five-star prison. His job was to work out how great a threat this individual posed to the lives of his men and others, and adapt his response accordingly. Not to think about nursery places, hospital beds and the renovation of rundown schools.

"Fire at will," Sivert Falkeid said.

No response. Just the wind and the sound of a helicopter in the distance.

"Fire," he repeated.

Still no acknowledgement. The helicopter was approaching.

"Can you hear me?" a voice said in his earpiece. "Are you wounded?"

Falkeid was about to repeat his order when he realised that what had happened when they were training in Haakonsværn had happened again. The salt water had ruined the microphone and only the receiver was working. He turned towards their boat and shouted, but his voice was drowned out by the helicopter, which was now hovering motionless in the air right above them. So he gave the hand signal to open fire, two rapid downward movements of his right arm with his fist clenched. Still no response. What the hell? Falkeid began to snake his way back to the inflatable when he saw two of his men walking towards him on the ice without even crouching in order to present a smaller target.

"Get down!" he yelled, but they kept walking calmly towards him.

"We've got comms with the helicopter!" one of them shouted over the noise. "They can see him, he's lying in the boat!"


He was lying in the bottom of the boat, with his eyes closed against the sun that was shining down on him. He couldn't hear anything, but he imagined the water lapping and splashing against the metal beneath him. That it was summer. That the whole family was sitting in the boat. A family outing. Children's laughter. If he could just keep his eyes closed, maybe he could stay there. He didn't know for certain if the boat was floating or if his weight meant it was caught on the ice. It didn't really matter. He wasn't going anywhere. Time was standing still. Perhaps it always had been, unless perhaps it had only just stopped?

Stopped for him, and for the man who was still sitting in the Amazon. Was it summer for him too? Was he also in a better place now?

Something was shading the sun. A cloud? A face? Yes, a face. A woman's face. Like a darkened memory that was suddenly illuminated. She was sitting on top of him, riding him. Whispering that she loved him, that she always had. That she had been waiting for this. Asking if he felt the same, that time was standing still. He felt vibrations in the boat, her groans rose to a continuous scream, as if he had plunged a knife into her, and he released the air from his lungs and the sperm from his testicles. And then she died on top of him. Hit his chest with her head as the wind hit the window above the bed in the flat. And before time began to move again, they both fell asleep, unconscious, without memory, without conscience.

He opened his eyes. It looked like a big, hovering bird.

It was a helicopter. It was hovering ten, twenty metres above him, but he still couldn't hear anything. But he realised that was what was making the boat vibrate.

Katrine was standing outside the boathouse, shivering in the shade as she watched the officers approach the Volvo Amazon inside the building.

She saw them open the front doors on both sides. Saw a suited arm fall out from one side. From the wrong side. From Harry's side. The naked hand was bloody. The officer put his head inside the car, presumably to check for breathing or a pulse. It took a while, and eventually Katrine couldn't hold back any longer, and heard her own trembling voice: "Is he alive?"

"Maybe," the officer shouted above the noise of the helicopter out over the water. "I can't feel a pulse, but he might be breathing. If he is alive, I don't think he's got long left, though."

Katrine took a few steps closer. "The ambulance is on its way. Can you see the gunshot wound?"

"There's too much blood."

Katrine went inside the boathouse. Stared at the hand dangling out of the door. It looked as if it was searching for something, something to hold on to. Another hand to hold. She stroked her own hand over her stomach. There was something she should have told him.

"I think you're wrong," the other officer said from inside the car. "He's already dead. Look as his pupils."

Katrine closed her eyes.

. . .

He stared up at the faces that had appeared above him on both sides of the boat. One of them had pulled his black mask off, and his mouth was opening, forming words; from the way his neck muscles were tensing it looked like he was shouting. Perhaps he was shouting at him to drop the revolver. Perhaps he was shouting his name. Perhaps he was shouting for revenge.

Katrine went over to the door on Harry's side of the car. Took a deep breath and looked inside. Stared. Felt the shock hit her even harder that she had prepared herself for. She could hear the siren of the ambulance now, but she had seen more dead bodies than these two officers, and knew from a brief glance that this body had been permanently vacated. She knew him, and knew that this was just the shell he had left behind.

She swallowed. "He's dead. Don't touch anything."

"But we ought to try to revive him, shouldn't we? Maybe—"

"No," she said firmly. "Let him be."

She stood there. Felt the shock slowly fade. Give way to surprise. Surprise at the fact that Hallstein Smith had chosen to drive the car himself rather than make his hostage drive. That what she had thought was Harry's seat wasn't.

Harry lay in the bottom of the boat, looking up. People's faces, the helicopter that was blocking the sun, the blue sky. He had managed to stamp his foot down on the revolver again before Hallstein Smith pulled it free. And then Hallstein seemed to give up. Maybe it was his imagination, but he had thought he could feel through the teeth, in his mouth, how the other man's pulse became weaker and weaker. Until in the end it was gone altogether. Harry had lost consciousness twice before he managed to get his hands and the handcuffs round to the front of his body again, loosened the seat belt and fished the key to the handcuffs out of his jacket pocket. The car key had broken off in the ignition and he knew he didn't have the strength to climb the steep, ice-covered slope back to the main road, or get over the high fences of the properties on either side of the road. He had called for help, but it was as if Smith had beaten his voice out of him, and the weak cries he did manage to make were drowned by a helicopter somewhere, probably the police helicopter. So that they would be able to see him from the air, he had dragged Smith's boat out onto the ice, lain down in it and fired several shots into the air.

He let go of the Ruger revolver. It had done its job. It was over. He could retreat now. Back to the summer, when he was twelve years old and was lying in a boat with his head in his mother's lap and his father telling him and Sis about a jealous general during the war between the Venetians and the Turks. Harry knew he would have to explain it to his sister once they'd gone to bed. He was secretly quite pleased about that, because no matter how long it took, they wouldn't give up until she understood the connections. And Harry liked connections. Even when he knew, deep down, that there weren't any.

He closed his eyes.

She was still lying there. Lying beside him. And now she was whispering in his ear.

"Do you think you can give life too, Harry?"

# Epilogue

Harry poured Jim Beam into the glass. Put the bottle back on the shelf. Picked up the glass. And put it down next to the glass of white wine on the counter in front of Anders Wyller. The customers behind him were jostling to be served.

"You're looking much better now," Anders said, and looked down at the glass of whiskey without touching it.

"Your father patched me up," Harry said. He glanced at Øystein, who nodded to indicate that he would try to hold the fort alone for a while. "How's it going in the unit?"

"Good," Anders said. "But you know, the calm after the storm."

"You know it's called—"

"Yes. Gunnar Hagen asked me today if I wanted to take over as temporary assistant lead detective while Katrine's on leave."

"Congratulations. But aren't you a bit young for that?"

"He told me it was your idea."

"My idea? Must have been when I still had concussion." Harry turned the volume up on the amplifier and the Jayhawks sang "Tampa to Tulsa" a bit louder.

Anders smiled. "Yes, my father said you took quite a beating. By the way, when did you figure out he was my dad?"

"There was nothing to figure out, the evidence told me. When I sent his hair for DNA analysis, Forensics found a match with one of the DNA profiles from the crime scene. Not from one of the suspects, but the profile of one of the detectives, which obviously we always need when they've been at a crime scene. Yours, Anders. But it was only a partial match. A family connection. A father–son match. You received the result first, but didn't pass it on to me, or anyone else in the unit. Then, when I belatedly found out about the match, it didn't take much to discover that the maiden name of Dr. Steffens's deceased wife was Wyller. Why didn't you tell me?"

Anders shrugged. "I couldn't see that the match had any relevance for the case."

"And you didn't want to be linked to him? That's why you use your mother's maiden name?"

Anders nodded. "It's a long story, but it's getting better now. We're talking. He's a bit more humble, he's realised he's not mister perfect. And I'm . . . well, a bit older, a bit wiser, maybe. So—how did you figure out that Mona was in my flat?"

"Deduction."

"Of course. Such as?"

"The smell in your hall. Old Spice. Aftershave. But you hadn't shaved. And Oleg had mentioned the rumour that Mona Daa uses Old Spice as perfume. And then there was the cat cage. People don't have cat cages. Not unless they're going to have repeated visits from a woman who's allergic to cats."

"You certainly come up with the goods, Harry."

"So do you, Anders. But I still think you're too young and inexperienced for that job."

"So why did you suggest me, then? I'm not even an inspector yet."

"So that you'd have to think it through, realise what areas you need to improve in, and then turn it down."

Anders shook his head and laughed. "OK. That was exactly what I did."

"Good. Aren't you going to have your Jim Beam?"

Anders Wyller looked down into the glass. Took a deep breath. Shook his head. "I don't really like whiskey. To be honest, I probably only order it to copy you."

"And?"

"And it's time I found a drink of my own. Get rid of it, please."

Harry emptied the glass in the sink behind him. Wondered if he ought to suggest a drink from the bottle that Ståle Aune had brought as a belated housewarming gift to the bar, a type of orange bitters called Stumbras 999 Raudonos Devynerios. He explained that it was because they'd had a bottle of it in the student bar, and that was where the bar manager had taken the number for the code on the safe, which in turn had lured Hallstein Smith into the monkey trap. Harry turned to tell Anders this when he caught sight of someone who had just come into the Jealousy Bar. Their eyes met.

"Excuse me," Harry said. "We're having a state visit."

He watched her as she made her way through the crowded room, but she may as well have been the only person in it. She was walking exactly the same way as the first time he ever saw her walking towards him across a driveway. Like a ballerina.

Rakel reached the bar and smiled at him.

"Yes," she said.

"Yes?"

"You have my agreement, I'll do it."

Harry smiled broadly and put his hand on top of hers on the counter. "I love you, woman."

"Good to know. Because we're setting up a limited company where I'm chair of the board, get thirty percent of the shares, a twenty-five percent job and we play at least one PJ Harvey track every evening."

"Agreed. Hear that, Øystein?"

"If she works here, get her behind this bar now!" Øystein snapped.

Rakel went over to Øystein, and Anders walked out of the door.

Harry picked up his phone and made a call.

"Hagen," a voice said.

"Hello, boss, it's Harry."

"I see. So I'm boss again now?"

"Offer Wyller that job again. Insist that he takes it."

"Why?"

"I was wrong, he's ready."

"But—"

"As assistant lead detective, there's a limit to how much he can fuck things up, and he'll learn a hell of a lot."

"Yes, but—"

"And now's the perfect time, the calm after the storm."

"You know it's called—"

"Yes."

Harry hung up. Tried to push the thought away. What Smith had said in the car about what was to come. He had mentioned it to Katrine, and they had checked Smith's correspondence but hadn't found anything to indicate that any new vampirists had been recruited. So there wasn't much they could do, and it had probably only been the wishful thinking of a madman. Harry turned the Jayhawks up another two notches. Yes, that was better.

Svein Finne, "the Fiancé," stepped out of the shower and stood naked in front of the mirror in the empty changing room at Gain Gym. He liked the place, liked the view of the park, the feeling of space and freedom. No, it didn't scare him the way he had been warned that it would. He let the water run off him, let his skin evaporate the moisture. It had been a long session. He had grown accustomed to that in prison, hour after hour of breathing, sweating, giving all he had. His body could handle it. Had to handle it, he had a long job ahead of him. He didn't know who the person who had contacted him was, and he hadn't heard from him in a while. But the offer had been impossible to turn down. A flat. A new identity. And women.

He stroked the tattoo on his chest.

Then he turned and went over to the locker with a padlock with a splash of pink paint on it. He turned it until it read 0999, the number he had been sent. God knows if the number meant anything, but it opened the lock. There was a padded envelope inside. He opened it and turned it upside down. A white plastic key fell into his hand. He pulled out a sheet of paper. There was an address on it. In Holmenkollen.

And there was something else in the envelope, something that was stuck.

He ripped the envelope apart. Looked at the object. Black. And beautiful in its brutal simplicity. He put it in his mouth, clenched his jaws. Felt the taste of salt and bitter iron. Felt the fire. Felt the thirst.

Jo Nesbo is a musician, songwriter, economist, as well as a writer. His Harry Hole novels include *The Redeemer*, *The Snowman*, *The Leopard* and *Phantom*, and he is also the author of several stand-alone novels and the Doctor Proctor series of children's books. He is the recipient of numerous awards including the Glass Key for best Nordic crime novel.

A NOTE ON THE TYPE

This book was set in Janson, a typeface long thought to have been made by the Dutchman Anton Janson, who was a practicing type-founder in Leipzig during the years 1668–1687. However, it has been conclusively demonstrated that these types are actually the work of Nicholas Kis (1650–1702), a Hungarian, who most probably learned his trade from the master Dutch typefounder Dirk Voskens. The type is an excellent example of the influential and sturdy Dutch types that prevailed in England up to the time William Caslon (1692–1766) developed his own incomparable designs from them.

Typeset by Scribe,
Philadelphia, Pennsylvania

Printed and bound by Berryville Graphics,
Berryville, Virginia